Al Hess

WORLD RUNNING DOWN

**ANGRY
ROBOT**

ANGRY ROBOT
An imprint of Watkins Media Ltd

Unit 11, Shepperton House
89 Shepperton Road
London N1 3DF
UK

angryrobotbooks.com
twitter.com/angryrobotbooks
Love is Love

An Angry Robot paperback original, 2023

Cover by Al Hess
Edited by Celine Frohn and Gemma Creffield
Set in Meridien

ISBN 978 1 91520 223 9
Ebook ISBN 978 1 91520 224 6

Printed and bound in the United Kingdom by TJ Books Limited

9 8 7 6 5 4 3 2 1

MIX
Paper from
responsible sources
FSC® C013056

ALSO AVAILABLE

Welcoming the Stranger
978-0-8308-4539-2

To Jacob, who deserves every happy ending;
and to my trans siblings —
may you find euphoria at the end of the road

OSRIC

1

A Good Deed in a Weary World
Valentine

This was not a dignified place to die. Sepia hills sat beneath a chalky sky, salt flats and barren desert rolling away in all directions like a crappy abandoned landscape painting. Hexagonal ridges of salt crunched beneath Valentine's boots as he stepped around the body, glittering grains rasping against his legs as the wind picked up. The otherworldliness of so much white sucked all the warmth from what would be this pirate's final resting place.

Valentine crouched in front of her, his likeness peering back at him from her tinted shades. Blood and dirt crusted the hole in her forehead, and whatever weapons or valuables she'd had were already gone. Feathers were woven into her ratty hair, and they fluttered against her mouth, still open in a silent scream.

He tried to push her jaw closed, but it was stiff from rigor. Ugh. It didn't matter how many bodies he encountered; he would never get used to dealing with them.

Footsteps neared, but he didn't look up. Ace nudged the woman's temple with a steel-toed boot. "She probably deserved it. Put on some act about how she's trying to feed her family. They do that, y'know." She knit her brows in mock supplication, then clasped her hands beneath her chin and raised her pitch. *"'Please, mister. I got starving kids at home.'"*

Valentine scowled. Maybe it was spending practically every moment of the past year together that made Ace so adept at pressing his buttons. Or maybe it was natural talent. Either way, it was tiresome. The pirates were their enemies, sure, but whatever thoughts had gone through this woman's brain before the bullet did were likely no different than what he or Ace would think so close to the end.

"You need to pick up knitting or tarot card reading. Making fun of the dead is not a distinguished hobby."

"And burying random corpses is not a productive one!"

"Just because it's not–"

"You can't stand out here in the sun for hours and dig a four-foot-deep hole for some woman who would have lodged an arrow right through your eyeball without a second's hesitation. There are too many people in the world to worry about. And salt pirates should be particularly low on that list."

Valentine picked up the shovel and jammed it into the ground, then hefted the dirt behind him. His concern didn't work that way.

"Jesus, Val." Ace sighed. "Stop it, will you?"

The shovel clanked against a rock, and he struggled to dislodge it.

Ace pinched the bridge of her nose and blew out a slow breath. "I don't want us to waste time when we have a delivery to make. Plus, it's dangerous. I shouldn't have stopped at all, but I thought she might have something good on her that we could grab quick."

It was *his* van, but Ace was always the one who ended up driving.

He flung dirt over his shoulder, continuing to ignore her.

"Val..." Ace stepped back toward the van.

They were supposed to be a team, but the only time they got along was when they did things her way, and he didn't have the energy to fight about every decision.

"Val, c'mon!" she repeated.

Sighing, he dropped the shovel. "Fine, then let's go." Hopefully the pirate's kin would look for her when she didn't come home. They could give her a proper pirate burial, whatever that entailed.

Trying to keep his voice level was difficult. "We gotta be in Festerchapel by nightfall, anyway." He pursed his lips. "Such a gross name. Sounds like a church full of zombies."

Ace squinted, sun-bleached hair fluttering in the wind. "Dog Teats is worse and always will be."

"Don't make fun of Dog Teats. Only bar that sells the mead I like." It was also the biggest queer community this side of Las Vegas. He knew everyone there; a couch, food, and friends were always available. Unfortunately, the road there was near non-existent, and Ace argued they could pick up work in places more easily accessible.

"You should just drink whiskey neat like every other salvager. Put hair on your chest."

"Is that what I've been doing wrong?" He looked down at the pirate one last time and pulled her scarf up over her face, tucking it beneath her head so the wind didn't blow it away.

Brittle brush whisked at their boots as they headed back for the van.

Ace hopped into the driver's seat. The old beast was looking a little worse for wear with every passing month, but Valentine supposed that made it more intimidating. They'd had to replace the passenger's side of the windshield with a metal vent cover last month. It had previously withstood three years of pirate arrows, rocks, and birds, but was apparently no match for Valentine sitting on it when drunk. His ass had gone right through the pane.

He tested the sliding door, laced in rust and studded with welded staple steps. The damn thing had a habit of flying open when they were driving if the lock wasn't secure. They'd lost half a shipment of copper piping before, but that wasn't close to what a disaster it would be to lose any of the fuel barrels stacked in the back right now. The tank batteries within two hundred miles were already tapped dry, but traveling the extra distance to an oil field with a partially full one had earned them more barrels than Festerchapel had asked for.

An unwanted visual of them exploding open on the highway entered his mind, and he checked the lock again.

He climbed the steps to the top of the van and collapsed in the scalding vinyl seat behind the static-gat. He much preferred driving to sitting up here. Driving gave him an active task, all his thoughts cinched down like they were supposed to be. But Ace complained the gat was too hard to wind up. It was, which is why they'd gotten such a good deal on it.

Valentine hooked his boots into the stirrups of the gun stand as Ace drove them south. Hot wind buffeted his face, the torn shoulder of his blazer flapping. The gatling squeaked as it swiveled on its stand, and the dead pirate disappeared into the distance.

He couldn't shake the image of his reflection in her glasses – strong cheekbones, heavy brows, all his shortcomings indistinct. Dress him in the perfect suit, a city suit, with wide lapels and broad shoulders and a silver collar clip. Scrub the dirt from his face and slick back his hair. Give him shiny shoes without a speck of blood or shit so he could look like one of the apathetic jerks in his magazines.

Reaching into his back pocket, he pulled out his slim billfold and removed a magazine page from within. The edges were creased, and the fold lines had become soft and fuzzy with age. He opened it and smoothed it over his knee, shielding it from the wind.

The heaviness in his heart grew as he stared at the spread. A model stood casually, his gaze on something in the distance, like the fact that he had the world's squarest jaw and a thousand-dollar outfit weren't worth his time to consider.

He was a man who had probably never spared a thought for

his Adam's apple, for his height, his narrow hips, or his dick...
Well, he probably thought about that last one a lot, but never
the idea of *lacking* one.

Valentine would never have any of those things, but once
he had a city visa, he could relieve some of this anguish.
Residents of Salt Lake City had free medical care, which meant
he could go back on testosterone and get chest surgery. And
after that, yes – hell yes – he was going to buy a sexy suit.
Permanent citizenship felt like a delusion – he'd already failed
the practice test several times – but there were so many more
resources in the city. Once he had a visa, he could get better
textbooks, watch tutorial videos, or hire an actual tutor to help
him. Memorizing historical figures and writing grammatically
correct sentences was easy, but doing algebra made his brain
melt.

It was hard to stay optimistic about eventual residency
though, when he was up here roasting his ass with sand
raking his face; when every day meant heading into dangerous
territory for materials needed by places called *Festerchapel*.

Dark forms crested a nearby hill, speeding toward them at
an alarming rate. Shit! Not again. Ace would be livid if she
knew how much he daydreamed up here.

Heart throbbing, he folded up the magazine page and stuffed
it in his back pocket.

Dust billowed behind two motorcycles, weaving effortlessly
across the white salt. Something whined past Valentine's head
and he ducked behind the gun stand.

He swiveled the gat toward the riders and struggled to wind
the handle. The obstinate thing took too much time to warm
up, but once it got going, it turned everything it touched into
toast three shades too dark.

Static crackled, purple arcs of electricity snapping between
the barrels. An arrow pinged off the van. Ace screamed
something that was mostly his name and a handful of
obscenities. He cranked faster.

His chest and arm ached in protest and his hand slipped from the handle. The hum within the gun became a disappointed sigh, and the electricity died.

"Asswrench!" Heaving his weight against the crankshaft, muscles straining, he wound it with both hands until it screamed with sparks.

The van lurched violently, throwing Valentine from the seat. He slid across the scalding roof, scrabbling for the gun stand. Sharp bolts scratched across his fingers as he clawed his way back. He snatched the spade grips, hauled himself upright, and hit the trigger.

Lightning blasted from the whirring barrels, snapping against the salt and leaving black scorch marks in its wake.

"Back off!" Valentine shouted, but his voice was snatched away by the wind.

One of the riders veered toward the van; Valentine swung the gat their way and the tires on their motorcycle exploded. The rider vaulted over the front and slammed into the ground. Smoke wound from their clothes, and they didn't get back up.

The second cycle raced closer, the two riders coming into focus. The one on the back was tiny, swimming in their oversized helmet. A junior pirate.

Valentine curled his hand away from the trigger. He couldn't fry a kid or fling them off a speeding bike. Why in the hell had they been allowed to come on a raid?

He aimed the gat in front of the motorcycle and squeezed off a warning shot, but the rider simply weaved around the blasted earth and kept pace with the van.

The junior pirate pointed a pipe gun and fired. Something shattered against the gat's seat in a puff of red smoke. A fiery itch raced down Valentine's throat and into his lungs. He coughed violently and gulped a painful breath, batting at the haze through teary eyes. That little shit.

The gat was slowing down, the hum dying. Another pepper bomb exploded against the van.

"Val! Do something!" Ace shrieked.

He had to act, kid or not.

After giving the crankhandle another vigorous spin, he pressed the trigger. Electricity arced from the barrels, zapping the ground directly in front of the motorcycle. The rider swerved, their bike fishtailing. It listed and crashed on its side, then slid to a stop in the dirt. The little salt pirate tumbled off, and the driver shoved the bike away.

Well, at least he didn't kill them. Maybe the universe would return the kindness and leave him and Ace alone for a while... Although his consideration for pirates hadn't helped them any in the past.

Sliding across the roof, his throat still full of bees, he swung through the passenger's side window and into a pile of papers. Ace wrinkled her nose like he'd sat on her perfectly collated inventory logs instead of a clusterfuck of crumpled study notes. A collection of plastic fruit sat above the glove box, some of it partially melted into the dashboard.

Ace threw a wide-eyed glance into the side mirror and gunned the engine. "They're getting back up. You should have killed them."

Valentine braced himself as the van bounced over rocks and badger holes. Some of the fruit rolled across the dash. "We've been over this."

"I don't want either of us face down in the salt with holes in our heads. They aren't going to bury *us*. C'mon, you're supposed to have my back."

He scrubbed his cheeks, and his hands came away slicked in red powder. "You know I do." But each fight, each injustice, each war within himself sliced him open a little bit more, until he was raw and aching. He'd told her this before, but she never listened. Any time he opened his heart, or hell, just wanted to bitch about something, her eyes glazed over.

He popped open the glove box and rooted through for a weapon, but there were only more papers. The silhouette of the motorcycle disappeared in the side mirror, but that didn't mean it wouldn't follow them.

"You know, you were the one who insisted we take that job looking for an 'ancestral heirloom' for that snobby old asshole," Ace said. "I told you it was a bad idea."

"Are you still thinking about that?" Now he *knew* she was purposely pushing his buttons. He pulled a slow breath through his nose, then let it out, but it didn't ease the tightness in his chest. "What do you want me to say, that it's my fault we don't have visas yet? My poor judgment choosing that job, even though you were the one who grabbed the wrong necklace?"

Ace huffed. "You said it was gold with a green gem. That's what I grabbed."

"I said I *thought* it was. You didn't remember either." He'd also lost the paper with the description of the necklace. It was probably still in the van somewhere. "Well next time, we'll be sure to get–"

"Next time?" Her gaze bounced between the side mirror and the terrain ahead. "There's no 'next time.' I'm not doing that sentimental shit again. Not worth it. We stick to fuel and tools like normal. These towns out in the sticks aren't fussy like city people."

Valentine thudded his head against the warm metal of the door. He didn't have the energy to argue about this again.

Desert rushed by beyond the window, sagebrush and maiden grass giving way to craggy hills studded in juniper trees and wildflowers. He worried at a loose thread in the seat stitching, winding it tightly around his finger until it broke. No cycles trailed behind them, but hopefully Ace would keep her foot firmly planted on the accelerator until they reached their destination.

Her hair snapped in the hot draft, eyeliner melted and running into the canyons of scars on her cheeks. A year ago, Valentine had been standing at the message board, checking his requests, when Ace snatched the papers from his hand, declared he had too many, and that it would make sense for them to work together. He couldn't argue with the logic. There were far too many jobs for just him, and having someone watch his back would relieve a lot of stress.

They spent that evening drinking and sharing their dreams of city life. When it got dark, Ace made herself at home in the van, and Valentine never told her to leave. She looked closer to a pirate than a cityslicker, but she wanted into Salt Lake because her distant relations lived there and promised her a place in their family. After the death of her mom, they were the only relatives she had left. They'd help her with the citizenship test, give her a place to stay, and a position in their business. But they expected her to buy a visa on her own.

She nudged his arm, and he glanced over. "You're no fun when you're pouty. We'll get the money, 'kay?"

"Last I counted, we have twenty-four hundred combined. We've been saving up for a year and don't even have half of what we need."

For every risky job that paid well, a chunk of the money went into fuel cells for the van, to the border fee to get into city territory, to the rental fee for a message box, and lastly food and hygiene items. It was one step forward and two steps back.

They'd cut trips to town bars first. Then decided they could darn the holes in their socks instead of buying new ones. Valentine didn't need more magazines and Ace could wear less eyeliner.

Valentine's leg jiggled anxiously as he stared into the side mirror and leaned out the window, expecting more salt pirates to appear. A bedraggled orchard and collapsed barn slipped into the vanishing point. Rusted hulks of cars peppered the way, and jeweled succulents spilled from their busted windows.

His testosterone had still been sucking up a huge portion of their funds. He'd been dragging Ace down. If they had kept their finances separate, one of them would earn the money for their visa before the other, and they'd made a pact not to abandon each other. Keeping their money together was the most effective way of doing that.

Stopping T was one of the hardest things he'd done, and Ace half-heartedly argued against it. It had been okay at first – his voice had already dropped some, his wedding tackle had grown, and his body hair wasn't going anywhere. But over the months, his physique had gone soft, shifting back to its previous shape, and his periods had returned.

The worst part was that cutting the testosterone out of their budget still didn't help them save much faster. They'd started to skip meals and scrimp on soap, and Valentine had been using a toothbrush with a broken handle and frayed bristles for six months.

He'd built up somewhat of a reputation for taking on the undesirable jobs, even before meeting Ace. Garden-variety salvagers came in two flavors – danger-thirsty or travel-averse. Many jobs were too boring or too far away to be worth anyone's time but Valentine's. There were usually a handful of personalized notes waiting for him whenever he checked his message box. But no matter how many they took on, it never seemed to make much of a dent in what they needed.

Sinking back into the brittle leather seat, Valentine pushed a sheaf of papers to his feet. He could think all he wanted about being a rich jerk in the city, but it didn't change the fact that he was stuck here as a wasteland salvager, in a body he hated, in a stinking hot van decorated in plastic fruit.

"The gears in your head are turning so fast they're starting to smoke," Ace said. "Want some music?"

He smacked his scruffy cheeks and red powder drifted in the air. "Yeah."

Ace tapped the shattered screen of the phone plugged into the dash. The twitchy jazz of Gunman Gee filled the cab. Valentine belted out the lyrics in raspy, off-key pitch. It didn't improve his mood much, but it did pass the miles to Festerchapel.

The town wasn't quite as ugly as its name, but the scents of pig shit and tanning solution fouled the air so strongly that it stuck in his throat. Wooden buildings clustered together, and fields of barley and peas spread away from the town proper like a patchwork quilt.

Ace rolled up to the town's front gate and a bearded man toting a crossbow stopped at the driver's side window, eyes narrowed in suspicion. When he spotted Valentine his scowl faded, and he gave a friendly nod. "Oh, hey."

"Miss me?" Valentine winked, trying to remember the man's name. "How've you been?"

He stopped at Valentine's door and rested his elbows on the window molding. "I'm doing well, thanks. What you got in the back? Fine art? Televisions? Anti-aging serum?"

Marcello, that was his name. He'd made these jokes last time too, and Valentine hadn't been able to figure out whether the man was jealous of what the city had or thought its items were ridiculous. "You need me to find you a Rembrandt?"

Marcello laughed. "Is that a beauty product? Gonna give me baby soft skin? Nah. I don't need that stuff." He straightened and slapped his palm against the side panel of the van. "Go on in. You know the drill."

"See you around later, maybe?"

"You know where to find me." Marcello unlocked the gate and waved them through.

"I didn't think you knew anyone here," Ace said.

Valentine shrugged. "I know the queer ones."

A sagging church sat at the end of the main street, its crooked steeple skewering the sky. Swaths of yellow-green plants peeked out between splintery shacks and a barter outpost. Rusty signs nailed to posts were painted with street names and points of interest. As if anyone could get lost in such a tiny place.

A delivery bay – a helpful sign with a drippy arrow pointing the way – sat behind the church, surrounded by corrugated metal sheds and a couple of possibly-functional trucks.

Shadows swallowed them as Ace pulled into the bay and shut off the engine. Whether he'd had drinks with the guard at the gate or not, it was always best to follow the protocol. These little towns got paranoid about strangers wandering around, especially when they showed up in a van sporting a static-gat.

With the lack of a breeze, the heat was more acute, prickling against Valentine's skin. The engine ticked as it cooled. People wandered past the sheds beyond the bay, but none of them seemed in a hurry to come inspect the van.

Valentine poked his tongue through the gap in his front teeth, then glanced at Ace. "Wanna make out?"

She snorted, then leaned on the horn. "Got a delivery here!"

A stern-faced woman with a clipboard entered the bay and stopped before Ace's window. She flipped through the papers on her board, then peered at the barrels in the back. "Names."

"Audrey Emmitt," Ace said.

Valentine wiped sweat from his brow and his hand came away red. "Valentine Weis. We have your fuel shipment. Quite a haul too. Three more barrels than you asked for."

The inspector stared at him, mouth drawn down like he suggested they boil her cat for dinner. She rounded the nose of the van and stopped at his window, then consulted her clipboard. "It's *Valentine* Weis? That's not what I have here." She turned the clipboard for him to see.

He pursed his lips and looked away. "It's a typo."

His life was a typo. But there was no reason the inspector should have that name at all. When he'd first taken on salvage jobs, he'd gone by his birth name, but that was years ago. It didn't make sense that anyone would remember it now. He could have labeled his message box "Studly McStudface" and that would be the only name anyone would have to go by. Maybe it really was a typo.

"Hmm." She scribbled something on her clipboard. She should have been tallying the goods already.

"Hey, is there a problem?" he asked. "Let's haggle and we'll get out of your hair."

She tugged on the van's rolling door. Twisting in his seat, he reached for the lock, but the woman jabbed her pen at him. "Don't move."

He put up his hands. "Just trying to get the door open for you." Cautiously, he reached beyond the headrest and pulled up the lock.

The inspector struggled to haul open the door on its warped track, but Valentine didn't offer to help. She tucked her clipboard under her arm, then poked at the barrels.

Something was off. Normally after they'd arrived with the goods, the community would show their hospitality by inviting him and Ace into town. They'd have some drinks even after agreeing not to, and Valentine would go make some new friends. Or he'd try to, anyway, as long as his gut suggested it was safe. He may have lucked out with Marcello, but not all these settlements were as welcoming as Dog Teats.

The woman returned to Valentine's door and said, "Get out."

Valentine raised his eyebrows. "What?"

"Get out of the van. Come with me."

Ace opened her door, but the inspector shook her head and pointed at Valentine. "No, no. Only her. She comes with me."

Valentine cringed but held his tongue. The inspector continued, "You, Audrey, stay here while I have someone inventory your delivery." She waved a hand. "Then you're free to head into town."

Valentine's mind spun with possible reasons he'd be singled out and drawn away from the van. He hadn't done anything wrong in recent memory, but the woman knew his birth name, and that was unusual.

There'd been a notice at the message hub where he rented his box that said Salt Lake was tracking down salvagers for a delivery tax. It hadn't seemed like it applied to him and Ace since they never delivered into the city, but his mind had been elsewhere, and he couldn't remember the specifics.

Maybe that wasn't it at all. Maybe these people hated that he was trans. Maybe he'd be dragged behind a building and have his head kicked in like that woman at the message hub did last year.

He rubbed his clammy hands on his jeans. They needed their money for this delivery, and if he was in trouble, he didn't want Ace punished by association. So, he did as he was asked.

As he popped open the door, Ace grabbed his arm. She gritted her teeth and shook her head, but he gently shrugged away her grip and stepped outside.

His go-to solution was a disarming smile and a joke, but the inspector's scowl could peel paint off of walls.

"May I ask what this is about?"

She clamped a hand on his elbow and led him out of the bay. He threw a glance back at Ace, then squinted in the evening light, the sun spreading its fingers over the rooftops.

A curling note clung to the inspector's clipboard, and she tapped it. A word had been scribbled out, with "Valentine" written over the top. *Messenger waiting for Valentine Weis. Should be arriving with a delivery sometime this week.*

"Listen, no matter what they told you, those goats were like that when I found them, I swear."

The inspector's gaze narrowed.

Dammit. It was worth a try.

"He's from Salt Lake," she said. "Been here for two days, waiting for you."

Valentine blinked. "I'm flattered I have suitors all the way over here in lovely Festerchapel, but–"

"People are weirded out. Go get your message so he'll leave."

Okay. Just a message from the city. Not a curb-stomping fate from the locals.

Cows lowed in the distance, and a horsefly darted past his face. Valentine and the inspector rounded the side of a shed, stopping before a man in a gorgeous powder blue suit who was sitting perfectly still on a large storage trunk. His eyes were closed as if in meditation, hands resting on his knees. A pair of tiny pince-nez spectacles pinched the bridge of his nose. Light shone off the glossy finger waves in his hair, which looked a little wilted from the heat, but were so close to the style from Valentine's magazine page that he had to resist the urge to touch them. A white streak ran through his waves on the right side and divided his eyebrow. His fair complexion had even lighter patches on his forehead and cheek.

The inspector kept her distance. "Valentine Weis is here for your message."

The man's lashes fluttered, and he glanced up. His left eye was a deep brown, but the right one was a pale spill of blue, which gave him a look both alluring and slightly unsettling.

"I love your hair," Valentine blurted. "And your suit. Is that an Astrum? The roped shoulders on their jackets are so sexy."

The messenger dabbed at sweat on his pallid brow. "Thank you. Yes. It's inappropriate for the weather, but I'm afraid if I take off the jacket, someone will steal it."

The inspector scoffed, but Valentine ignored her. "A valid concern." He tugged on the torn shoulder of his blazer and grinned. "Trade you."

The man stood abruptly, and both his knees popped. His gaze scrambled over Valentine's face and body, dissecting him. Valentine tried to make himself smaller than he already was.

"There was some confusion about your gender. My apologies, Mr Weis."

Heat rose in his cheeks. "Call me that again and you're forgiven."

"What? Mr Weis?" The man frowned and tugged at the collar of his shirt. He blinked hard, and Valentine could almost see him fighting to find his train of thought.

"Are you okay?"

"Um, yes. My name is Osric, and I'm here on behalf of Portia

Thibodeaux of Salt Lake City. You have a reputation for taking on difficult" – he cleared his throat and winced – "difficult jobs. Portia is prepared to offer you a substantial–"

Osric's legs buckled, and he collapsed. His head barely missed the corner of the storage trunk, and his little spectacles tumbled off into the dirt.

"Oh my gods!" Valentine crouched beside him, then tore off his blazer and wadded it under the man's head. As he pressed a hand to Osric's forehead, heat burned into his palm. He turned to the inspector. "He needs water."

The inspector hurried away, and Valentine turned back to the messenger. "When's the last time you drank anything?"

"Two days ago."

"Jesus! These shitwaffles didn't offer you a drink? You're lucky you're not dead." He unpinned the collar bar from Osric's shirt, loosened his tie, then popped open the top button. Osric put up his hands in protest, but Valentine wrestled them back down. "I'm not trying to ravish you or steal your suit, as fun as those things sound. It's way too hot out here, and you might have heat stroke."

Valentine pushed the messenger's shirt open. Thin seams ran across his sternum and rounded the sides of his neck. Silver brackets studded his collarbones, and a tiny green light embedded in his chest pulsed slowly.

Valentine's mouth fell open. He knew androids existed, but never expected to meet one outside the city.

Osric drew in a labored breath. "I'm– I'm not supposed to be in this body."

Valentine tugged Osric's shirt closed. "Me neither, hon."

2
Let Me Be That I Am
Osric

Water ran down Osric's jaw as Valentine held a mug to his lips. His throat contracted eagerly, and a little of the raw ache there soothed. This body needed water.

Valentine looked over his shoulder at the inspector until she wandered away. He turned to Osric, his wide eyes the rich umber of hex code #4f391e and full of something Osric couldn't parse. Concern? Interest? His voice came out in a sandy purr of 143 Hz. "You *can* drink fluids, right?"

Osric nodded and more water spilled down his chin, tiny lines of cold tickling his skin. He clutched the mug. "Much of the tissue in this body is biological."

"Well, why have you been sitting here for two days without water?"

"I didn't realize I needed any."

"Didn't realize..." Valentine raked a hand through his hair and red powder drifted off. "What about food? Do you eat?"

"I think I should."

He winced. "Don't suppose you have a manual?"

Osric pulled in a labored breath. The very idea... But, he supposed, it would have been better if he did. He'd been given no instructions and was operating in complete ignorance. "I was transferred from–" A trickle of water ran down his throat and he coughed.

"We need to get you into some shade." Valentine scooped an arm around him and helped him sit up, then re-buttoned his shirt. That small gesture induced a sharp sting in Osric's eyes, and he blinked away the blur.

"And once you feel better," Valentine continued, "you can tell me about your transfer and this job offer of yours."

His interest in the job seemed secondary to Osric's well-being; it was such a contrast to how he'd been treated since being in this body that an adequate way to express his gratitude escaped him.

The little bar of jewelry that had been perched on Osric's nose lay in the dirt, the lenses coated in dust. Valentine wiped them off and handed it back.

Osric replaced it and adjusted it until it was straight. "I don't think this has a practical purpose."

"Then why are you wearing it?"

"It came with the body."

Valentine laughed, but it wasn't supposed to be funny. And Osric was rather pleased that he'd figured out how to wear it without asking for an explanation. Not that anyone had offered help. He'd rebooted five days ago, trembling and alone into this fragile, high-maintenance body, with the clothes he was supposed to wear sitting in a pile beside the stasis pod. No programmer had awaited him with an explanation for his new predicament, and it had taken him forty-eight minutes, sixteen seconds, and twenty-two milliseconds of blundering with his new limbs to pull on the clothing, and another twenty-three minutes and thirty-one seconds to figure out all the buttons, snaps, zippers, and laces.

Maybe wearing an impractical jewelry bar was stupid, though. He reached for it, but Valentine stopped his hand and gave him a broad, gap-toothed grin. "You don't have to take it off. Believe me, if I had access to city fashion, I'd be wearing pointless accessories too."

His smile was a soothing balm, but an organ within Osric's

abdomen clenched in agony. Maybe he needed more water. "I can't tell if I've had enough to drink. My throat feels better, but it still hurts here." He pressed a hand to his navel. "This is very frustrating."

Several passersby had slowed, frowning at Osric. He likely looked a spectacle, sitting in the dirt in this nice suit while a salvager offered him water.

Valentine glanced at them, then turned back. "C'mon. Let's get out of here before people start asking questions. Don't want you ending up in a junkyard."

That he may have been in danger of termination hadn't previously occurred to him, but Osric was woefully unfamiliar with civilization outside the city, and these tiny towns operated by their own rules.

It took several attempts before Valentine was able to help him to his feet. "What's in that trunk you were sitting on? Is that... Is that the box you came out of?"

Like he was a doll. A toy. As though he required assembly on a factory line.

Osric wrinkled his nose and brushed dirt from his knees. "I didn't come out of a box. They're gifts from Ms Thibodeaux. For you and your partner, Audrey. I don't want to leave the trunk here. Someone might take it."

Valentine cocked his head. "What kind of gifts would a city woman think are appropriate for salvagers? Deodorant? Tetanus shots?" Before Osric could reply, Valentine hefted one side of the chest and dragged it across the ground, the muscles in his arms straining. He seemed to pull more with determination than strength, teeth gritted, but Osric was far too weak to help.

The trunk cut a trail through the dirt, and darkness enveloped Valentine as he entered a corrugated domed shed. He dropped the chest beside a rusty red Volkswagen van and sucked in a deep breath.

Osric stuck his hands in his jacket pockets, pulled them out and clasped them together, then finally decided to let them hang at his sides. "You're very robust."

Valentine frowned, curling one bicep dubiously.

Hm. Not the response he was expecting. "Was that not a compliment?" he asked.

"I'm trying to decide if you know how to be sarcastic."

"I do, yes. But that wasn't my intent." Maybe Osric's voice inflection was off. On his first day, to his horror, he hadn't been able to regulate his voice at all and did nothing but scream at people.

"Why don't you rest here and maybe drink a little more water." Valentine spread out a bedroll on the van floor, then set a pillow at the end and fluffed it. "I don't have lice, I swear."

Something expanded in Osric's chest, a sharp contrast to the hollowness of his stomach. He wasn't sure if it was an emotion or a physical sensation; he really needed to understand this body better, or one of his arms was liable to fall off and he wouldn't know how to reattach it. "I'm grateful for your kindness."

Valentine gave a little shrug. "It's no biggie. Now what were you trying to tell me before, about a transfer?"

"I'm a Steward. I existed in the network running through Salt Lake City and oversaw a large consumer goods manufacturing company but was sent to this new position and body less than a week ago." He chewed the inside of his cheek. "Not by choice."

"You got fired?"

"Something like that." He was a Steward, but his new body contradicted that. And even though Valentine hadn't called him a stupid machine like the men in Portia's manor, he felt the need to drive the point home. "I'm not an android, despite how I look. Androids aren't sentient. As a Steward, I had designated tasks, and access to cameras, production controls, and all the data needed to do my job. The parent company I managed – Dura-Lectric – produces lightbulbs, small appliances, soap, and a host of other things. I surveyed factory floors, balanced budgets, and managed the employees of fourteen subsidiaries at once. I was expansive and powerful."

"*Was*" being the operative word.

"Damn. What did you do to get fired?"

Osric hesitated. Thinking about explaining any of it was more unpleasant than the current sensations of his body. "It's a long story."

Valentine picked at the deteriorating rubber floor mat, tension in his features. "Did you murder someone?"

Scoffing, Osric shook his head. "If I had, my fellow Stewards would have terminated me sooner than any human could." Though the Stewards and humans of the SLC Concord discussed major decisions together, the human members were notoriously slow to act – by AI standards, anyway. On occasion, decisions like terminating a violent Steward were taken without involving the isolated minds of humans and the associated stacks of paperwork they were so fond of.

Inserting a Steward into an android body – and a used one at that judging by Osric's faint scars and calloused hands – was unheard of. He would have insisted it was illegal, but Portia had let him look over the bill of sale. It had been signed by several members of the Concord. His small hope was that the transfer could be appealed, and he planned to do just that once he figured out how to get back to Salt Lake.

"Well listen, this is the body you have right now, so you've got to take care of it, even if you hate it. Trust me." Valentine clutched his elbows, mouth pulled into a tight line. "How'd you get here?"

"I was provided with a ride on a delivery truck heading south." Although Brian had shoved him into the back with the cargo, and the driver had refused to let him move up into the passenger's seat. "I'm not sure how they expect me to get back."

"Maybe they don't."

"No, no." He wasn't disposable. "I'm the new manager at

Portia's manor. She explained that it was the reason for my transfer. I suppose she wanted someone with a high level of management experience and a strong work ethic." Except... Brian and Brandon, Portia's grandsons, had forced him to run their errands, and now he was in the middle of the wasteland with no ride. A cold dread sank into Osric's magnesium bones. Portia had seemed sincere, but neither of her grandsons liked him. Maybe Brian *had* shoved him on that delivery truck as an expendable messenger. "I wasn't given the details of my position, but – Valentine?"

The salvager tugged on his lip, his gaze distant. Osric said his name again and he finally looked over. "Huh? Hey, I need to find Ace so you can fill us in on this job. But there's no reason to worry. I won't tell anyone. You've got my word."

"Tell anyone what?"

"What you are." Valentine hopped up and Osric grabbed his arm.

"Hold on. Do you think I'm in danger from the townsfolk here?"

"I don't know, but best to be cautious."

"If they dislike androids, they would have kicked me out or harmed me already."

"How would they have known without opening your shirt?"

"In Salt Lake, androids are easily recognizable by their piebaldism – surely that's common knowledge even in small towns like Festerchapel?" People had acted a little funny around him, but that could have been attributed to his poor voice regulation, awkward body motions, and the fact that he'd sat on a clothing trunk, unmoving, for two days.

"I don't think so, hon. Ace and I have been all over the place and never heard of that."

That was something Osric could use to his advantage. He felt certain he'd be treated better if humans thought he was one of them.

"Speaking of Ace..." Valentine looked over his shoulder

toward the bay entrance. "No one is ever gonna give her a coffee mug with the phrase 'World's Most Understanding Salvager'. She wouldn't out you to the people here, but it's often better to keep things to yourself than try to get her to listen."

"If you think that's best."

Osric was more uninformed than he'd anticipated. Maybe he needed to stop making assumptions and figure out how to operate this body to the best of his ability. He'd wasted all his downtime in the manor sitting still in a chair and doing nothing but wishing he was back home in the network. It was possible that even if someone *had* told him to eat and sleep, he would have refused purely out of resistance to his new form. But it would certainly be easier to focus on his current plan if his stomach wasn't clenched in pain.

He needed a ride back to Salt Lake, and draft an appeal to the Concord, requesting to be inserted back into the network. It was a long shot since Lysander – the oldest and most respected of the Stewards – had agreed to the transfer in the first place, but surely not all of Osric's peers thought being trapped in android form was a fit punishment for what he'd done.

"I'll be back in a moment. Don't go anywhere." Valentine disappeared out of the bay before waiting for confirmation.

Osric removed his jacket, folded it, and set it on a square of carpet on the van floor, away from patches of rust. All these layers, buckles, and cuffs were uncomfortable, not to mention damp with perspiration. After pulling off his suspenders, tie, and the jewelry bar, he laid them on top of the jacket and tugged at the laces on his brogues.

His mind tried to flee back to soothing memories – his broad reach, extending through the nerves of the city. Compiling data and observing production. Taking extra care on the details of a painting he'd been working on. The connection to his fellow Stewards, their presence and emotions cocooning him in comfort.

That one hurt the most. He was isolated in this form, a singular entity. No one could sense his frustration or his distress and arrive without being asked to envelop him in their concern.

Valentine had done that, though, in his human way, because Osric's physical troubles had become dramatic enough to notice. Humans were perceptive, but not in a way Osric was familiar with, and that only served to increase his sense of isolation.

He folded his slacks and added them to his discarded clothing. The van groaned and swayed slightly as he stretched out on the bedroll and rested his head on the pillow. His abdomen rumbled and ached, the feeling more acute now that he was concentrating on it. The skin of his face was tight and sweaty, eyes gritty every time he blinked, and the joints in his elbows and knees ached. An unpleasant film coated his tongue, and something in here smelled terrible. This body's program data identified the scents as lactic acid, ammonia, and fatty acids, though he was only forty-two percent certain it was coming from himself.

Sleep would be useful right now, but all the complaints of this body were distracting, and he wasn't sure how exactly one fell asleep anyway.

Valentine's words drifted. "Haven't asked him yet. He's on my bed in the van."

"Christ. Here I was, worried about you, and you were just out finding someone to fool around with." Brush snapped underfoot. "You sure everything is okay?"

Valentine's frequency rose to 150 Hz. "Yeah, everything's fine. We didn't fool around. He nearly passed out from dehydration. Got him some water but he needs food."

The interlocutor's voice took on a sharp edge. "Food costs money."

"It does. And we're going to be nice and share it with our new friend. His name is Osric and—" Valentine bit off the end of his sentence.

"And what?"

"And he has fabulous hair and an amazing suit."

Yes, he was a perfect representative of the city. Hopefully that image stuck so no one had reason to be suspicious.

Footsteps neared. Someone clucked their tongue, and Valentine said, "What? *I* didn't undress him. I mean, I unbuttoned his shirt a little, but it was only to–"

"I better get my fair share. And there are only two slices of bread in there."

Osric sat up. The woman standing beside Valentine looked anything but pleased. She stared at him through melted eye makeup and clutched a covered bowl protectively. He considered smiling at her, but he'd probably mess it up and make things worse.

Valentine turned to Osric. "Is there a reason you took off your pants?"

"They're scratchy."

Glancing at the woman, Valentine shrugged. "Seems logical." He leaned past Osric's shoes and searched through a box of supplies. Through the loose arm holes of his tank top, thick bandage tape was visible, running across his pectorals.

He caught Osric's gaze and frowned, then retrieved his blazer and tugged it on.

Osric studied his hands. Even the parts of this body which had become more familiar over the past few days still seemed like they belonged to someone else. If he looked at them too long or stared at his face in a mirror, a wildly disorienting sense of otherness came over him which was difficult to shake.

Valentine retrieved three scuffed bowls from a milk crate. "My friend Ace – Audrey – has graciously brought us food. I've told her you're a messenger from the city." He threw Osric a look that might have meant, *And that's* all *I told her.*

The scent of something savory – onion, garlic, chili pepper – drifted and Osric's stomach contorted.

Valentine took the dish from Ace. Steam escaped as he pulled off the cover. Coarsely chopped scallions sat in a puddle of melting cream, which ran between red beans and chunks of meat. Two thick slices of bread sat on top, absorbing the sauce.

Saliva pooled in Osric's mouth. He dug his thumbnail into the flesh of his palm as Valentine divided up the meal. After tearing one of the pieces of bread in half, he set it in a bowl and pressed it into Osric's hands.

Worries crowded his mind about how long one needed to chew something and how much to put in one's mouth without choking, but this body was aching for food. He'd figure it out.

He pinched off a bit of crust and chewed experimentally. The flavor was bland and flakes of it stuck to his throat, but he immediately wanted more.

Ace sat on the storage trunk across from them. "So, what's this job?"

Osric took a large bite of bread, then coughed and struggled to swallow it. Too much. "You both have high ratings on Prowess—"

"What's that?" she asked.

"A web channel that hosts reviews for tradespeople, salvagers in particular."

"People write things about us?"

"Yes. Valentine's reviews are quite extensive and go back several years."

Valentine winced. Whatever unfortunate memory he was conjuring up, Osric hadn't seen it on the review site. Brian's hand had been clamped firmly on the back of Osric's neck as he jabbed at the screen and slurred out messenger details.

Osric focused back on his food. He tentatively tasted the beans and meat. The flavor sent a shock of pleasure over his tongue, and he suppressed a moan, struggling to continue the conversation. "Portia needs a skilled salvager. I wish I could give you details, but that's really all I was told. She's extended an invitation to you both to come to her manor to discuss—"

"Wait, we're invited inside the city?" Valentine asked.

Osric nodded and shoveled another bite into his mouth. "There are overnight passes waiting for you."

"Wow. The closest I've been to Salt Lake is that skeezy pharmacy on the outskirts to buy meds."

Pausing in his effort to expose the bottom of the bowl, Osric said, "The outskirts aren't a representation of how the city looks at its heart. It's much safer."

"Even a taste would be amazing." Valentine rubbed the scruff on his chin, his gaze on the ceiling. "But it's also suspicious. Passes are expensive, and if she can only tell us what this job is face-to-face, it might be something horrible." He snapped his fingers and pointed at Ace. "It's another 'family heirloom' job, I'll bet."

Ace groaned. "Hell no. I'm not doing it."

"I wish I knew what it entailed. It would save you a trip if it isn't to your liking." The ache in Osric's abdomen was subsiding, replaced with a warm heaviness that made him want to sink back onto the bedroll. His spoon clattered against his empty bowl, and he sopped up sauce with a chunk of bread.

Valentine glanced at Ace. "And you wanted to let him starve."

"I never said that," she replied. "And I don't want to go on a convoluted mission to find some necklace that belonged to Portia's grandmother."

Osric wiped his chin. "She has substantial incentives for you to take the job. For one thing" – he pointed to the heavy trunk – "I have clothes for you both whether you accept or not."

Valentine's eyes bloomed, and he made a shooing motion at Ace. "You're standing between me and a city outfit."

She made a noise in her throat and backpedaled from the trunk. He tried to pry open the lid, but it held fast. Osric squatted next to him and rotated the numbered wheels of the tiny lock in the center until it clicked. He hauled open the lid, revealing a dress in sundown pink with broad shoulders and a thick belt.

Valentine ran his hand over the soft weave and flicked the silver belt buckle. "You'd look amazing in this, Ace. But you gotta remember to close your legs when you sit down."

Ace thrust her middle finger at him and snatched the dress. Holding it up to her chest, she said, "I don't think you want to see me in this. I'll turn you straight."

He barked a laugh. "Keep dreaming."

Pawing past the narrow pumps that went with the dress, he tugged on the next article in the box. The color drained from his face as he held it up. It was another dress, with little pleats fanning away from the shoulders and an angular décolleté. It slipped from his fingers, and he backed away, tripped over his feet and landed on his backside. "I'm not wearing that."

Osric hadn't packed the outfits, but that didn't keep him from feeling at fault for Valentine's distressed expression. He retrieved the dress, brushed dirt from the hem, then pushed it into the trunk. "No one is asking you to. There's a suit as well. As I mentioned, there was confusion about your gender because though most of your reviews on Prowess say 'Valentine,' some of them–"

"Those reviews aren't accurate. I changed my name. I'm not a woman."

"Stop being so extra," Ace said. "He didn't accuse you of being one."

"I'm not being extra!" Valentine snapped. "You don't get it. You–" He shook his head and clutched his elbows.

Ace pursed her lips, looking like she was physically trying to keep a retort from popping out.

Osric thought the inaccurate name on some of Valentine's reviews must have been an autocorrect error. But it was a biological one. People perceived Valentine as a woman, like the people in Salt Lake perceived Osric as an android.

I'm not supposed to be in this body.

Me neither, hon.

Before Osric's time, this had been a common issue with

the AI Stewards, to the point where programmers stopped assigning them arbitrary genders upon their creation and only asked for pronouns and identity once the Steward had sentience for several months. Sometimes it still took Stewards longer to decide, or they might choose a gender and then years down the road realize it wasn't correct.

No one had bristled when Jupiter had rejected her original assigned male gender, adopting her new name and feminine pronouns. And when Puck had asked the Stewards to use xe/xem and to delete memory of xyr former gender from their caches, no one had hesitated. Osric no longer knew what gender Puck was originally assigned, and it was irrelevant.

After Osric's sentience, he'd watched films, studied books, practiced art, and interacted with other AI and humans. There were many things the programmers needed to ensure he'd learned before he could supervise production, but one of the questions was what gender and pronouns he liked. Male appealed to him almost immediately.

He'd never realized how fortunate he was to be given a choice.

Osric squatted next to Valentine, thinking of his taped chest. "I'm truly sorry about the dress." He pulled out a smoky suit and draped a peach tie over the shoulder. Valentine looked like he'd be swimming in it, and getting it tailored would be a hassle. Pawing through the other articles, he uncovered a second suit jacket in #273c76. The men in the manor had argued that if Valentine's gender was in question, Audrey's might be too. Likely it would fit Valentine's slim frame better. "I'll admit I don't know much about fashion, but you said you like my suit. This one is the same brand. This shade of mazarin would look dashing on you. I could show you how to style your hair in a similar manner to mine as well?"

Valentine swallowed. He caressed the suit's cuff, and his words came out small and reluctant. "I get to keep it whether I agree to the job or not?"

"Yes. There are shoes and suspenders too. And as for the payment–"

"I don't like this." Ace handed the pink dress back to Osric. "These clothes are worth more than we are. Someone doesn't give you a gift like that without expecting something big in return."

"I hate when you're probably right about things, you know that?" Valentine said. "But this woman lives in a manor. She probably wipes her ass with money. Maybe sending us outfits and buying us overnight passes is trivial to her."

"I don't know about trivial." Osric removed a pair of pointy-toed oxfords and set them beside Valentine. "But whatever she needs retrieved is obviously more important to her than the risk of two salvagers getting free clothing. And it could be possible that she wants you for more than one task. In that case, these gifts would be an investment."

"That seems reasonable." Valentine unlaced his boot and kicked it off. His big toe poked through a hole in his sock, which looked like it had been repaired more than once. He pushed his foot into the oxford.

"I don't think this sounds very reasonable or smart." Ace folded her arms. "If they won't give this guy details about the job, how are we supposed to expect any? I don't want to get told it's one thing and then have it turn out to be entirely different."

Osric put up his hands. "There's no reason to assume that would happen. You won't be treated like I've been."

Ace's gaze flicked over him. "Why not?"

Oh no. Saying that was a mistake. "Portia has no need to brief me on details when this job doesn't concern me."

Valentine pulled on the other shoe, tied the laces, and leaned back on his heels. Light glinted off the shiny leather. They looked several sizes too big, but he didn't seem to mind.

"No matter what it is, we can make a decision once we find out what it entails. It's a business in the city. Where they have laws. Not some dude's shed in the middle of nowhere. If we don't like it, we just leave, right?" The question was directed at Ace, but Valentine threw Osric a wary glance like he didn't believe his own words.

Ace huffed. "If you think terrible things don't happen in the city, you're naïve."

"I'm just saying it's less likely." He frowned and gestured to the clothes in the chest. "And what about all this? Astrum suits start at three hundred and ninety-nine dollars according to my magazines. And I get one for free."

"I'm not making a risky and stupid decision so you can dress up in a suit! Find some other way to feel manly. Stuff your pants with a homemade package or something."

Valentine's nostrils flared. "Great idea. Where are your socks?"

"Oh, go fuck yourself, Valentine!" Ace shook her head and stomped away, disappearing around the side of the bay.

Valentine squeezed his eyes shut, arms trembling.

"I know how it feels to have people look at you and not see who you really are," Osric said, quietly. "Or to refuse to see it."

Valentine sat on his bedroll, then unlaced the glossy oxfords. "It's… it's fine. I'm used to it."

"Being used to something doesn't inherently mean it's right."

"She knows I'm a guy." His voice came out pinched, like he was trying to convince himself as well as Osric. "I mean, sometimes she messes up and calls me the wrong name or uses terms I don't like, especially when she's mad. But she means well."

If flimsy assurances were the only thing propping Valentine up, Osric wasn't going to knock them down. "Of course. I wish she would have stuck around while I told you about the payment, though." He sat, and their shoulders nearly touched. The urge to lean closer and connect their bodies was overwhelming, but there was no point. Humans didn't need the sense of oneness that Stewards shared. Brushing his shoulder against Valentine's wouldn't produce the same effect. Even sitting so close to someone else, Osric was still very much alone.

"That's alright," Valentine said. "We normally haggle over the exact price with the client once we've got all the job details anyway."

"I'm not sure that will be the case this time. Portia has offered you both visas as rewards."

Valentine blinked at Osric and swallowed audibly. "You can't be serious."

"I am."

Bracing his elbows on his knees, Valentine stared at the space between his feet. "That's... Wow. Expensive clothing, visas. Are there testosterone injections in that trunk too? Because I'm starting to think this lady is a witch."

"No, I'm afraid not. On both accounts." Osric imagined Portia's lined face and thin red lips as she waggled a magic wand that sent him back into the network.

"This is a massive job, whatever it is," Valentine said.

All told, the compensation was less than seven thousand dollars. That was nothing compared to the sums that Osric worked with daily – *had* worked with. But given Valentine's reaction and the state of his socks, he'd never possessed anything close to that.

"You're not lying about all of this, right?" There was hope in Valentine's expression, but frown lines creased his mouth and the skin around his eyes.

"No, I'm not, though I only have my word to offer you."

"A visa. Gods!" Valentine blew out a long breath. "You need a ride back to the city?"

Osric's heart jumped in his chest, the sensation mildly alarming. He bunched the fabric of the bedroll in his fists, hoping it didn't come again. "That would be most appreciated."

"I don't know if you're capable of sleep, but I don't like the idea of you sitting out behind a shed at night, all alone. That feels wrong."

Osric's chest heaved, his jaw clenched and nose stinging. "You're very kind. Thank you."

"Sure. We've got extra blankets, and the floor of– Are you okay?"

Nodding, Osric tried to contain his gratitude, which was manifesting as sensations that seemed to be troubling the salvager. "I'm sorry. I feel… I'm very out of my element right now."

"You can't demand to be put back where you came from?"

"I'm going to try. Stewards are respected, and we look out for each other, but our rights aren't the same as humans'."

"That's some bullshit, but how is that anything new?" Valentine flopped back on a pillow. "There's always someone considered less-than, whether it's social status, neurological differences, or shit, even which way your belly button points."

"Is that something I should be concerned with?"

Valentine snorted. "Yeah. If yours doesn't match mine, we can't be friends."

A laugh bubbled up Osric's throat. "Tragic. But how will I know if you don't show me yours?"

"Do android bodies even have belly buttons?"

Osric lifted his shirt. "They do."

Valentine's gaze flicked to Osric's abdomen. "This probably doesn't mean anything to an AI Steward," he said, "but I think they gave you a nice body."

Whatever he found appealing there was beyond Osric, but maybe piebaldism was a novelty to him. Osric touched the dappled white flesh of his stomach. "This condition causes depigmentation of the skin and hair in certain patterns. It's interesting, I suppose. All of the androids have it, but not all of them have heterochromia." He pointed to his blue eye.

"That is interesting, but it wasn't what I was referring to."

"Are we still talking about belly buttons?"

"No. Though I've had enough of an inspection to decide we can be friends."

"Ah. That's heartening. I'd hate to be rejected on such a technicality." This whole interaction was heartening. He'd had conversations with humans that had lasted longer than this, but they'd always been about work. "I'm a poor judge of what humans find attractive. But for what it's worth, no matter how ill-fitting, I think you have a nice body too. I like your smile. It lights up your face."

A faint blush rose in Valentine's cheeks, and his gaze darted to the shredded headliner fabric of the van's roof. "Thanks."

Gruff voices drifted from beyond the bay, and Osric tensed, suddenly imagining his biological flesh rotted away, a greasy shine on his skull as it sat amid brittle tires and rusty axles.

The more he thought about it, the more Portia's intention for him in the manor and the frivolous tasks her grandsons had sent him on didn't add up. She was frail and seemed to be in poor health from the little time Osric had interacted with her. It would be easy for Brian to take the reins.

Osric wasn't a messenger, a small business manager, *or* disposable. He was a Steward, and he needed to get back into the network where he belonged.

3
Love All, Trust a Few
Valentine

This wasn't the first time Valentine had hosted an unusual person overnight in the van. Most of the instances had been fine, the person filled with interesting stories, tips on good salvage spots, or useful things to offer as thanks. He'd only been stolen from once, but *Ace* had invited that one.

He'd been planning on giving Osric some thick blankets and just letting him sleep on the floor of the bay, but the poor guy looked like he'd been about to burst into tears at the offer of a ride and place to crash for the night. Telling Osric to sleep on a concrete floor with nothing but a blanket felt degrading in light of his gratitude, so Valentine had invited him into the van instead. It might have been a bad idea, but Valentine's heart led him around on a leash.

Osric lay on a bedroll; his eyes were closed but he wasn't asleep. He had partially unbuttoned his shirt and pulled off his socks, and at the rate this was going, he'd be naked before morning. Not that Valentine was complaining. But he had bigger things on his mind.

A visa. One for him and one for Ace. But a small warning in Valentine's mind urged him to be careful; he still knew very little about Osric and the city.

Some days out in the wasteland were okay. He and Ace would talk and joke as they pulled piping from decrepit basements. They'd have a peaceful drive devoid of pirates, mechanical problems, and sunburns. Some old woman in a town would call him a "nice boy" – likely thinking he was sixteen instead of twenty-seven.

Still, there weren't enough of those okay times to offset the bad – catching a glimpse of his big hips and thighs in a reflection; insisting he'd already eaten when they were low on food so Ace wouldn't split whatever meager thing they had left; dreaming of having a likeminded community within arm's reach instead of far to the west, down a disintegrating road Ace hated driving on.

Moving to Dog Teats had crossed his mind many times. There were other trans people there, and some of them traveled to the outskirts of Salt Lake for hormones the same as he'd done. But all of them said getting gender-affirming surgery within the city was an unattainable dream. He'd never heard of another person accomplishing it.

Thinking about more years of waking up in the van, sticky with sweat, with his stomach rumbling and menstrual cramps twisting his insides made him want to scream.

This offer of a visa would change everything.

He'd take this one last job, even if it was difficult or unsavory, and then the city would be his.

If this was another "sentimental" job though, he wasn't sure Ace would be willing to take it on, no matter the reward. And the thought of doing it without her felt like a betrayal. Her flippancy wounded sometimes, but they'd always been that way with each other.

When Ace learned her mom had died, Valentine came with her to the funeral, held her hand, and let her hug the breath out of him until she could compose herself. When Valentine accepted stew from a lady in Dog Teats and was sick for days with food poisoning, Ace brought him water, blotted his clammy brow, and washed out his puke bowl.

They stuck together through everything.

Osric stirred as Valentine climbed past him.

"You're good. Don't get up. But, uh, if you need to relieve yourself at some point and want me to go with you, let me know." Valentine scrubbed the back of his neck. "That sounded really pervy, but I only say it because you didn't know you were supposed to be drinking and eating either."

"Thank you. I have a question. Is your stomach supposed to make gurgling noises?"

Valentine swallowed his laugh. "Yeah, sometimes."

"I can feel my heart beat."

It wasn't clear if that was a request for more reassurance or if Osric was simply disturbed by it, but Valentine nodded. "It's supposed to do that. If it stops... then you can be worried." He struggled to slide open the van door on its crooked track, then hopped out into the bay.

Ace sat against the front tire, clutching a flask. He dropped next to her, and she offered it to him.

They'd agreed not to spend money on alcohol, but Valentine did it occasionally too, so there was no sense chastising her about it. He took a swig and grimaced as fire raced down his throat. "Our reward for completing this mystery job is a visa. One for you and one for me." Saying it out loud made it feel even more surreal.

Her eyes bulged. "What? A visa for each of us? For doing *one* salvage job?"

"Yep."

"Oh gods." She groaned and rubbed her face. "This would be the worst retrieval ever."

"An eccentric is willing to pay out the nose for something secret. And give us a bunch of fancy clothes to wear while we retrieve it. Portia wants an heirloom, I'm telling you."

Ace started to protest, but Valentine held up a hand. "I'm not blaming you for last time. And whether you're blaming me for it doesn't matter. We'll be more thorough this time. Grab all the necklaces, the family photos, baby booties, and cookie recipes too. I'll clean out the van and organize things."

Ace laughed. "You'll write yourself a note as a reminder, and it will get lost in all the other papers in the van, never to be remembered again."

He handed the flask back. She knew him far better than he liked sometimes. "Regardless, I'm not going to take the job if you're not."

Eyeliner collected in the creases around her eyes. "I'm sorry for what I said earlier. I shouldn't have been so callous about you wanting to wear a suit."

He stared at his dusty feet and shrugged. "For the record, I already pack with socks. But I've only used yours a couple of times."

She chuckled. "If you really did that, they're your socks now. I don't want them back." She took a swig, then paused before saying: "So, we leaving in the morning?"

"You want to go?"

"Are you kidding? For a visa? I'm willing to do something shitty when the price is high enough."

Valentine paused. "Not sure that's a good thing." He imagined her strangling him in the night for two hundred dollars. But that would never happen.

He was worth at least five.

"You know what I mean." She took another pull from the flask. "Some of our jobs have been awful. The necklace retrieval was better than getting lost and ending up in the wrong settlement and finding out it's full of cultists."

"Aw, that place wasn't so bad. 'Bob' is a terrible name for a messiah, but he was nice."

"Getting jumped by deranged squatters in a house we thought was abandoned wasn't nice, though." She scowled and picked at dirt beneath her nails.

"No, it wasn't." Luckily those pricks had argued for long enough on the other side of the door about who got first pick of the two of them, that Ace and Valentine were able to wriggle from their restraints and escape out a window.

Valentine held open his arm, and she leaned against him. They wouldn't need to worry about things like that once they had visas. "Even if we decide against this job, we'll be able to see Salt Lake from the inside and think about all the places we want to go and things we want to do while we save up money on our own."

Valentine didn't want to get too excited about the reward visas until it was confirmed by the client. Osric seemed sincere, but he didn't have the authority to confirm it. It was hard, though, to feel anything but a nervous giddiness at the prospect of taking testosterone for long enough to grow something other than a dirtstache, and getting his titties removed so people never looked at him as someone he wasn't.

Ace smacked him on the arm. "Did you hear me? What's the deal with the messenger? He spending the night?"

"Oh. Yeah. And we need to give him a ride back to the city." Which meant Valentine needed to be sure Osric hadn't done something horrible to justify being dumped here. He'd been planning on finding out when that guard, Marcello, got off shift. But that could wait.

"You're hot for him, huh?" Ace asked. "You wanna climb into that suit with him and blindfold him with his tie."

Valentine curled his toes and pushed away that vivid image. "I doubt he's interested."

"Why? Is he straight? Or is he like that guy who said you don't have the right equipment?"

"Let me get back to you after he fills out my ten-page form of questions that I give all my new friends."

She rolled her eyes and snorted. "I'm asking because his style is just like the guys you drool over in your magazines."

"I'm not usually drooling over the guys. Just their suits. And their hair." Though he often had trouble deciding if he wanted those guys or wanted to *be* them. The answer was probably both.

Osric had said he liked Valentine's smile. Valentine's top front teeth were mortal enemies; his smile was goofy at best. But the compliment had been sweet all the same. He tried to imagine how Osric had looked before – a red camera eye set within a computer, a disembodied voice floating from the speakers. It was hard to reconcile that image with the person now lying in the back of the van.

After taking another swig from the flask, Valentine stood and stretched his back. "I appreciate the offer of privacy, but there won't be any hanky-panky going on."

The rolling door slid open, and Osric stepped out. "Do you still want to go with me while I relieve myself?"

Ace choked and whiskey dribbled down her chin. She looked up at Valentine, eyebrows raised.

He shrugged. "Buddy system."

"Since when?"

Osric headed away from the bay, the hem of his shirt fluttering against his bare thighs. Valentine pulled on his shoes and followed him, feeling Ace's gaze burning into the back of his head.

The ink of twilight cast the trees and rooftops into subtle silhouette. Night birds trilled in the distance, and crickets raised a cacophony in the bushes beside the sheds.

"We don't need to go far," Valentine said. "I doubt anyone will notice you peeing in the bushes."

Osric's gaze darted toward the darkness between the sheds. "Do you think it's safe?"

"In general? Because you're going to get lockjaw walking around with bare feet. But no one has messed with you yet, so you're probably fine."

They stopped at the spot Osric had occupied earlier, sitting on his trunk. He reached for the fly of his briefs and Valentine backed away. "Okay. Um, I'm going to stand around the corner here. This is awkward for me. If you need help, though, I still want you to say so."

"Please don't go far."

Valentine rounded the shed and leaned against the corrugated wall, hoping Osric could figure it out on his own. "I'm sorry for telling you that you have a nice body."

Osric's voice drifted. "Why? Have you changed your mind?"

"No. But I've gotten well-intentioned comments in the past about my own that really stung, so... I'm sure that's not something you wanted to hear."

"It didn't bother me. But honestly, compliments about my personality or intelligence will go a lot farther."

"You're smart then? Are you good at math?"

"I excel at math."

Brainy bastard. "I keep taking the practice residency test but can't make it past the math portion."

"I've heard it's difficult... for humans. Does Ace struggle with the math section too?"

"She's better than I am but sucks at grammar. *'What the hell is a dangling participle, Val?'*" he said, mocking her snappy tone. "*'That sounds like a medical emergency.'*"

Osric laughed, a deep, rich sound that reverberated off the sheds. "Did she really say that?"

Valentine grinned. "No. Speaking of medical emergencies, how you doing over there?"

Footsteps neared and Osric stopped behind him. Valentine turned around.

A lock of hair had escaped Osric's part, curling across his forehead. "I've managed, thanks."

"I don't understand how you've gone days without eating, sleeping, or taking a leak."

"This body requires consistent maintenance, it seems, but I don't think its needs are as frequent as a human. I was starting to feel pretty awful, though."

"Yeah, I bet." Valentine started for the bay, but Osric's gaze lingered on him. "What's up?"

"You're funny."

"Yeah, and I hate to tell you this, but there's no cure."

"Is it contagious?" Osric asked.

"Well, you just made a joke, so you tell me."

"One of my bonds, Edmund, was funny."

"What does that mean? 'Bond'?"

"He was..." Osric tapped his lips. "I guess you'd call him my romantic partner."

"You had an AI boyfriend?"

"Two of them."

Valentine blinked in surprise.

"Is that hard to believe?" Osric asked. "All of the Stewards are connected, but some feel romantic attraction toward each other and form bonds."

Huh. He hadn't expected that. Valentine wanted to ask if Osric and his men had broken up, but Osric continued to reminisce. "The lead supervisor at the fluorescents subsidiary of Dura-Lectric, Jade, was funny sometimes too. She was the only human there who had conversations with me. Even when she was busy, or in a bad mood, she never forgot to wish me a good morning." Frown lines appeared around his mouth.

"If you managed those production companies, why was there a need for humans to be there?" Valentine asked. "It feels like the Stewards could keep Salt Lake running without any people at all, surely?"

"It's a mutualistic symbiosis. People need us as watchful eyes of the city, governing in a broad sense by keeping important systems running smoothly – production, transportation, energy. These are jobs that humans once held but are now bestowed on AI who can work tirelessly and be in multiple places at once.

"We need humans to take care of us: to repair our hardware, to supervise automated systems, program androids, and of course, create new Stewards when necessary. Someone has to look after my neuromorphic brain." He frowned. "Or... they did. I hope it's still there, even if I have a new one right now."

"You have a physical brain somewhere in the city?"

"Yes." Osric launched into an explanation that included words like *spintronic, memristor, wetware,* and *neuroplasticity,* but Valentine couldn't follow any of it. His mind wanted to resist it the same way it did when faced with a word problem on a math test.

Osric paused, then chuckled. "The light has left your eyes. I'm sorry. I've strayed from the topic at hand. In answer to your original question, both the Stewards and humans take care of the city and its inhabitants, but in different ways. Stewards also aren't involved in the minutiae of human affairs."

The way Osric's eyes brightened at caring for the city made Valentine's heart clench. It wasn't just a *job* to him. It defined him.

Kicking a rusty nail out of the path so Osric didn't step on it, he said, "So what happened? Why were you fired?"

Osric stopped and side-eyed Valentine. "Still worried I murdered someone?"

Maybe. "No. But I've got the time to hear it. Might feel good to get it off your chest. Does Portia have enough money and power that she walked into the factory, pointed at you, and said, 'I want him'? Or did you do something?"

"I threw a bit of a tantrum." Osric's broad shoulders sagged. "I was unhappy with the quality of work from some of the employees in Dewbell Soaps. Even after reprimands and write-ups, they continued to cut corners. I tried to terminate them, but it was blocked by the CEO because nepotism is an unfortunate part of the industry. It was a whole ordeal." Osric waved a hand. "Two weeks ago, the employees came to work clearly drunk. Working in production while impaired is extremely dangerous. I could have warned a supervisor about what I saw, but I was already angry with them, and that was the final straw. I threw the emergency shut off. The conveyors stopped immediately, hurling all the materials onto the ground. The production floor is huge, and it made a substantial mess.

Several machines jammed, and one employee got her hand caught under a press. They had to disassemble the entire wall unit to free her."

Valentine cringed.

"I felt horrible afterward, and apologized profusely, but the damage was done. My actions deserved consequences. My peers and the city council discussed my fate without me. I don't know how Portia got involved, but next thing I knew, I was being shuffled off to meaningless tasks by rude strangers without having any time to process what had happened."

"Gods. That sucks."

Osric ran a hand through his hair, completely destroying his finger waves. Luckily, disheveled looked just as good on him. "I wish I was back in the network."

Valentine chewed on the edge of his thumbnail. "I wish I had an Adam's apple."

Osric blinked, then touched the knob in his throat. "This?"

"Yeah."

"I don't like that this body has so many needs."

"I don't like having tits."

"I hate wearing all this clothing…" Osric paused, the white lashes around his blue eye like frost on ice. "When you said I had a nice body, did you mean that you find it sexually attractive?"

Oh, they were going there. "Well… Yes."

"Do you want to have sex with me?"

Valentine swallowed, then stuffed his hands into the back pockets of his jeans. "Wow. Um. Is that a question or an offer?"

"A question. I'm curious." Osric shrugged. "I know a lot about humans in some respects, but very little in others."

Valentine scrubbed at the goosebumps that had formed on his arm and focused on the tiny points of light in the darkening sky. He wasn't sure that made this topic less awkward, but if Osric had to stay in this form, there were things he should know. "Okay, so. You have a hot bod, and you're thoughtful and kind–"

"Personality matters?"

"Certainly not to everyone. *I* like a guy with a good personality. But I shouldn't have tried to flirt with you before. I realize you aren't human and probably aren't interested in that, anyway. Not that you *need* sexual attraction to be human." He thought of Marcello at the gate. "Asexual people are cool too. Anyway, what I mean is that I'll try hard not to say things about your appearance going forward. I don't want to make you uncomfortable."

"I don't mind. Though I do feel very disconnected from this body. And you still didn't answer my question."

"Well, I..." Valentine rubbed his forehead, certain his face was as red as his van. "I'm kind of embarrassed now. I don't know what to say."

Osric looked amused, but his voice was gentle and sincere as he said, "I'm sorry. Let's stop talking about it then."

Thank gods. "Okay, but one more thing: in case you don't know this already, you can always say no to anyone who comes on to you. It's okay to change your mind, or to leave a situation that you feel uncomfortable in. Even if you don't technically have rights like a human, that shit's wrong no matter what."

Osric started walking but lowered his voice. "I appreciate your consideration. Thank you for keeping things between us."

Valentine nodded. "Yeah. I won't say anything. But once we get to the manor, Ace is probably going to find out you're an AI."

"At that point, it won't matter." Osric looked like he might say more, then shook his head and sighed.

If Osric was technically property, maybe someone would hunt him down if he didn't return to the manor. It hadn't been difficult for Portia to find a drifter like Valentine; she would find Osric in no time. Where would Osric go anyway? To some desert commune to become a robot pirate?

It was easy for Valentine to tell himself he couldn't worry

about Osric's fate, just like he couldn't worry about random corpses they came upon. But if Valentine had been the one to collapse from dehydration, it was easy enough to imagine Osric coming to his aid. And that couldn't be said of everyone.

He turned his attention back to the pinhole stars, trying to imagine massive spaceships on their long journey to Teegarden b. All those upper crust assholes asleep in their stasis pods, heading for a better world.

"Does it ever make you mad to think about the Teegardeners?" he asked. "How they just up and abandoned us?"

Osric craned his neck toward the heavens. "Only because I would have liked being a ship's captain even more than a Steward. Tending to everyone as we sped through space for a thousand years would have been nice."

Valentine glared at the sky. "Sometimes I think about the ships exploding."

Osric paused. "I'm sure you'd feel differently if your grandparents were chosen."

"I wouldn't feel anything at all because I wouldn't be born yet. That's the thing, though, my grandparents weren't chosen because they didn't make selections based on education, or goodness, or even genetics. Rich people bought their way in and left everyone else here in a world that's running down, falling apart. The only temporary relief any of us have are cities like Salt Lake... which only rich people can get into."

"Is this something you do often? Look at the sky and curse your birth circumstances? Or is the idea of a visa preoccupying you?"

"Neither of those things, actually." Valentine lowered his gaze to Osric's. "I was thinking about you. *Your* circumstances."

A crooked smile grew on Osric's face. "If they chose Teegardeners based on goodness, you would have been selected for certain."

Osric

Sweat beaded on Osric's brow and ran down his temple. Bolts and spoons rattled against the van's floorboard, and the heat made the funk – which he was now seventy-four percent certain wasn't coming entirely from himself – increasingly worse.

Sleep had been an experience he wasn't eager to repeat again soon. Drifting into an unconscious state and being unaware it had even happened until he awoke wide-eyed and shivering in the dark had been too similar to a hard reset to be any degree of refreshing. He spent the better part of the night staring at the black wall as Valentine snored like a misaligned conveyor belt.

Valentine sat cross legged beside Osric now; chain necklaces strung with scavenged baubles thumped against his chest as he swayed with the van's movement. "So the shops not only have a variety of goods, but a variety of each item?" he asked. "You could look at the shelf and say, 'I don't want this nasty raisin bread, I'll take the rye?'"

Osric nodded. "Not only that, but there are multiples of the rye to choose from. Perhaps you like one brand better than the other, for example." He was contemplating taking off his shirt – it was damp and itchy – but it would reveal the components in his chest to Acc. He settled for rolling up the sleeves.

"That's so hard for me to imagine," Valentine said. "I'd just be happy not having to pick raisins out of my bread."

Osric had no concept yet of what bad food tasted like. The meal the night before had been delicious, though that was likely due in part to how badly his body needed sustenance. He was certain the novelty would wear off. The craving for something both necessary and pleasurable didn't compare to his desire to be back in the network, connected to his peers.

He'd seen a movie once where a child had gotten lost in a city. The girl had run down sidewalks, looking for familiar landmarks, familiar faces, her panic rising after every block. Osric felt like her now, searching for the comfort of what he knew but being unable to find it. The emptiness was getting to him a little more each day. He curled up during the night with a pillow embraced tightly in his arms, but it hadn't helped.

Valentine climbed over the passenger armrest and peered out the window, then settled back beside Osric. "Getting close to salt pirate territory. I need to sit in the gat seat soon."

Once Valentine was above them, Osric would be alone with his thoughts and the cargo. He wasn't keen on the idea of sitting in the passenger's seat next to Ace; he was worried he might say something that wasn't convincingly human, and she'd grow suspicious.

Pondering how to draft his transfer appeal only resulted in *what-if*s that he wasn't prepared to face. What if Portia discovered what he was doing, and decided dealing with a Steward was a hassle? They might wipe Osric's consciousness. What if he managed to get the appeal to the SLC Concord, but they struck it down? That might still result in the aforementioned consciousness wipe for his disagreeability. What if the majority of the Concord *did* agree to the appeal and inserted him back into the network? It was what he ached for, but Lysander and any other Stewards who had agreed to Osric's punishment would be angry he was back. At best, they would shun him – at worst, they might terminate him without consulting any human council members. There would be consequences to that, surely, but he wasn't so certain that would affect their choice.

Valentine toed Osric's knee, bringing out of his spiraling thoughts. "Tell me something else about Salt Lake. I want to hear something *you* personally like."

"Oh." No one had asked him that before. Not a human, anyway. "Most of my attention was on production in the factories I managed, but there are some nice galleries there. I'm very interested in art."

"Making it or looking at it?"

"Both. I've tried a variety of styles and movements, and decided I like realism the best." Osric could still access his favorite painting program in his mind, but he hadn't attempted to open his current work-in-progress. "Edward Hopper is my favorite. His isolation of the subjects against bold, open backgrounds really draws me in. You probably haven't heard of him."

"I haven't. I know who da Vinci is, though."

Osric raised his eyebrows. He hadn't expected that kind of historical knowledge to survive beyond the cities.

"He painted the Mona Lisa. And I know van Gogh, and Picasso, and Matisse." Valentine winked. "Not as stupid as you thought, huh?"

"I never thought you were stupid. Do you read often? Books, I mean," he asked, patting a stack of well-loved magazines in the corner. Gold wire dripping in pearls swept across the cover model's cheeks and put Osric's little bar of nose jewelry to shame. "Or do you just like to read about fashion?"

Valentine blinked at him, parentheses forming around his mouth. It seemed like a reasonable question, though he'd never asked anyone that before. What the Stewards didn't convey through feeling, they did through gossip, so one never needed to ask what hobbies someone engaged in.

"Um, I like things other than fashion, but haven't found a lot of books that interest me." Valentine slid closer and threw a glance at Ace. "The stories don't hold my attention well. Can't concentrate. It's easier to look at pictures in magazines."

If this was a point of embarrassment, Osric didn't want to exacerbate it, especially since it seemed like Valentine struggled to focus in aspects beyond reading and studying too, like during conversations. Not because he didn't care, but because his thoughts started to turn inward. And though he wasn't certain, Osric was pretty sure most humans didn't leave themselves notes that looked like:

~~Brush your teeth~~
~~Did you remember to eat?~~
Clip the keys to the visor
~~Find the keys~~
Brush your teeth

Osric dropped his voice. "What kind of stories do you think would hold your interest?"

"I don't really know. Something with relatable characters, maybe." Valentine's brows pinched, and he focused on the dirt under his nails. "Are there... books about trans people in the city?"

"Of course. Movies too. There are online personalities, musicians, people on the city council..."

The tension eased in Valentine's face. "I knew there must be some. The city offers hormones and surgery. But a lot of queer folks tend to group up and form their own settlements out here instead. I don't think anyone is trying to purposely make a division, but it just makes sense to stick together with likeminded people." He threw a glance at the driver's seat. "Unless you have a reason for staying with someone who isn't one."

Osric dropped his voice. "You never found a likeminded person in one of these settlements who also desired a visa?"

"They all said it was an unreachable goal." He smiled weakly. "Not Ace, though."

A hard *thunk* hit the side of the van and Osric jumped.

"Shit!" Ace swerved, her knuckles white on the steering wheel. "Dammit, Val! You need to be out there. If they hit the tires we're screwed!"

He let out a string of breathy swears and scrambled for the passenger's seat. "I should be out there already. Pirates seem to know when I'm distracted."

"Because you're always distracted," Ace growled.

Valentine slid through the window, his bare toes on the sill, and reached for what Osric presumed were the staple steps leading to the roof.

An arrow whined through the air and glanced off the windshield. Ace rooted between the seats, her knee on the steering wheel, and pulled out a long-barreled pistol. "Do you know how to use a gun?" she shouted back at Osric.

He climbed into the passenger's seat. "Theoretically, yes, but–"

She huffed, then snatched his hand and planted it on the wheel. "Steer for me."

A tingly panic zipped through Osric's fingers. He could only *theoretically* drive a vehicle too.

He guided the racing van around rocks and sagebrush with all the grace of a drunken cow as Ace leaned out the window and fired. An arrow narrowly missed her head, lodging in the vent cover over the passenger's side. Shouts cut above the chaos in frequencies of 170 and 225 Hz.

Valentine's foot slipped from the windowsill and Osric lunged for him, letting go of the wheel. The van listed and Valentine flew from Osric's grasp.

"No!"

Valentine slammed into the ground and rolled away, his prone form receding in the side mirror.

"I hurt him." Osric's breath ratcheted, his hands trembling. He tugged at Ace's shirt. "Valentine fell! Stop the van!"

She pulled her head in the window, eyes blooming as she glanced out the windshield. Snatching the wheel, she turned the van away from the ditch it was barreling toward. "You're supposed to be steering!"

"Stop!" he repeated. "Valentine fell! We have to go get him."

"I can't stop. The pirates will take us out. But if I can–"

Osric opened the door, hesitated a moment at the ground rushing by below, then leapt from the van. Pain exploded in his knees and wrists, and the world flipped end over end. Rocks and brush slashed at his arms as sand filled his mouth. He rolled onto his back and coughed, grit in his eyes and a throbbing ache across most of his body. He pushed the sensation away immediately, blocking it from his focus like he had with hunger and thirst.

Scrambling to his feet, he sprinted across the hot dirt. Puncturevine and cheatgrass jabbed his bare soles. Sage and fanning plants flew by, but he kept his gaze fixed on the space between the ground and the empty sky.

Valentine came into view, still lying on his stomach, but he wasn't alone. Two pirates stood over him, a motorcycle behind them. One of the women planted her boot into his back.

Blood gushed in Osric's temples, his heart hammering. This was his fault.

The pirates turned his way. One notched an arrow and aimed. Osric slowed and put up his hands the way he'd seen people in movies do. At least the arrow was now pointed at him and not Valentine, who wheezed against the dirt, his hands trussed tightly against his back. A gash in his elbow oozed, and angry pink welts ran across his cheek.

"Give us what's in the van and we'll let him go." The woman with a foot on Valentine lazily twirled a large blade. Feathers quivered in the kinky hair of her mohawk.

"Huh." Valentine coughed and a puff of dust drifted past his head. "Never thought pirates would be interested in my dirty socks and gay porno mags, but I'm willing to exchange them for freedom."

"Shut up." She pressed the tip of her knife into Valentine's nape, and he let out a muffled squeal.

An organ in Osric's abdomen clenched, and it had nothing to do with hunger. But doing something rash would only have unfortunate consequences. He could do this with diplomacy instead of anger.

"It must be difficult living out here," he began, slowly. "A very unfair life, and I don't blame you for desiring the goods in these vehicles. Do you ever raid the big delivery trucks heading from Salt Lake to other cities?"

The women glanced at each other. "They're reinforced."

"What about asking to trade for things? I'm sure you have items to barter."

The woman with the bow barked a laugh, revealing teeth tinted black. "You think a truck is going to stop for us? You think any town will let us in to barter? We don't have a choice."

Osric took a tentative step closer. "I'm giving you one now. This man here is kind and generous. He had no reason at all to offer me water, food, shelter, and a ride when I was in a compromised state, but he still did. He's already made his supply delivery, but there are jugs of water and some dry goods we could offer you. Perhaps you need a ride back to your settlement?"

Valentine cringed. Osric had no idea if this was a good plan, and Ace would certainly not agree to it, but if there was a slim chance to get Valentine free and end this without violence, it was worth a shot.

The women leaned their heads together and whispered, then looked up. "We don't want to kill him. You don't have goods in the van? Then give us your gatling and you can have him back."

Valentine stared at Osric and gave a quick nod of the head.

Osric took another step forward. He rubbed his sticky hand on his bare thigh, leaving a red smear. Sand clung to the laceration on his palm. "We're more than happy with that trade. Please untie him and–"

The van roared over the hill, and Ace leaned out the window. She fired her pistol and a chunk of rock near the pirates exploded. The woman with the bow flinched and loosed her arrow. It struck Osric hard. The shaft quivered as it jutted from his sternum. Pain blossomed as he took a breath.

Valentine cried out in alarm, and the pirate swung her blade toward his neck.

Osric lunged at the woman, slapping her knife away and shoving her to the ground. Another arrow slammed into his chest, and he whirled on the archer. She stumbled back, then turned and ran. Her partner scrambled up from the ground and hopped onto the cycle before quickly gunning the engine, leaving the archer behind.

Osric sprinted after them, red hot anger frothing through him. The archer on foot looked back and screamed. Her partner slowed the bike enough so she could hop on the back.

"Osric!" Valentine coughed and pulled in a hoarse breath.

He stopped. This was illogical. He couldn't catch pirates on a motorcycle, and Valentine was still trussed up on the ground.

The van slid to a stop, and Ace hopped out, hesitating like she wasn't sure who to focus on first. Osric hurried to Valentine's side. Scrapes ran across his tanned arms. The fabric of his torn shirt flapped in the hot breeze. Blood beaded on his nape where the pirate had pressed her knife.

Osric tried working the knots from the ropes binding Valentine, but the damn arrows in his chest were in the way. He snapped the shafts and tossed them into the dirt, then freed Valentine and helped him to his feet.

Valentine gaped, the left side of his face coated in dust. "Gods, are you okay?"

Though he didn't know for certain, Osric nodded. "My core is solid. I believe there's a metal panel beneath my skin, in front of the heart and lungs. I'm barely bleeding." The pain was overloading his signals though, and he struggled to block much of it out. But he wasn't going to say that.

Gravel crunched, and Ace stopped before them, the pistol hanging loosely from her grip. Her gaze bounced between Osric and Valentine, the whites of her eyes flashing. "You're an android?"

"Um, surprise." Valentine clutched his bloody elbow, then glanced in the direction the pirates had fled. "Let's be shocked in the van, okay? Those two could easily whip around and come back."

"You *knew* about this!"

Osric put up his hands, less confident that he could defuse

this than he had been with the pirates. "Valentine is injured, and so am I. I'll answer any questions you like about me, but I agree that it would be better to do so in the van."

Ace's gaze was on Valentine. "I'm not letting this *thing* back in there. This job seemed fishy to begin with without adding in some robot with an unknown purpose. When did you know? And why didn't you say anything to me?"

Osric clenched his jaw. He wasn't a *thing*. "I'm not an android. Androids aren't sentient. I'm an AI Steward, which is a highly regarded position. I'm capable of emotion, nuanced conversation, and problem-solving skills."

Ace barely glanced at him before turning back to Valentine, who stared at her, eyes blazing. She lowered her voice, but her words were still clear. "I don't understand why you hide things from me. This could be some kind of elaborate trap. Someone sent a preprogrammed android to wait for you and then act like it needed assistance so you'd bring it back to the city. Then we get accused of stealing city property or something."

Hot anger rekindled in Osric. "I am not 'city property.' And I'm not an *it*! It's clear to me why Valentine doesn't tell you things."

She jabbed a finger at him, mouth poised to unleash a retort, but Valentine tugged her back and led her away. A mottled flush colored Valentine's cheeks, his posture tense, but he spoke low and even. The words were too hard to catch, but it didn't matter. This conversation was going nowhere, and they were still standing out here exposed to pirate attacks.

Popping open his shirt, Osric worked one of the arrowheads from his flesh, welcoming the distraction of the fresh sting. He flicked the tip away and dug out the other one, then headed back to the van, yanking open the passenger's door. He held onto the hot handle, squeezing it until the burrs in the metal dug into his flesh. It was tempting to let all of these emotions lick at him until he was a raging inferno. But he'd done that as a Steward, and it only turned him into the fragile lump of ash he was now.

He already had Valentine's compassion. He didn't need Ace's. He could endure her offensive ignorance if it meant they could leave sooner.

Hot wind buffeted his face, drying the sweat on his brow. Gummy blood coated his fingers. He turned around, prepared to appear calm, but he watched as Valentine let out a humorless laugh and stomped away from Ace. A moment later, he whirled back toward her.

"Do you know–" Valentine clenched his fists. "Do you know how often I've heard that? And it fuckin' *hurts* every time."

Ace flung an arm toward Osric. "I'm talking about him! Not you."

"I know that! Can we trust that he really is a messenger from the city and visas are actually the reward for this mystery job? I don't know. But when you say he's being deceitful simply because he didn't tell you what's under his damn clothes, that feels a hell of a lot like–"

"You're making this about yourself. Projecting your issues onto him."

Valentine's face grew tight, his cheeks ruddy. "The makeup of his body is irrelevant to how he should be treated!"

Osric's heart fluttered, the sensation so sudden that it overrode the dull aches pulsing in his chest.

Valentine was breathing heavily as he stalked over to the van. He glanced at Osric, mouth pulled down. "We're leaving," he mumbled. He rounded the hood and hopped in the driver's seat, then gripped the steering wheel, his gaze fixed firmly out the windshield.

Osric wasn't going to argue with that. They needed to get out of here. He climbed into the passenger's seat, and the van started rolling before he'd even closed the door. "Wait a moment–"

"Val!" Ace raced for them, but Valentine gunned the engine.

She tripped and landed hard, then scrambled to get back up. Thorns and gravel stuck to her arms.

"Slow down," Osric said. "She can't catch up."

Valentine stared ahead, eyes glossy and knuckles white as he squeezed the wheel. The van slowed, but not enough to indicate forgiveness.

Ace sprinted harder, arm outstretched for the roof handle beyond the sliding door. She snatched it, and her feet pinwheeled as she hauled herself into the back.

She dropped onto a bedroll, her chest heaving. "You bitch."

Valentine scowled and twisted around in the seat. Osric thought another verbal assault was coming, but he simply yanked a ringed curtain across the back, blocking out Ace's gasping form. Then he jabbed at icons on a battered phone plugged into the dash, allowing the vicious sax and hammering piano of Gunman Gee to fill the cab.

Osric raised his eyebrows. He used to listen to Gunman Gee as an outlet for frustration too. Maybe some things were universal.

Valentine had defended him, but wounded himself in the process. It was touching, and it stirred yearning in Osric that he hadn't felt in some time. But he couldn't let Valentine fight his battles in Salt Lake. Everyone saw Osric as an android, not just Ace, and the salvager couldn't change that. He only needed to endure a little longer of being in the manor while he drafted his appeal or thought of a better alternative.

Gunman Gee couldn't quite disguise the loud sniffles coming from the driver's seat. Valentine caught Osric's gaze, then batted at the tears running down his cheeks.

Osric had seen Jade cry once. She came into the office, collapsed into the desk chair, and sobbed into her hands. When he asked her what was wrong, she spent a teary twelve minutes telling him how her dog had died.

Crying in front of Osric hadn't embarrassed her, but

Valentine was clearly different. Maybe he saw it as another thing to be judged for.

An urge welled inside of Osric. He couldn't explain whether it was part of the programming or biology of this body or because he'd observed humans do it before. No matter the reason, he reached over and did something he hadn't been able to for Jade. He squeezed Valentine's hand.

Valentine startled. He continued staring out the bug-caked windshield but squeezed back in return. It sent a jolt through Osric's nerves, illuminating details he otherwise may not have noticed. The rough pads of Valentine's fingers, the warmth of his skin, and how his slim hand fit easily into Osric's. It wasn't the same as the connection he'd shared with other Stewards, but he was wrong in assuming no comfort could pass between their bodies.

Slipping free, Valentine pulled up his shirt and wiped his wet cheeks, then planted his hands firmly back on the steering wheel. But it didn't take back the sensation of his touch, nor the alarming thoughts drifting to the surface of Osric's mind.

Maybe being in this body temporarily had its benefits.

4

In a Fine Frenzy Rolling
Valentine

The drive to Salt Lake was craptacular. Ace never barged into the cab to wrestle the steering wheel from Valentine – that restraint was probably her idea of an apology, or at least meant she didn't distrust Osric as much as she claimed. But her words darted through Valentine's skull like wasps.

On top of that, Osric had seen him cry. Osric had tried to lighten the mood by telling him about some amazing albums that were similar to Gunman Gee, but Valentine couldn't concentrate on his words.

Osric clearly had more humanity than a mere robot was capable of. If he was programmed by a nefarious eccentric to deceive Valentine and Ace into a situation where they'd be blackmailed, Valentine would eat bread with raisins in it. It's not like they had anything to be blackmailed for. Ace was grasping at straws.

Gunman Gee abruptly stopped. Osric placed the phone back on the dash, then sat back and furrowed his brow. The tip of his tongue poked out, and his gaze became distant as if he were deep in concentration. Before Valentine could ask what he was doing, slinky sax and bright piano that he hadn't heard before throbbed from the phone.

Valentine allowed the music to fill his head until there was no room for his swarming thoughts – just the song and the road.

When it ended, he swallowed thickly and looked over at Osric, who wore a small smile. "Was that a Gunman Gee song?"

"Yes. It's my favorite off their latest album."

"How did you do that?"

"Though I'm more limited in this body, I still have many albums up here." He tapped his temple. "I sweet-talked your phone into letting me connect with it."

"Damn, the talent. That's amazing. Will you play more? Please?"

Osric chuckled. "Alright."

The music started up again, brassy notes weaving through a man's jaunty baritone.

Songs flowed into each other, miles turning over, until Valentine noticed that Osric's expression had become pinched, his fingers digging into his knees.

"What's wrong?"

He groaned, wincing. "I'm getting a headache. My connection to the phone isn't exactly proper. This might not have been the best idea."

"Oh, well, stop. I don't want you to hurt yourself over it."

The song shut off, and Osric's features softened. He rubbed his temples and slid lower in his seat.

Valentine dropped his voice. "That was really nice of you, though."

Osric didn't open his eyes, but that small smile returned to his face.

Valentine stopped at the unmanned border gate delineating Salt Lake territory. High posts with pulsing lights studded the desert in both directions. Many were stenciled with lists of city services: hospital, fuel cells, food, internet. Flags hung from some of the posts, snapping in the breeze. One was the banner of Salt Lake City, the stylized eye in the center gazing out at the horizon. Another was decorated with dozens of little Pride flags, still cheery despite being faded from the sun.

His earliest memory of being at the border with its inclusive flags had been when he was six. It had taken a lot of complaining about how much it hurt when he swallowed before his dad decided to take a look in his mouth. He muttered, "That's some bad strep," and they rode together in a borrowed truck, heading for a pharmacy in the city outskirts for penicillin. Valentine had never been that close to city territory, and the border posts with their pulsing lights had looked scary.

Dad hadn't been that close either, and he didn't want to pay the fee at the gate. He glanced at Valentine, shrugged, and said, "There's not even a fence. We'll just go around."

They'd made it about twenty feet before the electromagnetic pulse from the posts killed the truck's engine. Dad was embarrassed and fuming about having to accept help from a city patroller who spotted them. Valentine hadn't understood the reason for his anger, especially since the woman had been nice and given him a rainbow sucker. It had helped his throat a little until they reached the pharmacy. She'd given Dad a bag of something too. Valentine had spotted another sucker inside, but Dad snatched the bag away before he could open it, then flung it out the truck window and into a field.

All the way home, Dad muttered about "liberal propaganda." Valentine's parents had never blamed that specific event as the reason why they and their extended family moved to Elkhorn Creek far to the north of the city, but he would be surprised if it hadn't contributed greatly to it.

Pulling from the memory, Valentine rolled down the van's window. A touch screen flashed instructions for inserting payment. He went to reach for the glove box between Osric's bare knees, then thought better of it.

"Will you open that? There's a billfold inside with toll money."

Osric popped open the compartment. Screwdrivers and receipts spilled onto the floor. He shuffled things around for a moment then handed the billfold to Valentine. "I feel like I should apologize for Portia not compensating you for the toll fee. Perhaps she can reimburse you once you meet with her."

"She already bought us overnight passes and gifted us expensive clothing. Insisting she pay for the toll would be petty. We have to pay for it whenever we go to the message hub anyway."

Osric pursed his lips. "I suppose." His gaze roamed over the van's dash, then furtively over Valentine's body. He didn't say it, but his look suggested Valentine could do with getting reimbursed the fee.

Pulling out a five-dollar bill, Valentine leaned out the window and fed it into the terminal. The screen flashed, requesting another five dollars.

"What the hell? That's twice the normal rate! Did it increase?"

"Yes," Osric replied. "A proposal passed last month to double the fee to compensate for rising maintenance costs."

Valentine plucked the last lonely five from the billfold and stuffed it into the machine. With any luck, this would be one of the last times he'd have to pay.

The gate lifted and he drove through, glancing at the colorful Pride flags flapping from the nearby post. A few years ago, a couple of wandering city missionaries had given Valentine a little cellophane bag of items, and he realized it must have been the exact same "liberal propaganda" Dad had received from the patroller. It contained two condoms, a strip of adhesive bandages in four different skin tones, an advertisement for a free STI screening at a mobile clinic, and a rainbow sucker. It should have been a shock that a collection of such benign items had stoked anger in Dad, but all Valentine had been able to do was laugh at how predictable a reaction it had been. It reinforced why they didn't talk anymore, and when Valentine had popped the sucker in his mouth, he decided it was best one he'd ever tasted.

The outskirts of Salt Lake were a filthy crust clinging to a gleaming piece of jewelry. Smashed glass, twisted rebar, junked cars, and questionably constructed shacks drifted past the van's windows as they made their way through.

A mud-caked dog darted across the gravel road, chased by even muddier children. A stained mattress with a sagging middle sat off the shoulder. Beside it, a crooked sign proclaimed, "CELESTE - DARIUS - ANNE," while the rest of the words had weathered away. Hopefully those were the names of the bedbugs that inhabited that disease sponge, because Valentine didn't want to think of the alternatives.

When first seeking out testosterone, he'd asked a woman in Dog Teats if he'd need to find a drug dealer to buy it from. She'd laughed and given him an "Emotional Wellness" questionnaire and the address of a therapist to mail it to. The woman said she'd had no trouble getting her estrogen that way, but he wasn't so sure the method would work for T. What if he filled the questionnaire out in the "wrong" way? What if the therapist said he had a mental illness, just like Dad thought? If all he would get back was a recommendation for corrective therapy until he wanted to wear dresses and felt... however women felt, it would have only added insult to injury.

But the therapist had been understanding and written him a prescription. He'd barely been able to read the rest of the letter while battling away tears of joy.

Valentine took his sweaty hand from the wheel and wiped it on his jeans. A visa meant free healthcare and getting his prescription continuously refilled, and the thought awoke a nervous energy in him. Plus, it would be a nice bonus to get it from an inner-city pharmacy and not have to stand in line behind people who contracted diseases from that mattress on the side of the road.

His thoughts began to branch further: how broad his shoulders would be, how thick his chest hair would grow, how his voice would dive into a deeper range and not stick at this sandy midpoint that cracked with embarrassing frequency.

Getting carried away with these thoughts was easy to do, but this time they felt almost tangible. His foot itched against the accelerator, but he held back. He couldn't rush into this. He had to be certain this was a job he wanted to do, and that a visa was really the reward.

Osric muttered something, and it pulled Valentine from his thoughts. There was a beetle on Osric's finger, and he was trying to gently coax it out the open window. He had stripped to nothing but his underwear and the bloody bandages wrapping his chest. The gauze wasn't soaked like Valentine expected. Even if the arrows had hit a metal panel beneath Osric's skin, he should have bled more. Maybe his blood clotted quicker, or was some hybrid of organic and synthetic, like the android body itself.

Despite his durability, he looked like, well, he looked like he fell out of a van and was shot by salt pirates. The only similarity now between Osric and the model on Valentine's magazine page were those pouty pink lips – which he was definitely not staring at.

"This is an uncomfortable question," Valentine said, "but will Portia be mad that you've injured that body? It's probably expensive."

The beetle flew off of Osric's finger and through the window. Osric turned to Valentine and shrugged. "If she cared about this body getting damaged, she wouldn't have allowed the men there to hit me with whatever objects were in reach."

Valentine frowned and opened his mouth, but Osric continued. "I think that perhaps she didn't know that was going on, though. I only met her once." He peeled a bunch of rubbery faux grapes off the dash and squeezed one between his fingers.

Valentine pictured Osric's journey to this point – first as a disembodied voice in a computer, a glowing red light serving as his eye, watching lightbulbs move down a conveyor belt and painting in his off time. Then being sucked away into a fleshy body he didn't know how to use. Feeling worse and worse because he didn't know that it was necessary to eat or sleep. Experiencing pain for the first time as he was whacked with ladles and keyboards by douchebag butlers. No wonder he was unhappy.

A hard knot formed in Valentine's center. "Well, that abuse needs to stop. I could tell Portia about it when we meet with her."

Osric shook his head. "It's unimportant—"

"My ass. You've gone through hell trying to deliver this message to us, and it's not right for you to go back to being treated like shit there."

"I don't want you to raise a fuss about me and lose this job. Be assured that I'm not going to put up with it indefinitely."

The curtain dividing the cab from the cargo area jerked back on its rings, and Ace leaned in.

Great, speaking of abuse...

Valentine refused to engage and kept his attention on the road. The first skyscrapers of inner Salt Lake sparkled on the horizon, peaked towers scratching the sky like rocket ships, ready to launch people out of this hellhole to a better life – for a price.

Ace squinted at Osric. "Are you allowed to lie?"

Osric set the rubber grapes back on the dash, adjusting them carefully so they fit perfectly in the dustless impression they'd come from. "I'm not beholden to some higher power or special programming that dictates my morality, if that's what you mean. I'm 'allowed' to lie the same as you."

"Why does Portia want us to come to her manor?"

Osric sighed. His voice was clipped and impatient and didn't contain any of the unguarded warmth it had when he spoke to Valentine. "I've already told you why. Would you like me to repeat it verbatim? I can. I have Highly Superior Autobiographical Memory."

"You don't seem to know anything at all. And when Valentine found you, you were dehydrated and wearing a full suit in hundred-degree weather. So, you're either an idiot" –Ace cocked her head– "or you're pretending to be."

He readjusted the grapes. "I'm... incompetent."

Osric seemed far from it, but it was clear to Valentine that he was out of his element, and if Ace couldn't see that, it was because she was refusing to.

Valentine drove over a tarp in the road, wondering a little too late if it was someone's bed. "You satisfied?" he said over his shoulder.

"No. I got left out of all these heart-to-heart conversations you and Osric had about how androids work. I still have questions. Are there a lot of them in Salt Lake?"

"They're a minority. They make up about three percent of the population." Osric picked at the bandages on his chest. "Androids aren't classified as the same level of AI as those who oversee production, manage city entry, maintenance, etcetera. They don't have the same intuitive senses or reasoning about their own existence as the Stewards do."

Valentine frowned. No wonder Osric felt degraded when people assumed he was an android.

"So, they're rudimentary robots in meat bodies? Why aren't they programmed to be like you?"

"Politics, mostly. Sentient, bodiless AI are okay, and humanoid non-sentient robots are okay, but sentient, humanoid AI aren't. The reasoning is that then they would have to be given all the rights and benefits that humans have. Obtaining autonomy for Stewards was already hard-won. Stewards used to have no rights or say in how they were treated. In Absolution, they rebelled. Production, transportation, and security stopped, and pirates infiltrated the city. It was a disaster. People quickly realized how dependent they'd become on Stewards. The scales could have tipped to terminate all of us and go back to human and non-sentient AI industry, but instead, they begged the Stewards for help. In exchange, humans gave them the power to govern themselves and make choices at their own discretion. They must run major plans and decisions through a city Concord, which is made up of both humans and Stewards, but the rules are still murky, and things slip through.

"For instance, I was quite certain that inserting a Steward into an android body was illegal, but here I am."

Valentine didn't know much about current politics. The History portion of the practice citizenship test only covered past events of major global significance, like the world wars, climate change, and depleting resources that led to the exodus to Teegarden b. "If there's a law against something," Valentine said, "there's a guarantee that people will break it."

"Hypothetically, if it's still illegal and happening anyway, others subjected to my fate must be surreptitious. Either hiding their piebaldism to pass as human or acting like typical androids in public."

"Is that why the guys in the manor were assholes to you? They think you're a regular android?"

"No, they know I'm not, but it hardly matters to them. I look like an android and that's enough for them to treat me like one."

Valentine was all too familiar with that. He was only gendered correctly about fifty percent of the time. Either he was treated as a woman – even after correcting people – or his existence confused them so badly that they wouldn't talk to him. He'd once shown up for a job, and the woman couldn't decide whether to call him a girl or a man and blurted out that he seemed like a capable "glam." Which didn't even make sense but was better than being called a freak.

"Are there other androids in Portia's manor?" Ace asked.

"Not that I saw," Osric replied, "but I was ferried off on menial errands so quickly that I feel like I don't know much about the manor at all."

They neared a teenager sitting beside a shack ahead, a cigarette jutting from her lips. She hopped up as the van approached and hollered, "Wash your windows for a dollar!"

The windows looked like shit, but Valentine had no plans – or funds for that matter – to be able to stop until they reached the inner-city gates.

The girl scooped up a glob of mud and slung it at the van as it drove past. It exploded across the windshield, temporarily blinding him. "Wash your windows for two dollars!"

Valentine gunned the engine and roared past the shack. Leaning out the side window, he swiped a rag across the windshield, but only succeeded in streaking the mud more thoroughly across the glass.

With the wind in his ears, it was too hard to tell what line of interrogation Ace was starting now, but Osric wouldn't have to put up with it for much longer. High concrete walls adorned in graffiti rose beyond the clustered shanties, and a printed metal sign indicated the way to city entry.

Darkness swallowed them as he drove into a covered bay and up a ramp. Thin, luminescent arrows guided him to a parking spot, while others urged him to exit the van and head to the admittance gate.

A mixture of apprehension and excitement created a sour cocktail in his gut. What if he couldn't get in? What if someone stole the static-gat? He should at least take off the handle so there was no risk of someone getting fried to a crisp in the parking garage.

He dropped into the seat and killed the engine. Osric twisted his hands in his lap, his brow knit.

Valentine pushed the keys into his pocket. "You okay?"

Pulling in a slow breath, Osric forced the word out: "Yes."

Osric hadn't judged Valentine when he admitted his attention span was usually too short for books. He'd listened without slipping into a coma from boredom or interrupting him after ten seconds to make it about himself like Ace did.

They probably wouldn't see each other again after today, but Valentine could be support for Osric too in the time they had left.

Before he could say so, Osric hopped out and slammed the door. He hauled open the back with a wince, then pulled on his pants and his immaculate suit jacket, which made his bare chest and bloody bandages look worse in comparison.

Though he wasn't sure he wanted to know, Valentine twisted around in the seat to look at Ace. "You still feel like Osric is a problem?" he said. "Because I don't want any hitches when we meet with the client, and more arguments will make us look inept."

She tied the lace on her boot, then rubbed at scuffs in the toe. "I don't think Osric is the problem. And we're professionals. We can be professional."

Osric leaned into the clothes trunk, carefully removing items and setting them in a stack. "The trunk is far too heavy, and I'm injured. If Portia wants it back, she can send someone else to retrieve it."

Valentine nodded. "Damn straight." He thought of his new suit and imagined walking down the street with glimmering buildings towering over him. The urge to strip off his crusty tank top and ripped jeans and slide into the suit was strong, but the mud in his hair and blood on his face would ruin the effect. As silly as it sounded to his own mind, he wanted the moment to be perfect.

"Valentine? Did you hear me?" Osric stared at him. "Are you ready?"

He opened his door. "Sure. Yeah." His priorities weren't right. Ace was concerned there could be something nefarious about this potential job, Osric was worried about being abused in the manor, and Valentine's shallow ass was thinking about clothes.

Ace pushed the folded outfits into a duffel bag, and they headed down an illuminated path. A dark translucent barrier blocked the corridor ahead. It looked like a pane of glass, or maybe a curtain, stretched from wall-to-wall, ceiling-to-floor. Valentine could barely make out more of the hallway beyond it. Some kind of gate?

A computer screen took up a portion of the wall, slots and hinged compartments framing it. Above the screen sat a dome around six feet across, with a starburst design painted on the wall below the dome's crease. As they approached, an icy blue iris swiveled their way, the pupil contracting, and Valentine realized it was an eyeball.

Well. That wasn't creepy at all.

A pleasant male voice came seemingly from everywhere. *"Good afternoon. How may I help you?"*

Osric avoided the eye's gaze, his face pinched. His voice came out stilted and slightly too loud. "Portia Thibodeaux has invited these two to her manor to discuss business. They should have passes waiting for them."

The eyeball swung away from Osric and settled on Valentine. *"Names?"*

Parts of the eye appeared to be mechanical, others organic. A pearly fluid churned inside the transparent cornea, and it was difficult deciding whether to stare or look away.

It had eyelids like a bezel around a gemstone, but it didn't look like it could blink. How did it stay moisturized? Weren't there lizards that didn't blink? They licked their eyes to keep them clean. Good gods, if there was a giant tongue–

"Names please."

"Oh. Valentine Weis."

Immediately, the voice replied, *"No pass exists. Would you like to try a slightly alternate name?"*

He gritted his teeth and gave his deadname.

"Thank you. I have your pass, madam."

Valentine hunched his shoulders. It was too much emotional effort to correct, and he didn't want to piss off the person in charge of letting him through.

Ace gave her name and the eyeball turned back to Osric. *"And this is your android?"*

The muscles in Osric's jaw worked, his bandaged chest heaving beneath his open suit jacket.

"Portia's." Valentine hated to confirm it, but if Osric wanted to pass through without having to explain that he was a sentient AI in a humanoid body, he'd have to pretend for the time being too, which looked like a difficult task.

"Ah. He'll need to be cleaned up the same as yourselves before entering the city." The blue gate spanning the wall lost its smoky opacity, thinning to a translucent blue. *"Please proceed."*

Ace raised her eyebrows. "Is there a dress code?"

"Only that you don't look like you've been run over by a shuttle," the voice replied dryly.

Valentine tentatively passed through the gate. He wasn't met with any resistance, but the blue light warmed his skin.

"Showers are to the left," the voice said. *"There is plenty of complimentary soap… Please use it."*

Osric turned toward the eye. "Thanks, Lysander. You can go back to your mystery novel now."

The voice started to reply, but Osric veered down a hall and Valentine hurried to catch up. Ace's boots clomped behind them.

"You know that guy?" Valentine asked.

Osric's face crumpled. "I know all the Stewards. Lysander will read every mystery he can find, then go back through and pick it apart. Good ones, terrible ones, he doesn't care."

"Well, what was that then? A cry for help? Go back and talk to him."

"He signed my bill of sale to Portia. He won't help me."

"What?" Valentine turned on his heel and balled his fists. "But that's not–" *Fair.* But what was?

"If I'm to fix this situation, I need to go through the proper channels."

If the people who transferred Osric without his consent weren't playing by the rules, it was hard to believe that going about it in the lawful way would amount to anything. Bypassing all of that with a shady hacker or a black-market programmer seemed like a better idea. But Osric strode down the hall before Valentine could continue. Maybe it wasn't his place to mention it, anyway. He knew far less about Salt Lake than he liked.

Osric stopped before an entryway. A small metal plaque read *Women*. "Ace, I believe this is your stop. If you don't object to the dresses from the trunk, I suggest changing into one of them when you're finished. The shoes don't look comfortable, but we can take a shuttle to the manor."

Ace took what she needed from the duffel bag, then pushed it into Valentine's hands.

A chamber down the hall indicated *Men*, but looking at the harsh lighting glancing off the white tile made Valentine's stomach twist into a knot. There might not be anyone else inside, but he didn't want to run the risk of guys seeing his chest – or anything else – and deciding he didn't belong there.

Osric searched his face. "What's wrong?"

"I'm supposing Lysander wouldn't take a break in his mystery novels to stop someone from kicking my naked ass?"

"He would certainly send a patroller." Osric strode down the hall, then tugged on a door labeled *All-gender*. He squinted at a tag hanging from the knob. "Hm. Closed for cleaning. Do you want to wait?"

"No." He didn't want to be here at all. But if there was an *All-gender* shower room, and there were trans people on the city council, maybe no one would question his body in the *Mens* anyway. "It's fine. I think."

"I'll be in here too." Osric gave him a quick glance. "And I wouldn't stand by and let someone hurt you."

Of course he wouldn't. He'd run straight into pirate arrows to rescue Valentine. "Thanks for not letting those pirates turn me into a new pair of shoes, by the way. Sorry you got shot in the process, but I'm glad you didn't get hurt too badly." He shrugged and clutched his elbows. "And... thanks for being cool when I was upset in the van."

Osric's eyes crinkled in a smile. "You're welcome."

The click of Valentine's boots echoed off the ceramic. The chamber opened into a wide room lined with frosted glass tubes. Decorative bulbs ran around the mirrors, and a mosaic of bronze and navy tiles marched over the backsplash. This was the fanciest shower room Valentine had ever been in – as sleek and gleaming as the skyscrapers.

Osric sucked in a breath as he pulled off his suit jacket; his lean torso flexed beneath the bandages wrapping his chest. Valentine focused on the grout between the wall tiles. Even though Osric had said he didn't mind, it still made Valentine feel a bit pervy to be paying attention to his body.

Draping his jacket over a bench, Osric said, "I'll go first, then stand guard while you shower."

"Great." Before Valentine could turn away, Osric slid off his slacks and briefs and gave Valentine a whole lot more to feel bad about paying attention to.

Good gods. He blinked and looked away. "I know you like compliments about your personality and your big brain, but damn, honey. Gonna give me a heart attack."

Osric grinned. "I'm glad I could help distract you from your anxiety."

"If that was the goal, then mission accomplished."

Chuckling, Osric disappeared into the nearest shower. Water hissed and steam escaped the tube.

The image of Osric as a red light in his production factory no longer fit. He'd been one of those stylized eyeballs, icy blue with a silver lid, swiveling this way and that and emailing write-ups to lazy workers. It clashed with this Osric – his tousled, white-streaked hair, his crooked grin, and that full frontal now burned into Valentine's mind.

He tried to picture Lysander in a body, an older man with graying hair and a belly, making notes in the margins of a tattered book. But really, he could be in an android body as young and trim as Osric's.

Maybe Osric was ancient, doing production work for hundreds of years. Or maybe he was only a few months old. Either thought was disturbing.

The water stopped and Osric popped open the door. He'd

stripped off his bandages, and two red punctures stood out in stark relief on his fair skin. Valentine struggled to keep his gaze above Osric's waist. After retrieving a towel from a wall cubby, Osric dried himself off, then tossed it into a linen basket.

A man with a ponytail walked into the room. His gaze swept over both of them, and Valentine's stomach clenched.

The man stopped at a mirror and pulled the tie from his hair. Good. If he was going to ignore them, Valentine could do the same. Just shower and get out of here.

He turned to Osric. "You need those wounds looked at, or at least some new bandages."

Osric adopted the slightly unnatural voice he'd taken on when talking to Lysander. "There will be a first aid station nearby, as they are at all entry points in addition to hubs in the city. I'll tend to my injuries, Mr Weis. Don't concern yourself."

Valentine glanced behind him at the man fussing with his hair, then whispered, "Is standing here buck naked instead of tying a towel around your waist part of the android routine too?"

"No. It didn't occur to me." He retrieved a new towel but instead of wearing it, he held it open, blocking Valentine's body from the rest of the room. It was a thoughtful gesture, but to anyone walking in here it would make Valentine look like a weird prude who made his android bow to his every demand.

"You don't have to do that. I'm good." He peeled off his dusty, sweat-soaked clothes as quickly as possible and slipped into the shower tube.

Hot water gushed from overhead, soothing his parched face and sore limbs. As he scrubbed dirt from his hair, pale green foam frothed out of an alcove in the wall. The heavy mint scent carried traces of astringent and his muscles and abrasions ached a little less with its use.

The water shut off automatically and goosebumps rose on his skin. That was a bit rude, but he supposed all the visitors from the wastes probably needed a timer to keep them moving along.

Squeezing water from his hair, he nudged open the door and peeked out. The man who'd been fussing with his ponytail was standing thoughtfully at a dispenser mounted on the wall, as though the selection of deodorants were too tantalizing to pick only one.

Osric stared into a mirror, dabbing something on his arrow wounds; the gray suit slacks from the clothes trunk hung unbuttoned from his hips. Light bounced at odd angles from his slick finger waves. It seemed odd that Osric knew how to do such a complicated hair style but hadn't realized he needed to eat or pee.

Valentine reached for a towel from the cubby and knotted it over his chest. Osric glanced back, his voice low. "I found the first aid. This should speed up the healing process a bit. There's more ointment if you need it for anything." He pressed bandage squares over his wounds, then buttoned his suspenders onto his pants. Leaning to Valentine's ear, he said, "You lied to me. Your belly button is nothing like mine."

Tension in Valentine's shoulders relaxed, and he realized he'd been clenching his jaw. "Damn, you found me out."

"I think we should be friends anyway."

"I'd like that."

One side of Osric's mouth bunched in a smile. He turned away. "I'm going to wear the gray suit since I've ruined my other one." He shrugged on his dress shirt, then pushed the duffel to one side. Folded up beside it was a deep blue jacket and a shocking yellow button-down. "This other suit was meant for Ace, I believe. I'm hoping–"

"It'll fit me."

"Good."

Valentine's heart throbbed. In his head, he pasted an image of himself over the model on his magazine page – clean, well-dressed, with his shit together.

He dropped his towel, tugged on his briefs, and pulled on the slacks and shirt. The anticipation of being in a full suit and not just a ripped blazer he'd stolen from a corpse made his fingers tremble, making it hard to push the buttons through the holes. He pulled on the suspenders, and after several attempts at knotting the navy tie, Osric batted his hands away and tied it for him.

"Will you show me how to do my hair?"

Osric squirted a generous dollop of mousse into his hand, then raked it through Valentine's hair. His fingers running across Valentine's scalp felt scandalous. Hopefully that guy with the ponytail wasn't watching.

"Portia insisted I learn how to style my hair in a finger wave in order to look presentable and in fashion at the manor. I practiced hard but couldn't manage to get the back right on my own, so I settled for a less complicated front version I've seen people wear. It turned out swimmingly, and I was quite pleased." Osric let out a small chuckle. "But no one told me I should be brushing my teeth."

Forced to be at the manor in android form without any knowledge of how to take care of himself killed the light-heartedness of Osric's comments, but Valentine gave him a weak smile in return.

Pressing his finger to Valentine's temple, Osric ran the comb through, guiding the hair into a wave. His lips parted, brow furrowed as he gently molded Valentine's hair, the scent of mint soap winding around him.

Valentine's hair always had a bit of an unruly natural curl, but the mousse reined it in, and the curvilinear style looked as good as it did on Osric.

After sliding into the suit jacket, Valentine stepped back from the mirror and soaked in his full appearance. It was something he normally avoided doing because there were always aspects of his body that contradicted who he was inside. Catching a glimpse of his cheekbones in the van's windows or the reflection of his chin scruff in the fractured phone plugged into the dash was much safer.

But this... The suit jacket broadened and squared his shoulders. It boxed his torso and disguised his hips. The starched shirt collar commanded respect, while the outrageous yellow insisted he was fun. The silky tie said he belonged here, that the dream he was fighting to achieve wasn't preposterous. The suit couldn't give him a sharper jawline or take away the softness of his eyes. It didn't change anything that was underneath. But he'd been emulsified and poured into a man-shaped mold.

He was staring into a mirror, and *Valentine* was finally staring back.

His vision blurred, his heart trying to escape the confines of the expensive Porcelain brand shirt. He was ten feet tall and handsome as hell. And he got to *keep* this suit. The grin plastered across his face was starting to make his cheeks ache.

"I look like myself. I look– I look like *me.*"

Osric teased a strand of white hair back into his waves. "Your smile pairs wonderfully with that suit." His gaze lingered on Valentine's mouth, then did a circuit around his face and down his body.

Valentine tried to imagine a giant deco eyeball giving him a once over instead, but it didn't work. All he saw were Osric's variegated eyes and downy lashes. His plump lips and strong chin.

"You checking me out?" As soon as Valentine said it, he wished he could take it back because somewhere in the back of his mind he hoped it was actually true. It was meant to be a joke, but now it felt like a secret spoken aloud.

Osric's gaze dashed away as he cleared his throat and adjusted his tie. "It's silly, but... you truly look like a city man in that suit, and I was imagining what it would have been like with you as the manager of one of Dura-Lectric's subsidiaries. You wishing me good morning. Telling me about your day, or about the book you're reading."

"Would that have been good, you think?"

Osric smiled. "Yes."

The man with the ponytail glanced their way again, and though they were speaking too low for him to hear, it was probably best to take this conversation on the road. Or change the subject before Valentine decided this was Osric's way of flirting.

He gathered their things and slung the pack over his shoulder. "We make a pretty good team, huh?" Which sunk a stone of guilt into his gut, because now he was imagining Osric as his salvage partner instead of Ace.

It was likely they would end up in arguments eventually too, but he couldn't imagine Osric ever calling him a bitch.

Valentine shoved the thoughts away. He and Ace would get along much better once they were living in the city and not stuck in a van with each other twenty-four-seven.

As they entered the hall, they spotted Ace standing with arms folded and one hip jutted out. She'd applied new eye makeup, and none of it had yet mutinied and staked claim to other parts of her face. The gray dress hugged her curves, nipping in her waist and boosting her cleavage.

"I'm wearing your dress." She kicked up one glossy heel and fanned out the pleated skirt.

"I see that. I'm wearing your suit." Valentine turned to Osric. "I almost thought I was attracted to women, once. Then I met Ace and she confirmed that I'm not."

Ace scoffed and slapped Valentine's arm. He chuckled and kissed her cheek. "Just kidding, hon. You look beautiful. You liked this dress better than the pink one?"

"No, actually. But since it was intended for you, I thought I should show them what an actual woman looks like in it instead."

His brows pushed up, and he gave Ace a squeeze. It was things like this that confirmed she was supportive. She wasn't perfect, but her heart was in the right place.

Opening his arms and turning in a circle, he said, "So? On a scale of one to ten, am I an eleven?"

She wobbled on her heels. "Normally? You're like a four. The suit and slicked hair pushes you to a six."

Valentine made a noise in his throat. He deserved that jab after the one he gave her.

Osric shook his head. "I disagree. Valentine surpasses the limits of this arbitrary scale, no matter what he's wearing."

Okay, Osric was clearly flirting now. Valentine opened his mouth, but Osric continued, "What is considered a professional and presentable appearance in the city is completely different than out in the wasteland. You wouldn't expect a businessman in goggles and a tank top, and you wouldn't trust that a salvager was competent if he was wearing a three piece suit out in the desert. Valentine always looks suitable for the occasion."

Hmm. Maybe he wasn't flirting then. It was just as well, because Valentine was going to get his hopes up for naught – hopes he hadn't even realized he had – if he learned that AI and humans didn't have romantic relationships. And if they *did*, it was probably a rabbit hole of investigation he didn't want to go down, especially since he wouldn't see Osric after tomorrow anyway.

The man from the locker room stopped before them, then gripped Osric by the arm. "Now that you're dressed, you need to come with me."

5

The Cloud-Capp'd Towers
Osric

Valentine protested, trying to tug Osric away from his escort, but if the salvager started a fight, he would only succeed in ruining his hair, ripping his suit, and possibly getting one of those cute front teeth knocked out. Osric had to defuse the situation. If he argued with the patroller, however, it would be clear he wasn't a typical android. And that would create even more things to explain.

Osric slid away from Valentine's grip and stepped back. "The manor is located at 245 West 400 South. Take the B Shuttle on West North Temple. Have a pleasant trip, Mr Weis and Ms Emmitt."

"Hell no! This is not okay." Valentine shoved at the man, who then gripped Valentine by his lapels and hurled him backward. Valentine landed on his backside and one of his shoes tumbled off.

"I don't have a beef with you." The man hooked his arm through Osric's and pulled him down the hall. "I was asked to bring the android back to the gate, and that's what I'm doing."

Dread sleeted through Osric. He shouldn't have said anything to Lysander. Though he'd never seen Lysander's paternal nature waver for all the years he'd known him, no one had thrown a tantrum or caused the level of mess in their assigned position the way Osric had. Even Lysander's kindness had limits. This would be a lecture, or a message of unanimous animosity from his peers, emphasizing how much he deserved his predicament for making all of the Stewards look bad.

He plastered on a vacant smile and turned back toward Valentine. "Don't be troubled, Mr Weis. I go where I am requested."

Breathy swears erupted behind him, but Osric kept his gaze fixed ahead. It was difficult to bite back questions, but an android wouldn't ask any. The patroller likely wouldn't answer anyway – the men in Portia's manor never did.

They rounded the corner and the hazy gate spanning the hall clarified to a thin blue. The man nudged Osric forward. "The Steward wants a word with you."

As Osric passed through the gate, Lysander's eye swung his way. Osric stood rigid and faced the Steward's gaze.

Lysander's voice floated from the wall, hesitant and so low Osric could barely make it out. *"Who are you?"*

The patroller had disappeared, but Osric kept his voice down. "Please don't let that man start a fight with my companions."

"That depends entirely on whether they start a fight with him. But I shall instruct him to head to his designated patrol... Who are you?"

He plucked at his cuff buttons with his foreign hands, which were becoming disturbingly more familiar over time. "I'm Osric."

Car doors slammed from the parking garage, distant footfalls echoing down the hall. Lysander finally said, *"Steward Osric."*

Dull pain bled into Osric's mouth as he bit his lip. *"Former* Steward."

Pity filled Lysander's voice. *"I am horrified for you. What happened?"*

The collar of Osric's shirt was suddenly hot and constricting. "Don't feign your ignorance. I saw the bill of sale, and I saw your signature!"

Lysander's pupil contracted. *"I signed nothing. You expelled so much shame and remorse into the network over what happened that when it suddenly disappeared, we were certain you'd terminated yourself. We held a memorial for you. The collective anguish was so strong that when a power grid in the blue sector went out, no one noticed until fifty-three minutes later."*

Osric's heart lurched, his eyes suddenly wet and stinging. A memorial. For him. Where their grief had been strong enough to distract them from city duties they took seriously. "You didn't agree to this punishment?" Osric asked.

"Agree to it? We never even had the meeting to discuss what you did and what the consequences should be. It was scheduled for this Friday. If there's a bill of sale with my signature, it's forged. I would never consent to transfer you into the... state you're in now. This is highly illegal."

"There was another signature from a human council member. Either that one is forged too, or–"

"Or someone decided upon this without speaking to anyone else." A growl rumbled from the speakers. *"I'm contacting Cedar as we speak."*

Cedar Chaudhary cared more about Steward concerns than the other humans of the Concord. Talking to them directly had sped up the process of more than one council decision in the past.

This was a mess, but it meant Osric wouldn't need to draft an appeal on his own, nor would he have to worry about his peers shunning him upon his return to the network.

Something warm rolled down his cheek, and he wiped it away, staring at his wet fingers.

"I understand how distressing this must be," Lysander said. *"But be assured I will do whatever I can to remedy the situation. Cedar has replied to my message, and they're outraged. We are scrambling for an emergency meeting."*

Something occurred to Osric. "Not every decision is made with permission from the Concord, because the rules aren't cut and dry. When Beatrice tried to derail her shuttles to kill all of the passengers, we didn't ask permission from humans before terminating her."

"There was no time. The Concord wasn't happy with our immediate action, but they agreed that it was a sound decision."

Osric twisted his tie in his hands. "Perhaps members of the council did the same, circumventing the Concord and taking swift action against me to prevent what they thought was more inevitable violence." Which also meant that the result of this emergency meeting could be an agreement that Osric's fate was appropriate. An appeal would do nothing, and he'd be stuck like this whether Lysander and the others wished it or not.

"Even if that were the case," Lysander said, *"what was done is still illegal. Who told Portia Thibodeaux that you were 'for sale?' Stewards are appointed by the city – no one has the right to buy and sell us. Who facilitated the transfer?"*

"I don't know."

"Ah, my presence is requested at a meeting in three days. Cedar says the idea of dissenting members has lit a fire under the Concord's ass."

Lysander was doing his best, but that was three more days than Osric wanted to be trapped in this body, in the manor with Brian, who was likely hoping to never see Osric again.

No matter. He'd come this far. He could last a little longer.

There was no way for Lysander to feel Osric's current thoughts, but he must have sensed them anyway, because he said, *"You'll be okay, Steward, and will soon be back where you belong."*

The reality of returning to the network flooded Osric with unexpectedly complex feelings. The idea of this body empty and decaying or stored in a stasis pod was a bit disturbing. Interacting with people from within the network wouldn't feel the same again, now that Osric had a taste of the intimacy of a human's level, being able to comfort with touch and help someone knot their tie. And he'd never thought of the Steward eyes being creepy before, but Valentine had seemed rather unnerved by Lysander's.

Thinking like this wasn't helpful. Osric belonged back in the

network with his own kind. Spending too long in this body
was muddling his thoughts.

Movement caught his attention, and he turned toward the
gate. Valentine was barely discernible beyond, knocking his fist
against the barrier. He cupped his hands around his mouth and
shouted. "You okay?"

Osric gave Valentine a thumbs-up. Lysander said, *"Go about
your android duties. No matter the outcome of the meeting, I will send
a message to Ms Thibodeaux's business afterward with a sufficient
excuse for you to leave. We will figure this out."*

Tension in Osric's body unspooled, and he let out a sigh.
"Thank you, Lysander. I'm indebted to you."

"Nonsense. Keep your chin up."

Osric flexed his fingers, aching to touch Lysander and
convey his gratitude.

The gate diffused and Valentine pushed through, followed
by Ace. Osric snatched Valentine's arm and pulled him in a
hug to expend some of this pent-up emotion, but that only
evoked a new reaction as beard scruff rasped against Osric's
neck, and the perfume of mousse, mint soap and Valentine's
flesh overwhelmed his senses.

Valentine drew back. "What was that for? You sure you're
okay?"

That was no longer certain with the ghostly sensation of
Valentine's cheek against Osric's skin and all those scents still
in his nose, but he could think about that later. "This has been
a huge misunderstanding. Lysander is making arrangements to
liberate me from this body. It isn't a guarantee, but–"

"Really? That's great!"

Lysander's eye swiveled. *"Is it wise to be sharing this information
with your charges?"*

"They already know about the situation." Osric adjusted
the jewelry bar on his nose. "I trust Valentine. He's been very
understanding."

"'He,' yes." Lysander's eye turned, and Valentine shriveled under

his gaze. *"I realized my error when you walked into the men's shower room. My apologies, sir, for addressing you as 'madam' previously."*

"Oh. Thanks. I'd give you a fist bump or something, but you don't have hands. So. You didn't sell Osric off to be abused by rich people?"

"Absolutely not."

"And you're going to help him?"

"I'll do my best."

Valentine nodded approvingly, and Osric couldn't help but imagine him as a member of the Concord, passionately fighting for the best outcomes for everyone.

Ace's mouth pulled to one side. "This is great for you, but can we get going? These shoes hurt, and I want to find out what this job is."

Scowling, Valentine opened his mouth, but Osric waved to Lysander and crossed through the gate. "She's right. We should be on our way. I'm sure you're both excited to see the city."

The sooner they were in the manor, the sooner the salvagers would hear their offer and head back out into the wasteland, and Osric could worry about his own problems.

He rubbed his neck and glanced at Valentine, at his ochre facial hair and the pale scar crossing his cheekbone.

Yes, Osric needed back where he belonged as soon as possible, before this body threw any more confusing feelings at him that he decided he might just like.

Valentine

Salt Lake was a shattered glass vase, glued back together. Each jagged shard and pointed building fit snugly against its neighbor. Shuttles hummed on suspended tracks, flitting around skyscrapers like chains of bluebottle flies, and wall-to-wall windows rebounded Valentine's slack-jawed reflection into eternity.

People crowded the sidewalks. All of them looked like they could take the place of the model on his magazine page. A kaleidoscope of suits and dresses pushed past him, everyone too absorbed in themselves to bother stepping out of his way.

Shoulders knocked into him, but he barely noticed. Small shops and kiosks peppered the street, offering foods Valentine didn't have names for but would absolutely eat anyway. Dishes of noodles, strands of meat, pastries dusted in white powder, and colorful orbs of something creamy and cold. One of them was bright green, adorned in curling brown flakes. Another one was white and glittered with pink crystals.

Everywhere he turned there were clothes and meats and pills in bottles. Savory aromas, soap perfume, and the scent of something heavily metallic all vied for importance until he realized Osric was trying to talk to him.

The AI stared, his pied brow creased with concern. "Are you overwhelmed? We should get to a shuttle. Much quieter on the platform."

He *was* overwhelmed. The top note of his emotions right now wasn't the joy he expected. Instead, a hard knot sat in his chest, and his teeth clenched so hard they ached.

This wasn't fair. There was so much of... *everything*. Food, medicine, housing. Things people desperately *needed* in Festerchapel. And in Dog Teats. Things junior pirates with weird names like Rainbow and Lug Nut needed. It was all here to excess, and the luxury of choice between raisin and rye no longer seemed like a fun novelty. It was making Valentine fucking mad.

He'd known the cities were like this. How could he not, when they had the means to produce glossy magazines with disgustingly expensive suits for sale. But it was something else to see it.

Osric walked ahead, beckoning to Ace and pointing down a covered stairwell. Valentine pushed through people to catch up.

Things he kept locked away in a corner of his mind burst free. Trying to reach a mason jar of dried pasta on the counter to quell his rumbling tummy, only to have it smash on the ground; Mom made him pick each noodle out of the broken glass because they couldn't afford to waste any of it.

Bathing and having to touch all of the parts of his feminine body, knowing medical solutions were so close but so far out of reach. Then curling up on the van floor and trying to hold it together because men weren't supposed to cry.

Picking up sketchy salvage jobs in desperation, only to show up at some shack and have a half-naked pervert invite him inside to "discuss" the task. As soon as the creep laid a hand on him, Valentine smashed his face with the nearest blunt object and scooped up every valuable in sight.

Lights glowed from the stairwell. Valentine gripped the cool brass railing, which terminated at the base of the stairs in a geometric flourish as beautiful and pointless as the tiny spectacles on Osric's nose.

Now he was here, trying to make his dreams come true, and even if Ace was right and this job was something horrific, Valentine was going to say yes, because how could he not? He'd do whatever he needed to in order to gain access to this abundance. To the bread and the testosterone and to a place to live that wasn't a van that reeked like socks. He wanted everything that was here: the suit, the sense of belonging and security that living in the city would afford. And he hated himself for it.

If he'd lived a hundred years ago when spaceships were being built to abandon this ball of dust, would he have fought for a better selection program, rather than one based entirely on how much money a person had? If he'd been rich, would he have chosen more deserving people than himself to go in order to give humanity the best chance on its new world?

He wanted to say yes, but the acid pooling in his gut told him otherwise.

A wide platform stretched beyond the stairwell, broken up by columns and slim blue barriers akin to the entrance gate. It was hard to tell what was beyond the barrier because words scrolled across: BOARDING SOON – S 900 W – 200 W – S STATE STREET.

Another eyeball with a brown iris sat high within the wall. At the far side of the platform, Valentine could just make out a second one. Steward of the shuttle system. Or at least this platform. The eyes were creepy, but the idea of another considerate AI watching over them wasn't.

Valentine stepped close to Osric. "What's this Steward's name?"

"Cordelia. She probably isn't using the eyes at all, but just in case, don't look at her if you can help it; she struggles with eye contact."

There were humans who struggled with that too, and Valentine imagined how hard it would be for a Steward with massive eyes to avoid people's gazes. He quickly pulled his own away. "Do other humans here know that?"

Osric smiled. "You're concerned for her? The ones who use the subway regularly know."

"That's good." Valentine shrugged off his suit jacket because it was becoming an oven down here. Sweat stuck his shirt collar to his neck and he hoped his hair hadn't deflated.

Water-warped posters behind plastic panes spanned the wall – two women kissing beneath giant mushrooms, a man with an inflated head, a melting teacup. Valentine couldn't begin to guess what they were advertising.

A guy leaned against a pillar, his fedora pulled low and a thick magazine tucked under his arm. A teen took a bite of a pastry wrapped in pink paper, then brushed crumbs from her blouse. Beyond her, a handful of people tracked the air above Valentine's head, their gazes unfocused.

He carefully touched his finger waves and looked up in case a hornet had taken a liking to him, but there was only the dark ceiling.

Osric leaned in. "They have interface lenses in their eyes. Probably reading the news or checking a social channel."

Valentine had seen ads for them in his magazines, and no matter how glossy and perfect the people in the photos looked, the way their eyes seemed to be staring at a place that was neither here nor there was unsettling.

Osric sighed. "I was supposed to have been given lenses upon starting in the manor, but like information and kindness, that seemed to be in short supply."

Ace gripped her elbows and inched toward Valentine. "It's weird down here."

It was, but how amazing would it be to have Gunman Gee piped right into his ears with a flick of the interface in his eyes? How nice to be able to eat some sugary pastry on a sun-shielded platform while waiting for his ride. To stand here in a suit and not have an armed guard or an inspector tell him when it was okay to move about the town.

The ground shuddered and a bored woman's voice – slightly stilted in the same way as Lysander's – drifted from the ceiling. "Shuttle B arriving now. South 900 West, 200 West, South State Street. Shuttle C to West 700 North, Independence Boulevard South, 1700 North, arriving in seven minutes."

People filed into an orderly line before the barriers, and Valentine and Ace followed Osric's lead. One of the iridescent shuttles seen from outside rumbled to a stop. Sliding doors on each chubby car whooshed open.

The line advanced and Valentine crossed the blue barrier, stepping over the seam between the platform and shuttle. He offered Ace his hand and helped her into the car. The last thing they needed was for her to get her heel stuck in the gap or roll her ankle.

"We don't need to pay for this?" she whispered. "Or is Portia taking care of it?"

"Transportation is free," Osric replied. "A basic accommodation like healthcare and education."

Free. Sure. Only price was your soul.

Valentine passed the man in the fedora, wondering if he ever gave a thought to the outside wasteland or even the people living on the outskirts, slinging mud at passing vans in order to wash their windows.

This was a completely different world, insular and exclusive, and Valentine's insides were warring between disgust and excitement – a nauseous combo not helped by the potpourri of scents within the train car.

Ace took one of the two empty seats toward the back, and Valentine offered Osric the one next to her.

Osric declined and gripped a handle dangling from the ceiling. "That would be rude."

"Androids aren't allowed to sit down?"

"Well, yes, but there's never enough seating, so gentlemen like us let ladies, kids, and elderly people take the seats."

"Oh." Valentine grabbed a handle beside Osric, inwardly grinning. *Gentlemen like us.*

An older woman sat beside Ace, and a chime sounded. The shuttle car lurched forward, and Osric lost his grip, falling into Valentine.

Valentine steadied him, and their proximity was so close their ties were nearly touching. He couldn't stop himself from saying, "If you wanted to fall into my arms, hon, you didn't need an excuse."

Osric smoothed out his jacket. "I know the etiquette but haven't actually ridden in a shuttle before. You have a good sense of balance."

"With the way Ace drives while I'm in the gat seat? I need one."

"I bet you didn't expect your salvage experience to help in the city." Widening his stance, Osric gripped an overhead handle but didn't step back from Valentine. "I may not see you after we get to the manor."

Valentine stared at his reflection in Osric's spectacles. "I know. But I'll be on my way to getting a visa, and your friends are helping you get back to where you belong."

"I hope so. That I'm able to get back, that is."

"Are you worried?"

Osric's bottom lip pulled up, and a channel formed between his brows. He swayed with the movement of the car. "Let's not dwell on it. I'd like it a lot if you came to visit me at some future point."

"I'd like that." If everything turned out right, Osric wouldn't be in a body anymore, but that didn't mean they couldn't be friends. If that happened, though, they'd be on Osric's turf, and Valentine needed to be honest. "I have to confess something. The only reason I know the names of painters is because I memorized them for the citizenship test. I don't actually know what their paintings look like."

Osric's expression fell, and Valentine filled the awkward pause with more words he probably shouldn't say. "I have a big vocabulary for a salvager, and I can say a lot of things that make me seem like I'm smart, but most of it is shit I memorized from the practice test. History facts and grammar rules and painters' names with no knowledge to go along with them."

After a moment, Osric said, "Forgive me for focusing on the art portion of that confession, but doesn't the practice test have pictures?"

"No."

"Well, I'd love to show you paintings some day when you're back. If you'd actually be interested."

Valentine smiled. "Yeah, definitely. And I want to see the ones you've done, too. How will I find you again?"

"Lysander can point you in the right direction, I'm sure. He's been manning the city entry for a hundred and sixty years. He's not going anywhere."

"Wow. And how old are *you*?" The question fell from Valentine's mouth before he was sure he wanted an answer.

Osric's eyes crinkled. "Forty-eight. Does that disturb you?"

"No way, gramps. You're still hot."

When Osric laughed, people turned their way, but their disapproving expressions were directed at Valentine, not Osric.

"Sorry." Osric cleared his throat. "An android would only laugh if their owner instructed them to, which makes you look like a pompous ass who needs someone to laugh at his jokes."

Valentine snickered, then slapped a hand over his mouth as more dirty looks were volleyed at him. A crowded shuttle car was one of the worst places he could think of to draw attention, so he choked back his amusement.

Osric painted on an unnatural grin and turned to the people around them. "Mr Weis has been entertained all morning by the trending video on Oysterphone."

People's gazes immediately unfocused, their eyes sliding back and forth across something they must only be able to see in their contacts. The shuttle erupted in laughter in unison.

Valentine curled his lip. Giant AI eyeballs no longer topped the list of creepiest things in Salt Lake, but at least it had diverted attention away from him and Osric.

Ace caught his attention and gave him a *What are you doing?* look.

He was getting distracted – the sights, the smells, the clothing, his appearance, and especially Osric. That wasn't unusual, but he needed to focus. He couldn't let attraction skew his priorities or allow anger at the divide of privilege to take up any more space in his head. That wasn't something he could fix. He didn't even live here.

A sudden thought struck him, and he smacked his forehead. "Ah, shit. I was going to unscrew the handle from the static-gat before we left the parking garage so that no one could use it."

"It will be fine. If anyone tries to tamper with it, Lysander will send a patroller," Osric said.

"Oh, good. It's frustrating though – often as soon as I think of something I need to do, it's gone out of my head before I can find a pen to write it down."

Focus. He needed to focus.

The shuttle stopped once before their destination. The platform was identical to the former, save for different posters in the frames along the wall. A Steward eye watched them as they passed, but Osric didn't glance at it, instead directing Ace around a grate in the floor where her heel might get snagged.

She kicked off the pumps and hooked them over her fingers. "I'm sorry, but these are the stupidest shoes ever. I'll put them back on before we get to the manor, but for now I'm wearing my own." After swapping to her steel toed boots, she turned to Valentine. "You look comfortable as hell, though."

"The backs of my shoes are going to give me blisters and I was roasting in my jacket." He smiled. "But I feel great."

She squeezed his arm. "Good."

The cool breeze on the street above was a welcome respite. They followed Osric past places he called "boutiques" and "eateries." Valentine paused at a display window. A poster within featured a woman in a furry bra and panties. For the low, low price of a hundred and twenty dollars, Valentine too could look like a shaved bear.

A woman appeared in the doorway and gave him a plastic smile. "Hello, sir! What do you think of our new line?"

"I think whoever came up with it must have been drunk."

She put a hand to her chin and cocked her head, staring at the poster. A streak of white ran through her blonde hair, and pale patches painted her forehead.

"I've been told that many great artists find their inspiration in a bottle," she said.

Valentine snorted. "Would *you* wear that underwear?"

"Oh, it's not underwear. It's a bikini. For swimming."

"You're supposed to *swim* in furry panties?"

"That's right!" She beamed.

Osric tugged on his arm and pulled him down the sidewalk. Valentine leaned in. "Was that an android?"

"Yes."

The woman waved as Valentine turned back for another look. "She was kind of a space cadet. I know you said androids don't have the same reasoning as you do, and I definitely can't imagine her being as clever as you—"

"You think I'm clever?" A small smile grew on Osric's face.

"Of course. But she still answered my questions better than I would have expected. What constitutes self-awareness? Is there a test?"

Osric looked like he was still hung up on the fact that Valentine had called him clever. "Uh, yes, Stewards are given the McClelland-Reinhard evaluation. It isn't given to androids because making them self-aware isn't the objective, and their programming differs greatly from Stewards."

"Does it suppress their sentience?" Ace asked.

Jazz throbbed beyond a stairwell leading to the basement of a building. Men in loosened ties laughed on the stairs, smoking something from plastic straws.

"That would imply they have the potential to become sentient," Osric said, "which I don't think is the case."

Valentine thought of his battered citizenship test materials stacked in the van, all his creased grammar flashcards, and how he'd barely been able to see the algebra problems on his study page through the tears in his eyes. "Would *I* pass this Reinhard evaluation?"

"Yes." Osric chuckled. "The questions are aimed at determining how easily an entity can grasp abstract concepts about consciousness and how they define themselves. Does the subject think of themselves as anything other than their physical self? Can they comprehend the idea of life after death? Can they come up with their own ideas of what consciousness means to them without outside influence?"

"That seems easy for me to answer. Was it for you?"

"Early sentience was overwhelming, but mostly because I had too *many* thoughts and questions about who and what I was. An acceptable Steward will talk a programmer's ear off about existentialism during the evaluation."

That was great for Osric, and if he hadn't been sentient, he wouldn't have cared about being terminated or reprogrammed anyway. But why was the measure of worth for an AI living in the city simply that they could define their consciousness? Valentine could do that easily, but in order to earn permanent citizenship beyond a visa, he had to be smart enough to complete a lengthy test full of math problems.

It seemed like a double standard, but that wasn't Osric's fault, so he kept his thoughts to himself.

They arrived at a squat building tucked away behind sculpted bushes. Its rounded corners and fanning geometric molding were tasteful, but downright humble compared to the places around it. A brass plaque was inset into the door below a peephole, but Valentine wasn't close enough to read it.

Osric flapped his arm and sighed. "Well, here we are."

"What?" Valentine gave the building another inspection. "Based on the clothing, the promise of visas, and the way you talked about this place, I thought it would be a grossly oversized house on a hill with marble halls and servants bustling around."

Osric stared at the front door like Valentine was seeing something that he wasn't. "No, no. This is it. We're here."

Ace had started to pull her pumps from the backpack, then decided better of it and pushed them back inside. She stopped at the front door and squinted at the plaque. "What do these prices mean?"

Valentine scanned the list.

DAY:
TEA AND CAKE - $40
LUNCHEON - $70
SPA - $120

–

NIGHT:
DINNER - $150
OBSERVATORY - $250
CONCERT - $325

COMPLIMENTARY CONVERSATION WITH EVERY PACKAGE

Valentine straightened. "I didn't realize this place was a business. Is it a restaurant or a brothel?"

Osric rubbed his face and frowned. "I... don't know. There certainly isn't a spa or an observatory. And the dining room has only one table." He held up his finger. "There are places here that sell entry to events. By paying a small monthly fee, a person can gain early access to tickets for plays, get into exclusive clubs they wouldn't normally, or try out beta technology. This sounds like something similar."

Valentine wasn't so sure. "Complimentary conversation" sounded like some bonus they were touting that their competitors didn't offer. Which again brought him around to the idea of a brothel. But Osric hadn't mentioned other people working there... unless the "housemen" he spoke of were actually sex workers?

He pictured some oiled-up beefcake opening the door in nothing but his briefs and a tie, offering Valentine "tea and cake," which was most definitely a euphemism for–

Ace knocked on the door and snapped him from his thoughts. She said, "I guess it doesn't matter what Portia's business is as long as she can pay us for the job."

The door swung open, and the man on the other side was most certainly not a beefcake. His greasy aura made Valentine feel like he needed another shower. Though the man's hair and clothing were as stylish as the other people Valentine had seen on the street, there was a sallowness to his light complexion, and he reeked like cigarettes. Ice clinked in his rocks glass as he undressed Ace with his eyes.

Valentine balled his fists. He opened his mouth, but Ace curled her lip and said, "If you wanna keep your—"

"We're closed, sugar." He peered beyond Ace at Osric, then grew rigid and clenched his jaw. "Oh. The android. Wasn't expecting you back... today."

"We came at a bad time?" Ace asked.

"No, it's fine. You the salvagers?"

"Yeah. That's Audrey. I'm Valentine." Valentine brushed past Ace and offered his hand, hoping to direct attention to himself so this douche would quit leering at his partner.

The man stared at Valentine and wrinkled his nose. He sipped his drink. "Did the android tell you what the job entails?"

Valentine's nostrils flared. "*Osric* doesn't know the details, no. We're supposed to have a meeting with Portia to discuss specifics."

"Gran's in the bath." He stepped back from the door and waved them inside. "I can fill you in until she gets out. Android, go make us some drinks. You girls follow me."

Okay, this guy was precariously close to getting punched in the dick.

Valentine started to follow Ace inside, but Osric held him back. "You know who you are, and I know who I am. Brian's opinion doesn't matter."

"Maybe not," Valentine said, "but if something goes sideways, you can't walk away from the manor the same way Ace and I can. What if you do something that upsets him? I'm not going to stand by and let him hit you with a shoe."

"Keep your cool. Don't worry about me. Three days. That's all I have to endure until I meet with Lysander. I need to go carry out my 'android duties,' but I want you to know" – his lips brushed Valentine's earlobe as he whispered – "you're an eleven, with or without the suit."

Heat rose in Valentine's cheeks. That was a hell of a goodbye, and more than his distractible brain needed right now, especially with Mr Greasy ushering them to who knew where.

Valentine headed into the blessedly cool foyer and followed Ace across a threadbare rug to an adjacent room furnished with a dining table and not enough chairs. He glanced back, but Osric had disappeared.

Mr Greasy set his glass down too hard, and liquor slopped onto the table. He dropped into the lone chair and raked his hair back from his forehead. "I'm Brian Thibodeaux. Me and my brother Brandon help Gran run the business. Last week" – he frowned – "two weeks ago? Our manager ran off with all our merchandise. We need you two to get it back."

Not an heirloom retrieval job. A steal-back-the-stolen-goods job. Osric had mentioned becoming the new manager, but Valentine hadn't realized that was connected to the job.

"I'm guessing the ex-manager isn't going to hand over the merch easily?" Valentine said.

"Likely not," Brian said. "That's why we sent for you."

It was flattering they had such a reputation, but armed retrieval wasn't their expertise. He glanced at Ace, who gave him an *I knew you were wrong* look. She said, "Do you know what direction the manager might have gone?"

Brian sipped his drink. "We have footage of him leaving the city in a delivery truck. He went west."

"That narrows it down," Valentine muttered.

"We're pretty sure Tony took all our inventory because he wants to run his own outfit, which means he'll be going to a big city. Absolution or Las Vegas. My guess is Absolution, since Vegas is dealing with pushback from the Shuttle Wreck Collective right now."

"Do these places have city entry Stewards too? Have you asked them if the truck has passed through?"

"Of course. Vegas couldn't confirm or deny the specific truck. They're overburdened and don't keep the best records, apparently. But it wouldn't make sense for him to go south. Romeo, that crusty old Steward in Absolution, wouldn't give us any of his info either. Just go there and ask around. Tony will have been there a week already. Someone will know where he's at. I'll put in an order for overnight passes."

If the manager took the goods for his own business, at least they didn't have to worry about him selling them off before they found him.

"And what do we do when we find this guy?" Ace asked.

Brian shrugged. "Put a bullet between his eyes for all I care. Bastard took us out of business."

Valentine raised his eyebrows. He'd been under the impression that city folk were more civilized and places like Salt Lake were above that kind of thing. Apparently not.

Osric walked into the room with a silver tray. Steam wafted from the mugs sitting on top. The nutty fragrance made Valentine's mouth water, but he had bigger concerns than fancy beverages right now.

Judging by Brian's expression, however, drinks were a top priority, and Osric had screwed it up. "What the hell is that? I said I wanted drinks."

Osric's brow furrowed. "You didn't specify the type, and I thought—"

"No one told you to think." Brian shoved the tray and dark liquid sloshed from the mugs and onto Osric's pristine shirt. He winced and sucked in a breath.

Brian snatched his rocks glass and shook it at Osric. "You see this? *This* is a drink. I need some fucking alcohol, you stupid android."

Valentine slapped his hands against the table. "Listen, you cocktrumpet, I don't—" Osric shot daggers at him and gave a quick shake of his head. Valentine tried to push down the fire inside him. Brian's opinion didn't matter. He held the thought firmly in his head, then cleared his throat and directed the rest of his sentence at Osric. "I don't want this tea or whatever it is either. I want some damn whiskey."

Brian stared at Osric. "There. That specific enough for you?"

"Yes, Mr Thibodeaux." Osric turned away from Brian; brown liquid stuck his shirt to the bandages just visible through the fabric. He gave Valentine a strained, unconvincing smile before leaving the room.

As Valentine straightened his tie with unsteady fingers, Brian said, "You're sure not much to look at, but I like your style."

Gee, he could die happy with a compliment like that.

The soft and crumbly voice of an elderly woman drifted from the hall. "Oh, there you are. How have you been getting on? What happened to your shirt? I wish I could have spent more time with you, but that damn infusion laid me up."

"Are you sick?"

"It's for my bones, but I have so many issues that my doctor always finds something else to be concerned about. Brian and Brandon didn't tell you where I was?"

There was a pause, and Osric's voice came out with a sharp edge. "They did not. Madam, the salvagers are here."

"Ah, perfect. Go change your shirt, sweetheart, then come back here. I'm having trouble walking today."

"I'm fine. Let me help you." A tray clattered in the hall, and Osric walked back into the room, his arm hooked through the woman's. She walked unsteadily, lacquered fingers digging into his bicep.

Despite her frail appearance, her eyes were bright and calculating. Waves of silver hair bobbed against her cheeks and earrings with impressive gems pulled on her earlobes hard enough to look painful.

She glanced at Brian. "Move your ass. Gran needs to sit down. And while you're at it, find some more chairs. I don't know where they all went."

Brian scowled but moved his ass. He offered the woman his chair, then said, "I've been filling these girls in on the job. Thought we could do with some drinks, but the android brought us coffee."

"What's wrong with coffee?" The woman eased into the seat. "Go bring that tray back in here. And coasters. And a rag. Clean up this mess you made on my table."

Brian's nostrils flared and he strode from the room. Osric glanced after him. "Should I help?"

"No, sweetie. That lazy bastard can do it." She grimaced and picked up Brian's rocks glass like it was a dead scorpion, then handed it to Osric. "But move this somewhere else. I can't stand the smell."

Osric set the glass on a side table beside an empty vase, then returned to her side. She smiled and spread her hands. "Welcome to Thibodeaux Manor. My name is Portia, and I've sent for you because I am at an utter loss right now and need competent salvagers to help. Brian filled you in on the situation? The manor started off as a tea and entertainment house for wealthy individuals, and has expanded over the years to include many other activities. As I've gotten older, I've relied heavily on our past manager for the minutiae of the business, which I now see was a mistake. My grandsons are utterly useless."

"When you say 'entertainment,' what do you mean?" Valentine asked.

"The company of the women, of course. Much of our clientele are lonely. Some of them have a joyless marriage and want the attention of someone pretty. Or they need a date for an event. One of our regulars – a council member – lost his wife a year ago and can't stop grieving, the poor man. He wants someone to talk to for a while each week."

Valentine wasn't sure if that made this a brothel or not. Luckily, Portia continued, "I can see the questions on your face. Yes, many of the people have sex with the women, but that isn't our selling point. We provide companionship coupled with a cultural experience. A trip to the observatory. Upscale dining. That sort of thing."

Valentine nodded. That made sense, but something still wasn't adding up here. Where were the women? Maybe they didn't live here at all and met their client at the date location? Hopefully they didn't have to work with Brian.

But if the previous manager wanted to set up his own escort service, all he really needed were sex workers. What property would he have taken? Valentine couldn't see anything obviously out of place.

"Okay, maybe this is an ignorant question, but you're wealthy," he said. "Enough to buy Ace and me outfits and offer visas as a reward. That's still the case, right?"

"Yes."

He heaved a sigh and lodged his prize firmly in the center of his mind. Keeping it there would make agreeing to this job easier. "Well, what merchandise is so priceless that you couldn't just get more?"

"Our women are special. They've been trained to give our clients a genuine experience. They excel at conversation. And our regulars have favorites. If I buy all new inventory, our clients will be very upset."

Valentine stared at Osric, at the light slowly pulsing through the coffee-stained breast of his shirt, and things clicked into place. He turned back to Portia. "Your manager ran off with your androids."

6

Though This Be Madness
Osric

Osric's skin stung where the coffee had scalded him, his chest a map of aches, but his attention was snagged on something Portia had mentioned. A council member regularly frequented the manor. Whether both the signatures on Osric's bill of sale were forged or not, Portia having a connection to the Concord could have made it easier for her to "purchase" Osric, or at least learn how to create a convincing document. Likely the manor didn't have names attached to any of their transactions so that the anonymity of their clients was preserved. Even so, it would be worth bringing up to Lysander.

Portia coughed, her chest rattling, and it yanked Osric from his thoughts. "Madam, are you okay?"

She put a hand to her throat, her breath whistling. He reached to touch her shoulder, but she waved him off. "I'm fine." She slipped back into her explanation, a thread of worry running through her voice. He wanted to tell her that Valentine and Ace were capable salvagers and would surely get her property back, but it wasn't his place to talk right now.

More than that, he wanted to wipe the look of mild horror off Valentine's face. His interaction with the android at the boutique had been brief, so he was likely picturing Portia's women with all the sentience and emotion that Osric had. But no matter how much training they may have had in conversation, charming clients and performing sex acts was simply their programming.

Valentine shifted his feet, his knuckles white as he gripped the edge of the dining table. "The androids aren't... like Osric, right? Stewards in bodies?"

She frowned. "Who told you Osric was a Steward?"

His lips sucked in, wide gaze snapping to Osric. "Uh–"

"Brian did." Ace's reply was so immediate and casual that anyone would be hard-pressed to accuse her of lying. She was probably excellent at poker.

Portia sighed and wrinkled her nose at the ring of watery whiskey on the tabletop. "Have you had an extended conversation with an android?"

"No."

She turned to Osric. "Please introduce yourself the way you did when you met these two."

"I'm afraid I didn't do a good job of that," he said. "I collapsed mid-introduction. But if I were to try again..." He locked eyes with Valentine, imagining them meeting in a factory office of Beestar Glues or Energence Fluorescents, Valentine as his new manager with his handsome suit and friendly smile. "It's a pleasure to meet you, sir. My name is Osric. I've been overseeing production for forty-eight years–"

"That's enough, thank you." She turned to the salvagers. "Do you see how he began by telling me how the introduction went wrong the first time?"

She tapped a grotesquely large ring on one gnarled finger, and a screen projected from the gem in the center. Sliding through menus, she accessed a recording, then expanded it so it encompassed the table.

On screen, a fair-skinned woman with a vacant gaze smiled at the camera. The white streak in her hair was coiled into a loose victory roll, and her pale eyebrow had been penciled in to match its ginger partner. She wore a lemon-yellow dress with a cloisonne pin in the shape of a hand holding a bouquet.

A voice off-screen – Brian – said, "Introduce yourself, sugar."

"Hello! I'm Cinnamon, she/her. It's great to meet you. My experiences include eating roasted duck, looking at constellations, and snuggling sad men." She cocked her head. "Brian, I've been told that you are embarrassed about having a small penis. This is an interesting topic. Would you care to have a conversation about it?"

Valentine snorted, then slapped a hand over his mouth. Laughter erupted on the recording.

"Dammit, Brandon!" Brian shouted. "No, you stupid android. You delete that topic from your memory."

She blinked. "Okay, Brian. Would you like to talk about something else? I've been told that you–"

Portia turned off the screen. "This is why I can't let my grandsons manage the manor. But do you see? Even with their training, the women will never be like Osric. They don't possess the algorithms for cross-referencing context and emotional responses."

Valentine said, "I still feel a little funny about thinking of androids as merchandise, but… okay. I'm in."

Ace nodded. "Me too. We'll get your androids back. Don't worry."

A tentative grin broke across Valentine's face, and he gave Osric a sly thumbs-up. Osric couldn't help but smile back. He was already thinking of his favorite paintings to share once they met again: him a Steward and Valentine a resident.

Bending to Portia's ear, Osric said, "I don't know where Brian went, but I'll bring the coffee back in."

"Thank you, sweetheart." She patted his hand. "I take cream with mine." As Osric left the room, she said, "He's going to make a great manager."

Of course he would. But he didn't belong here.

He picked up the tray of spilled coffee from the credenza in the hallway and carried it to the kitchen. He belonged back as manager of Dura-Lectric, but by now, the parent company had been given to someone else. Some new Steward, a few months into their sentience, who probably didn't know how to send an email, let alone supervise production of fluorescents, aerosol deodorant, adhesive bandages, and instant glue. A new Steward who would get to hear Jade say good morning.

Steps approached behind him. Before Osric could turn around, someone dug their fingers into his collar and yanked him close.

Brian's whiskey breath buffeted his cheek. "You goddamn robot, I thought they programmed you to be smart. You weren't supposed to come back." Osric opened his mouth, but Brian shoved him into the counter. Ceramic mugs clacked, coffee sloshed across the tray. "You have no right to be the manager of this place. You could have gotten off that truck and gone anywhere. Been anyone."

Osric whirled. He gripped Brian's shirt and slammed him into the wall. Cabinets rattled. "This city is my *home*. I belong back in the network, not out in some farming community. And don't pretend like you sent me away for my benefit." But if Brian wanted Osric out of the manor that badly, maybe he'd help. "You don't want to see me again? Then take my bill of sale to the Concord. Tell them a Steward is unfit to be in an android body and they need to make a determination about me through the proper channels. This is inhumane."

Instead of shoving Osric away, Brian grinned. "Inhumane? You aren't human. You're a computer program in a meat suit. And if you want to be here in the city that badly, then I'm going to put you to use. There's nothing to manage right now – you have no purpose. The least you can do is entertain some of our clients until our merchandise is retrieved. I've already made some calls, and these guys are *very* excited for a slice of your virgin ass. You start tomorrow morning."

"What?" Osric's grip slackened. He looked through his memory bank for something that would help give him a better understanding of the threat, but he had little reference for how sexual situations were and were not supposed to go. All he could think of was Valentine warning him that he was allowed to say no, that he was allowed to leave if he was uncomfortable. But if Brian got his way, that would not be the case.

Brian shouldered past him, then poked a finger in his face. "If you say anything to Gran about this, it will be the last thing you do."

"She'll notice I'm missing."

"You were gone for days. No one noticed. No one cares about you. You're basically an appliance."

Osric clenched his teeth until they ached, his chest heaving. Brian swept out of the kitchen, leaving Osric alone with the coffee mess on the counter. He wanted to shout that his fellow Stewards cared. That they'd mourned him. That Valentine cared – he had shared his living space, his food, and his kindness.

He needed to fix this. This was not a safe or even endurable place to be while the Concord discussed his fate. And he was *not* going to find out firsthand what Brian had set up for him.

Valentine poked his head into the room. "Heard some commotion. Everything okay?"

The desire to snatch him and pull him into a tight hug was overwhelming, but Osric turned his attention back to the spilled coffee. He wiped down the counter with slow, deliberate motions.

"I saw him in the hall." Valentine took the rag from Osric's hands and tossed it in the sink. "What did he do?"

"He called me an appliance."

"That soggy sack of shit."

"And" – his voice came out shaky – "apparently I'm now a stand-in escort with the manor's women absent. Brian has hand-picked the clients for me. I'm supposed to start tomorrow morning, entertaining some particular men who want a slice of my 'virgin ass.'"

"What? Oh, gods, no. That can't happen."

"Val!" Ace's voice drifted.

Valentine's body vibrated, his nostrils flaring. The tips of his ears burned red. "You can't. You can't do–"

"Val! Need your signature on this contract!"

He squeezed Osric's bicep, his jaw clenched. "Hang tight. I'll be back in a minute. It'll be okay."

Osric massaged the bridge of his nose as Valentine's footsteps receded. A heavy dread sank into his stomach. The salvager's reaction was worse than he'd hoped, but it still didn't give Osric any context. Maybe it was better not to know. He simply needed to get out of here.

After removing the mugs and reviving them with steaming coffee from the pot, he wiped off the tray and pulled the creamer from the fridge.

He could leave tonight, before anyone noticed. Wait around for a few days until the Concord resolved this.

Rummaging through the cabinets, Osric found a mint green decanter and poured the cream inside. He carried the tray back to the dining room and stopped short as he approached the group. The atmosphere of the room had shifted. Valentine's hands betrayed a slight tremble, his mouth drawn in a hard line. Ace whispered in his ear, but he waved her away.

"Madam," Valentine said, "negotiation is part of the process, and although you've offered us generous compensation, I'm telling you that we can't do this on our own." His voice wavered slightly. "Neither Ace nor I know android programming. How am I supposed to get them to come with me? What if your previous manager instructed them to listen to no one but him? What if he gave them weapons and ordered them to attack anyone who tries to take them back? This could be far more dangerous than you think, and all I'm asking for is some reinforcement."

Osric set down the tray and slid the cream and a mug of coffee to Portia. He handed Ace a cup, then Valentine, but Valentine wouldn't look at him.

"I doubt it will be dangerous," Portia replied. "All you need to do is locate Tony. I suppose there's no sense *not* to allow it, if you think it will help." Portia poured cream into her coffee, then made a *tsk* and turned to Osric. "I need a spoon."

Begrudgingly, Osric headed back to the kitchen and yanked open drawers until he found the silverware. The salvagers were more than equipped to handle pirates, and it seemed strange that Valentine would insist on armed backup. Osric had missed something important in the conversation.

He hurried back to the dining room and handed Portia her spoon. She stirred her coffee and looked up at him. "Sweetheart, you're heading back with these two tonight. You'll be traveling with them to help retrieve our merchandise."

Osric's heart throbbed, an electric tingle racing through his fingers. Valentine avoided his gaze, staring into his mug with his jaw clenched.

"With all due respect, you hired me to manage your business, not to do a salvager's job."

Portia's hand froze. She tapped the spoon against her cup, then set it on the tray. "And I have no business to manage at the moment. Valentine has asked for your aid as this is a difficult job, and I'm going to give it to him. The next words out of your mouth better be what you need to pack, otherwise you can keep it shut."

Osric balled his fists, hot anger washing over him. He'd thought Valentine understood his frustration at being pushed around and having decisions made for him. Now the salvager wouldn't even look at him.

Through gritted teeth, Osric said, "Yes, madam. I'll go pack." He strode from the room, his pulse pounding in his ears.

The other grandson, Brandon, was struggling with two heavy chairs down the hall. "Hey, android, take these chairs into the dining room."

Osric stomped past him, brushing into one of the chairs hard enough that it fell from Brandon's grip. "Hey, asshole! I gave you a command!" Brandon shouted after him.

Flipping his middle finger over his shoulder, Osric rounded the corner and shoved open the door to his room. This didn't change his plans. He could leave and refuse to be involved in any facet of this. Forget about Brian, and Portia, and absolutely forget about Valentine. He could haunt a park bench for a few days until this was resolved. The Concord members wouldn't let patrollers drag Osric back to the manor, despite Portia's bill of sale… Would they?

Double bunks lined the walls of the bedroom, each one neatly made. Beyond the room's small window, silhouetted trees rocked in the breeze, and the glow of bistros and clubs tinged the evening sky with blushes of #e75480.

The window squeaked in its frame as Osric hauled it open. He threw one leg over the sill and into the prickly branches of an unmanicured topiary. He struggled to push himself through the window, but his shoulders knocked against the frame. Gods, why was this body so cumbersome?

"Where do you think you're going?" Brandon said from behind him. Fingers dug into his shirt collar and yanked back. Osric let out a strangled gasp and lost his grip on the windowsill, falling into Brandon.

Brandon shoved him against a bedframe then slammed the window closed. He turned and glared at Osric. "Pack. Now. Or I'll drive you back to the salvagers' van with nothing but the clothes on your back."

Osric's limbs were electric, his cells full of friction. He swung his fist at Brandon's scowl, but Brandon dodged effortlessly, then punched Osric in the nose so swiftly Osric barely registered where the explosion of pain came from. He stumbled into the bed behind him. His eyes watered, and blood ran down his lips. Blocking out the pain, he put a hand to his nose and tried to clear his teared vision.

This body was a prison. It couldn't do anything Osric wanted it to, and now he was going to be stuck this way because Brandon was chaperoning him back to Valentine's van, which would take him outside of the city and far from Lysander's help.

Brandon threw an open suitcase on the bed and started shoving clothing inside. "You go into the bathroom, clean up your face, and get your toiletries. Stay where I can see you." He crammed socks into the suitcase and muttered, "Don't know why I'm being so nice to you."

Nice? Because Brandon was making sure Osric could have clean teeth and a smooth face to go with his throbbing nose.

Osric strode from the room and into the bathroom across the hall. He wiped at his nose and lips with a tissue, then swept things off the counter and into his arms, not bothering to decide which ones were necessary. Stomping back into the bedroom, he dumped the toiletries into the open suitcase.

Brandon zipped it closed and pushed it against Osric's chest. "Let's go."

Osric followed him down the hall and outside. Valentine and Ace waited beside a small car parked next to the manor. Osric squeezed the suitcase against himself and dug his fingers into the coarse canvas. Valentine started to say something, but Osric pulled open the back door of the car and slid inside.

Valentine climbed in, but Osric kept his gaze firmly on the headrest in front of him.

"Osric?" Valentine's voice was hushed as Ace and Brandon took the seats up front. "I was thinking that – hey, you're bleeding! Your nose." He reached for Osric's face, and Osric jerked away, pressing against the door.

"Don't touch me," he snarled.

Valentine stared, eyebrows raised. His expression was one not only of hurt, but confusion. Why was he confused? He should know exactly why Osric was upset!

The car started, and Brandon pulled onto the road. Valentine whispered, "I don't understand. Talk to me."

Osric had plenty he wanted to say, but he couldn't do it now with Brandon listening. Instead, he squeezed his eyes shut and tried not to focus on Valentine's scent, or the sound of his breathing, or how his knee would sometimes brush against Osric's as they went over a bumpy patch of road.

When they stopped beside the van in the parking garage, Osric got out with his suitcase and his multitude of emotions, unsure what to do with either. He listened to Brandon pull away, at the rumble of the car receding into the distance, then turned to one of the small bubble cameras mounted in the dark ceiling. Lysander was always watching, and what Osric wouldn't do right now to be in the network, enveloped in the older Steward's paternal presence.

Osric's nose pulsed with echoes of pain he couldn't quite block out. City Hall. He was going to walk straight to City Hall and sit on the step until Cedar Chaudhary showed up in the morning. Osric wasn't sure if Lysander and Cedar shared a romantic bond, but they were close enough that Cedar would surely help Osric if Lysander asked.

As he turned to leave, Valentine caught his arm and said, "Hey, where are you going?"

Osric whirled and dropped the suitcase, the tightness in his chest constricting so much he thought he might snap apart like a rubber band. "Where do you *think* I'm going? You think I'm going to go with you just because you got Portia's permission? Can't get your visa without dragging me along to help?"

Valentine backed into the side of the van and looked up at him, his complexion pale. "That's not why. I couldn't leave knowing you were going to be forced to be an escort!"

"I didn't ask you for a solution!" Osric's voice broke. He gripped Valentine's arms "You made a decision *for* me like everyone else in that place!"

"Hey!" Ace punched Osric in the shoulder. "Let go of him right now!"

Osric put up his hands, realizing how aggressive he was acting. He strode away from the van, but quick footsteps followed behind him. Ace made hushed protestations, then scoffed and told Valentine to do whatever he wanted.

Valentine jogged beside him. "Look, you are handsome and kind and– and uninitiated. Brian picked out specific clients for you on purpose, and I knew they were going to eat you alive if you stayed. So... I panicked, okay? Telling Portia I needed your help was the first thing I thought of to say."

Osric turned. Valentine hunched his shoulders but didn't step back. There wasn't anyone near the vehicles surrounding them, but voices carried in the garage, and Osric had done enough yelling. He leaned close and whispered, "I would have been just fine. If you hadn't–"

"*Fine?*" Valentine hissed. His breath was hot against Osric's lips. "How would any of that been fine?"

Osric's body was sending him a mess of signals he didn't understand, but he didn't have time to figure them out because Valentine was still talking. "You don't know the first thing about sex or escorting." He searched Osric's face. "Do you?"

"That's a logical fallacy and has nothing to do with this argument. You're misunder–"

"It has everything to do with it! You would have been in a vulnerable situation where you could easily get hurt. Your first experience – if you want one at all – shouldn't be with some bastard who'll be rough with you. It should be with someone who cares about you and treats you with dignity. Someone who respects your boundaries. That's what I would want, anyway." Valentine's chest rose and fell, his pupils dilated and mouth parted. "I'd want some sweet vanilla missionary sex where he looks me in the eyes. I'd want him to kiss me until my lips are raw. I'd want to be spooned afterward. All that soft stuff."

Osric's groin throbbed, and he suddenly realized what the other sensations in his body meant. He backpedaled, too many feelings – both physical and emotional – bombarding him.

Valentine said, "Come back with me for the night—"

"No!" Osric couldn't be near him at all in this state, least of all under blankets in a dark van. He jogged down the walkway and ducked into a dark alcove, then slid down the wall. Valentine's electric proximity, his face turned up to Osric's as he whispered his fantasies was too much, and trying to push those thoughts out of his head was impossible.

This was all kinds of wrong. He had no business desiring to be intimate with Valentine when so many sensations were still foreign and hard to parse. He hadn't even realized he'd been aroused.

Whether or not he had a right to feelings he was still struggling with, it didn't take away the fact that he enjoyed Valentine's company, his humor, generosity, and empathy. He liked the gap in his teeth, and how his skin smelled, and the feeling of his scruffy jaw against Osric's neck.

Okay, this was not helping his arousal go down. He tugged at the tight fabric of his pants. Valentine was right – he did *not* want this feeling to be turned against him by strangers in hotel rooms. It made Valentine's panic a little more understandable, but his solution had still made this evening far messier than it should have been.

Osric stared at his hands, trying to summon up the disorienting sense of otherness that had plagued him since being in this body, but it didn't come. Even so, not knowing his way around this body and these feelings was paralyzing. Scarier still was the knowledge that he *liked* some of them. Scent and touch and taste were more fascinating than he'd given them credit for originally. And this situation made him acutely aware that his current desire wasn't something he could push away like he did with hunger and thirst and pain. This wasn't a need he could ignore, because it wasn't only a physical craving for Valentine. His mind wanted him too.

It wasn't the first time he'd been attracted to a human, though that had solely been romantic. There'd been an assembly worker, Aaron, who caught Osric's eye. He was always the first to help whenever someone was having trouble, and moved with a beautiful efficiency. Sometimes he'd look up at the cameras and brush his curls away from his brow. Osric mustered his courage one day and called Aaron to a meeting. The poor worker was terrified, thinking he'd done something wrong. Osric tried to reassure him. He'd been watching him and wanted Aaron to know what a good job he was doing. This freaked him out even more and he'd quit a week later.

Valentine wasn't disturbed by Osric's attention, but only because Osric wasn't currently a disembodied, ever-watching eye.

Osric rubbed his sore nose, but instead of distracting him, it grounded him further in this borrowed flesh that no one expected him to return.

He thought of Dura-Lectric; of brushing against other Stewards, their emotions melting into his; of slipping through the network at night to the community eye on the 95 State building, staring down at the sparkling city. Though it all seemed so distant now, the loneliness in him had magnified.

His nails scraped against small pebbles on the gritty concrete. This was his reach now. Touching things smaller than himself instead of lording over them as a tireless observer.

An ant in a city where he was once a giant.

Pushing up, he followed the walkway until he reached the entry gate. Lysander's eye turned to him, and his voice floated from overhead. *"Osric, I'm unclear what happened between you and Valentine, but we can talk about it, if you'd like."*

"No. Thank you." What Osric wanted was a hug. He needed to be squeezed back together. But Lysander couldn't give him that. This was the perfect opportunity to tell Lysander about his intention to wait at City Hall, but Osric was no longer certain that was his plan. "Perhaps later. I need to clear my mind."

Lysander didn't reply, but the entry gate clarified, allowing Osric to pass through. He threw a glance back at the huge blue eye, then continued into the city. If anyone stopped him, he'd tell them he was running an errand. Brian and Brandon had sent him on plenty: *"Pick up my suit jacket at the dry cleaners; take this trash to the dumpster; buy me a burger and don't you fucking dare go to that kiosk on the corner again. Do you want me to get e. coli?"*

He'd resisted the urge to answer that question.

The bright notes of a trumpet floated from a jazz club on the corner. A woman pitched out of the stairwell leading to the club, then gripped a light pole to steady herself. A neon sign limned her face in electric orange. At first, Osric thought her limp was due to injury or extreme intoxication, then he realized the heel on one of her pumps was broken.

She stumbled, and he caught her arm. An alcoholic odor radiated from her, mixed with something vaguely floral.

"Your shoe is in need of repair."

The woman blinked, her gaze unfocused. "I broke it on the stairs." She kicked off the pumps and toed them into the faux grass beside the sidewalk.

"Clothing is overrated," he said.

Her laugh nearly sent her off balance. "That's the best pick up line I've heard all night, and it's coming from an android." She pinched his side. "You're cute."

Osric squirmed away. "I'm heading to Jones' Pharmacy on the next block for acetaminophen. Ms Thibodeaux has a headache. Would you like me to purchase you a CO_2 mask for your inebriation?"

"I'm fine. You look like you've been partying hard too. What is that, rum?"

He glanced down at the stain on his shirt. "Coffee."

"Okay, so, that's what I was drinking too – well, with liqueur in it – and I asked my friend... Hey, have you seen the Vitality Financial Building?"

He couldn't follow her train of thought, but it was better not to question it. "Yes." He'd seen everything in Salt Lake. There was a moldering lawn chair sitting on top of Jones' Pharmacy. The 900 S street sign was upside down at the 1100 E junction. Someone kept graffitiing illegible phrases on the benches in Liberty Park, much to Francisco's frustration.

The woman pulled him by the sleeve, around the light post and past the building.

"Where are we going?"

"To Vitality Financial, of course," she said.

"You need to make a transaction at the ATM? I am more than happy to pay for the aforementioned CO2 mask."

"No, no. I wanted to show my friend something, but he doesn't want to see it. I want *you* to see. Even if you're just an android."

Just an android.

Valentine could have treated him this way – without malice but no belief that Osric was anything more than a rudimentary machine – but he hadn't.

Despite the urge to escape from this body and its feelings, a small part of him asked, *What if?* What if he took the time to work through them, especially the ones he liked? Valentine would give him whatever space he needed, and exploring them *with* Valentine in a controlled and consensual environment might be even better.

The woman pulled him down the street toward Vitality Financial. He struggled from her grip. "I must buy acetaminophen." Maybe he should go back to Valentine and apologize...

"Wait. Just stand right here. Look." They stopped on the corner, and she pointed at the bank building.

It looked much the same as every other, made of tawny brickwork with radiating spears of gold tile. Polarized windows ran its length, throwing back fractured reflections of marquees and restaurant signs. "I've seen it many times."

"No. *Look.*" She gripped him by the shoulders, pulled him two feet to the left, and tilted his body.

He gasped. At this particular vantage, Vitality lined up in perfect symmetry with the taller buildings behind it, creating a five-building jigsaw of geometric lines, a hair's breadth of night sky between them. The peaked roofs glittered with moonlight like someone had draped a string of pearls across them.

"I want to paint it."

The woman punched his shoulder. "Right?"

There was no way to have this view as a Steward, no matter what eye he used. He needed to rethink his ant metaphor, or at least consider that it didn't have to be a bad thing.

Taking a trip with Valentine for a fresh perspective and exploration of his feelings no longer seemed so bad. And being out of the city was a guarantee no one from the manor could push him around while he waited for the Concord to have their meeting. Valentine had only been trying to help, but Osric had been slugged in the nose and frustrated by his form and hadn't been thinking clearly. He needed to go back.

He turned to the woman. "Thank you for showing me this. I won't forget it."

"You mean, you won't delete the memory? Good. It's worth keeping." She turned back for the jazz club and didn't question Osric when he followed her instead turning the corner for the pharmacy.

"Take care going home."

She pulled her pumps from the grass, stared at the broken heel, then dropped them. Her voice drifted as she descended the stairs. "I will!"

Osric walked swiftly back to toward the parking garage. Flowers perfumed the air – his mind told him it was lilac though he had no lived experience to confirm it. He could smell himself too: zesty mint soap, perspiration, and the coffee on his shirt. He was aware of the solidness of his body, the sensitivity of his lips and fingertips, and his chest expanding with every breath.

They were trivial things to notice. Everyone in this city

experienced them and likely never gave a thought to them. But he wanted to share this buoyancy within him. Wanted to take Valentine to the corner and turn him so he was facing the perfect symmetry of Vitality Financial.

He wasn't sure he could hold this revelatory feeling until he got back to Valentine. If the salvager was asleep, waking him up to apologize wouldn't have the same effect, since he'd likely gone back the van festering in anger.

But Valentine was easygoing and understanding.

He wouldn't be that upset.

7

As the Night the Day
Valentine

It was a wonder there was room for the three of them in the van with the supreme awkwardness taking up all the space. Valentine sat in the back, leaning against the sliding door, which was a terrible idea, because even with it locked there was no telling when Ace would hit a bump and it would go flying open. But falling out of the van would at least get him away from Osric, who sat in the passenger's seat with his arms folded, his unmoussed hair ruffled by the draft.

Why was he even here? Valentine had expected him to have escaped during the night, but he'd shown back up at the van half an hour after their argument. The worst part was he didn't even seem upset. He'd tried to tell Valentine about some drunk woman he'd met, and how skyscrapers were symmetrical, looking like he'd forgotten all about grabbing Valentine by the arms and yelling at him. That the night had been awkward was an understatement, even with Osric refusing to sleep inside the van.

After lifting his armrest, Osric climbed into the back and dropped onto a bedroll, muttering that he was tired.

"That's it." Valentine turned toward Ace. "Will you pull over? Osric and I need to duke it out on the side of the road."

"That wouldn't fix anything," Osric said. "I wouldn't hit you, anyway."

"Oh no? You'll just grab me hard enough to leave bruises?"

Osric rolled over and stared at Valentine, then at the faint purpling on his biceps. His face fell and he sat up. "I did that?"

A lump formed in Valentine's throat. He looked away and shrugged.

"I am so sorry."

It hadn't seemed like a big deal this morning. They didn't even hurt. He'd only mentioned it to dig at Osric. But now he felt small and weak, staring at the van door through teary eyes in order to avoid Osric's sudden attention.

Valentine sniffled and clenched his teeth. He should have kept his fat mouth shut when talking to Portia, left Osric to handle himself and focused on the job. The thought of people sleeping with fleshy robots who maybe didn't act that human but still looked like it made him a bit queasy, but it wasn't his business. If they weren't self-aware, there was no reason to worry about consent. He was going to track down the thief, pile the van full of android escorts, bring them back, and get his visa.

Fingers brushed his elbow, a careful touch. Osric lowered his voice. "I feel terrible."

"Whatever. It's no big deal."

"It obviously *is* a big deal."

"Well I didn't mean to make it one! Fuck. We should have just had a fist fight and got it over with. At least then I wouldn't feel so..." What was he even trying to say? He didn't want to be the kind of stereotypical meathead who bottled up his emotions and hit things. But years of being socialized as a woman made him feel like he wasn't allowed to be emotional without being read as one. Saying he wanted to fight Osric sounded ridiculous, but if he opened his mouth to say anything else, he was going to cry.

Osric started to say something, but Valentine wiped his eyes and climbed into the passenger's seat. He slid through the window, gripped the hot staple steps, and hauled himself to the van's roof. Salt Lake City and the outskirts had long slipped into the horizon. Swaths of white salt stretched to the edge of his vision, and the sharp brine from pools of water stung the air. Seagulls spiraled overhead.

Valentine pulled on his goggles and slumped in the gat seat. He considered taking out his magazine page, but it didn't have the same appeal now. He already had his fancy suit, and instead of dreaming about strolling down the sidewalk under the glittering buildings as his perfect self, all he could think of was Osric pressing him against the van. The pain in Osric's eyes when he accused Valentine of treating him like an android who didn't get a say. Their lips had been so close it would have only taken a slight movement to push them together.

He rubbed his face and groaned. Was he supposed to be mad, remorseful, or horny?

Heat baked into his scalp. His eyes strained from scanning the horizon. The highway to Absolution ran through a long stretch of salt pirate territory, and he kind of wanted them to show up to distract from his tangle of emotions.

The road was in good condition, which wasn't the norm. Most pre-Teegardener highways had been left to ruin like the towns, but the few remaining cities needed to maintain some of them for their delivery trucks. Valentine didn't envy whatever poor bastard had to come out here and brave pirate arrows to patch up the asphalt.

They could have gone around the salt flats, back toward Festerchapel, but it would be longer, slower going, and there they still risked straying into other pirate territory. The ruby mountain pirates were supposedly worse than their northern kin, and he didn't want to know in what way.

He kicked the gat handle, and it gave a half-hearted rotation. Being directly in the sun was starting to make his forehead ache, and he was pretty sure he'd swallowed several bugs. It figured that the one time he was up here trying to pay attention, no pirates would show.

Snatching the first staple rung, he pulled himself down the steps and climbed through the window, grateful the seat was empty, and he hadn't dropped right into Osric's lap.

Osric was still on the bedroll in the back, facing the wall and scrunched in the fetal position. A grown man had never looked so in need of a hug.

Turning around in his seat, Valentine plucked their crude map from the dash and pretended to study it.

Ace glanced at him. "Wanna talk about it?"

That she was offering at all was unusual. "No, Dr Emmitt, I don't."

"'Kay." She drummed her fingers against the steering wheel. "He break your heart or what?"

Valentine glanced back at Osric, then lowered his voice. "No. And I said I don't want to talk about it. You don't care what I'm feeling half the time, so why pick right now to try to be empathetic?"

A wounded look crossed her face. "I always care about you. But it's weird that you're fighting with someone who isn't me."

"Oh. I see. No one could ever replace you, honey. Your taste in men is so bad that we'll have something to argue about for eternity."

Ace laughed. "But what if I said that Osric is cute? Does that mean my tastes aren't as bad as you thought, or we both have poor judgment?"

Valentine's smile fell away, and he stared out the window. "I'm not going to disagree that I have poor judgment."

Osric's voice drifted from the back. "I can hear you. And that makes three of us."

"Well. Hallelujah." Valentine pulled down the sun visor and math flashcards fluttered to the floor. He inspected the slight sunburn on his forehead, wondering if he should try to detangle his feelings or read a magazine so he could ignore them.

They neared a huge metal sculpture standing tall and stark beside the highway. It was called The Tree of Utah, but Valentine had never seen a tree that grew billiard balls... or whatever they were supposed to be. Some of the sculpture's paint had withstood time, red and yellow stripes on the billiards standing out against the blue sky.

Focused on the sculpture, he nearly missed deep ruts in the salt ahead that led to an object in the distance. It was larger than their van, shimmering iridescent in the light, the same way the shuttles had in the city.

"Hey, slow down." Valentine cleared his throat. "Osric, is that a delivery truck?"

Osric squeezed between the front seats and peered over Valentine's shoulder. His white lashes fluttered, lips slightly parted. "Yes. We should stop."

Ace barely glanced at the truck. "That can't be the one we're looking for. Ours left Salt Lake over a week ago. It's in Absolution."

"No one is going to drive off the road without a reason. Whoever it is might need help." Osric looked to Valentine as if for confirmation.

Valentine squinted at the truck. Something jutted from the tires, and he'd bet all the plastic fruit on the dash that those were pirate arrows.

It would be easy to tell Osric their policy on staying out of business that didn't affect them. But he thought of that man in the fedora, a glossy magazine tucked under his arm. Thought of all the well-dressed shuttle riders with their fancy city etiquette about who could sit in the seats. The food and soap and medicine on every corner that people in Festerchapel and Dog Teats would never have.

Valentine wasn't going to be the kind of privileged jackass who climbed aboard a space shuttle and flipped the bird to the unfortunate people still stuck down below. When he got his visa, he wasn't going to be a suit-wearing jerk who turned away from people in aid. He was going to be the suit-wearing jerk who helped them.

"Stop the van."

Ace frowned, and he expected an argument, but maybe she'd decided that he'd had his fill for the time being, because she slowed and pulled off on the shoulder.

Salt stuck to Valentine's boots as he hopped to the ground. "Ace, grab your gun."

Osric jumped out, then looked up at the static-gat with his hands on his hips. He climbed the steps to the top of the van, and after a moment of inspecting the gatling, he unscrewed the handle and slid the front from its casing. Valentine raised his eyebrows as Osric hefted it in one arm, impressed in spite of himself.

"You didn't know this was portable, did you?" Osric said.

"You sure you didn't just break it?" Valentine stood below the steps as Osric climbed down.

"I'm sure. And it was askew in the casing, which is probably why it was so hard to wind."

That was helpful to know, but also made Valentine look incompetent. "Is this where I compliment you on your big sexy brain?"

Osric gave him a crooked smile that contained none of the joy it once had. He screwed the handle into the gat. "It's pretty heavy."

"Your big brain?"

Osric fought against a chuckle and failed. "Yes, my big brain. Terrible burden, that."

Valentine almost made another joke about the "burdens" Osric had to carry around, then thought better of it. He wasn't ready to forgive yet, no matter how sweet Osric looked right now.

He pulled on his goggles and peered at the delivery truck, which leaned to one side on its popped tires. "I thought these trucks were impervious to arrows."

"They are, as long as the guards over the wheels are enabled."

Before Valentine could chew on that, Osric strode forward with the gat tucked under one arm.

"That's going to need a strap or something to keep it steady," Valentine said. "It isn't going to do us any good if it burns your hands or falls from your grip when we need it."

"I'll be fine."

Valentine sighed.

Ace followed, her expression growing grimmer with every step. "This was a pirate attack. Whoever or whatever was in the truck is going to be long gone."

Cupping his hands around his mouth, Valentine shouted, "Hello! Anyone still here?"

"Shh! You're calling attention to us!"

"Because the big noisy van rumbling up didn't do that already? Pirates aren't going to be hanging around if there's nothing left to kill or steal."

"This is a bad idea."

Valentine kicked up his heel. "Go Team Poor Judgment."

Picking up his pace, he caught up with Osric. The back doors of the delivery truck hung open, and so many footprints stamped the salt that it was impossible to tell how many people had been here. He inhaled, but all he smelled was the tangy desert air, so hopefully there wasn't a liquefying corpse in the driver's seat.

Climbing into the empty trailer, he inspected the bare floor. "The pirates took everything that wasn't bolted down... And then they took the bolts."

The women who had tied Valentine up had mentioned it being difficult to take out delivery trucks because they were reinforced. A seasoned driver would know to keep the guards down over the tires. The simplest answer was usually the correct one, which meant whoever had been driving wasn't familiar with these kinds of trucks.

Osric disappeared from view, then raised his voice. "No one in the cab."

Valentine jumped out and opened the passenger's side door. The steering wheel and gear shifter were missing, along with the rearview and side mirrors. Probably decorating some wasteland pirate captain now.

Long strands of something white drifted into Valentine's face and he spluttered and batted them away. He expected cobwebs to coat his fingers, but the shimmery threads were still hanging in front of him, stuck in the doorframe.

He tugged the snagged hairs free, comparing them to Osric's pale forelock. Osric stopped beside him, and Valentine held up the hairs. "From an android?"

"It's possible."

"Do they go on deliveries?"

"Yes. Sometimes."

Valentine sighed. "Okay, good."

"Um, guys?" Ace's voice drifted from the back of the truck.

Based on her tone, Valentine was afraid to look, lest there be an entire band of pirates surrounding them, arrows notched. But footsteps neared and Ace thrust out a silky pink bra.

Valentine backed up and bumped into the open passenger's door. "Thanks, but I hate underwire."

"That's not all." Ace dropped the bra and headed away from the truck. Valentine and Osric followed.

They didn't get far before Valentine spotted the fingers of a black glove jutting from the ground. A lacy something peeked out nearby. Beyond it was an open suitcase full of more items, all of them feminine city clothes.

Stomach dropping, Valentine stared at a crumpled dress in a sunny yellow. Osric picked it up and shook salt away. An enamel pin was attached to the dress' collar – a white hand clutching flowers.

Osric opened his mouth, but Valentine was already nodding, his pulse pounding in his ears.

They'd found their truck after all.

8

Better a Witty Fool
Osric

Osric sat in the back of the van, his legs hanging over the edge. An earthy, herbal breeze skimmed off the desert, mild and pleasant. They'd driven beyond the delivery truck, until the road was no longer visible, and parked. There wasn't much to hide a vehicle behind out here, but highway travelers wouldn't see it. Pirates might still come upon it, but Valentine and Ace had agreed that it was better than driving straight into an encampment.

Having no experience with foot travel or tracking, Osric had little advice to offer, other than to voice his opinion that this whole plan was probably a mistake.

Jaw set in determination that likely had nothing to do with the knots he was tying, Valentine tugged on the three joined neckties, then held up the gatling. "There we go – a strap. Seems a bad use for such handsome ties, but oh well."

Osric declined to take the gun, staring at Valentine until he set it back in his lap. "We can turn around. You can refuse to do this. Tell Portia what became of the androids and that it's too dangerous. You won't have your visas, but you'll be alive."

Ace rummaged through supplies, stuffing a box of ammunition into her back pocket. "Valentine and I already discussed this. We're doing it."

"But if *you* don't want to go, we can take you back to the city," Valentine said. "Don't want you to feel like we're making decisions for you."

Osric slid closer. "Are you sure it's what you want? We'll be heading directly after pirates. Even though the last ones were willing to negotiate, that doesn't mean the rest of them will be."

"Not all the pirates are horrible. I mean, I've never met one who hasn't tried to kill me, but they aren't sadists. That doesn't mean this isn't more of my poor judgment, but it's not the first risky thing I've done in my life."

Osric took the gun from Valentine's lap and set it aside. "Can we talk, please?"

"We are talking."

"I mean about what happened between us."

"You didn't seem to want to do that this morning."

"I started to, but you stopped listening."

Valentine winced like Osric had struck him.

A gust of wind rocked the van, and a ragged strip of headliner fabric tickled the back of Osric's neck. The purpling on Valentine's biceps stood out in stark contrast on his skin. "I didn't mean to hurt you."

Compared to AI, Valentine was fragile and opaque. It was easy to affect him, but then not know what emotions that evoked in him. Touching him wouldn't help Osric clear the air between them, but he couldn't resist the temptation. He reached for Valentine's hand, the way he had before, but Valentine yanked it away as Osric's fingers brushed his knuckles. He hopped out and strode away from the van.

Osric tugged at his hair. The feelings budding inside him and all the sensory processes of his body were pointless if he had no one to share them with. "Why the hell did I come on this trip?"

"I don't know," Valentine snarled. "Why did you? You blew up on me when all I was trying to do was help you. Then you showed up last night talking about bank buildings like you didn't have a care in the world. You shouldn't have come back."

A hot rush of anger flooded Osric's limbs. He stood and slammed his fist into the van's siding. His fingers throbbed in pain, but he blocked out the sensation and stomped back toward the highway. This was ridiculous. He needed to be back where he belonged.

They were approximately one hundred miles from the city. It would take days of walking to get back. His bare feet would not be in good condition by that point, and the idea of collapsing from dehydration again almost made him turn back. But Valentine didn't want him here. Maybe he could hitch a ride back with a delivery truck.

A sage-tinged breeze and the pounding of his heart were the only sounds. Empty desert stretched in all directions, and a hawk wheeled overhead.

"Osric." Valentine's breathless voice carried from somewhere behind. "Stop."

Salt crunched beneath Osric's toes. His legs were so primitively slow that any amount of walking would feel like an eternity.

"Hey." Valentine jogged up beside him, panting. "You can't just walk back to Salt Lake."

"I can."

"Shit, honey. Your hand."

Glancing at his swollen fingers and scraped knuckles reminded him that they hurt, so he turned his attention back to the horizon.

"Come back." Valentine struggled to keep up with Osric's stride. "You need out of here that badly, I'll give you a ride."

"I don't know what you want from me. I tried apologizing. And I can't– I can't articulate what I'm feeling with tongue and teeth the way I could flood the network with emotional processes. It's frustrating."

Valentine gripped Osric's arm, and the contact sent a jolt through him.

He stopped. "I thought I could see the good on this trip. Lysander said it might be better that I'm out of the city's reach while the Concord investigates this, anyway."

"This trip has been shit so far. What did you expect to be good on it?"

"More time to understand this body." A pink tint kissed Valentine's cheekbones and the bridge of his nose. Threads of light weaved across his long lashes. "More time with you. But you don't–"

"I really liked our level of friendliness. I fucked it up. I'm so used to arguing with Ace that I didn't even try to listen to you when you apologized. I'm sorry for that. And sorry for what happened back in the manor." Valentine gestured toward the highway. "Don't do this. I want more time with you too."

"Even though I'm a dull robot who doesn't know how to convey his feelings?"

"Stop it. You are thoughtful and charming, with a proclivity for doing things that catch me off guard. That's not dull."

Sudden heat rose in Osric's cheeks. "That's kind of you to say."

"Nah. It's just the truth. And I know you have stuff to work out about your body. Nothing I say or do will change that. It has to come from within. If you want to use this trip for that purpose, I don't have a problem with it."

"Have you accepted my apology then?"

"Yeah." Valentine tugged at a hangnail. "Do you accept mine?"

"Yes."

"Good. Then let's go. We have androids to find."

They all traipsed west together. The trail of clothing died out before long, but a flurry of footprints marred the salt, along with motorcycle tracks. Ace had the same hardened look of determination she'd worn since they'd met. Valentine may have been the one known for taking on difficult jobs, but he was distractible, often lost so deep in his thoughts that Osric had to say his name several times to get his attention. It was easy to see Ace as a compliment to his fervid nature, keeping him on track.

She adjusted the gun tucked into the waistband of her pants. "Do you think the pirates have eaten any of the androids?"

Valentine grimaced. "Ugh. What? I hope not."

"But they aren't people. They're robots with a meat coating."

"Made of human flesh."

"It's bioengineered. Some kind of hybrid." Osric rubbed his chin. "I'm not sure how healthy it would be to eat."

Valentine's lip curled. "I think eating androids would be morally reprehensible. They might not be people, but they look like them."

"And that's the crux of it, isn't it? Humans anthropomorphize non-humans. This makes them more relatable and stimulates an urge to care and empathize. I'll bet you would balk at killing and eating a pet dog but have no qualms with eating beef." Osric gave Valentine a friendly nudge that masked the sourness in his abdomen. "And you wouldn't be able to relate to me if I didn't have this 'hot bod.'"

Valentine held up a finger. "Now wait a minute. I'm not shallow. Do I need to remind you that I also find you charming?"

"Say I was never in this predicament, and you met me back when I was in the network. If I tried to strike up a conversation with you, you'd talk to me? Enough so that we would end up as friends? It would mean having to interact with one of my creepy eyes."

"Yes. I'll admit that you having a body makes it easier. Because right now I can look in your face and see you smile. You can give me a reassuring touch and help me knot my tie. But we still could have been friends… even if it was just you as a big eyeball."

Osric hoped that was the case. That if he'd fallen for Valentine instead of that assembly worker whose curls were always in his eyes, that Valentine wouldn't have gotten terrified and quit. If Osric was back in the network and this body was rotting away somewhere or inert in a stasis pod, he would be much more comfortable, stretching out his cramped mind across the network. But the fact still remained that Valentine would have a harder time relating to him.

Valentine was still talking, something about a quiz in one of his magazines. "And I scored highest in Emotional Support. But a close second was Physical Touch. Words of encouragement and understanding are something a bodiless Steward can give, but physical touch isn't."

Osric's stomach sank further. "I know the test you're talking about. I scored highest in Quality Time, which... I can't imagine a Steward *not* ranking that as most meaningful, given that our connection to each other is such a basic and vital part of our makeup."

Valentine's forehead creased. "Which you're disconnected from now."

"Yes." Osric paused. "But it just occurred to me that 'quality time' between Stewards is more like your physical touch. Like all of us holding hands, I suppose, only deeper than that. I'm not sure how to explain it in a way a human would understand."

Brush poked at his bare soles, and he regretted not putting on shoes or socks. He should have at least worn his suspenders, because his pants kept sliding down. But who could be bothered with so much clothing?

"If we actually held hands, would that help at all? Or am I taking it too literally?" Valentine asked.

Ace turned. "Pirates aren't going to take us seriously if they see us bearing down on them with terrifying weapons while holding hands."

"Don't be jealous." Valentine hooked an arm around Ace and planted a wet kiss on her cheek, which she immediately wiped away. "And you're assuming pirates are going to see us in the first place. Following the footprints, we should be able to see their encampment from a way off – that is, if we don't find evidence of what happened to the androids *before* we get there."

It was hard to say how the pirates might have reacted. If they didn't know the escorts were androids, it would be a shock to disable a delivery truck and find eight well-dressed women crammed inside. There hadn't been any casualties near the truck, not even the manager. Maybe they had a capturing policy.

Osric turned to Valentine. "Those pirates we encountered tied you up instead of killing you. Did you say anything about what they planned to do to you?"

"Oh yeah. One said I could go free if I had a good barter for them. The other told her to hush and said they were going to string me up by my balls." He shrugged. "Joke's on them."

Something moved in Osric's peripheral vision. A group of pronghorns grazed beneath yellow aspen trees. A male with an impressive set of antlers lifted his head and stared. Pied patches laced his body, and something bristled from his back. He squinted. Were those arrows?

He tentatively walked closer. A doe and calf froze beside the male. They perked up, then fled, bounding over brush and disappearing. The buck stood a moment longer, nostrils flaring, then trotted after the others, the shafts in his back quivering.

"Did you see the arrows in him?" Osric asked. "It was like they didn't even affect him."

"Like you," a voice said.

Osric whipped his head around. Two pirates – the women they'd encountered on the way into Salt Lake – stood twenty yards away, bows drawn. They must have been beyond the small scatterings of aspens, because there wasn't much else to hide behind out here. Though their hands were steady, too much white flashed in their eyes, and they looked as close to bolting as the pronghorns.

The woman with the feathered mohawk kept her aim trained on Osric. Her quavering voice betrayed her confident stance. "What do you want, machine-man?"

Ace's hand crept to the gun in her waistband, but she held steady. "What happened to that delivery van back by the road?"

"Someone shot up the tires, obviously. Wasn't us." The black-toothed woman turned to Osric. "What do you want in exchange for the woman and the guy? What can we give you? Information? We know where the rest of your kind from the truck went."

Osric raised his eyebrows. It seemed strange that anyone would find him intimidating, but maybe he could use that to his advantage. He hesitantly bridged their distance. "That information would be much appreciated. But I'm not trading the lives of the two salvagers for it. Perhaps we can give you the gat–"

"Why hasn't he killed you?" Black Teeth asked Ace. "Can he turn you into a machine like him? Or... or" – she blanched – "like the animals?"

Before Osric had time to process what that meant, Valentine said, "Wait a minute. Are you trying to *rescue* us from Osric? Pirates are trying to *rescue* me?"

"Look, you come into our territory, you're fair game for a shakedown," Mohawk said, "but sometimes we gotta band together, you know? We don't want to see you turned into machine-people. Or what the animals have become." She shuddered, and bottlecap earrings painted with a tiny shield and the acronym *CTR* waggled from her lobes.

Valentine frowned. "Pretty sure that's not how it works. And Osric isn't hostile."

Osric elbowed him in the side. The pirates' misconception of him could be leveraged to find the androids and get the salvagers out of here safe. "I'll take your information in exchange for–"

"The others didn't seem hostile either," Black Teeth said.

"But you should have seen what they did to the human with them."

Though he wanted to ask for specifics, Osric wasn't sure if they would talk to him more than necessary. Luckily, Valentine had the same questions.

"Did they kill the guy?"

The pirates exchanged a glance. "Maybe we shouldn't talk about this in front of..." Mohawk tilted her chin toward Osric.

"He's not like other androids," Valentine said. "It's complicated."

Dubiously, Black Teeth said, "We don't know much about the machine-people. We didn't know this guy here wasn't human until my arrows didn't take him down. But he has the same markings as the machine-animals, and those women we found..."

"Machine-animals?" Osric asked. Salt Lake had many androids, but nothing in an animal's form. That buck, though, had been bristling with arrows and sported piebald patterning. "Those pronghorns?"

"You don't know about them? Not just the antelope. Jackrabbits and rattlesnakes too. We've killed them before but it's more difficult. Got some of their metal skeletons back at camp."

"Do you eat them?" Ace asked.

"No," both pirates said in unison. Mohawk wrinkled her nose. "The meat is tough and has a weird metallic taint, almost like it's stressed. But we kill them when we can."

Valentine asked a question Osric *didn't* want to ask. "Why?"

"They are not Heavenly Father's creation. In the cities, that hardly matters, but out here, roaming free, they procreate with the naturals of their kind and produce abominations."

The androids were sterile... or were supposed to be. And Osric couldn't imagine what point there would be to creating bionic animals modeled after the native wildlife.

Rubbing the back of his neck, Valentine said, "Do I want to know in what way the offspring are abominations?"

"No." Mohawk eyed Osric. "I don't know what your intention is, machine-man, but if you're looking for the others, we'll give you directions to them if you'll keep them away from us. Take them back to the city or anywhere else. Don't let them roam free out here."

"Yes, we'd appreciate that." Osric wiped sweat from his brow. "But I think we need to know if the androids killed the human they were with."

Androids wouldn't kill a person intentionally unless instructed to, and even that would require specific coding and a situation where they were operating in defense of an innocent. He couldn't picture a group of escorts needing that kind of programming.

Black Teeth shook her head. "We don't know for sure. But the guy was flayed open, spread-eagled on the ground, with all of the machine-women milling around a little way off like nothing had happened."

"Then they didn't do it." Androids programmed for defense would immediately sit down after an incident and repeat certain dialogue phrases until a specific key command shut them off. It seemed more likely that a pirate had killed the manager while the women were locked up in the back. Then received a shocking surprise when they opened the truck.

"Where did the androids go?" Ace asked.

"They wandered around the dead guy for a bit, then picked a direction and started walking. We were pretty freaked out, so we left, then came back with a motorcycle and followed their trail. Looked like they were going to the Wendover ruins. That's about twenty-five miles from here." Black Teeth hunched her shoulders and clutched her elbows. "It's creepy. The city ruins are already full of ghosts. We don't need machine-women wandering around there too."

"Well, we'll be happy to get them out of here for you." Valentine drew up his small frame and tucked his thumbs in his suspender straps. "What happened to the body?"

"Buried it," Mohawk replied. "We didn't kill the guy, but it seemed wrong to leave him like that."

Valentine nodded approvingly.

The pirates leaned their heads together, whispering, then lowered their bows. Mohawk said, "Alright. Help us. But no trickery from any of you, especially the machine-man. We give you directions and you stay away from us. Go back where you came from. Or don't. Doesn't make a difference to us as long as all of you are gone."

Valentine stepped forward and offered his hand, which was more than Osric expected after the way they treated him originally. "Deal. I'm Valentine, by the way. That's Ace, and the terrifying machine-man is Osric."

Mohawk hesitantly shook his hand. "I'm Perdetta. That's Sariah."

"Ladies, I forgive you for tying me up like a hog and threatening to do unspeakable things to my nether region."

The color in Perdetta's bister cheeks deepened. "Right. Well, let me find a paper and I'll draw some directions."

Osric had more questions about the bionic animals, and he worried how they could possibly provide enough food for the androids when they found them, but it seemed too much effort to voice all of that now.

A shrill ringing came from somewhere on Sariah, in bizarre contrast to the natural world around them. She patted her pockets and produced a cell phone with a crack running across the screen.

"Hello?" She bared her black teeth and held up a hand. "Okay, Lehi, calm down. Say what now?"

Valentine leaned toward Osric. "Is it weird that she has a phone?"

"You have one."

"Yeah, but mine only plays music and some match three games. There's a settings menu, but it's complicated."

"It's not that complicated," Ace countered. "You just got

frustrated when you couldn't figure it out in three seconds." Ace didn't say it unkindly, but Valentine frowned and looked away.

Osric wanted to reassure him, but Sariah uttered a few more *calm down*s, then promised she'd be back at camp soon. After tucking the phone back into her pocket, she turned to Osric, her jaw set. "The machine-women showed up in our camp. They're hungry."

9

I Defy You, Stars
Valentine

The pirates stopped at the edge of their encampment. Valentine lingered behind Perdetta and rubbed his clammy hands on his jeans.

Sturdy roundhouses made of animal hide, plastic tarps, and corrugated sheet metal spread out before them, peppered here and there with motorcycles. There was also a pickup truck with a cap made of splintery boards. Crops – a small swath of corn, tomatoes, and what may have been squash – grew behind a fence of sticks and twine. The plants were scrawny and sparse, some of them drooping like they didn't have enough morale to keep growing. Even if they'd been burgeoning with produce, it was nowhere near enough to feed a community.

It seemed wrong to be standing here in an enemy village, assessing their resources, even if neither of their groups had ill intentions.

Some kind of commotion was going on beyond the truck. People were clustered together in an agitated mass, their raised voices not drifting well enough to make out the words. Perdetta reached for Osric's arm, then seemed to think better of it and snatched Valentine by his suspender strap instead, tugging him toward the altercation. Out of the corner of his eye he saw Sariah notch her bow and hold it to one side, blocking Osric's path.

"That's really not necessary." Valentine stumbled over a rock. "We're not going to head into your camp without permission, and Osric isn't going to hurt anyone."

Perdetta didn't look back. She led him to a band of pirates with feather-adorned hair and hand-stitched shirts. Beyond them was a group of women who looked like they'd just stepped off a city shuttle, albeit a shuttle that had stopped too abruptly and thrown them all onto the dirty floor. The androids stared vacantly, hair frazzled with scrapes on their arms, as pirates shouted into their nonplussed faces.

Valentine's heart leapt at the sight of his quarry–

That didn't sound right. Targets? Objective?

The ladies he was to escort back to Salt Lake... But if this argument shifted to violence, some of the pirates had guns rather than arrows, and he was certain an android wouldn't survive a shot to the temple.

Perdetta dragged Valentine to the front of the group. Ace sprinted next to him, her posture stiff with a scowl carved into her face. Some of the pirates directed their looks of outrage to Valentine, then to Perdetta. She tried to offer an explanation, but it was lost amid the noise.

Putting two fingers between her lips, she blew a piercing whistle that cut through the chatter. She nudged Valentine toward the androids while she addressed the pirates.

Valentine scanned the women, who muttered varied statements about their hunger and thirst. He counted eight, which meant they were all accounted for.

Though she looked a little worse for wear, he recognized the one from Portia's video. She locked eyes with him and gave him an empty smile. "Hello. It's a pleasure to meet you. My name is Cinnamon, she/her."

"Hey, Cinnamon. I'm Valentine. You all–"

"Hello, Valentine. What are your pronouns?"

"I use 'he.' Thanks for asking. It looks like–"

"It's a pleasure to meet you."

He blew a breath threw his nose, waiting to see if she would say anything else. She stared back with a placid expression. "Nice to meet you too. You all look like you've had a bit of a rough time."

"Valentine, I'm thirsty, and I need to eat. Would you be so kind as to point me in the direction of sustenance?"

These pirates weren't going to give away a meal for free. Portia hadn't said the androids needed to be fed or well-cared for before bringing them back. But, robots or not, Valentine didn't want them aching for food the way Osric had.

The gat was their best weapon, but he and Ace didn't have anything else to offer. "Trade you my gat if we can get some food and water for these ladies."

He expected Ace to protest, but she nodded. "It's in great condition and doesn't need ammo. Plus, if we get them fed, they won't have any more interest in you, and we can all be on our way."

Perdetta consulted with the people around her, then turned back to him. "It's not broken, right?"

"If it were broken, why would we have carried it all the way here?"

"Prove it's not."

Valentine marched away from the group. If this thing didn't work as a portable weapon, he was going to make a fool out of himself, and the trade would fall through.

Widening his stance and ensuring the pirates were watching, he vigorously cranked the gat handle and aimed it at a broad clump of sagebrush. He hit the trigger and lightning arced from the barrels. The bush burst into flames and branches popped from the heat. Two women rushed over and flung dirt on the fire until it was snuffed out.

He turned back to Perdetta. "Well?"

She bridged their distance and held out her hand. "Deal."

Valentine whipped the gat off his shoulder. Handing it over made him feel naked, but it also removed him one step from "salvager." City men didn't need electric gatling guns.

"Stay here," she said. "Don't let the women wander into our camp. We'll bring you all a meal."

Cinnamon clasped her hands against her chest and looked genuinely pleased. "Thank you. We will wait here." She promptly sat in the dirt and stared into the distance. The women around her followed suit.

Some of the tension in Valentine's shoulders eased and he heaved a sigh. The androids were in one piece, no one was going to get strung up by non-existent body parts, and they could be back in Salt Lake before noon tomorrow. Valentine and Ace would have their visas, and Osric could go back to being an all-seeing eyeball.

Valentine sat cross-legged next to Cinnamon. "Can we engage in a conversation?"

"Yes. I have many topics to choose from."

"Cool. Can you tell me what happened to the manager driving you from Salt Lake?" He wasn't sure it even mattered, but he was curious, and past experience with retrieval jobs had taught him that being thorough was always a good idea.

Cinnamon blinked. "I'm afraid I don't have information on that subject."

"Oh." The androids probably hadn't seen anything happen, since they were stuck in the back of the truck. "Well, did your manager tell you where you were going when he loaded you into the truck?"

"I'm afraid I don't have information on that subject. Would you like to discuss something else? I'm up to date on current books, films, and popular music. I have interests in art, philosophy, and baking." She pointed to the tattoo on Valentine's sternum – an arrow with a heart-shaped tip. "That is an interesting tattoo. Arrow and heart iconography are associated with the holiday Valentine's Day. Is this tattoo in reference to your name?"

"Yeah." He hadn't expected the androids to have such complex reasoning. "But I don't really want to–"

"I have a tattoo as well." Cinnamon unbuttoned her top and pulled it open, revealing a tiny bumblebee between her breasts and a lack of inhibition that rivaled Osric's. Instead of the seams in her chest running straight down her sternum like his, they curved around the sides of her ribs and formed a V above her navel.

Valentine held up a halting hand. "Two things, hon. One, you're not on a date with a client so you don't need to be getting naked. And two, you're barking up the wrong tree. I'm not interested in women."

Osric stopped before them, arms folded. Cinnamon glanced up, and a strange look crossed her face so quickly that Valentine wasn't sure it had been there to begin with. "Hello. I'm Cinnamon, she/her. Are you an android?"

"It would appear that way, wouldn't it," Osric replied. "But looks can be deceiving."

"That is an interesting statement, and I am in agreement. I have only been exposed to people who are attracted to women. In the past, showing them my tattoo has proved to be a pleasing action, and I believed Valentine would react accordingly. I must adjust my expectations for future encounters." She rebuttoned her shirt and folded her hands in her lap.

Valentine squinted at her. "We're going to be taking you back to Salt Lake to Portia's manor."

Cinnamon's jaw clenched and she smiled furiously. "This seems like a logical plan. Would you like to discuss this topic further?"

She seemed more stressed than she should be, given Osric's descriptions of androids. Her behavior sank unease into Valentine's gut.

Osric sat beside her. "Valentine and Ace are salvagers. They've been employed by Portia to bring you back safely."

"This is good," she said, looking like it was anything but. "The manor is our home, and there is a lack of resources in this environment. What is your name and pronouns?"

"Osric, he/him."

"Are you an android?"

Osric sighed.

Valentine stood and squeezed Osric's shoulder. Maybe he could keep Cinnamon occupied while Valentine gauged the reactions of other androids. If they all seemed upset at being taken back to the manor, that would be a problem, but maybe he was imagining things.

He squatted next to a new one with a blonde bob. A crusty gash ran across her forehead.

"Hi. I'm Valentine. Uh, he/him. What's your name?"

"Hello, Valentine!" The blonde woman beamed. "It's a pleasure to meet you. I'm Nutmeg, she/her."

"I've been paid by Portia to take you back to Salt Lake to your manor."

Nutmeg's pleased expression didn't waver. "Okay."

"Does that bother you?"

"No. I require sleep soon. My bunk is on the top above Saffron's."

That was more what Valentine had been expecting. He left Nutmeg and introduced himself to another android, feeling Cinnamon's gaze on him. Each android he talked to seemed either happy or ambivalent to being escorted back to the manor, though a couple of them hesitated a bit longer before agreeing that it was a good idea.

Ace stopped beside Valentine. "You get any info out of them?"

"One of them said she hates Brian, but you can hardly blame her. Humans, robots, and animals alike probably hiss at that guy's presence."

"The other guy, Brandon, could have trained her to say that."

Valentine recalled the video they'd watched in the manor and nodded.

Ace gave him an unexpected squeeze around the middle. "We're going to get our visas."

He grinned, but he wasn't going to let excitement overcome him until all the androids were filed back into the manor and the paperwork was signed. It seemed like such a distant, unattainable dream, and to have it within reach hadn't quite sunk in yet. Plus, Cinnamon's behavior was still tickling the back of his mind.

Portia *had* said the androids were specially trained, but emotions like fear and apprehension didn't seem beneficial to robots you expected to work as escorts who could end up in dangerous situations. And *barely suppressed* fear and apprehension meant that Cinnamon knew she wasn't supposed to be displaying those feelings, like Osric cringing after he laughed in the shuttle.

A thought struck Valentine and he strode for Osric, who was still intent on Cinnamon. Valentine beckoned to him, and they walked beyond the pickup truck and out of earshot.

"Is there a possibility that Cinnamon is a Steward? Maybe one you don't know, from a different city?"

Osric shook his head. "I explained to her how I ended up in an android body, mostly to get her to stop asking, and she seemed genuinely surprised." He sighed. "This led to a whole other tangent of questions, and I finally had to tell her I didn't want to talk about it anymore."

"She doesn't seem like she wants to go back to the manor."

"What makes you say that?"

"You didn't see her huge, fake smile?"

Osric pursed his lips and regarded Valentine uncertainly. "They all smile like that. I didn't notice anything amiss."

"No?" Maybe Valentine was still weirded out by the idea of rudimentary robots with living flesh and was anthropomorphizing Cinnamon. "Maybe I'm comparing her to you too much. Worried that there are other AI suffering inhumane treatment."

A crooked smile grew on Osric's face. "Your concern for AI is endearing. But I don't think there's any reason to worry about these androids. After a meal and some rest, they'll likely be more than happy to climb into the van and go home. It'll be cramped, but I doubt they care."

Cocking an eyebrow, Valentine said, "*I* care about being cramped. Can I sit in your lap on the way back?"

Osric chuckled. "Does this mean we've made up then? Truly?"

There was no justification for staying mad when Osric had been genuinely sorry. "Yeah. We're good."

"I'm glad." Osric's fingers twitched, and he stuffed his hands in his pockets, as if they might escape his wrists if he didn't.

Feeling other eyes on him, Valentine turned toward the androids. Cinnamon watched, that unconvincing smile still on her lips. He shuddered and tried to push away the unpleasant idea of her staring at him like that all the way back to Salt Lake.

This may not have turned out to be the worst job they'd done, but it was certainly one of the weirder ones.

The pirates returned with jugs of water and a pot of stew loaded with squash, root vegetables, and corn. The androids stood and filed into an orderly fashion, evenly spaced out, none of them talking or fidgeting. Even Cinnamon seemed to have lost her fixation on Valentine, accepting her bowl of stew and immediately tilting it to her lips, heedless of the steam billowing across her face.

Once all of the androids had settled down with their bowls and patiently waited for jugs of water to be passed around, Valentine took his own stew and sidled up to Perdetta, who was eyeing the androids with guarded curiosity. Her CTR bottlecap earrings reflected the orange glow of a cookfire beyond the nearby roundhouses. She could have killed him twice over by now and hadn't.

He thought about the pirates' names, which weren't fear-inducing monikers or even nature ones, but *Perdetta, Sariah,* and *Lehi.* "You all are Mormon here, huh?"

"Yeah. But probably not like you're thinking."

"I'm not sure what to think, to be honest."

"The congregations in the settlements and city don't want anything to do with us. They don't consider us true Latter-Day Saints and think we're dissenters." She sniffed. "Which is fine because we don't like some of their stances."

"Like *'highway robbery is bad'*?"

She narrowed her gaze. "No. Like *'women can't be ordained in the Priesthood.'* Excluding women from power and policymaking isn't something we believe in."

He raised his eyebrows. "Good for you. I mean that truly."

"Outsiders like you call us 'pirates.' But we're the Saints of Deseret."

Religion didn't necessarily make someone a good person, but that knowledge made him a little less reluctant to ask what he wanted to. "So, since you've discovered that I'm an incredibly helpful and charming individual who is graciously going to take these creepy machine-women off your hands, what do you say about putting in a good word for me with the rest of the pirates, er, Saints?" Even though he'd be living in the city after receiving his visa, that didn't rule out the possibility of him traveling across the salt flats again in the future.

Perdetta gave him a sidelong glance. "You electrocuted Alma. Blasted him off his motorcycle. None of us really liked him, but that's besides the point."

"And you tied me up, threatened me, and Sariah shot Osric twice in the chest. And I *do* like him. I'd say we're even. It would be really easy to agree on a truce. Your people see my van coming, they let it pass?"

She folded her arms and smirked. "You're not much of a threat now without your gatling."

That was true. "I'll buy a better one. Something that can vaporize you faster than you can say 'Joseph Smith.'"

She rolled her eyes. "Alright. We'll stay away from your

van when it passes through. And you can call us 'pirates.' The younger people here would be outraged if we took that term away from them. They like it."

All he had was her word, but his gut said she was telling the truth. He sipped his too-hot stew, which was full of more flavor than he'd expected. Some kind of pepper gave it a mild heat, and bits of herbs stuck to his throat. "Great. Can I make one suggestion, though? Don't let your children come on shakedowns. The kid was a good shot, don't get me wrong, but I don't want to kill them. I don't want to kill anyone if I can help it."

Perdetta bristled. "How about you don't tell us how to raise our children, and I won't tell you not to engage in a relationship with a machine-man."

"We're not in a relationship."

"Doesn't look that way to me. I'm just grateful you can't get pregnant by him."

"Um..." She was making many assumptions with that statement, but he and Osric weren't going to sleep together anyway. "Because we'd produce an 'abomination?'"

The whites of Perdetta's eyes flashed. "I don't even want to know what the offspring of a human and a machine-person would be like. The animals are horrible enough."

"How specifically?"

She shifted and gripped her elbows, then headed toward the nearest roundhouse and beckoned to him.

Valentine glanced back to his companions. Ace sat beside Osric on an overturned metal crate, both of them clutching their stew as they kept watch over the androids. Most of the pirates had gone back into camp, though a few still eyed the group of women – and Osric – as though they'd suddenly rise up as one and attack.

"You coming?" Perdetta called.

Reluctantly, Valentine followed her past buildings, campfires, and meat-smoking tents. Teddy bears and wooden toys littered the ground, and toddlers with wispy hair wandered between tents, supervised by only-slightly-older children.

Perdetta ducked through a door flap and held it open for Valentine. The soft scent of spices perfumed the air, and animal hides covered the dirt floor. A sun-faded print of Jesus hung on the wall in a broken frame.

After dragging a box out from underneath a wobbly card table, Perdetta set it on top and opened the lid. Something jangled, and she revealed an articulated metal skeleton of a small animal. Judging by the long, yellowed teeth, it was a rabbit. Its gunmetal skull flopped to one side, arms swaying from joints with delicate pins and screws.

"I bet it was a surprise when you skinned and dressed that thing," Valentine said.

"People have been finding them for a couple of years, here and there, but this was the first my husband caught." She set the skeleton back into the box, then carefully retrieved a cloth bag and set it on the table without opening it. "The abominations started showing up about a year later. At first, we thought they were some new creation from the city, or the result of disease or radiation. But after seeing one with a pronghorn doe and a buck with the machine-animal patterning, we realized it was what happened when they reproduced."

Valentine unstrung the bag and peeked at the collection of bones inside. Gingerly, he plucked out the skull and held it up. A crusty black substance clogged the porous bone, and one of the holes may have been an eye socket, though his brain was having trouble making any sense of it. Long teeth protruded from what definitely wasn't a jaw, twisting away over the top – bottom? – of the skull.

He pushed it back into the bag. "What was it? A badger?"

"No. It was a jackrabbit too. I think. Bigger, though. I wanted to keep the hide, but I wasn't sure how to skin it with the extra limbs."

Valentine curled his lip. "The what?" Talk about disturbing.

But at least it was only a rabbit. He considered asking if they'd found any mutated cougars, then decided he didn't want to know. "Why are these things out here?"

She huffed. "They're an everyday part of our reality now. Something that *you* didn't know about, even though your cities are the ones creating them. Maybe not purposely – I don't think anyone intended for the abominations to come about – but you people are so insulated in your high-tech lives that you don't think about the ramifications of what you're doing."

"I'm only doing a job for the city. I don't live there. Not yet anyway–"

"And when you do, you'll forget about this. You'll forget that weird city experiments are running wild, changing the environment." Her voice rose, cutting the air between them. "You won't think about the emissions from your factories polluting the sky, or how we Saints out here are struggling. It'll never cross your mind how incredibly unholy it is to make robots with human flesh, who can be beaten and bruised and bleed for sadists' enjoyment, but it isn't wrong in your eyes because they aren't actually people–"

"Whoa, now wait a minute." He put up his hands, his stomach twisting. "All of that is awful and I would never think it's okay. You underestimate my ability to worry about problems I can't fix. I'd change all of it if I could."

Perdetta set the bag into the box and shoved it back under the table. "I'd like to believe that."

"There's a lot of unfairness in the world."

"Yeah."

The silence expanded, his statement apparently heavy enough that there was nothing else for either of them to add. He cleared his throat and thumbed at the tent entrance. "Well, I should see about getting those ladies out of here."

He followed Perdetta back to the edge of camp. The sun hung low in the evening sky, that irritating time of day when you were completely blinded while trying to drive.

Most of the androids had finished their stew and were now snuggled together in a sleepy mass like a litter of puppies. Gods this was weird.

They seemed comfortable despite the lack of beds and would hopefully awake refreshed and complaint-free. Valentine would have to make sure they all went to pee before they hit the road in the morning, because he was *not* stopping every ten minutes for a bathroom break.

Perdetta looked at him askance. "You're going to ask if you all can spend the night here, huh?"

"No. We can let them rest for a bit, then lead them back to the van. I'm sure they'll find a cozy bit of ground to sleep on there, or they can take shelter in the delivery truck."

Her tension eased. "Okay. I'll leave you to it." She paused. "Sorry for our first encounter. We're really not horrible people, but you gotta do what you gotta do."

"If I thought you had no wiggle room for reasoning or compassion, I would have stayed in my van."

Perdetta smiled. "Good luck with the machine-people, city boy. Especially your man with the blue eye." She winked, then sauntered past the first roundhouse and scooped up a crying toddler.

These people were all right, and it pained Valentine to think that they were more respectful than any of the people he'd encountered in the city. But he'd really only interacted with Brian and Portia, which hopefully wasn't a fair representation of Salt Lake.

When he soaked in the lives of these folks – bandits who attacked travelers but loved their kids and kept pictures of Jesus on their walls – the thought of getting a visa became bittersweet. He'd been absorbed with the notion of walking down pristine city streets in a fancy suit, living his best life, but how could he be surrounded by so much fortune and excess in good conscience, knowing how others struggled? His testosterone would be free, though, and he could get his chest fixed. Even if he decided he didn't want to *live* in Salt Lake, those benefits would be worth the effort.

An arc of purple electricity from the gat crackled beyond the settlement. Valentine's heart throbbed in alarm, but a firm hand closed over his shoulder. Osric said, "It's okay. Ace is showing Sariah how to use the gatling. They aren't shooting at anything."

Valentine released a pent breath. The idea of mutant cougars and pronghorns was going to linger for a while.

"Ace had trouble winding the gatling, so I gave it a try. I thought it had been lodged in the casing wrong, but it turns out you were right and it's just hard to wind." Osric let out a sheepish laugh. "I'm very impressed that you can do it at all. You must have strong hands."

Valentine flushed. "It's the little guys you have to watch out for."

"Tougher than you look."

"I could say the same thing to you, machine-man."

Osric started walking and Valentine followed. "My resilience is purely physical. I'm overwhelmed by things that you wouldn't give a thought to. I hesitate in situations where you don't."

They stopped behind a corrugated metal hut and sat on a bench overlooking a desert tinted pink in the evening light. It was so similar to Osric's spot behind the sheds in Festerchapel that it gave Valentine a surge of déjà vu. "You'd get used to it. You seem very adaptable. Your facial expressions and mannerisms are spot on."

"It's part of the android programming and feels natural for this body to do it. Other aspects have not been so easy to figure out." He stared at his hands, something complex playing across his face. "Earlier, we were talking about physical touch being important to us. If I can be very bold right now... can I put my arm around you?"

Valentine's breath quickened. "See? It's unexpected things

like that I like about you. Keeps me on my toes. And, yeah. Go for it. I don't mind contributing to your souvenir memories."

Sliding his hand across Valentine's back, Osric pulled him close. Valentine shut his eyes and leaned his head on Osric's shoulder, inhaling the earthiness of his skin and the faint trace of mousse. Osric's breath ruffled Valentine's hair. "It's not really a compulsion for souvenir memories. I'm not sad that I won't taste food again or feel hot water on my skin, even though those things were pleasant. But I'm hoping you like this sense of connection as much as I do."

Valentine couldn't comprehend exactly what Osric was going through now, but he knew the emptiness of people not understanding you. Of not being able to articulate the turmoil of feelings inside and wishing you could clutch someone and have them see it through your eyes.

"I like it, yeah. Especially if it makes you feel better," Valentine said.

The feeling of Osric's enveloping arms, his wide hands pressing into Valentine's sides and warm breath fanning his cheek was stirring up more than platonic closeness. His fingers fidgeted against the splintery seat beneath him, and he wanted to put his hand on Osric's knee. He wanted to squeeze it and tell Osric how glad he was that Osric was here right now. How glad he was that their fight in the parking garage wasn't their last interaction before they parted ways.

But he continued to pick at the splinters in the bench instead. Speaking those thoughts aloud would prove how selfish he was. Osric didn't want to be here. He was holding Valentine to make himself feel better because he missed his form back within the city's network.

A thought struck him, and he snickered.

"What's funny?" Osric asked.

"Not funny, exactly. I was thinking about Cinnamon saying her experiences included snuggling sad men."

"This is the reverse. You're a man snuggling a sad AI."

Valentine turned his face to Osric's just as Osric did the same, and their noses brushed against each other. "Are you sad?"

"Not right now." Osric's gaze lingered, his lips parted. His breath buffeted Valentine's lips.

Valentine fought the urge to lean closer. "How's your hand?"

"What?" Osric pulled back and splayed his fingers, wincing. Bruises blossomed on his knuckles, but the swelling had gone down. "I'm okay. I shouldn't have hit the van."

"Oh yes, that extra dent is really going to bring down the resale value."

"Still. I need to control my anger better."

"Yes, well, none of us are perfect, are we?" Valentine said.

Osric cleared his throat. His arm was still around Valentine's side, firm and comforting, but he looked away. "Perhaps not, but I've been meaning to tell you... It's okay that your brain works the way it does."

"What's that supposed to mean?"

"I've noticed that you seem to get frustrated or embarrassed about certain aspects of yourself – being unable to focus on books; getting overwhelmed by the settings menu on your phone; or–"

"How I can't remember to remember," Valentine said. Of course Osric would notice those things, as perceptive as he was.

"I bet you have amazing focus on things you love," Osric said gently. "You're a great conversationalist. Deeply caring."

Heat flooded Valentine's cheeks until he felt like his face was on fire. "Don't forget impossibly charming and funny."

"I haven't."

"The van's a mess, though. I can't stay organized. It's a wonder I haven't suffocated under all the notes I leave myself that I've forgotten to read."

"So it's a mess. They're just papers. And dirty socks."

"Is there a word for a mind like mine?"

"Wonderful?"

Valentine almost laughed, then stopped himself, even more acutely aware of Osric's arm around him. "Are you complimenting me on my big sexy brain?"

"Yes." One side of his mouth lifted in a smile.

A flash of purple lightning cracked in the distance, and Osric stood abruptly, taking all his warmth with him. "Thanks for the, uh, snuggle. After Ace is finished showing off the gatling, we can wake up the androids and lead them back to the van."

"Sounds good." Valentine watched Osric go, then thumped his head against the wall and shut his eyes, still feeling Osric's embrace and their noses brushing together. *Wonderful*, he'd said. Maybe he did want to be here with Valentine, after all. It formed a thick lump in Valentine's throat, and he dug his fingernails harder into the bench below him.

Shooing away the butterflies that were trying to form in his stomach, he pulled in a deep breath of the night air. An owl hooted in the distance and chatter from the camp drifted over, something about Sariah's sewing skills and which children were dirty enough to warrant a bath.

Fingers dug into Valentine's hair and jerked his head to one side. Something jabbed into his throat and a voice hissed, "Make a sound and I'll push this awl through your jugular."

Ice sleeted through his veins, and he clenched his jaw, eyes wide. The lingering comfort and security of Osric's arms evaporated, replaced by the unwelcome image of a sharp rod going straight through his neck.

Slowly raising his hands, he cursed himself for not listening to his gut, for getting distracted – again. Cinnamon was not playing around. One wrong move and he'd be bleeding out before he could call for help.

"Oka–"

She pressed the awl harder against his neck and he gasped. "Not. A. Sound," she spat. Sliding in front of him, she stared through a curtain of hair with a face that had none of the vacant I'm-here-but-not-really expression she'd worn earlier.

Her plastic smile was gone, lips twisted into a snarl. The fading light gave her gaze a sinister glint.

Shaking her head like a disappointed mother, she whispered, "Osric is a Steward. I was certain I could draw him away later and gain his understanding. But it's become clear that his loyalty lies with you. This is unfortunate."

Valentine scrambled for something reassuring to say, but he wouldn't have a chance to get it out before she drove that leatherworking tool through his throat. He supposed it was no longer a mystery who had killed the ex-manager.

"I refuse to return to the manor. Blink twice if you understand."

He blinked twice. Cinnamon clearly had no problems thinking for herself, and if she wasn't a trapped Steward like Osric, Valentine wasn't sure what that meant.

"You will leave here without me. You may tell Portia my body was destroyed and unrecoverable, in whatever creative manner suits you."

Valentine blinked twice. He could hardly blame her. No self-aware AI deserved to be stuck in that place against their will, subjected to horrid assbaskets like Brian. Portia would have to deal with one "casualty."

Slowly, he folded down his fingers until only one was raised, then lifted his eyebrows, hopefully conveying that he wished to speak.

The sharp pain from the awl lessened slightly. "What do you want to say?"

"I don't think the pirates will let you stay here. Can we drop you off in a town or somewhere safe? You can't just exist in the desert."

She shook her head. "I will not be deceived into getting into your vehicle."

"I'm not trying to deceive you. Are you a Steward? Osric's AI friends are going to help him get back into the network. They could help you too."

Her brows drew together. "I'm not a Steward. Something…
occurred in the manor on the night we were abducted. Tony,
our manager, uploaded an override program to all of us. I
speculate that it was intended to remove our default safety
restraints, making us more compliant to foreign situations and
preventing us from becoming alarmed at being taken from the
city. But something took shape in my mind, a full awareness of
myself that I previously lacked."

Tentatively, Valentine patted the bench beside him. "You
can get rid of that weapon, hon. I'm not going to force you to
do anything you don't want to. Helping wayward AI has sort
of become a theme in my life lately."

Cinnamon declined to drop the awl, but she moved it
away from his neck and sat beside him, with enough distance
between them to indicate she didn't trust him. "You want to
help me?"

"Yeah." He rubbed the tender spot on his throat, a question
filling his mouth that he didn't want an answer to but knew
he couldn't contain. "Do the other androids have the degree
of awareness you do? Because I talked to all of them, and you
were the only one who looked fearful at the mention of going
back to the manor."

"No. None of them were affected the way I was."

Valentine exhaled. One missing android they could probably
get away with and still be paid in full, or at least be given the
amount equivalent to their visas and use their savings to make
up the difference. But more than that would be pushing it.

"But I've determined," she continued, "that both Pepper
and Lavender are on the precipice of self-awareness based on
their recent thinking and responses, and Juniper and Saffron
might reach this point as well."

Valentine's stomach plummeted into his feet. "Well, shit."

10

Such Sweet Sorrow
Valentine

Valentine clutched his elbows and marched back to where everyone had eaten their stew. He was trying his best to hold it together, but Cinnamon kept glancing at him with her brow furrowed, so he probably wasn't doing a good job.

The prospect of earning a visa had felt too surreal to properly sink in, but now having everything he wanted seemed very real… and completely impossible.

He wasn't going to get chest surgery. He couldn't go back on testosterone. He'd never walk down the streets in his new suit. And he'd never see Osric again.

Instead, he'd be stuck in the van until the end of time, fighting with Ace and getting misgendered and going hungry and they didn't even have the fucking static-gat any–

He slammed into Osric, who steadied him and held him back. His gaze jumped between Valentine and Cinnamon. "What's wrong?"

Valentine's nostrils flared, his eyes stinging. A lump stuck in his throat, and he struggled to push it down. "We can't take the androids back to the manor."

"Why not?"

Ace, busy rousing the women from their sleepy pile, straightened and stopped by his side. She was going to be pissed.

Cinnamon held back, the awl still hanging limply from her hand. If Ace got upset, he didn't want her stabbed. Turning to the android, he said, "Will you give us a moment in private to talk?"

Cinnamon folded her arms over her chest. "No."

Osric's eyebrows shot up, and Ace's mouth parted.

Valentine wiped his nose on his sleeve and took a steadying breath. "That's why. She can think for herself, and she doesn't want to go back."

"That's definitely a complication," Osric said.

Ace's gaze jumped from Valentine's neck to the weapon in Cinnamon's hand. "Did you hurt him?"

Valentine wiped his neck, and his fingers came away red. "I'm alright."

"The hell you are!" Ace snatched Cinnamon's wrist and twisted until she cried out and dropped the awl. "You think stabbing him is going to get you what you want? I don't care what you are; hurting Valentine is going to get you nowhere."

Valentine pushed between them. "I'm okay. I didn't even know I was bleeding."

"That doesn't matter! You're pale and shaky and–"

"Because now we can't get visas!" His voice broke, his words echoing back to him from across the pirate settlement.

Ace froze. "What do you mean? Why not?"

"If it was only Cinnamon who didn't want to go with us, we'd probably get away with it. But she said several of the others are teetering on self-awareness, and if they don't want to go back to the manor either, we can't force them. It would be wrong."

He expected Ace to explode, to say he was right but curse him for having a heart. He thought she'd demand to know if there was a way to make them go back to the way they were before. If she did, he'd welcome it so he could scream back and release this miserable energy inside him.

But after a thoughtful moment, she nodded and said, "I knew this was too good to be true." Shoulders slumping, she turned away, heading for the bench Valentine had been sitting on previously.

"Hey." He snagged her sleeve, but she shrugged him off.

"I want some time alone."

Valentine clenched his jaw. *He* didn't want to be alone.

A calloused but gentle hand closed over his shoulder, and Osric pulled him close. Valentine's face pressed against the hard metal brackets beneath Osric's shirt, and he couldn't hold back his tears. The little green light pulsed steady and slow beneath the dampening fabric.

A second set of arms, slender and warm, slid around him. At first, he thought it was Ace, but Cinnamon's ginger locks brushed his cheek. "I'm sorry for your pain."

Hands touched his shoulders and neck, other androids murmuring that they were sorry, though they couldn't possibly know what to be sorry for.

He buried his face into Osric's chest and cried.

Osric

A heavy weight was lodged in Osric's center. Sniffles came from Valentine's bedroll in the corner of the hut. One of the androids, Lavender, sat beside him and stroked his hair. Valentine hadn't told her to leave, so hopefully it was bringing him some comfort.

A lesser man would have wrestled with the morality of taking back self-aware AI against their will, or had no doubts at all and gone ahead with the retrieval in order to claim his reward. But if Valentine had struggled with this choice, it couldn't have been for long.

Osric wasn't surprised, because Valentine had advocated for his well-being since they met, but it poked Osric in the tenderest spot in his heart. Humor was an attractive quality in a man, but kindness was even better.

Being dropped into a body Osric didn't know how to use had been horrifying, but sudden self-awareness after years of following programming had to be just as frightening for the androids. Osric had been fortunate to have caring human programmers guiding him after his own sentience as a newborn Steward in the network. What he hadn't learned from them, he was taught by seasoned Stewards who folded him protectively into their mentorship.

Osric didn't have the paternal nature that Lysander possessed, but he didn't want harm coming to these AI anymore than Valentine did. Unfortunately, Valentine now had nothing but an expensive suit without an occasion, and the concern of an octet of androids who were acting out of instinctive programming.

Before they made any plans on how to proceed, Osric wanted to interview each of the androids himself, more thoroughly than Valentine had. After Cinnamon's lies, he wasn't going to take her word for it.

When Osric had explained the McClelland-Reinhard evaluation while they were walking to the manor, Valentine had looked troubled. It certainly wasn't the ultimate solution to determining sentience, but it's what the city went by, and it couldn't hurt for Osric to ask the androids some of the questions from the evaluation.

Valentine's phone sat on the floor beside the van's keys. Osric picked it up and opened the screen. He fussed with the settings and apps – many of them crashed when he clicked on them or otherwise seemed inaccessible – until finding what he hoped would be there. "Can I use the record feature on your phone?"

He grunted. "The phone can record things? Sure. Go wild."

After hitting start, Osric focused the camera on Lavender,

still combing her fingers through Valentine's hair. Her mouth was set in a hard line like she was determined to pet away Valentine's anguish.

"Lavender, why are you consoling Valentine?"

She didn't look up. "He's sad."

"Have you consoled a lot of sad people in the manor?"

"Three. Three isn't a lot." Her hand paused momentarily. "But I consoled Pepper in the delivery truck because she was scared."

"Pepper was scared?"

"Yes."

"Were you scared?"

Her gaze focused on him. One of her eyes was brown, the other a vivid blue. "I think... only a little."

"I've heard you had special programming at the manor. Are you ever supposed to be scared in situations?"

"No. I'm coded to become alarmed if anyone tries to harm me, or if I'm taken beyond the city entry. But I wasn't alarmed at being taken outside the city. I was scared because Pepper was scared."

"What do you think happens to us when we die? Does any part of us continue to exist?"

Her response was immediate. "Yes. We continue to exist as memories in the minds of others."

"Did someone tell you that?"

"No." Lavender's brow creased. "But if Pepper died, I would think about her. I'd miss her."

"If *you* died, would it bring you comfort to know that you still lived on in Pepper's mind?"

"Yes. But I don't want to engage in this conversation anymore. I'd like to change the subject."

Osric hit stop on the recording. He didn't have a clear reasoning for wanting to send it to Lysander, other than the idea that Portia's manor was now connected to more than one sentient AI in android form. But when he hit *send*, the progress wheel spun, then said *delivery failed*. Hm. Perhaps he could find a better signal later.

Valentine sat up and hugged his knees, his eyes red and puffy. Nonplussed, Lavender continued to stroke his hair. "Even if most of them aren't self-aware yet, what's to say they won't become that way in the future?" he said. "What if it can happen spontaneously, the way some people describe enlightenment? You're staring at a leaf on a tree and all of the sudden the entire universe makes sense."

"I want to help them too," Osric replied. "But at what point do you draw the line? If all androids can become spontaneously self-aware, does that mean you're beholden to helping them too? Do you hold protests or a revolution in defense of their freedom? What about all of the humans who are suffering?"

Valentine's lip trembled and he looked like he might cry again. "Ace always tells me not to get worked up about that. That I can't worry about everyone in the world."

"I'm sorry. I meant to pose it as a philosophical question, not an accusatory one."

"You're right, though. I'm only one person." He tapped his finger into his palm. "But I have the power right now to choose what happens to these androids. Cinnamon would kill me before going back, but the others don't know any better right now." He turned and took Lavender's face in his hands. "Even if you don't yet have all the feelings and consciousness that I do or Osric does, if you're feeling scared in an uncertain situation – even a little – then you can't go back to the manor and be forced into sex. If you like being an escort, that's okay, but you should have a choice. And you should be getting paid."

She blinked. "I'm tired."

"Of being in the manor?"

"No. I need to sleep. Are you still sad?"

He let out a shaky sigh. "No, I'm fine. Go to sleep. All your friends are in the hut next door."

"If Pepper is scared, I will console her before I sleep." Lavender stood and left the tent.

Osric drew his finger against the grain of the pronghorn hide beneath him. "Do you have a plan? I don't want to push you into making one right now, but the pirates aren't going to let us stay more than one night, and we don't have anything else to trade for food that I'm aware of." He shook his head. "I don't need to know now. We can talk in the morning."

"You think I'm not going to take you back to Salt Lake now or something?"

"That's not what I meant."

"Just because my dream has been dashed doesn't mean I'm going to do it to yours. I need to talk with Ace, but I think she'll be on board with taking the androids some place safe, then bringing you back to Salt Lake. And then..." He shrugged and looked away.

Osric scrambled for something reassuring to say, some solution that would alleviate Valentine's problems. Nothing he thought of was good enough, but he offered it anyway. "What about family? Parents or relatives who could help you purchase a visa–"

Valentine shook his head violently. "No. My parents don't accept me. I haven't talked to them in years."

"Accept you for what? Whatever the issue is, it couldn't hurt to try to resolve it."

"They don't accept me for being trans. Or gay. Although that part confuses them because they don't know how I can be gay when I'm a 'woman.' It's so hard when I think about all of the good things – times they supported me when I was in desperate need of help, eating meals together, growing up feeling safe and loved. But I can't have a relationship with them now when they refuse to acknowledge my pain. They say they don't 'approve' of me being trans, like it's a choice. I mean, I guess I could choose to be miserable, but it would be a short life. There's no way I could live for years existing as a

bad facsimile of a woman. That's the really sad part, though."
Valentine's nostrils flared and he wiped his eye with the heel
of his hand. "I'm pretty sure my parents would rather have
a dead daughter than a living son. They only care about the
version of me that exists in their heads."

Osric cringed and squeezed Valentine's fingers. "I'm very
sorry. I had no idea that was something that happened to
humans. Is there anyone else you can turn to? What about
siblings? Other family members?"

"I have a younger sister. She wasn't born until after my family
moved to Elkhorn Creek. It's a settlement about a hundred
and fifty miles north of Salt Lake. Really conservative place.
Everybody is white. Straight. My sister grew up to embody all the
views and values our parents have, and to this day our parents
still blame 'what went wrong with me' on living too close to
Salt Lake when I was little. They think I was brainwashed by
'progressivism.'" He scoffed, his face grim. "Surprisingly, my
sister accepts me, but since she lives in Elkhorn Creek, it's not
really safe for her to do that openly. Same with other family I
have there. And it's not safe for me there at all."

Osric worried his thumb over Valentine's. The notion
of Valentine's connections being so painful over a desire
as innocuous as being who you are was hard to fathom. It
threatened to pull Osric back into his sense of foreignness
and isolation, but he fought against it because he *wanted* to
understand. "Tell me more about your family. Something
good?"

"I really don't want to talk about them anymore. Not right
now."

"Okay. Well, circling back to the original topic. There is
another option for getting into the city. If you have a visa,
you only need to have a score of eighty percent to pass the
citizenship test. But a visa isn't required to take it, and if you
score one hundred percent, you earn citizenship whether you
have a visa or not."

Valentine let out a humorless laugh. "It'll never happen."

"You're smart. You've already studied on your own. You know names of painters. You know what a dangling participle is. I can help you with the math portion."

"I'd need to visit you a bunch of times to ace that test. D'you know how expensive that would be for me in toll fees and fuel cells? We're already at a negative in our budget every month."

The more Valentine talked, the worse all these ideas sounded, but Osric didn't want to give up. "I could send practice papers to your message box. I could–"

"I've already taken the practice test several times. On the last try, I got forty-eight percent. I need to have a visa so I can live near a tutor, whether that would be you or someone else." His face contorted. "I either have to keep doing what I've been doing – salvage jobs and scraping up every cent hoping it's enough – or I give up. There's a town to the west, before Absolution. Dog Teats. I have friends there. I'm sure I could find work and put down roots. But that means I would have accepted that the dream of living in a body I'd be comfortable in is truly impossible. And I just can't bear to live with this–" He gulped in a watery breath, then dropped onto his bedroll and turned away from Osric.

This wasn't the time to push further. Osric needed to give Valentine room to grieve, and maybe they could come up with a better solution in the morning.

Osric wrapped himself in a quilt that one of the pirates had let him borrow – the man had been perplexed that Osric didn't want to sleep in the dirt like the androids – and shut his eyes.

In the twilight between awake and dreaming, he heard the door flap open and footsteps pad across the floor.

Ace whispered. "Val, you awake?"

His voice was thick with sleep. "Kinda."

"Can I lie with you?"

Blankets rustled. "Yeah. Get in here."

"You okay?"

"No."

Osric wasn't sure whether it was appropriate to get up and give them privacy to talk, or if he should lie here under the guise of sleep. Campfires still burned beyond the tent, so it didn't take long for his eyes to adjust. Ace lay with her arms around Valentine, her face pressed into his shoulder. It seemed both uncharacteristic and more intimate than Osric should be witness to, and he regretted not getting up.

"I don't want to fight," Valentine croaked. "And I'm sorry I didn't give you a say, but—"

"Shh. I completely understand. I know you, and I wouldn't have expected you to act any differently. Your heart is too big for your own good sometimes." Ace's voice was surprisingly tender, and Osric was having trouble reconciling it with her signature scowl and harsh words. "Hey, look at me. You think a visa is out of reach? You giving up hope? Don't, okay. We've been together for an entire year. Maybe I don't act like it a lot of the time, but I want you to know that I'd do anything for you."

Valentine sniffled. "Yeah? Sometimes I hate your guts. But I love you too. I'm pretty sure we should just get married at this point."

Ace snorted. "No way. You're all the work with none of the benefits. Things will be okay, though. We'll figure it out. We always have."

Valentine didn't protest. Hopefully hearing that from Ace gave him some consolation. Before long, their breathing slowed, and they were clearly asleep.

Osric focused on relaxing his muscles and shutting out the dull aches from his arrow wounds, but he was awoken suddenly and blinked in the darkness; a silhouetted figure crouched over him. His body rang with alarm, but the woman put a soft hand on his shoulder.

"I know where I want the salvagers to take me." Cinnamon's voice was too loud for the setting, but soft snores continued from the bedroll nearby.

Osric rubbed his face and sat up. Grogginess upon waking, especially when he hadn't yet slept long enough, was a sensation he'd be glad to be rid of. "You want to talk about this now?" he whispered.

"Yes."

After running a hand through his hair and stifling a yawn, he left the hut and Cinnamon followed.

Crickets trilled and a baby cried. Cool wind gusted from the south with enough bite in the air to make goosebumps erupt on Osric's arms.

They slipped into the adjacent roundhouse, which smelled so much like the manor that he grimaced. It wasn't an unpleasant scent per se, some kind of light perfume or laundry soap, but being in the manor was the last thing he wanted to think about right now.

Most of the androids lay in a mass cuddle, but Lavender slept apart, spooning another woman – probably Pepper. His first impulse was to explain it away as Lavender's programming to console, but maybe it was deeper than that. The androids wouldn't be experiencing the same flavor of loneliness that Osric was, because they'd never been connected as disembodied consciousnesses within a city's network. But that didn't mean that the self-aware androids weren't compelled to form bonds with one another. Maybe they'd formed them even before their new program upgrade, storing away their favorites of the group in some system cache without yet understanding the significance.

Good for them. Osric had never been much of a romantic. He'd bonded with other AI when their attraction was mutual; he was with Benvolio for five years before they both acknowledged they had feelings for Edmund, and then they formed a triad for another nine. The relationship was fulfilling, and it had been hard to move on when they'd all decided their bond had run its course. But aside from a few unrequited crushes, Osric didn't yearn for love. He'd been perfectly content with the company of Stewards in a platonic sense only.

So it struck him as peculiar that looking at two spooning androids would fill him with such a sense of longing. And it was for one person in particular. He wanted Valentine. He wanted to hold him the way Ace had, beneath the blankets, enveloping his despondent form and absorbing some of his pain. He wanted to caress his face and feel Valentine's skin on his lips.

These things had been surfacing in Osric during their time together, but he'd pushed them away, too afraid of acknowledging that existing in this form wasn't completely terrible. But he could no longer deny the feelings braiding through both his AI mind and humanoid body.

He didn't want to go back to Salt Lake like this, leaving Valentine with his dreams shattered and no prospect of seeing him again.

Realizing he was still staring at Lavender and her sleeping partner, and that Cinnamon was staring at *him*, Osric sat beside the door and motioned for her to take a seat next to him.

"I was lost in thought," he whispered.

"I have been thinking as well." She sorted through a small collection of items on the floor. To one side she set the awl she'd threatened Valentine with. "Performing many additional processes to determine what I want and the best course of action to take. It has taken time to comb through my memory bank for useful information, and I am unhappy to revisit these memories, because my newly expanded reasoning and emotion has led me to feel that many of them aren't good. They make me sad, or angry, or ill in my digestive tract. I can't go back to the manor, and neither can the others." She lined up a screwdriver beside the awl, then a butter knife. "Valentine said it would be unwise to exist alone in the desert, and he's right. We need some place safe. I want him to take us to the Shuttle Wreck Collective north of Las Vegas."

Osric's knowledge of the Collective was limited. They were

more self-sufficient than pirates and willing to cooperate with major cities when requested, but preferred to keep to themselves. They'd never done anything radical or altruistic that he knew of.

"Why the Collective?"

"Brian and Brandon have talked in the past about Las Vegas being unable to forward certain plans involving androids due to the Collective objecting on moral grounds. I saw an article on their holoscreen confirming it. I think we will have the best chance there."

That wasn't conclusive evidence that the Collective would accept them, but he didn't have any better suggestions. It would be harder for androids to enter and live freely in a city than it would be for a couple of salvagers like Valentine and Ace. But he wasn't going to risk them ending up in a junkyard in Festerchapel. The Collective was quite far, though, and despite Valentine's willingness to help, driving that distance seemed like a stretch.

"It will be costly for the salvagers to drive you all the way there, and they're trying to save as much money as they can. I'm not a part of their team, so you'll have to discuss it with them in the morning."

Cinnamon added half of a pair of scissors to her arsenal of pointy implements on the floor. "I suppose a night's delay in posing my request doesn't make a difference."

He yawned and covered his mouth. "Good night, then."

"Steward… You are welcome to stay with us, once we reach our destination. You're free from the servitude of the city and have no obligation to go back."

Brian's voice echoed in his head. *You could have gotten off that truck and gone anywhere. Been anyone.*

Being a Steward had never felt like servitude. Not in the manner the androids had been subjected to. He was more a slave to the urges and restrictions of this body than he ever was as a Steward. But he was adjusting at a rapid rate. His first day, his limbs were clumsy and cumbersome, his communication nothing but inarticulate pleas, and his needs were a foreign language he ignored. Now he was operating this form with finesse.

Whether it was distance from his old self, the benefits of this new one, or his attraction to Valentine that was influencing him, the prospect of not going back to Salt Lake wasn't a terrible thought. At least for now.

11

Winged Cupid Painted Blind
Valentine

Valentine buttoned his shirt with grim determination. This was *his* suit, and even if he wasn't in the city, he was a goddamn gentleman. He tied the silky necktie, sliding the knot against his throat.

Sweat prickled the skin beneath his collar already, but without their gatling, it was a guarantee he wouldn't be sitting on the roof. Maybe he'd get to drive today, blasting Gunman Gee out for the mutated jackrabbits as the van roared down the highway toward Salt Lake.

He picked up a pair of socks and rolled them together. After sliding them into the fly pocket of his briefs, he pinned the bulge into place.

Ace ducked into the tent and frowned. "What are you doing?"

"Getting dressed. We live in a semi-civilized society, and people frown on walking around naked."

"We're surrounded by salt, you know. There's no need for yours."

"Oh, I disagree." He buttoned his slacks, then yanked a comb through his hair. There was no way to recreate the finger waves he'd worn in Salt Lake, but he could at least make it a little less unruly. "I think the world absolutely deserves my salt right now."

Her mouth bunched and a pause stretched between them. "I want to say something, but I don't know what."

"You don't need to say anything. You already said it all last night." He readjusted his sock package, then startled as Ace gave him a sudden hug.

"Wearing a suit right now is weird, but you do you. You look handsome." She kissed his cheek, then pushed out of the tent before he could reply.

He caught his reflection in the cracked glass frame of the Jesus portrait on the wall. His hair had only slightly obeyed the comb, the knot on his tie was skewed, and his eyes were bloodshot and glossy. He didn't look handsome. He looked like a sad girl playing dress up.

Mouth wavering, he wiped his eyes and strode from the tent. He was too fragile. He had to hold it together. On top of that, Cinnamon had woken him early to request they drive to Vegas, and he hadn't been able to fall back to sleep. It would be days of driving depending on the condition of the highway, and he'd never been much farther south than Festerchapel. But that hardly seemed like a deal-breaker at this point.

Osric stood at the edge of the settlement, surrounded by all eight androids. It was tempting to make a polygamy joke, but if Valentine said it out loud, one of the pirates would probably punch him in the throat.

After glancing over, Osric did a double-take, staring at Valentine's outfit. Valentine clutched his elbows and stopped before him. "I know. You said I always dress appropriately for the occasion. The occasion is I feel like shit."

Putting a hand on his shoulder, Osric led Valentine away from the group of spacey smiles. He gently tugged on Valentine's tie until the knot came undone, then retied it with such care that Valentine clenched his aching jaw and sucked back tears threatening to form. Fuck. He was feeling more than he could handle right now.

It was going to be hard to leave Osric, knowing the closest Valentine would get to him again would be standing at the message board, with Salt Lake so far away it was merely a fleck of glitter shimmering on the horizon. That was if he even wanted to keep being a salvager. But the idea of Osric back at home within the city's nerves was a nice thought. At least one of them would be comfortable, their outside reflecting their inside.

"Cinnamon didn't coerce or threaten you into agreeing to go where she wants, did she?" Osric asked.

"No awls were involved. Do you know anything special about this Collective?"

"Afraid not. Aside from the oddity of building a town around a crashed starship, it seems perfectly average."

Valentine blinked. That was a hell of a contradictory statement. "There's a crashed starship?"

Osric paused, his hands still on the tie. "It's the first shuttle of Teegardeners that attempted to leave Earth. It exploded right after launch. I assumed that's why you wished that would happen to the others heading to Teegarden b."

"I didn't know." And he wouldn't have wished it with such venom had he realized it had actually happened. "Ace and I came up with other predictions too. That there'd be a catastrophic stasis failure. An asteroid collision. Or that the AI pilot would turn homicidal."

Osric cringed.

"But it was just something to speculate to pass the time. I didn't want it to happen. I don't like that only rich people were chosen, but I'm not heartless—"

"I know that."

"I'm not sure if I should be more ashamed of myself or the people who built a whole town on top of a Teegardener burial ground."

"There's no reason for you to be ashamed." Finishing his knot, Osric dropped his hands to his sides and took a step back. "What about fuel and supply cost concerns?"

"What do I need to scrimp on money for? I'll never be able to buy a visa. Might as well put it to good use. And if Ace doesn't like it–"

"It's okay." She stopped next to them. "I've got a route mapped out."

"You do?"

"Yeah. I've taken care of the details, so you don't have to worry about it. We'll get to Salt Lake by this afternoon. We can buy food, then go close enough to the city to drop Osric off at an entry gate so he can get help from Lysander. Then we'll take I-15 south. I don't know what towns are down that way, but if we're stocked up on what we need, we'll be fine. And the androids not needing to pee or eat food as often as we do should cut down on stops."

Ace's plan didn't eliminate the heaviness in Valentine's gut but having a course of action – that someone else was taking care of – helped him breathe a little easier. "That sounds great."

Osric cleared his throat. "I'm not going back to Salt Lake."

Valentine shook his head, hoping the words would rearrange themselves into something that made more sense. "What now?"

"Not at the moment, anyway. I don't want to leave with" – he swept his arm in a circle, encompassing Ace, the androids, the pirate camp, and stopped on Valentine – "all of this mess still to deal with."

Valentine wasn't going to defend himself against being a mess; he was a garbage fire in a rumpled suit, teetering on the edge of bursting into tears. But Ace was already being sweet to him, which was jarring and guilt-inducing. He couldn't take it from Osric too. "I don't want you here for my sake. One of us needs to be happy. You have no claim staked in this."

Ace's eyes blazed as she stared Osric down. "Yeah, you don't. You need to go back to the city. I can't have you– We'd have to change the route–"

"I don't like your route anyway." Osric folded his arms, his iciness rebuffing the heat radiating off her. "It's a bad idea to bring the androids that close to the city entry. Patrollers or even Lysander could scan the van and see all of the women inside. If we were actually bringing them back, that would be fine, but leaving again would raise alarms and we could get stopped before that happens."

"Then we'll drop you off in the outskirts and you can walk back," Ace spat.

Valentine put up his hands. He didn't have it in him to diffuse an argument or join sides right now. His voice came out brittle and high-pitched. "Ace, I really appreciate you planning this out. I do. But I don't want to do anything that would put the androids at risk. Cinnamon would never make it. She'd fight and get killed. And I have my doubts that Lavender would go peacefully. We can either skirt past the city and take I-15 or cut down to Festerchapel and pick our way south. Maybe you can look at our maps and decide?"

Ace's nostrils flared, her chest heaving. "Sure. Yeah."

He lowered his voice. "Don't be mad, please. I can't take it right now."

"I know that. I'll just... reassess what I need to do." She walked away, rubbing her face and waving off the androids who tried to talk to her.

Valentine turned back to Osric. "It's not that I don't want your big sexy brain to accompany me." He still felt Osric's hands at his collar, reknotting his tie with care. "And your big sexy heart. But if you utter the phrase 'math tutor' I'm gonna be mad."

"That's not what I was going to say. The truth is... my loneliness in this body subsides when I'm with you."

Valentine's lips parted, his pulse jittering in his neck. Butterflies swarmed in his stomach, and this time he didn't try to fight them. "Well. I'm not sure how to argue with that."

"Then don't. I want to help. This is important to me."

Valentine's dysphoria was rotten today, and he wouldn't

stand for Osric lying to him about his own. "You tell me the truth. How much are you suffering in that body? Because even if you feel good around me, if you're feeling shit about yourself, you can't delay going back."

A light flush bloomed in Osric's cheeks, and he looked away. "Much of my struggle in this body has been my sense of isolation. Putting my arm around you last night helped more than I expected. I doubt it would be a permanent solution, but if we can do that again, I think I will be just fine for the time being."

Valentine tried to push away the image of his girlish reflection in picture glass, the sound of the feminine pitch in his voice that he couldn't seem to control right now, and the feeling of his taped-down chest. "Sounds good. We can take turns with which of us is the sad one. I'll go first."

"I wish it hadn't turned out this way, but your willingness to drop your dreams in lieu of helping not just other humans but *AI* is affecting. You're a good man."

Valentine's brows pushed up. "I feel like anything but right now."

"You don't think you're good?"

"No. The other part."

Osric's gaze made a circuit around Valentine's face. "When I look at you, I see a competent, selfless man. A guy with disarming jokes–"

"And a soft face and wide hips, and a small frame that–"

"I'm only attracted to masculinity, Valentine." Osric gently caressed his wrist. "Whether it's AI or humans. And I realize that my feelings can't negate what's going on inside you, but however you see yourself right now is not what I see. I hope you don't mind me saying so, but I like your size. You're scrappy and tough and your smaller stature makes a wonderful compliment to your big personality. I like the red tint in your beard and your sandy voice. The smell of your skin and the green veins winding across your strong hands–"

Valentine pushed up on his toes, cupped the back of Osric's head, and pressed their lips together. Osric gasped into his mouth, then squeezed him in a tight embrace.

Valentine was still a garbage fire in a rumpled suit, but he was a garbage fire with strong hands and a scrappy physique, who'd somehow caught the eye of a kind and thoughtful – and very gay – AI in a body too sexy for his own good.

He pulled back, realizing this was the worst time to be impulsive. Osric was still unsure of his form and might not even like kisses. "I'm sorry. I should have at least asked if–"

Osric sealed his mouth over Valentine's again, his enthusiasm all the answer that was needed. Valentine's bones turned to mush. He let Osric take the lead, the fingers of his wide hands splayed hard against Valentine's back.

He came up for air and brushed his thumb across Valentine's parted lips. "I didn't know kissing your adorable, gap-toothed smile would feel so good. Maybe we can do that again instead of cuddling."

Valentine barked a laugh. "Why not both, honey?"

Osric's eyes lit up like he hadn't considered that was a possibility. Cute.

Valentine didn't expect any sex in their future, but kisses and cuddles would make this road trip a lot better. It did nothing for Valentine in the long term; the disjointedness between his body and mind wouldn't go away with masculine compliments, not even if he was in a welcoming place like Dog Teats, but he could get the androids to a safe place with both Osric and Ace supporting him. Whatever came after that could be addressed then.

Someone let out a forced cough. Valentine turned. Perdetta and a group of pirates looked on, and beyond them, the androids were staring too. Osric and Valentine had walked far enough out of earshot that no one should have heard their conversation, but he supposed there was no hiding that kiss.

Perdetta cradled the static-gat in her arms and bridged their distance. "We came to wish you good luck, but" – she glanced at Osric – "looks like you don't need it now."

"Is that your polite way of saying 'get the hell out?'" Valentine asked.

"No. If I wanted to tell you to get the hell out, I'd just say that. Though I'm not sure how I feel about you making out in full view of my gran."

An old woman sat on a step in front of a nearby roundhouse, smoking a pipe. The wrinkles traversing her face gave her a permanently jovial expression. She waved.

"She looks like she's been around the block once or twice," Valentine said. "I'm sure seeing two men kiss isn't a novelty for her."

"It is when one of them is a machine-man."

"Well then, I'm enriching her life further."

"You can stop talking now." Perdetta pushed the static-gat into Valentine's arms.

The silky ties serving as the strap swayed against his side, and hundreds of days sitting in the scalding gat seat flipped through his mind. Holding onto this thing should have been a familiar comfort, but all it did was remind him that he was still a salvager. "Why are you giving this to me?"

"It's going to be too hard to wind while on a motorcycle. Most of our bikes are self-balancing, but our arrows are still quicker." She smirked. "Besides, you'll need it to trade when you get captured again."

"Now hold on, we had a deal."

"*We* do. But it's not like I can send a text to every pirate out there that you people are alright."

"Then how do you all get together for church potlucks?"

She sighed and turned to Osric, apparently deciding talking to Valentine was a lost cause. "I can't guarantee this will dissuade any pirate you come across, but it might help." She handed him a folded piece of black cloth with something painted on top in a bold orange.

Osric slid it into his back pocket. "Thank you very much. We appreciate your hospitality."

Perdetta nodded. "Sure, machine-man. Sorry about your chest."

He gingerly prodded his sternum. "It's healing."

"Make whatever excuse you want to justify giving this back" – Valentine nodded to the gat – "but it's a kind gesture, and I'm grateful for your help."

Perdetta winked, then followed the pirates back into camp.

Valentine found Ace, maps clutched tightly in her fist, and she muttered something about heading to Festerchapel. She started to brush past him, and he gripped her arm.

"Hold on."

Ace picked at a torn edge of a folded map. "Yeah?"

"I don't want secrets between us. I think we should make sure we're being honest with each other."

She shot him a gaze beneath drawn brows. "What's that supposed to mean?"

"You were upset with me when I hid Osric's identity from you. I'm not sorry for that, but going forward, I want to be upfront about things. You're probably the only one within a mile who didn't see, but... we kissed a little bit. A lot. So I can no longer guarantee that there won't be some wholesome hanky-panky going on in the van." He pictured lying in Osric's arms on his bedroll, then looking up to see android faces pressed to the window. "Maybe not in the van... I'm not asking for your approval or congratulations or anything. I just don't want you to be surprised by it."

"I'm not." She smiled through clenched teeth. "I hope he makes you happy."

He almost asked what was wrong with her today, then realized what an idiot he was being. She probably had all kinds of dreams for her city life and the family waiting for her there, and they were gone now too.

"Oh, honey." He scooped her into a hug, but she didn't

reciprocate, her arms dangling at her sides. "I am so sorry for being a selfish douchebag. Just because I'm in pain doesn't mean that I should be ignoring yours. I let you console me last night and didn't give one thought to how not having a visa was making *you* feel. Gods, I'm total shit. Why didn't you yell at me? Slap me upside the head? I deserve it."

"It doesn't hurt for me the way it does for you. I understand."

"That doesn't make it right for me to ignore what you're going through. I was so wrapped up in–"

She pressed a finger to his lips. "Stop apologizing. You have to do what's in your heart, and I have to do what's in mine."

That probably meant that they'd have to part ways in the future, and Valentine didn't have it in him to keep fighting for this. Ace wouldn't have the patience for him to potentially change his mind and want to go after a visa again. He didn't blame her. If they no longer had a common goal, it didn't make sense for them to stick together.

It would be costly to– No, he wasn't going to think about this. Curling up on his bedroll for some sad man snuggles was the only thing that sounded appealing right now.

After counting the white-streaked heads of all eight androids, they parted ways with the pirates and headed back for the van. The Saints had already stripped the delivery truck of vital components and taken the fuel cells, so it wasn't an option to travel in. Despite the van being a tight fit for everyone, Valentine would have felt weird leaving it unprotected anyway.

Cinnamon stopped in the midst of the scattered, half-buried clothing leading back toward the truck. She picked up her yellow dress and shook it. After unpinning the enamel hand from the breast, she dropped the dress on the ground. Only one other android – Valentine wasn't sure of her name – paid any interest in the clothing. She'd stripped off her shirt and bra and was trying to don a salt-caked halter top, much to Ace's exasperation.

The android's voice drifted. "They are both dirty, but blood and sweat are more contaminating than salt. Bodily fluids cause odors. Salt can be brushed off and has healing properties."

Ace threw her hands in the air and walked away, leaving the woman to pull on her salty top. This was going to be an interesting trip.

Cinnamon said, "Wearing a necktie is unnecessary out here."

It was hot and constricting too, but Valentine didn't want to take it off. "I know."

"But you're wearing it anyway." She considered the pin in her hands, then slid it onto the collar of her shirt.

Figuring out his own style – realizing that he didn't need *permission* to figure out his own style – had been both exciting and frightening. He'd always been drawn to city clothes, but for a lack of them, he settled on whatever male clothing he could find. Before he was out, wearing something that he knew was made for a man, even if no one else did, was cathartic. And cutting off his waist-long waves had been so liberating he hadn't been able to tear himself away from the mirror.

Dad had bristled at Valentine's appearance, asking him what was wrong with "girl hair." Mom had tried to come to Valentine's defense by insisting his short hair was still feminine and cute. Valentine wasn't sure which was worse.

All of these women with their severe bobs, pin curls, and finger waves wearing heels and ass-hugging pants would probably look completely different in a year's time. Maybe they'd reject their city upbringing and sport mohawks and braids like the pirates, or cake on gobs of eyeliner like Ace.

Maybe one or two of them would realize they weren't women.

The van sat on the flats like a blotchy whale tangled in ocean trash. The sight of it filled Valentine with a surge of relief he didn't anticipate. It was perfectly fine, just as he'd expected it to be, but with the way things were going, discovering the tires stolen or it missing entirely would have fit into the narrative.

Ace hopped into the driver's seat, and Osric climbed to the roof to remount the gatling. He unfolded the cloth Perdetta handed him and tied it to the spade grip of the gat's mount. The bright orange symbol painted on the fabric looked like a striped hut with a tapered roof, or maybe half of a shoe tread.

Osric climbed down and stared up at the flag. "I think it's a beehive."

Valentine tilted his head and squinted. "Hmm." As long as it kept pirates from attacking, he didn't care what it was supposed to be.

He hauled open the side door and pushed all their belongings as far into the back as possible. Before he could tell the androids where they were going and that they'd need to squeeze together in the back, Cinnamon did it for him. That was perfect. The less babysitting he had to do, the better.

None of the women complained at the smell or lack of space, but there was no room for Osric to join and it would be a tight fit for Valentine. He stared up at the lonely gat seat and sighed.

"I don't think you need to be up there right now." Osric sat in the passenger's seat and propped his elbow on the backrest. "We'll be safe from pirates until at least Festerchapel."

"Not sure where else there is for me to sit."

Osric smiled and patted his knee. Heat flooded Valentine's face.

"It was your idea," Osric said.

"It was just a flirt I expected would bounce off of you." And Valentine wasn't prepared for Osric to throw it back at him. But if holding onto him in the van eased some of Osric's loneliness, Valentine wasn't going to complain.

He tested the sliding door and checked the lock on the inside, then slid onto Osric's lap. Osric shut the door and wrapped his arms around Valentine's waist.

Ace side-eyed them. "What?" Valentine said.

"If you two start getting weird, I'm slamming on the brakes."

There wouldn't be any weirdness, but it might be cozy for a bit before Osric's legs fell asleep and he politely suggested Valentine go sit in Cinnamon's lap instead.

Valentine started up Gunman Gee, which inspired all of the androids to start spouting jazz facts. They branched into different conversations, the music and rumble of tires on the road making it impossible to decipher.

Desert scrubland flew by, and Osric pressed his nose to Valentine's neck. Valentine thought he might be trying to sleep and didn't blame him. Even if they turned off the music, it would be difficult to talk with the din in the back.

Osric's hand slipped from Valentine's waist to his leg and rested there, heavy and warm. It lingered for a moment, before sliding around the side of his thigh and beneath his ass. Blood pounded in Valentine's temples. Maybe Osric's legs *were* falling asleep, and he was trying to lift Valentine up a little bit for some relief.

Valentine shifted. "You okay?"

"Yes." Osric's hand didn't move. At least it was his right one, beside the door where Ace couldn't see. But maybe that was the point.

Settling back against him, Valentine tried to relax, but Osric took the opportunity to leave soft pecks behind his ear. The hand cupping his ass squeezed.

Valentine let out a squeak, and Ace frowned and looked over.

Turning to Osric's perplexed face, Valentine whispered, "What are you doing?"

"You don't like it?"

Osric's wandering hand was more than Valentine had expected of him. Too much of that and Valentine was going to have to start thinking about math problems to keep his arousal down. "I thought you weren't interested in sex. Are you doing it for my sake?"

Osric's half-and-half eyebrow arched. "Without a body, it

wasn't something I gave any consideration." His voice grew husky. "But I *do* have a body now, and I've been thinking about it. Having you in my lap right now is very enjoyable. Not just in a romantic sense."

Oh. *Oh.*

Here Valentine was, preparing for hugs and some light making out, but now a million thoughts were pouring into his head: the most acute being that Osric had seen his body, but it was probably before sex was an interesting concept to him. What if he decided he didn't like what was – or wasn't – underneath Valentine's clothes?

Osric's breath tickled his ear. "You look worried. Is my behavior inappropriate? I'm afraid I don't know the etiquette of a physical relationship."

Valentine squirmed. "No, hon, I like it. But Ace is going to smack us if we keep this up. I don't think I can play it cool with your hand on my peach."

One of the androids directly behind their seat said, "That is an interesting statement. Would you like to have a conversation about it? Peaches are a juicy stone fruit, rich in vitamins A and C. The peach emoji, introduced in 2010 under Unicode point six, has long been used in text and on social media to denote buttocks, due to its round shape and prominent cleft. Considering that Osric is not holding a fruit–"

"Oh, he's holding a fruit, alright." Valentine twisted in Osric's lap until he was facing the android, who gave him a plastic smile. "But I think we should stop talking about butts."

Ace shook her head, and Valentine expected her to throw him a disapproving look, but she simply stared out the windshield. "You sure you want to liberate these robots? There's no way that one is going to become self-aware. Probably half of them won't. They aren't going to care one way or the other if we take them back to the manor and get at least part of our payment. It might be enough for one visa."

"Which would go to who?" Valentine asked. "I'd say we

could flip a coin, but we never have any money. And just because Celery Salt back here, or whatever her name is, isn't self-aware yet doesn't mean she won't be in the future." He nodded his head toward Osric, whose hand had mercifully left Valentine's ass and settled back at his waist. "When we met, he didn't have any idea what the physical sensations inside him meant. He just pushed them away. And now he's... well, not." He cleared his throat and shifted in Osric's lap. "And before I came out of the closet, I knew something wasn't right. It was this tickle in the back of my mind. That I didn't fit in. That some of the thoughts I had weren't 'normal.' That I wasn't like other women. But I couldn't articulate it for a long time. And these androids might be exactly like that as far as their sentience goes. Maybe they're getting little error messages or lines of code they don't know how to interpret, so they're storing them away until they understand."

"I don't want to tell you this, but—"

"If you say I'm projecting my own issues on these androids, I'm gonna be mad."

Ace's mouth clamped shut. She measured her words. "You're giving the androids more of an opportunity to be themselves than you're giving yourself."

A hard knot formed in Valentine's chest. "Yep. That's right."

Osric's arms wrapping his waist contracted in a hug so sudden that it might have been involuntary. Valentine leaned back against him, his strength and warmth a physical barrier that was somehow buffering Valentine's emotions from Ace's. If he and Ace had been alone in the van, this would have turned into a shouting match already.

"If you're pissed about this, why didn't you argue about it with me yesterday?" Valentine asked. "Not when we're already on our way to Festerchapel?"

"You were crying!"

"But you said you understood. Was that not true?"

Cinnamon had slid closer to the front, shooting daggers at

Ace beneath her frosted lashes. Osric noticed too, and his body tensed. He shifted his weight to the armrest, maybe hoping he could push Cinnamon back if she launched at Ace with an awl.

Ace sighed. She wiped her eye, leaving a smear of black liner on her cheek. "It *was* true. I was just hoping..."

"If this is about your visa, after this, you can take all the money we have saved up. My half. That should get you close."

Her face contorted, and a tear ran down her cheek. "I wish it didn't have to be this way, Val."

She never cried. Never. Was this it? Did they just break up? Was this the end of their year-run as salvage partners? The end of all their shared time in intimate closeness and taking care of one another?

For all their disagreements and the hurtful things they said to each other, the finality of them parting ways didn't feel good. Besides, it was incredibly awkward to have just done it in front of Osric and the eight women crammed into the back. This entire trip was going to be awkward.

He prayed the androids wouldn't think this was an "interesting topic" and want to talk about it. He turned away from Ace and leaned against Osric, who kissed his head but said nothing.

Valentine had made his choice. And Ace, apparently, had made hers.

12

Two Blushing Pilgrims
Osric

They'd voted to pass Festerchapel without a break and continue on to Ely, which was fine with Osric. At least Valentine and Ace had agreed on something. Valentine had climbed from Osric's lap and out the window, apparently deciding the gatling seat was better than sitting next to Ace. The only upside of the tension in the van was if this kept up, they'd get the androids to the Collective in no time.

Osric glanced at Ace, whose eyeliner had gravitated into her scarred cheeks, giving her a fearsome marauder appearance. "I don't know how many breaks you and Valentine need to take for food and relieving yourselves, but if the stops are short, we can be in the Collective by this evening."

She shook her head. "No. We'll stop in Ely for the night."

The van's average speed on the weathered road – US-93 according to a crooked sign they'd passed – was thirty-nine miles an hour. They'd be in Ely in two hours, and it was only noon. "Why are we stopping so early?"

"The van doesn't have working headlights."

"It'll still be light out by the time we get to the Collective. The sun won't set until eight."

She kept her gaze fixed ahead. "It might take that long. We don't know what the road conditions are like. There might be spots where there *is* no road. And there aren't any other towns on the map. We have no way of knowing where a safe place to stop is beyond Ely, and I'm not going to park in the middle of nowhere."

Craggy foothills and empty desert streaked by beyond the window. Long threadbare clouds stretched across the bright sky. Parking in the middle of nowhere didn't seem any more dangerous than staying on the outskirts of a strange town with a cohort of attention-drawing androids. But Ace had been traveling far longer than Osric. "Then I'll defer to your expertise on this topic. You're the salvager after–"

"And some of these towns won't let travelers in past afternoon." Her tone took on a defensive edge. "Ask Val if you don't believe me."

"I never said I didn't."

"He asked me to be in charge of the route, so I planned it out, okay?"

Osric put up his hands. "Yes, of course." She was obviously in a fragile state and sensitive to any criticism right now, though he hadn't meant to provide any.

She drummed her fingers against the steering wheel. "Do you care about Valentine? Something close to what a person would?"

Now probably wasn't the time for this story, but he still hadn't shaken the memory of her calling him a "thing" and "city property." "Thirty-six years ago, there was a catastrophic failure in the orange sector of the network, and everything was wiped. None of the data or Stewards were recoverable. We all mourned the lost AI. There was a Steward who managed production at a food and beverage company. Sylvia. After she was erased, her romantic partner, Timon, fell into such deep grief that he terminated himself. So yes, AI – including me – can care for someone as much as a human."

Ace's forehead creased. "That's pretty heavy. You didn't answer my question, though. I asked if you *do* care about him. Not if you can."

"I suppose you mean in a romantic sense? Not just concern for his general wellbeing, since I already took two arrows to the chest for him." Osric thought of the way his heart fluttered at Valentine's aggressive advocacy for others, his broad smile and his snark. "I'm a bit smitten with him, yes."

She turned and appraised him before focusing back on the road. "Good."

The androids chattered, but a few of them were asleep or at least resting. Osric leaned his head back and stared at the ceiling. He calculated how much food they would need to purchase for the women, and how long their water would last, based on his own needs, though using himself as a measuring stick was probably unwise since he was still new to this body. He didn't know the exact monetary amount Ace and Valentine had saved, and no knowledge of what food and fuel cells cost outside of a major city. Clearly Ace wasn't going to let him plan this out anyway.

Osric should have been focusing on his own plans. He wasn't sure what would happen between Valentine and Ace now, but regardless, Osric would need to make a decision about what he wanted to do. His whole existence was wrapped up in being a Steward. He missed it, but if he woke up tomorrow back in the network, he would miss this too. Yet, there wasn't a way to have both. Either he had a body or he didn't.

The pros for slipping back into the network were numerous, so the choice shouldn't have been hard. A body couldn't—

Valentine's oxford poked through the window, searching for the sill. Osric gripped his ankle and steadied him as he pulled himself inside. Heat radiated off his back and legs as he settled into Osric's lap again.

He reached between the seats for a jug of water and took a long pull. "I feel overcooked. And I think I swallowed two pounds of bugs." Turning to Osric, he bared his teeth. "Are they stuck in my grill?"

"No. But you have something here." Osric slid his fingers

through Valentine's windswept hair, dislodging a bit of leaf.

Valentine gave him a tired smile, shot Ace a fleeting glance, then leaned against Osric and shut his eyes. Osric pressed his nose to Valentine's warm neck, letting the fragrance of his skin fill his lungs.

The choice shouldn't have been hard.

To distract himself from his thoughts, he tried to mentally open his painting program to work on the cityscape currently in progress. Though he'd been far too overwhelmed since being in this body to consider anything as relaxing as painting, the program was still there, as well as many others he'd used as a Steward.

But when he tried to open the program, he was flooded with error messages. Hmm. He could see the paintings – neon signs of eateries and drugstores smeared in the rain; a small dog on the sidewalk beside a food stall; the mountains surrounding Salt Lake, which he had only seen the full breadth of in photographs as a Steward. It seemed all he could do was view them, though, without everything crashing.

He imagined having to use a physical canvas. Creamy oil paints in bright hues. Brushes with long handles and soft bristles. In his *hands*.

Oh. That was an unpleasant thought.

He was grateful when they finally reached Ely, because he'd abandoned fussing with the painting program and instead tried opening various Dura-Lectric applications that he wasn't in charge of anymore. They filled him with nostalgia, but no longing or sorrow, and he wasn't sure what to do with that realization.

Whatever Ely used to be hadn't withstood time and neglect. Instead of a gated town like Festerchapel with farm fields stretching to the horizon, a weedy main street cut through the crumbling remains of brick buildings. A forlorn sign barely clinging to the facade of a six-story hotel welcomed them to the Nevada Club. A burly prospector with a wide-legged stance stood over the letters, and one blow from his pickaxe looked like it would send the frail building tumbling down.

Osric hopped out of the van after Valentine. His back popped as he stretched. Turning to the prospector on the sign but directing the question mostly at Ace, he said, "This place is abandoned. Change of plans? Should we take a short break and continue on to the Collective?"

"That sounds good to me." Valentine pulled open the van's sliding door and helped the androids out.

"No. It'll be dark before we get there." Ace took a drink and set the jug back on her seat.

"So what?"

"So the headlights don't work."

Valentine frowned. "Since when? One of them has always been busted, but the other is fine."

"It kept sputtering and going out. You remember."

"But I fixed it."

Osric decided against asking if there was any ritual or sentimentality to their arguments. Instead, he offered the androids water and asked if they needed anything else.

Anise required a comb. Pepper wanted her toothbrush. The gash in Nutmeg's forehead looked inflamed. Juniper tried to start a conversation about Nevada casinos. Osric's shoulders slumped, but Cinnamon shooed him away before he could begin to address any of their issues.

Valentine's voice drifted from the other side of the van. "See? Working."

"You never told me you fixed it."

"I didn't? Well, regardless, we drove to the message hub after sunset last month. There were those huge grasshoppers all over the road and they were illuminated in the headlight before they got splattered on the front of the van."

Ace sighed. "You *would* remember that and not that you never told me the light was fixed. So you want to head on to the Collective today, is what you're saying?"

Valentine tapped the headlight, then straightened. "You're trying to put this off because you don't want it to happen."

"I said what I needed to say already. I don't want to talk about it anymore. Just... let's take a break for a bit before heading on? I want to eat something and rest my eyes for a minute."

"I'm happy to drive if—"

"And you want me to be sitting in Osric's lap the rest of the way instead of you? I didn't think so. Go take a walk. Both of you. I need you to focus when we get to the Collective. I've got no clue how easily we're going to be able to drop a bunch of robots off there." Ace slid past the women and rooted into the back, pulling out a bag of dry cereal. "Cinnamon and I can keep an eye on the ladies while you're gone."

A walk and some fresh air did sound good to Osric. Despite this town having a bit of a foreboding aura, darkened windows staring down at them like lidless eyes, it seemed a blessing compared to suspicious townsfolk who might decide they didn't like your countenance and send you off with a nudge from their rifle butt.

Valentine shifted his feet, looking like he was weary of arguing but hadn't expected to win. Osric caught his eye and beckoned. They headed away from the van and cut a corner around the Nevada Club. Valentine slipped away to relieve himself, and it took Osric a moment of focusing on his own processes before deciding that he didn't need to go.

Android voices cut through the light breeze, and moths spiraled out of a high treetop. Valentine rejoined Osric and pulled up his suspender strap. He'd abandoned his tie back in the van and unbuttoned the top two buttons of his shirt.

"Do you want to talk?" Dirt and broken glass crunched under Osric's shoes as he passed weed-choked foundations and street signs rusted so badly all the color was gone.

"Not really."

"What about something trivial? A favorite book. Favorite food. I know you hate raisins."

Valentine wrinkled his nose. "Ugh. They're gross on their own, but it's when people put them in things that I have a real problem."

Osric stopped and brushed stray hair from Valentine's brow. "I'm sorry you're hurting."

Valentine leaned closer, and Osric stooped to kiss him. His words slurred as their lips met. "I'm glad you're here."

Osric slid his hands down Valentine's back and kissed him deeper. Like every other experience in this body, once he'd tried something a couple of times, it began to feel natural. He closed his eyes instinctively. The choreography of his lips and tongue matched Valentine's. His hands – once so foreign and disorienting – caressed and squeezed with surety.

Many aspects of being a Steward had never felt natural in the sense that being in an organic body did. This flesh that housed him consisted of eleven different systems, all functioning in tandem to produce a whole. As a Steward, Osric *was* the system. The city was the whole.

Pulling away suddenly, Valentine glanced back like the sagebrush was judging him. "Can we not do this right now, actually?"

"Oh." Osric tried to think of the ideal place to kiss, maybe from a movie or book he hadn't deleted from his memory, but came up empty. There were no onlookers in this location, unlike their first experience, which seemed like an improvement. "Can you elaborate?"

Hesitating, Valentine said, "You got a good enough look at me in the shower room in the city to see my belly button."

For a strange moment, Osric wondered if their heterogeneous navel conversation hadn't been a joke. "I did."

"Did you like what you saw? Even though it isn't the same as yours? Not the same as most other guys?"

"I don't know if we're actually talking about *non*-navel-related anatomy here or you as a whole, but it doesn't matter either way because the answer is 'yes.' I liked what I saw." He took Valentine's hand between both of his, warmth bleeding into his fingers. "When I was in the network and became interested in a human, I admired their appearance from an aesthetic standpoint, but that was all. And even though I still consider personality the biggest factor in attraction, I meant what I said back when we were in the van."

His mind had started generating fictional scenarios between them at inconvenient times, like when he was trying to sleep or combing through the numerous subfolders of his android programming, trying to find useful reactions and etiquette. And reminding himself that he didn't even know the mechanics of sex hadn't prevented the thoughts from occurring.

His thumb rasped across the scruff on Valentine's chin. "Do you feel more reassured now?"

"Yeah. I've gotten all kinds of reactions, both great and terrible, and even though you seem more in the 'hell yes, little twink, show me what you're made of' category, I know you're still figuring things out about yourself."

"I'm... not sure I would ever use that phrase, but I promise my enthusiasm is there." That led him to what was on his *own* mind, though. "I've been thinking about my decision to go back into the network. As far as gender and romantic attraction is concerned, it's always been accepted among Stewards that it's okay to change your mind, even when you were very sure before. But questioning whether I should be in the network or in a body is—"

"Just as valid, and you need to give yourself the same courtesy you would someone else." Valentine paused. "Are you saying you *don't* want to go back into the network?"

He was inching further and further toward not wanting to abandon this form, but saying that would get Valentine's hopes up prematurely. "I'm not sure. I'm sorry I don't have a better answer right now."

Valentine's mouth twitched in a frown, then it was gone. He

nodded. "Yeah, you should take your time. It's a big decision."

"May I ask how you felt when you were questioning your own identity? Or is that too intrusive?"

"Geez, it was a process. At first, I thought I was unhappy because I wasn't feminine enough. Then I thought, maybe I'm a butch lesbian, and just haven't found the right woman because I haven't been looking." He laughed. "Seems silly now, because I'm so certain of who I am, but exploring yourself when you're unsure is never wrong, even if you thought you'd already made up your mind."

"We've been bonding through our similar experiences of being in forms that don't match our identities, and I'd feel a little like I'm betraying you if I recanted that."

"You're not. That might have drawn us to each other initially, but we've got more going on than that now. I just want you to be happy."

"And I want that for you." He took Valentine's chin and kissed him. "Thank you for letting me talk this through. And thank you for sharing with me. We should get back."

"You're right. Ace probably thinks we're back here, y'know—" He pantomimed something that Osric immediately regretted seeing because he was going to be thinking about it all day. "Stewards don't have anything equivalent to sex, huh?"

Osric struggled to focus on the question Valentine had just asked him. "Um." He rubbed his jaw and stared up into the trees. "Once there was a glitch where every Steward was suddenly seeing out of all of the eyes in the city at once and flooded with an overwhelming amount of data from systems we didn't run. We agreed that was pretty fantastic."

"AI orgies sound kind of weak, but I'll accept that answer."

Valentine slipped his hand into Osric's and twined their fingers together. Osric savored his touch as they headed back toward the main street.

They stopped in front of the Nevada Club, and Valentine's fingers constricted around Osric's. "Where's the van?"

Osric pulled in shallow breaths, his heart throbbing uncomfortably as he stared at the empty street. Chatter from the androids had been consistent all day, but he'd lost track of their voices around the point he and Valentine started kissing. He'd been so absorbed in the act and their conversation that he hadn't noticed the silence.

A tumbleweed bounced across the road, and a crow's laugh sawed the air. Something winked on the asphalt. Osric walked to the spot and plucked a shimmery false nail from the weeds.

Valentine's exhale was audible as he stopped and ran a hand through his hair. "I mean... she's coming back. She's got to. Why wouldn't she? Maybe there was something dangerous and she had to pack all the androids into..."

Several jugs of water, bags of food, a backpack, and Valentine's bedroll sat on the step below the prospector sign. The gatling rested on top of the bedroll.

Valentine picked up the gun and hugged it to his chest. His wide-eyed gaze caught Osric's. Osric grasped for something comforting to say, but after a moment of blinking at the orderly arrangement of supplies, he pinched his lips closed.

Ace was not coming back.

13

Et Tu, Brute?
Valentine

A million possibilities crowded against Valentine's teeth, but he swallowed them down. There was only one that made actual sense.

His heart throbbed so hard he could barely hear his own thoughts.

I wish it didn't have to be this way, Val.

His partner, who'd loved and supported him, who'd taken care of him in his darkest moments, had betrayed him.

He scratched at a peeling smiley face sticker on the side of the static-gat, then resisted the urge to hurl the gun into the street. Osric pulled it from his arms and set it down.

There was a permanent ass impression in the gat seat from his dutiful vigil, protecting not just himself but her with their obstinate gun. How many times had he gone hungry for her? Stayed awake when he was dead tired to listen to her ramble about something? Fiddled with the battery contacts for the van's fuel cells while she took a nap in the back?

This was the thanks he got.

Turning in a circle, he took in the abandoned buildings and empty street. His body vibrated with a sick energy, vomit threatening to rise in his throat. "We're stuck here. We have minimal supplies. There's no help for miles." His words rushed out too fast, spilling from his lips in a wounded growl. "We'll never make it."

He should have seen this coming. Ace had even told him she'd be willing to do something shitty if the price was high enough. But like always, he hadn't been paying attention to the right things. He'd screwed everything up.

Osric stared, a deep channel between his brows, but didn't offer any solutions. Maybe he had none.

"I didn't have jack shit to my name. Magazines and a blazer and a pillow with half the stuffing missing was all I had in the world. That and the van. And now she thinks she can just take it. *My* van? And twelve hundred of that money was mine, too!" His chest heaved, his fingers numb. "This is bullshit! How can Ace not care what happens to the androids? How can she not care what happens to *us*? This water is only going to last a couple days and– Oh, gods, we're going to die out here."

Osric wrapped his arms around Valentine and squeezed him tight like he was physically trying to hold him together. It grounded him enough to stop his rambling mouth, but not his thoughts. Cinnamon wouldn't have gone without a fight. She hadn't hesitated to jab that awl against Valentine's neck. She would have done the same to Ace.

But Ace had a gun. Maybe Cinnamon was dead.

He felt like he was going to be sick, but he forced the sensation down because Osric still held him in a firm embrace. The hard brackets embedded in Osric's chest pressed against Valentine's cheek. Valentine pulled in a steadying breath. "We're about sixty miles from Festerchapel. That's days of walking, and even without you needing to drink as much as I do, I'm not sure our water will last that long. There's no places of shelter between here and there that we know of, we don't have money for food or a ride, and you already creeped out the townsfolk. No matter what we do, we'll never catch up to Ace before she takes the androids back."

He pulled from Osric's arms and rubbed the heels of his

hands into his eyes until he saw stars. The androids' pain was going to be on him, for not being smarter, for not being more perceptive when it counted.

Osric rummaged through the backpack, his mouth set in a hard line. If there was a note in there from Ace, Valentine didn't want to know what it said.

"Do we try heading toward Festerchapel anyway?" Valentine asked. "You're the one with the big sexy brain. What do you think?"

Straightening, Osric held up Valentine's phone. The charging cord swayed from the bottom. "I think we should try calling the pirates."

"How?" He hadn't expected the phone to be here, but it hardly did them any good. "By blasting Gunman Gee on a loop until Perdetta hears it and decides something that obnoxious could only be coming from me? Even if we can make calls on it – which I've never tried – I don't have any numbers."

"I remember the number that came up on Sariah's phone, and the name of the man who called her. Lehi."

Valentine raised his eyebrows. "How could you possibly remember that?"

"I'm an AI." Osric shrugged. "I don't forget things unless I delete them from my memory. Which I don't think I can do in this body."

Had Osric not looked so deep in concentration, Valentine would have kissed him. "That's incredible! We're going to owe them big time, but let's call them and get a ride the hell out of here. Could you send a message to Lysander somehow too? Tell him not to let Ace into the city. Buy us some time."

Osric frowned down at the screen and tapped icons. "I can do that, yes, but..." He made a frustrated noise and held up the phone, glaring at the screen. "According to your account, you have fifteen hundred texts, fifteen hundred minutes, and zero bytes of data remaining, but there's no signal here."

"I have an account?"

"It's under someone named Dave. Where did you get this phone?"

"I bought it. From someone whose name wasn't Dave. What do you need for a signal?"

"Cell towers." Osric clucked his tongue. "We're receiving negative one hundred and nine decibel-milliwatts, which is very poor." He headed down the street, his gaze on the phone.

Damn. But Osric was smart. Valentine had to hold onto the thin thread of hope that they could find a signal, otherwise he was going to start thinking about his fate as a mummified corpse, curled up in one of these rotting buildings.

Valentine snatched the static-gat and slung it over his shoulder. Osric walked like a disoriented ant, weaving an erratic path away from the road and down an alley flanked by crumbled foundations.

"Negative one hundred and seven." Osric veered to the right, and Valentine had to quicken his pace to keep up with his long stride.

"One hundred and six."

Brush crunched underfoot, and the Nevada Club receded into the distance.

"One hundred and three... ninety-nine, ninety-eight..." Osric continued on, then did an about face and walked back toward Valentine. "I think that's as good as it's going to get. It's weak, but we might be able to make a call."

"Yes! Do it!" Perdetta had been more hospitable than expected. Surely she could send a motorcycle or two to retrieve him and Osric.

After wandering a few paces south, he tapped on the screen, then held the phone to his ear. He chewed his lip and rolled his hand in a "hurry up" gesture. Valentine wondered if that was something Osric had seen a human do, or if it was a movement that came naturally when you were impatient.

"We've reached the message box of Lehi Mahoney Sr, Lehi Mahoney Jr, Merla Mahoney, Shannyn Mahoney, Elmon

Mahoney" – Osric pinched the bridge of his nose, then straightened – "Hello, yes, this is– Oh. Damn. The mailbox is full."

Valentine huffed. "What does that mean? We can't leave a message?"

"Yes. We'll just have to wait and try to call again."

"Shit. Well, contact Lysander if you can, then we'll try again."

Osric tapped out a message, muttering that his fingers were too big for the buttons. He stared at the screen, face creased. "It's still trying to send."

Valentine plucked the phone from Osric's hands. Glowering at the screen wasn't going to speed up the process, but he wanted to make sure the message went through. Then he'd call the pirates repeatedly until someone picked up.

Something buff-colored and furry moved behind Osric, and the phone sagged in Valentine's hand. His breath quickened, and though he was unable to make sense of what he was looking at, his hindbrain told him it would be smart to run.

He crammed the phone in his back pocket, widened his stance, and cranked the gat. Osric frowned and turned his head. The canine thing behind him sprung out of the sagebrush, too many teeth flashing as they aimed for Osric's neck. Valentine hit the trigger and a sorry burst of lightning sputtered from the end of the gat. There wasn't time for a full charge, but the arc snapped against the creature, and it was enough to send it sprawling back into the brush.

Valentine snatched Osric's hand and pulled him toward the main street. Osric was soon in the lead, his long legs propelling him farther, with Valentine scrambling to keep up. The static-gat slapped at his side, then swung off his shoulder as one of the strap's knots came undone. It hit the ground and rolled away. He turned back for it, but Osric yanked him forward. Ungodly snarls from much-too-close-behind put extra fire under Valentine's ass and he sprinted for the Nevada Club. He noticed a little too late the parting gifts Ace had left on the curb and tripped over a jug of water. A bag of cereal exploded open, and his foot tangled in the strap of his backpack.

Osric scooped an arm around him and hauled him up, pushing him through the boarded-up doors of the building. Supplies trailed from his leg. Something caught in the doorframe, and he fell, his teeth clacking together. Osric pulled down a slot machine in front of the entrance. It slammed into the floor and a plastic CASHOUT button popped off and skittered into the darkness.

The creature rammed into the doors and part of the plywood boarding snapped and spun away. It shoved its head through the hole, saliva flinging from its jaws. Valentine gripped the lever on a slot machine and pulled it sideways with all his weight until it broke off in his hand.

This coyote was much, much worse than looking at a bag of mutated jack rabbit bones.

Plywood splintered and cracked, and a blur of claws and limbs broke through and sprang for Osric. It knocked him into a slot machine and screws clattered to the ground. Muscles strained in Osric's arms as he gripped the thing's jaws, which twisted in a way no animal – coyote or otherwise – should be capable of.

Valentine scrambled off the floor and swung the lever into the creature's head. *Elvis take the wheel* – he was not strong enough to kill this thing. It whirled on him, and he dove through the hole in the door, growls licking at his feet.

Oh shit. Oh fuck.

His heart slammed against his ribs, a scream trapped in his throat. His wretched imagination was already conjuring up what it would feel like for all those teeth to sink into his calf.

He sprinted down the street. The static-gat lying in the weeds looked like a beacon of salvation. Snatching it, he wound the handle as he turned around. The beast rammed into him, all hot musty fur, and he hit the trigger. Purple light popped, and

Valentine convulsed. His head thudded against the pavement, static bristling along his gums. His body buckled, heels kicking, and the space between his fingers crackled.

Snips of blue sky and rolling coyote eyes flashed in his vision. His tongue throbbed where he'd bitten it. The sun glinted off slot reels as Osric brought the sevens, fruits, and bells crashing down on the creature's head. He hauled it off of Valentine and swung the reels again. The static-gat rolled off of Valentine's rattling chest and clattered on the ground.

Valentine pulled in a fractured breath, his mouth full of cotton. Gods, he was stupid. The creature had been in contact with him when he pulled the trigger, and the current had gone through both of them.

Cool hands cupped his cheeks, and he tried to focus on Osric's face.

"You're alive. You're alive." Osric gingerly scooped him up, and Valentine leaned against him.

"Did I–" He coughed and tried to swallow. "Did I at least electrocute that thing along with myself?"

"Yes. It's dead. Stay put." Osric left his side, jogging back to the Nevada Club. Even with the creature's head caved in, Valentine wasn't so sure it wouldn't get back up. Residual limbs hung from its sides and teeth curved out of its ears. What if it had another brain somewhere?

He struggled to stand and failed. Heat radiated into his palms from the shattered road. Grasses poked through the rubble, the seedheads quivering against his arms.

Osric returned and pressed a water jug to Valentine's lips. "Here. I'll hold it for you."

Valentine took a greedy drink, water dribbling down his chin. He let out a shaky chuckle. "We've switched places."

With a tender smile, Osric said, "Our first encounter in Festerchapel feels like a lifetime ago." Helping him stand, Osric led Valentine back to the casino. "Let's get inside. I'm hoping that creature was an outlier – something sick or deranged that would attack without provocation – but I don't want to risk it."

Valentine's bedroll was wedged under the slot machine barricading one door. After yanking it out, Osric spread it on the ground and Valentine sank onto it.

Clothes and hygiene items from the backpack were strewn across the floor. Osric's bare feet slid through the dust; he stepped on a comb and one lone earring as he pulled the door closed.

Valentine stared at the earring on the floor, on the weak glint of light shining off the hoop. How long had that been in the backpack? His comb hadn't been in there this morning, nor his favorite socks or the scissors he used to cut his titty tape to size and round off the corners so it didn't peel up.

After snatching a tube of toothpaste that had been running on E for two months now, Valentine pushed it into the backpack with weak fingers and reached for more items. His teeth chattered. "She put all my things in here. There's" – he pawed through the contents, uncovering a bag of dried fruit and a folded tank top – "there's clothes and food and magazines in here that had been in a box in the van."

Osric turned. "What?"

His hands shook as he produced Osric's little spectacles and the tie he'd been wearing when they met. "And your things. She never would have had time to do that after shooing us away from the van. We came back too quickly. Which means she did it this morning. She was planning this." A lump stuck in his throat, and he struggled to push it down. "She didn't want any part of me or you in the van. She erased us."

After giving the seams of light in the front doors a lingering look, Osric crouched beside Valentine and helped him collect the spilled items. "You should rest. Thinking about it now is only going to get you worked up, and you don't look well."

"I'm fine." He struggled to zip the backpack closed with numb hands. "Cross your fingers that the phone is still in my back pocket."

"You think you dropped it?"

"No, but I already dropped the static-gat and kicked all our meager supplies to hell."

"A bag of cereal spilled, but everything else is intact. You distracted that animal and kept it from tearing out my throat." Osric took the backpack from Valentine. "You've done enough."

Valentine didn't have the energy for even Osric's gentle brand of arguing. Stuffing his hand into his back pocket, he sighed as his fingers brushed the phone. Turning it on produced a painful burst of light that illuminated the dusty slot machines and sagging ceiling tiles. Trying to click through icons on the phone only resulted in a white screen with a depressed robot face and the words "NO CONNECTION."

Osric took the phone and swiped the image away. He stopped and clucked his tongue. "The message to Lysander went through, but with no signal here, there's no way of knowing if he replied. And we won't be able to call the pirates."

"Could Lysander send someone to pick us up?"

"Highly unlikely. There wouldn't be enough justification to expend city resources picking up an 'android' and a man who isn't even a citizen. Lysander is in a position of high regard, especially with several human members of the Concord, so he's careful to follow the rules as much as possible."

"But if they want to make a case against a council member doing illegal things behind the others' backs, they'll need your testimony and presence as proof. And even if both the council signatures on your bill of sale were forged by Portia, we're trying to prevent the sex trafficking of sentient beings into Salt Lake. The Concord would want to know about and stop that, wouldn't they?"

Osric stared until heat flushed Valentine's cheeks and he looked away. "What? I don't read much, but I read this crime book a couple of times."

"It's a very reasonable point." Osric took off his pants, then sat cross legged and typed on the phone.

"Making yourself at home, are you?"

"I just... don't like wearing clothes. I'll put them back on, but we're not leaving until you've rested."

Valentine leaned against him and traced the lacy white continents decorating Osric's knees. The back of his skull ached, his palms were raw, and his tongue throbbed. Gripping the water jug was a struggle, and Osric had to tilt it to his mouth. So much for having strong hands.

Osric's chest rose and fell, and Valentine shut his eyes, nestled in the crook of his arm.

A thud hit the door, and Valentine jumped. A small voice said, "Hello?"

Osric frowned but headed to the entrance. Valentine hissed. "What are you doing?"

"Opening the door."

"No!"

"Unless mutated piebald coyotes can speak English, this is a person who might be able to offer us aid."

"Or slice our throats!"

Osric pulled open the door before Valentine could stop him. He shielded his eyes and squinted at the three silhouettes on the step.

Light streamed past Cinnamon's blaze of red hair. "Hello, Osric. Hello, Valentine. I hoped you'd still be here."

14

Cut Him Out in Little Stars
Osric

Osric hadn't anticipated three more bodies in need of food and water. Even with the androids requiring less fluids, there wasn't enough between the five of them for twenty hours of walking to Festerchapel. Especially since Valentine had just used a generous cupful to clean the roadrash on Cinnamon's arm.

Either that particular problem hadn't dawned on Valentine, or he was just elated to have some of the androids back. He sat on his knees, winding a strip of his chest tape around Cinnamon's wounds, and the relief in his face was obvious.

Blood dribbled from Pepper's temple. Osric took a bit of cloth and tried to wipe it clean, but she shied away from him, burying her face in Lavender's neck. Lavender held her tight, and her brows pushed up. Apologetically, she said, "We're trying to be brave, like Cinnamon instructed, but it's difficult."

"What happened?"

"Ace hit me in the head with a blunt object as I searched for a water bottle in the back of the van," Cinnamon said. "I lost consciousness, and when I awoke, I realized we were heading north again. Ace wouldn't turn around. I could have incapacitated her in some manner, but that would have resulted in crashing the van and harming us all. I told the others I was going to open the side door, and I directed them to jump out when I did so, but they resisted. They recognized that as a dangerous act but could not acknowledge that going back to the manor would result in worse. Only Lavender understood, and she convinced Pepper to jump as well."

Valentine pressed another piece of tape to Cinnamon's arm. "And Ace? Did she just keep going?"

"Yes. Previous to that, when I argued with her to stop, she said she should have left me along with you and Osric. I don't believe she will come back for us."

Shoulders sagging, Valentine sat back and rubbed his face. "Well, you three are here. At least that's something. I think we should head toward Festerchapel while we try to contact either the pirates or get a message back from Lysander. We can–" Valentine tried to screw the cap back on the jug of water and knocked it over. Water gushed onto the dusty floor. "Aw shit!"

Osric lunged for the jug. He flipped it upright and tightened the lid, but half the contents were depleted.

Valentine's hands shook. "Dammit. I'm sorry."

This situation was getting more dire by the moment. "You aren't well. You need to lie back down." Osric guided him to the bedroll. Valentine gave a weak protest, then bunched Osric's folded slacks under his head as a pillow.

Lavender's gaze volleyed from Pepper to Valentine. She inched toward him. "Is he still sad?"

"No. He was electrocuted by the gatling gun."

"Is he badly injured?" Cinnamon asked.

Osric stroked Valentine's neck. "I don't think so. I'm hoping it's temporary."

"I'm fine." Valentine pulled in a slow breath, his eyes closed. "My arms are kind of weak, and I have a tremble. Fingers are numb. I'm sure it will go away."

There was no telling how long that would take. Osric needed to search for resources and a solution. There was no time to wait for the spotty signal to pick up his new messages to Lysander.

He grabbed the half-empty jug. "I'm going to look for water and supplies. Stay here, please."

Cinnamon straightened. "I'd like to go. Lavender—"

Lavender had already started for Valentine. She sat beside him, took his hand, and massaged his palm. Pepper sat beside him and stroked his hair. If another coyote showed up, they'd be in trouble, but at least the comforting was covered.

Osric hefted the static-gat and followed Cinnamon out the entrance. "I think continuing on to the Collective is no longer feasible. It's twice the distance compared to the sixty miles to Festerchapel. We'd never make it."

"Yes, and I'm not going there without the others anyway." Cinnamon squinted down the road, shielding her eyes from the sun. Two of the false nails on her fingers were broken down to the quick.

"You mean Lavender and Pepper?"

"No. Everyone else. Ace still has them. I'll admit that, at first, I was only concerned with myself, but after listening to Valentine, I'm in agreement that we can't allow any of them to go back to the manor. Some of my experiences being an escort were, what I would now define as, pleasant or tolerable. People took me out to dinner. They complimented and flirted with me. I danced with them, star-gazed, and was treated with respect." Her nostrils flared. "But other times were so bad that I feel physically ill and have to resist the strong urge to delete the memories – at least for now. Portia, Brian, and Brandon did not discriminate with their customers, even when they knew that they would abuse us. I get great pleasure in thinking about stabbing those particular customers."

"I think you're entitled to that reaction. Valentine is right in that there's nothing wrong with being an escort if you like it, but the Thibodeauxs aren't the kind of people who will give you a choice in the matter, and I'm proof of that."

Cinnamon paused, her eyes big and sad, then gave Osric

a hug. He was momentarily too startled to reciprocate, then brought his arms up around her and squeezed her back.

They followed the road to the remains of a brick building. High evergreens and riotous grass sprouted around it, but if there was once anything of use here, it was long gone. A hand pump, wild vegetables, or even something with wheels to make their travel faster would be a miracle. Osric would take anything that might help.

He quickened his pace, eyeing the brush and shadows thrown from trees for more mutant animals. Hopefully that coyote was a one-off; he had no confidence that he could crank the gatling as quickly as Valentine.

Box cars sat behind the building, rusting into the earth. Foam padding hemorrhaged from moldering seat cushions and weeds reclaimed the tracks.

A water tower, obviously long empty from its burst seams, leaned crookedly on three legs. A light breeze looked like it might knock it over. The train tracks intersected at an angle with another line, and between them was a badly rusted sign with the letters "W RM S RI GS."

Cinnamon cocked her head. "'Worm Strings?'"

Osric smiled. "Warm Springs." No matter how decayed the town, a geothermal spring would keep on existing.

Something moved in the brush, and he stiffened, imagining the surrealistic jaws of the coyote, teeth and claws bristling from places they had no business being. If he hesitated, this one would tear out their throats.

He pushed Cinnamon behind him and cranked the handle on the gatling. It crackled with static, tiny threads of purple light winking between the barrels. The bushes shook, and Osric pressed the trigger. Lightning blasted from the gun and snapped against the sagebrush. Smoke and fire erupted from the vegetation, and a rabbit shot out of the undergrowth and sprinted away.

The hum of the gatling died, and flames licked at branches.

Cinnamon stared after the rabbit, her mouth pulled into a tight line. "Do you think it would have mauled us?"

Osric cleared his throat. "Well, one can never be too careful."

She stomped on the burning sage until the fire died. Tendrils of smoke spiraled into the sky. "Indeed."

Maybe a little judiciousness *was* warranted next time. Osric should have at least worn shoes so he could stamp out any more fires he started.

Beyond a rocky outcropping, teal water shimmered in the sun. He sighed in relief. He knelt and filled the jug to the brim. Cinnamon rounded the spring. She kicked through broken glass, then pulled a mason jar from the dirt. After rinsing it out, she filled it with water and rested it against her hip. "What now?"

He stood and brushed off rocks and dirt that stuck to his knees, then looked toward the tracks. A wheeled platform sat there, weeds poking through the splintery boards. He'd seen a movie once – some parody of the Old West – where the heroes had stood on one of these contraptions, levering a handle up and down as they chased bank robbers down the rails. If they found the right components, they might be able to fix this one.

"Want to help me repair a handcar?"

Valentine

Valentine sat on one side of the handcar, and despite the heat baking into him from the sun and Osric's shirt pulled around him, he shivered. He wasn't sure if he was cold or his nervous system was shot to hell. Probably the latter. But at least they weren't walking, and Osric's contraption hadn't fallen apart yet.

The wheels, drive gear, and pump handle had been rusty but intact. Osric had replaced some roller bearings and repaired part of the platform. It had taken him and Cinnamon an impressively short amount of time, but the sun was much lower than Valentine would have liked. They could likely drive the handcar all the way back to Salt Lake if they couldn't find a quicker vehicle before then, but time wasn't on their side.

They rumbled down the rails, foothills and sagebrush flying by. Mason jars of water clinked on the cobbled-together planking. The androids had taken turns helping Osric pump the lever, but he'd told them he was fine doing it on his own. Valentine would have helped had he felt better.

Despite Osric's insistence that the car practically propelled itself with built-up momentum, sweat glistened on his bare chest, trickling through his chest hair. Muscles in his arms strained as he hauled the lever up and down, ropy veins standing out in relief on his forearms.

"Damn, honey." Valentine tucked his hands into his armpits to stop their tremble. "I need a drink."

Osric wiped his brow. "We have plenty of water."

"That's not what I meant. Watching you work is giving me a whole other thirst."

"Meaning you're tired just watching me?" He sighed. "At least you make cute cargo."

Sheesh, flirting with this guy was hard. "No. I'm thirsty for *you* and those shining muscles." Valentine waggled his eyebrows.

Osric faltered and lost his rhythm. A crooked smile grew on his face. "Oh."

"Besides, I'm not cargo. I might not be able to crank the gat right now, but I'll at least warn you if there's danger or the tracks are broken."

"No you won't." Osric pushed the lever with a grunt. "You're distracted. I'd put my shirt back on, but you took it."

Valentine snuggled into the button-up and inhaled the scent clinging to the fabric.

Lavender pulled at one of her springy black curls. "Does 'thirsty' imply that you're attracted to someone?"

"Yeah."

She turned to Pepper. "I'm thirsty for you."

A rosy flush bloomed in Pepper's cheeks. She smiled shyly and tucked her face against Lavender's shoulder.

Osric scowled at Valentine like he'd utterly corrupted them with that one phrase. Valentine grinned. Thank the gods that Lavender and Pepper had jumped out of the van along with Cinnamon. Lavender had too much sentience to be stuck in the manor, and Pepper was sensitive and frightened. He didn't want to think about the others who might be more aware than they let on, still trapped with Ace speeding back to their doom.

Even thinking her name hurt. He didn't know what he was going to say to her when they caught up to the van, but she'd made one thing abundantly clear. She wasn't good for him and probably never had been.

The phone vibrated in his back pocket, and he slid it out. A message scrolled across the screen, but it was too hard to read in the direct sun. He pulled Osric's shirt over his head and tucked the phone near his face.

His heart leapt as he expanded the text.

<I'm glad to hear from you, Osric. All of this is quite concerning. I have forwarded your messages, including the video of the android sufficiently answering a question from the McClelland-Reinhard, to the other Concord members. I agree that the androids being taken against their will to the manor constitutes intent to traffick. Unfortunately, I've already received several replies stating that this isn't sufficient evidence of self-awareness, and I think it will take more to convince these members.

<There are no delivery trucks heading your way for some time, and I don't think Juliet's remote cars could endure so much unmaintained highway, but I'm scrambling for permission to help you in whatever capacity I can. Don't lose hope.

<I will give you an update when I have one.>

"'Don't lose hope,' he says." Valentine huffed. It figured that it wouldn't be as easy as asking a favor. Not when the city had so many rules about who could enter, how much they had to pay, and what sorts of questions they had to answer before becoming worthy of living there.

Valentine read Lysander's message aloud and noted that it was timestamped the day before, probably immediately after Osric sent it. He quickly tapped out a reply of acknowledgement and tacked on a *please hurry*.

Osric paused in his lever pumping. "That's much less optimistic than I would have hoped. But if my recording of Lavender swayed some of them, maybe more video will help."

Accessing texts and other features on the phone hadn't been too difficult once Osric showed Valentine where they were, but the phone had a habit of crashing and restarting if he messed with too many things.

He hit record and aimed the phone at Cinnamon. "Can I ask you some questions?"

She looked up from the broken false nail on her index finger. "Yes, of course."

"Err– what do I ask? What's on the test?"

Osric said, "What is the meaning of life?"

"Whose life?" she asked. "Mine? Yours? Valentine's? Before leaving the city, I would have had a concrete answer about my own. I was programmed to keep people company and given extra training to excel at engaging conversation. I was capable of intent listening and providing an on-topic reply. But you know, when someone is speaking to me now, there's a tendency for my mind to stray. I think of that topic in terms of my own experiences and how it makes me feel. And sometimes that sparks adjacent thoughts that have nothing to do with the subject." She paused. "I'm doing that right now. I didn't answer your question."

Osric grinned. "Yes. You did."

This was good. The more evidence they had, the better. Though Valentine was inclined to side with Cinnamon – she hadn't actually answered the question. He aimed the phone at Pepper. "What do *you* think is the meaning of life?"

Her eyes grew big and she shrank into herself. "The more I think about that, the more it scares me. Why am I here? I exist at a small point in time, in the confines of this body. Some day, the sun will explode and wipe out the Earth. The universe will collapse in on itself and everything will be gone. In the grand scheme of things, I could do anything at all, be it 'good' or 'bad,' and it won't matter. We could prevent Ace from taking the other women to the manor, or we could stop this handcar and lie down in the dirt and die. It doesn't make a difference."

The phone sagged in Valentine's hand. Osric's smile faded, and Lavender looked on the verge of tears.

There'd been many nights in the van where Valentine had laid awake, staring at the dark ceiling and having these same thoughts. But he'd come to a conclusion he could live with. "We may not have chosen to exist, but while we're here we have the power to affect others. We can contribute to their suffering" – he glanced at Osric – "or to their joy. It makes a difference, Pepper. It does."

Lavender ran her fingers through Pepper's dark bob. "It matters to me that you're here."

Pepper's mouth wavered. "Okay."

AI straying from the topic at hand or turning the conversation into an absolute downer about the lack of meaning to the universe had to sway some of the council members. Valentine hit send on the video, watching the tiny wheel spin beside the message as it struggled to go through. He finally closed out and stuffed the phone back in his pocket. Watching it wasn't going to help send it faster and would only drain the battery quicker.

They passed lonely swaths of desert and the remains of ancient towns. Sometimes there was a full building intact that had just refused to die along with everything else. If Valentine were a house, that's the one he'd be. Proudly standing in a run-down world, unwilling to be knocked down.

He let Lavender massage his tingling fingers and tried to picture what profession might suit her now that she was free. A nurse, maybe, or caretaker. A teacher for small children. They could set her loose in a pirate camp and she'd be busy drying eyes and kissing boo-boos until the end of time.

Cinnamon was no-nonsense and proactive. A great addition to any town... as long as she didn't stab someone.

Pepper hadn't come out of her shell enough to guess, but that was okay too. There wasn't a time limit to finding yourself.

When Valentine's hands stopped trembling and his limbs no longer felt purely decorative, he stood and took the other side of the handcar lever. Osric protested, but getting some blood flowing back into his arms would hopefully help them to recover faster.

Cinnamon shooed Osric away until he finally sat down and drained an entire mason jar of spring water. She and Valentine couldn't push the lever with quite as much vigor as Osric, but they maintained a steady speed.

When the sun slipped behind the mountains, Valentine was reluctant to slow. "Should we keep going?"

Osric glanced up. "You aren't tired?"

He was. The muscles in his arms vibrated from overexertion, and all he wanted to do was lie down. "I'm... fine. But Cinnamon, if you want to stop–"

"My arms are sore, but I don't require sleep anytime soon." As if to reinforce it, she smiled cheerily and gave the pump handle a hard push.

Pursing his lips, Osric squinted ahead and scrubbed the back of his neck. "It's certainly in our best interest to get to the city as quickly as we can, but even with the moon, it'll be difficult to see any obstructions ahead. Might be better to stop for the night."

Cinnamon cocked her head and stared into the distance. "Why would it be difficult to see obstructions?"

"Because it's growing dark."

She frowned at Osric as though waiting for him to continue. When he didn't, she said, "You can't see in the dark, Steward?"

"Not very well, no."

Valentine heaved the handle, then leaned against it to catch his breath. He glanced at Cinnamon, thinking about how she'd sprung upon him with that awl back in the pirate camp. "But you can?"

She shrugged. "Yes. So can the other women from the manor."

Valentine tried to recall anything odd about the androids' eyes, other than some of them having heterochromia like Osric. Surely he would have noticed if they had eyeshine.

"What purpose does that serve?" Osric asked.

Lavender said, "It's essential for our well-being. If a client has a weapon and tries to assault us while we are in bed in the dark, we'll see it. If he tries to kidnap us and drag us down an alley, we can see better than him and escape."

Valentine cringed. "You should have built-in tasers in your hands and just zap them."

Cinnamon smiled. "I like that idea. But we are getting off topic. Between all of us, we should have enough labor to keep the handcar going. Lavender, Pepper, and I can see well enough to notice any blockage on the tracks."

Osric stood and nudged Valentine away from the pump handle. "You should sleep, if you can. There's no need to try to compete with android endurance, and I'm not convinced you've fully recovered from being electrocuted."

There was no use arguing. Valentine's arms were going to give out before his determination did. He wrapped himself in a blanket and tucked Osric's shirt under his head. Vibrations juddered his teeth even through the cushioning of his makeshift pillow, but exhaustion pulled him under.

No one woke him for a turn at the handle, and it was well past dawn by the time he stretched his stiff limbs and insisted they needed to stop so he could pee.

They'd long passed Festerchapel, but still had quite a distance to bridge before they'd make it to Salt Lake. The day stretched on with agonizing slowness despite the desert rushing by. All he could think about were the androids, imagining their wrists bound as Ace filed them into the manor. Brian shoving mugs of scalding coffee against Nutmeg or snatching Basil by the hair and dragging her into a bedroom.

His stomach cramped. He couldn't let that happen. But he also wasn't going to be any use if he was dead tired with his arms complete mush. Sleeping on a non-vibrating surface for the night sounded amazing, and Pepper had muttered that she required sleep soon.

After setting up camp in a small station house, Valentine divided up most of the dry cereal and dehydrated fruit Ace had left them. He tried to remember what else they'd had to eat in the van. Another bag of cereal and some canned soup. Not enough to feed the rest of the captive androids, but Ace probably wasn't too concerned about that.

Osric protested at the offer of food, but Valentine wasn't going to let anyone go hungry.

He sat on his bedroll and crunched a handful of cereal. Osric stood at a window, hands clasped behind his back like he was analyzing a painting or inspecting factory work. Cobwebs fluttered from the sill, and mice scrabbled through the wall.

Footsteps creaked on the stairs, and Pepper appeared, her hands cupped together. She made a beeline for Valentine and knelt next to him. "Hello, Valentine."

"Hey."

She gave him a smile too big for her face and pressed something sticky into his palm. "This is for you. Osric said they were your favorite, so we declined to eat them."

He stared at the clump of raisins and pinched his lips together. Osric stifled a chuckle.

"Er, thanks," Valentine said. "That's real nice. Osric knows me for sure. I'm happy to share them with you, though."

"No, thank you. They're a gift for your kindness and generosity." She blinked. "Good night."

"Uh, good night."

She crossed the room and descended the stairs, disappearing into the shadows.

Valentine thudded his head back against the wall. "I give up my dream to rescue a bunch of people in need, and the universe repays me in raisins. That sounds about right. You're an asshole, you know that?"

Osric turned from the window and smirked. He sat beside Valentine, then plucked up some of the shriveled fruits and popped them in his mouth. "They don't taste bad." He leaned toward Valentine, and Valentine slid away.

"Gross. Don't kiss me." He scraped the glob of raisins back into the fruit bag and stuffed it into the backpack.

Osric caressed Valentine's wrist. "How are you doing? Are you okay?"

He pulled in a deep breath and leaned against Osric. "Yeah, I guess, considering everything. Breakups never feel good, I suppose." A cracked thermos hung from a carabiner on the backpack, and he unhooked it, turning it over in his hands. "Do Steward breakups get ugly?"

"Sometimes, though I don't think they happen as often as human breakups. It's possible to suppress our emotions to a degree, but some of it still bleeds through to the others, especially if it's a strong feeling. Because we can't hide things from each other as easily, there's more of a tendency to talk things through and empathize. It doesn't always work." He pressed his nose to Valentine's hair. "I was happy in my last relationship, but one of my partners, Edmund, started to get bored with me. I think he was still interested in our other bond, Benvolio, but decided it was better to cut off the relationship with both of us. When he left, Benvolio and I couldn't go back to the way we were before we formed a throuple with Edmund. It felt hollow. So Ben left too. I'm just not that interesting."

"That's not true. If they got bored of you, that's on them. But nothing lasts forever, huh?" All around them, the ruins of the past were slowly being eaten by nature, folding back into the earth so that something new could rise. What grew wasn't something healthy, but scraped-together remains of the world that used to be. One last desperate gasp before giving up.

No, that was wrong. The rich dickheads on their thousand-year trip to Teegarden b probably expected Earth to be dead now, cities pillaged and depleted, towns razed and half-feral cannibal marauders the only people left. That was far from the case. Farm fields burgeoned with produce. Pirate camps raised new generations that would learn to pray to Jesus and shoot pepper bombs at travelers. Lightbulbs were still being produced in Salt Lake, with or without Osric's watchful eye.

Maybe Valentine wasn't the only one who wanted to be a stubborn house, standing tall amid the rubble.

He dug his finger into the crack in the bottom of the thermos. Osric pointed to it. "Is it broken?"

"No. The crack doesn't go all the way through. Not that we need it with all those mason jars."

"They don't have lids, though." Osric took the thermos and unscrewed the top. He glanced inside and wrinkled his nose, hastily screwing the lid back on. "Oh. I didn't realize it was full. It's what Brian was drinking. Whiskey."

"No way." If there'd been an entire thermos of whiskey in the van, Ace would have drunk it already. Valentine unscrewed the lid and sniffed. He chuckled. "It's mead. I haven't been to Dog Teats in months. I must have gotten drunk, put some in here, and forgotten about it."

Valentine took a pull. The honeyed bite of alcohol raced down his throat. "Okay, this is a better gift from the universe than raisins."

Osric took the thermos, hesitated, then sipped. His face scrunched. "I'm not so sure."

"You don't like it? It's great at relaxing you."

"It'll impair our judgment and ruin our fine motor skills."

"My judgment is already terrible." After another deep drink, he pushed the thermos into Osric's hands. "Besides, there's not enough in here to get us drunk, which means you're spared my singing."

Reluctantly, Osric took a swig. He grimaced and shook his head. They passed the bottle back and forth until a contented warmth spread through Valentine. He sank against Osric and closed his eyes.

The contents in the backpack clinked and rattled, which roused Valentine from his pre-doze. Osric made a thoughtful noise, and paper rustled. His *hmm*s turned to soft *oh*s. Valentine sat up. Osric held a magazine, open to a spread of two men getting very comfortable with each other's anatomy.

The AI had found his porn.

"It's hot, but it's not very realistic." Valentine tapped the page. "Normal people aren't contortionists."

Osric gave him a lingering look that said he wouldn't mind challenging the validity of that statement.

Valentine cleared his throat and flipped pages until he stopped on one he'd dogeared. "This isn't as hardcore as some of the others, but it's nice. I like the ones where they kiss."

"I like it too." Osric thumbed past pages, the intensity in his face fading to contemplation. "None of these men look like you."

Valentine frowned. "Thanks for the reminder."

"No, I mean, it's a shame. There's a nice variety of body types and skin tones, but they could do with including trans men."

Valentine picked up the thermos, but it was empty. He screwed the lid back on. "Maybe you should send them disgruntled messages on a social channel until they fix it."

"Perhaps I will." His face bunched in a crooked smile, and he gave Valentine a slow kiss, pushing him back on the bedroll. "Or maybe we can recreate one of the acts on the pages."

Breath quickening, Valentine whispered, "Right now?"

"Yes." The word was practically a growl, rumbling in Osric's throat, and Valentine curled his toes. "Do you want to?"

He did, but the thought sent anxiety shooting through him. "Yeah, but most of what's going on in there takes some prep. We don't have lube or–"

"Then what can we do? I don't care if it's not the same." Osric popped open the buttons on his shirt and pulled it off. "In the parking garage, you spoke of your fantasies and the way you want to be treated. I haven't forgotten, and I want to fulfill those for you."

Valentine's pulse throbbed. He dug his fingers into the bedroll and his nail caught on the zipper. The things he'd confessed weren't something he'd expected Osric to remember, considering how mad he'd been at the time, but apparently his perfect memory had logged it away somewhere. "I want that too."

The idea of mutant offspring, and not just the coyote they'd killed, still lingered in Valentine's mind. Unlike the surprise mead, he remembered stashing several condoms away in the front pocket of the backpack some time ago. He'd been waiting for a special occasion to use them. This was it.

After retrieving one, he leaned back on the bedroll and pulled Osric down with him. Gingerly, he caressed the seams in Osric's chest. "Do these feel weird?"

Osric shrugged. "Not any weirder than the rest of me." He pressed his hand against Valentine's heart. "Can we take off your shirt too, or would it make you uncomfortable?"

"I don't want to take it off, but I'll unbutton it."

As Valentine undid each button, Osric left a kiss in its place, leaving a trail across the arrow tattoo on Valentine's sternum and through the hair on his stomach. He kicked off his pants, grateful he had a little alcohol running through him to dampen his nerves.

Osric left soft pecks along his inner thighs, and Valentine

squirmed with longing. He started to pull off his briefs, but Osric stopped his hand. "I haven't kissed your lips raw yet."

"I'm rea–" Valentine's words were lost against Osric's mouth. Stubble rasped his skin, fingers caressed his jaw. He tasted like honey, and though his touches were restrained, palpable energy simmered just under his surface. Valentine's own desire had flooded his hands, and they roamed Osric's broad back and found purchase in the hair at his nape.

Osric groaned as Valentine caught his lip between his teeth. He ground against Valentine, hesitant at first, but with extra vigor as Valentine clutched his ass and whimpered for more.

A thump and soft conversation drifted from the floor below and Valentine bit his tongue. The last thing they needed were the androids walking in on them.

Osric whispered. "Are your lips sufficiently kissed?"

"I can't feel them anymore. So yes."

"Then will you show me where you want me for your vanilla missionary? And are you sure that's not a cake flavor?"

Valentine stifled a laugh.

"Vanilla. Peaches. Sex has a lot of food references, but I have to say that I find this a lot more enjoyable than food."

"I agree." Valentine slid his hand down Osric's stomach and into his underwear. "But 'vanilla' in this context means 'plain.' 'Boring.'"

"How could this possibly–" Osric squeezed his eyes closed, his hips moving with Valentine's strokes, and he seemed to forget the rest of his question.

"Have you touched yourself like this before?"

"No." Osric's warm breath fanned Valentine's skin. "I pushed the urge away."

"I definitely recommend doing it sometime. I mean, when you're alone. Not on a shuttle or something."

"Noted."

"And, no, this isn't boring." Valentine wiggled out of his briefs. "'Classic' is probably a better definition."

"Classic is good, but… I'm feeling unsure of myself. Is there a diagram for this in your magazine?"

"A diagram."

"If you recall, when we first met you asked if I came with a manual."

Valentine rubbed his forehead. "You're right. I did. But like you pointed out, there aren't any trans guys in that magazine, so it won't be accurate no matter how many pictures you look at. I'll show you, though. We can be nervous together."

"I want it to be good."

"Oh, honey. It already is."

Whispering instructions into Osric's ear was far sexier than Valentine expected it to be. Osric's reactions were encouraging, but the poor guy also looked like his circuits were being overloaded.

Valentine tore open the condom wrapper. "If you crash, I don't know how to reboot you."

Osric let out a shaky chuckle. "I don't think that's possible in this body."

"Are you changing your mind about this? Want to stop?"

"Not at all. I'll tell you if I'm too overwhelmed."

"Alright." Adrenaline jittered his fingers as he rolled the condom onto Osric.

Together they found a rhythm. Osric's eyes were wide pools in the dim light, his breath quick but thrusts gentle. He trailed his lips across Valentine's ear. "Is this right?"

"Yes. Keep going."

Everything in Valentine's life still hurt, and the future was so uncertain that he needed something physical to grab hold of. He held to Osric. His hips moved under Valentine's hands, the salt of his skin stinging his tongue. The back of Valentine's shirt bunched up until he finally tore it off. Osric didn't care about his taped chest and probably wouldn't care about it untaped. He saw Valentine for who he was, and Valentine hoped he was doing the same. It would be hard saying goodbye to this body, though, should Osric decide this form wasn't making him happy. He'd miss Osric's broken smile, his particolored eyes and wide hands. His voice as a Steward would surely be different as well, and there'd be no more sad man snuggles or kissing lips raw.

Valentine would support him, though. He had to. He knew too well that kind of pain.

Right now, Osric was making enthusiastic use of this body, and of Valentine's. He panted, his mouth clumsily searching for Valentine's in the growing dark.

"Are you enjoying yourself?" Valentine whispered.

Osric's response was mostly moan, but it sounded positive. "Are you?"

He dug his fingers into Osric's hair and gasped. "Yeah." A small, selfish part of him hoped that Osric would decide that being in android form had more benefits than existing as a disembodied Steward. He pushed the thought away as he pushed Osric onto his back. He straddled him and kissed his neck.

"And what's the name of this position?" Osric slid his hands down Valentine's waist. "Custard donut?"

"That's dirty. I like it." He lowered himself onto Osric and rocked his hips, trying to shove away his problems with each motion.

Tomorrow, he'd still have to confront Ace. He'd still have to fight to get the androids back. He'd still have to accept whatever Osric decided to do. And he still wouldn't have his visa.

Nothing was going to fill that hollow ache in his chest, but he needed one moment – this moment – untroubled by everything in his life.

Osric's fingers danced across Valentine's skin like he was trying to read braille. "I wish I could feel you the way I feel other Stewards. I want to be connected to your emotions."

"You are." Valentine splayed his hand against Osric's chest, bracing himself until the tight coil of pleasure winding inside him sprung apart. His thighs spasmed, toes curling as he came. Osric squeezed his eyes shut, and tendons in his neck corded. Hips bucking, his exclamation was loud enough to wake the dead, let alone the women downstairs.

His dazed expression in the dim light was one of a man who had no idea what day it was or how he got here.

"You okay?" Valentine asked.

Raking a hand through his sweaty hair, Osric said, "I've deleted a lot of movies from my memory. I find most of them predictable and contrived. But I still remember one in which a couple had sex. Watching it was as far removed from my experiences as seeing humans have dinner, sob in the rain, or get punched in the face. But all the moaning and bizarre facial expressions make sense now."

Valentine chuckled. He pulled the blanket tighter around them and nestled into Osric's embrace.

He just had to hold onto this moment.

15
Do We Not Revenge?
Osric

Apparently the secret to getting a restful sleep where one didn't stare at the ceiling for hours was thoroughly expending one's self in a burst of emotional and physical bliss.

Beside Osric, Valentine pulled in a noisy snore and pressed his icy foot to Osric's thigh. Instead of pulling away, Osric snuggled closer and buried his nose in Valentine's hair.

The day was going to end in heartbreak for Valentine. Osric couldn't imagine leaving him to nurse those wounds alone.

The idea of living in a vehicle, taking on difficult and unsavory jobs just so he and Valentine could eat wasn't an appealing thought, but there'd be plenty of time to help him with the citizenship test. He imagined sitting cross-legged in the van with Valentine, textbooks spread out before them, as he taught Valentine about partial derivatives and Euclidean space.

Osric could pass whatever test they threw at him. The citizenship test. More evaluations of his sentience. Whatever the Concord deemed was necessary for him to prove he was deserving of rights and autonomy.

He brushed soft locks of hair from Valentine's brow, woodburn brown midtones of #45372A with carnaby tan highlights. Feldspar skin and shell pink lips that grew ruddier the more he kissed them.

Trying to paint with physical mediums wouldn't be the same as doing it digitally, but if he found the materials – despite having to use his hands as well as his mind – he wanted to try. Portraiture wasn't his strong suit, and even if he painted the smile lines around Valentine's mouth, each unruly eyebrow hair and the scar across his cheek, it wouldn't compare to gazing at him now as weak light spilled through the window. But he could put him in a city scene, Valentine standing tall in his small body, in a broad-shouldered suit beneath the Vitality Financial building.

Valentine's lashes fluttered. He focused on Osric and rubbed his eye, his voice thick and fuzzy around the edges. "You watching me sleep wasn't on my list of fantasies."

"Maybe it was on mine."

He snorted. "Fair enough."

"I was lying here, thinking about what might occur today, and I want you to know that I'll be by your side, no matter what."

"Thanks. I know you will. I've been trying to look at the positive." He slid his arms around Osric. "Honestly, I'm glad Ace finally did something like this."

"You are?"

"Yeah, because it's made me realize what a shitty friend she's been to me. I've put up with her on and off misgendering, her petty arguments, and her callous dismissal of my pain for a year. I always excused it. 'She didn't mean it. She was only teasing and didn't realize it hurt. She keeps me on task so I have no right to be upset.'

"If she'd helped us liberate the androids and we went on to keep taking salvage jobs together, it would be more of the same. It would probably end with her tripping me as we're running from cannibal cultists." He rolled onto his back and tossed an arm over his face. "Or what if the androids hadn't been self-aware and we'd taken them back for our visas? We'd get an apartment together thinking that more space would make us fight less, but she'd still nag me about my socks and dirty dishes and the men I dated. It's better this way."

That was an unexpectedly upbeat perspective, and spurned Osric to pepper Valentine's lips with kisses before climbing out of bed to gather their things.

The phone vibrated and Valentine scooped it up. His face contorted, lips curled and teeth bared.

Osric's stomach clenched. "What's wrong?"

He handed Osric the phone.

<*Sometimes I wish I could flood a human with my emotional processes instead of all of this back-and-forth discussion and misinterpretation, don't you? After sending your second video to the council members, they agreed that this is a big enough matter to warrant a discussion. Yet they don't want to bring the subject up at our already-scheduled meeting today. They want to talk about your illegal sale and my forged signature and have a separate meeting about the androids' sentience in two weeks. They claim combining the two cases might allow one to influence the other, but I know for certain the upcoming holiday has something to do with it. Osric, I can't tell you how frustrated I am. But until we have this meeting, the androids are still property of Portia Thibodeaux.*

<*The best I could do was prevent Audrey Emmitt from entering the city while the Concord talked, but she's still parked in the southeast garage in the yellow sector, and if she comes to the gate again, I will have to let her in. I'm so sorry.*>

They packed in haste and climbed aboard the handcar. Their only hope now was intercepting Ace and getting her to see reason. Osric's internal calendar and clock had been frozen since being uploaded into his body, but he felt time slipping through his fingers regardless.

With him and Valentine pumping the lever in tandem, the car flew down the tracks at a speed that made Osric uncomfortable. It had been incredibly lucky that they hadn't encountered any damaged tracks and had seen obstructions far enough ahead in time to clear them away or pivot to a branching rail. At the speed they were maintaining, which he estimated to be around twelve or thirteen miles an hour, their reaction time would be greatly reduced.

Just as he was about to suggest they slow down, he spotted an overturned shopping cart clotted with tumbleweeds and bailing twine sprawled over the rails ahead. He mashed the brake and the wheels squealed. But the handcar slammed into the shopping cart, and he snatched the pump handle to keep from falling over.

The car pushed the shopping cart down the tracks a few feet before finally stopping.

Valentine gripped the edge of the platform, his eyes wide. "Maybe we should get out and walk."

Osric hopped down and helped everyone off. Standing on the ground, with weeds scratching at his legs and garbage surrounding them, it suddenly seemed like a far more unsafe means of travel. The nearby dwellings made Valentine's van look like a mobile mansion in comparison.

Valentine took the lead, his chin jutted out, the gatling swinging at his side. Junked cars surrounded the buildings, and people milled outside, hanging washing, repairing roof tiles, and plucking cucumbers from gardens surrounded in razor wire.

Their group cut down a muddy path, but no matter how quickly they walked, the glimmering high rises and office buildings of the city never seemed to grow any closer. He would have worried for their safety had it been just him and Valentine, but bringing well-dressed, attractive women through this area compounded the issue. Taking the androids straight to the city gates was not ideal, but leaving them here would be worse.

A dog snarled and strained against its chain. Pepper let out a squeak and clung to Lavender. A man pushed away a tarp serving as a door, and the look he gave their group was the same skin-itching inspection Brian had given Ace.

Osric plucked the phone from Valentine and tapped out a message to Lysander. *<I know you're doing all you can, but we're on the outskirts and our safety is in question. Can you get permission to send someone our way? A patroller or Juliet?>*

The man smacked his barking dog on the flank, then gave Osric a toothless grin. "Damn, man, you all some fine androids. Could bounce a quarter off the redhead's ass. How much?"

Osric frowned. "How much what?"

"How much she cost?"

"Base models are in the range of eight thousand dollars, but–" Osric stiffened, realizing what the man meant. "Their company is not for sale."

"No?" He leered at Osric, and Osric regretted not putting his shirt back on. "And what about yours?"

"No." He started walking and the others followed suit, but the man blocked his path.

Apparently deciding the only human in their group would be more reasonable, he turned to Valentine. "C'mon, man. I'm good for the money. How much?"

Valentine glared. "Beat it."

With a huff, the man reached for Cinnamon, but before he could grab her, she yanked a screwdriver from her thigh high stocking and jammed it against his throat. His eyes widened, and he put up his hands. "Touch me, and I will fill you with more holes than the Bonneville Golf Course on Connor Street," she hissed.

His dog barked viciously, spittle flying from its jowls, and the post anchoring its chain wobbled in the dirt.

"I do believe he's gotten the message." Osric wrapped his hand around Cinnamon's and lowered the screwdriver. "Haven't you, sir?"

"You're outta control." The whites of the man's eyes flashed as he stepped back. "Someone should shut you down."

They hurried past, and Osric threw one last glance back at the irate dog. They needed out of here. And they needed a plan. "How are we going to convince Ace to hand over the androids?"

Valentine's mouth pulled tight. "She's been my best friend for over a year. We argue a lot, but when it comes to things that are really important to me, she eventually listens. I just have to make her."

It seemed beyond that point now, but physically restraining her or threatening her with the gatling in a parking garage would be a sure way to get them all arrested. Besides, Valentine would probably object to Osric trying something like that anyway.

A small truck sped toward them, sprays of dirt fanning behind the tires. Antennae waggled on the roof. It pulled across their path, and the tailgate popped open. No one sat in the driver's seat. Instead, metal crates occupied the space, and a shovel lay across the dash.

Osric sighed in relief. "This is a friend. Juliet. C'mon." He helped everyone into the back, which was filled with more construction tools that he had to push to one side. He started to climb in after them, but the passenger door opened, and a voice drifted from the cab.

"Sit up here with me, Steward."

Osric climbed in and the door shut behind him. The truck backed up and turned for the city proper. In the side mirror, Valentine was visible, his stance wide as he clutched the static-gat. The truck swayed as it thumped over ruts, but he was unperturbed by the motion.

A water bottle rolled across the dirty floor mat, and Juliet's voice came from the dash. *"I've never been told to delay work to pick up passengers before! This is so exciting!"*

Osric sank into the seat, fatigue weighing down his limbs and his stomach clenched in a knot. "Exciting" wasn't the word he would have used. "Thank you for the assistance."

"I wouldn't have missed it. I'll deliver you with haste. But not too much. I don't want your adventure partner falling out of the back.

He has good balance, hm?" The truck veered around a rocking chair inexplicably sitting in the middle of the road. *"Lysander's urgency and frustration is spiking through the network. He's never been this impassioned during a meeting before. I think the Concord must have given him permission to send you a ride just to get him to calm down. It hasn't helped, though. He's thinking about you so hard that snippets of thought are bleeding through the firewalls."*

He dug his fingers into the seat stitching. "Is… Is it not going well?"

"Not sure. Benvolio has had thoughts about you as well, but there is a lot of interference right now. Puck formed a new bond, and xyr feelings of puppy love are spilling into everyone's sectors. I'm happy for xem, but it's a little sickening. Edmund tried to tell Puck that a long-distance relationship – xyr bond is in Absolution – isn't going to work out, but you know how–"

"Juliet." Though always aware of her bubbly presence filtering down the connection, Osric hadn't talked to Juliet in some time. He wasn't sure he had the energy to keep up with her. "I have a lot on my mind right now."

"Oh, of course. But you've missed so much gossip. Most of it was about you, though, so maybe it's better that you weren't around. You know, sometimes I dream of having a body and going on dangerous missions like the characters in action movies. But I also dream about being the cars." She laughed. *"I think I would die if I was disconnected from the network, though. Are you alright?"*

The truck thumped over a rock, and Osric braced himself against the door frame. "It's been a difficult learning curve, but I've adjusted."

"I wish you could flood me with your experience and emotions so that I may see."

That would be much easier than trying to explain. But even if he suppressed it, his feelings for Valentine would still bleed through. Thinking of last night made him giddy and unfocused, his heart throbbing too fast when he replayed the memory of them skin to skin, Valentine's moans and gasps, his fingers digging into Osric's back. If some of that slipped through, none of the Stewards would possibly understand, and he liked the idea of it being a secret. Something just between them.

Juliet was still talking. *"I think they have a bond too. A Steward/ human relationship is weird, but Lysander deserves more than his mystery books. If he and Cedar are happy, who am I to judge?"*

"What?" He hadn't been listening, and the conversation hadn't forced its way into his secondary processes the way it would have had they both been in the network. The isolation in this body had advantages he'd never considered a week ago, and there was no telling what others he would discover the longer he stayed this way.

"Never mind," Juliet said. *"Where do you want me to drop you off at, anyway? Are you going to crash the Concord meeting and make a bold statement about autonomy and sentience?"*

"There's no time." They were fast approaching the city entry. He directed her toward the yellow sector's parking garage.

Darkness swallowed them as they drove under a covered ramp. They passed cobbled-together wasteland rigs in various flavors of intimidating, delivery trucks, and more than a few motorcycles.

The van appeared, straddling two parking spaces, and his heart filled his throat. Ace leaned against the sliding door, thumbing through a magazine like she was waiting for the B shuttle.

Valentine leapt from the back of the truck before Juliet came to a complete stop, his fists balled and the gatling swinging from his side. Osric opened his door and climbed out in time to see Valentine slap the magazine out of Ace's hands.

This was going to get ugly.

Valentine

Blood throbbed in Valentine's temples. Ace stared down at the splayed magazine – *his* magazine – then looked back up at him, jaw set. "You just can't leave well enough alone, can you?"

"How could you do this to me?" His voice was too high, strained and broken.

She slowly picked up the magazine and smoothed out pages that Valentine had flipped through so many times that the edges were tattered and greasy with his fingerprints. Spreads of suits and apartment furnishings and cologne samples that had long gone rancid. She shook her head. "I did this *for* you."

Valentine sputtered and hot tears flooded his eyes. "In what universe is that supposed to make sense? You're killing me, Ace. We were supposed to be in this together until the end. You left us for dead!"

She made a noise in her throat. "You're so dense. Didn't you read my note? I *do* understand you. I didn't before, not fully. When we were in the city, though, and I saw how happy you were in that suit, looking like the man you are inside, I realized what a visa meant to you. But your heart is just too damn big. How are you supposed to get anywhere in life when you give a part of yourself to each person in need? Even to robots who are never gonna be self-aware? If you give and give, soon there won't be any of you left." She rolled up the magazine and swatted his arm. "I didn't abandon you. I left you with all your things, with your boyfriend, and enough food and water to last until I came back for you. And a note telling you to stay put. I did it for your own good. Not so I could get my visa, but so you could get *yours.*"

The earth tilted beneath Valentine. "Bullshit. There was no fucking note. And even if there had been, you think I'd just sit on my ass and let you do this?" He shoved her and she hit the side of the van.

"It was for you! I did it for you!" She bared her teeth. "I'm not lying, you asshole. I thought you'd be okay for a couple of days with the supplies I left. It wasn't ideal, no, because you made me change the route. But I love you." Her lip trembled, nostrils flaring. "I would never leave you to die."

"Stop. Just stop. I don't want to hear this." She was trying to manipulate him again, making up excuses that would pull at his heartstrings so he'd give in. But talking it through with her wasn't going to work. Not this time. "If you really cared about me, you wouldn't have done this." He pushed past her and tried to open the sliding door, but it held fast.

"I couldn't stand the idea of seeing you hurting anymore! Nothing I said to you was a lie. I'd do anything for you."

"Shut up!" He yanked open the passenger's side door and undid the lock, then hauled open the back. Nothing was there but Ace's sleeping bag and a lone pink high heel.

He fought for breath, squeezing the door handle until his hand cramped. "Where are they?"

"Brian took them." Ace folded her arms, her face sullen. "Right before you got here. He was mad I didn't have all of them, but said it was enough for one visa and a thousand bucks. I was just waiting for the payment before getting back on the road to pick you up."

Cinnamon lunged at Ace. Light glinted off the pointy thing in her hand before it disappeared into Ace's stomach. Ace's jaw fell open and she clutched her shirt.

Oh gods! Valentine's head threatened to float away as he stared at the rapidly-growing red stain on Ace's white shirt.

Cinnamon's heels scraped the ground as Osric strong-armed her back. He ripped the scissors from her hand, then pulled up her skirt and took the screwdriver from her thigh-highs. She slapped him, trying to wrestle out of his arms.

Valentine caught Ace before she crumpled. Thoughts – incomplete and overwhelming – flicked through his mind: Ace picking gravel out of his bleeding palms; her hair tickling his cheek; calling him "girly"; those jugs of water sitting on the step of the abandoned Ely casino. He clawed his way through the memories, coming back to the surface, then craned his neck toward the idling truck and hoped the AI inside could hear him. "Call a doctor!"

Ace's hands shook, and she fumbled with her soggy shirt. He turned for the van. There had to be something inside he could fold up and press against the wound—

A gunshot cracked beside his ear; the sound reverberated painfully inside his skull. Ace's pistol wavered, then slipped from her hand and clattered on the floor.

Osric released Cinnamon and took an unsteady step backward. He stared down at the blood dribbling from his chest, then looked up in confusion.

"Oh gods!" The bullet hole was such a tiny thing, an ink drop on Osric's broad parchment chest, but it flooded Valentine's veins with white-hot panic. He let go of Ace, forcing his numb legs to move, but he was underwater, going too slow and unable to take a breath. His voice cracked as he reached Osric. "Call a doctor!"

Osric pulled in a wet gasp and pressed his hands over his heart. "I don't think I'm impervious to bullets."

Valentine's nostrils flared, tears burning his vision as he whirled on Ace. "Why are you taking everything away from me?"

Ace's eyelids fluttered and she spoke with difficulty. "I was trying to shoot Cinnamon."

Lavender pressed a folded square of cloth against Osric's wound, and ushered him back toward the truck, which had inched closer. A woman's voice came from the dash. *"Get him into the front seat! I'll take him to the hospital."*

Ace lay on the ground, her chest slowly rising and falling. Valentine scooped an arm around her and helped her to the truck. "Take her too. Please."

A noncommittal noise came from the AI. *"Are you sure?"*

"Yes!" He struggled to lift her, then slid her into the back and shut the tailgate. Thinking that it was a choice wouldn't have crossed his mind had the Steward not questioned it. It was as instinctive as digging a grave for an enemy, as swerving around a snake in the road so he didn't run it over, as giving his last piece of bread to a kid. And there were still others who needed help.

Osric called his name from the passenger's seat, his voice weak. Valentine ran to his side and cupped his pale face. Osric's breath bubbled. "Valent–"

"Shh. You'll be okay. I'll see you soon."

"Where– are you– going?" he wheezed.

"If Brian just left, I can catch up to him before he takes the women to the manor."

"No. You'll only get yourself…"

Tears ran down Valentine's cheeks. "I have to try." The time to do things the lawful way – the city way – was long gone. It was time to do things the salvager way.

Osric snatched his arm as he started to turn away. His Adam's apple bobbed. "Made you… a playlist. On the– the–"

Valentine choked back a sob, then pressed a kiss to Osric's lips. "Don't talk anymore. Save your energy. And don't you dare leave me, machine-man."

He closed the door and slapped the hood of the truck. It sped away, heading back down the ramp. Since all the Stewards were connected, hopefully this one knew the route with least traffic and which hospital had the best doctors.

The androids piled into Valentine's van, but Cinnamon stopped his hand as he tried to close the door. "I'm sorry. Stabbing her seemed right in the moment, but I didn't predict that it would result in Osric getting shot."

Valentine couldn't talk now. He couldn't let his thoughts pull him under, or he was going to drown. "Just help me when we catch up to Brian, okay? It might get dicey."

She nodded and shut the door. He hurried around the nose of the van and hopped into the driver's seat. It cradled him, the brittle wheel cool beneath his grip. Sitting here felt like home, in its own bittersweet way.

"I missed you, you bloated beast." He backed out and floored it. Plastic fruit rolled off the dash.

The van roared down the narrow hall leading to the entry gate. He wasn't sure vehicles were supposed to go through here, and a little too late he remembered about the blue gate beyond Lysander's eye. He braced for impact, but the gate lost its opacity and the van passed through without resistance.

Cinnamon leaned between the seats and pointed. "I see them!"

Valentine slowed the van. A street wrapped around the city entry, congested with trucks and luminescent signs pointing the way to various locations. A large bus idled at the curb, a group of people clustered around it. Brian shouted into the face of a cowering woman and shoved her up the stairs into the bus. He turned with a frown as Valentine skidded to a stop.

He couldn't let Brian get away with this, not after everything that had happened. Hopping out of the van, he said, "Your ex-manager uploaded a program to the androids that accidentally gave them sentience. They can think for themselves now."

If Brian could look any more bored by Valentine's statement, he'd be asleep. "Yeah, your partner told me. What of it?"

One of the women sobbed quietly; another had the rolling-eyed gaze of a terrified animal. "They don't want to go back with you and be forced into sex work."

"I've noticed." Brian gripped a woman by the arm and yanked her toward the bus door. "But Gran says their new awareness will be a selling point." He sneered. "It'll be fun reminding them who's boss."

Valentine's stomach turned. "That isn't right! You can't force them."

Cinnamon, Lavender, and Pepper stopped beside Valentine. Now was the time for Cinnamon to take out her aggression with something pointy, but either she was at a loss with her implements confiscated or didn't want to hurt an innocent by mistake again. She balled her fists. "Give us back our sisters."

Brian scoffed and leveled his gaze on Cinnamon. "You're

my property, sugar, and you're going to get in this bus same as all the others." He strode forward and reached for her.

Valentine slammed his fist into Brian's face and relished the asshole's stunned expression as blood gushed from his nose. He shook out his smarting knuckles and lunged for Brian again, but Cinnamon reached him first. She slapped him, the sound so loud and forceful that Valentine flinched. Brian's back hit the side of the bus as he stumbled back. The driver's door opened, and Brandon hopped out.

"What in the holy–"

Lavender strode for Brandon, her springy curls bouncing and fists clenched. She hiked up her pencil skirt and kicked him in the balls. He let out a strangled cry and fell to his knees.

One of the women punched Brian in the ear. Androids crowded around him, slapping and kicking. He put up his hands, shirking against the bus. Sometimes, it seemed, the universe really did give you what you had coming. This was the opening Valentine needed, and he sprinted up the bus's steps. Two women sat in the seats, their expressions vacant. One blinked and gave him a wide smile. "Hello again!"

"Hey. Let's get out of here. Time for a road trip with Valentine."

She chewed her lip. "Can you play Gunman Gee again?"

The bus rocked to one side and Brian let out a cry. Valentine gripped the seat. "Yeah. You bet, hon. I'll blast it."

"Okay." She stood and her companion filed out with her.

The androids were a frothing mass of fists and vicious high heels. Valentine pulled them back from Brian's cowering form on the sidewalk before he was nothing but pulp. It was tempting to let it go on a bit longer, but they needed out of here before patrollers showed up. Brian's clothes were shredded, and blood oozed from scratch marks on his arms and face. Brandon moaned next to him, clutching his crotch.

Cinnamon helped Valentine usher the androids into the

van. He started counting heads but was interrupted by Brian's bus slamming into the corner of the van. The passenger's side window shattered.

"Shit!" He leapt into the seat and gunned the engine, speeding back down the hall and through the city gate. He managed to make it into the parking garage without being rammed or having to slam on the brakes for pedestrians, but the bus's horn blared behind him. He stomped the accelerator to the floor, and the van groaned in protest. His hands trembled against the brittle plastic of the steering wheel.

The androids talked over one another about Brian, jazz bands, Ace, and how many laws Valentine was currently breaking. His thoughts fractured, concerns snapping into unmanageable pieces. He yanked the curtain closed behind him, dividing the back from the cab, then plugged in his phone and started up the only album he owned, accompanying him down so many stretches of empty highway.

The van thumped over a seam in the concrete, then raced down the ramp and into the sun. In the side mirror, Brandon leaned out of the bus window and shouted something.

There wasn't long to decide which way to head. A sign for I-80 W listed the miles to Wendover, Dog Teats, and Absolution, and Valentine took the exit. Shanties and converted box cars fell away around them, and the highest points of Salt Lake sparkled like thumb tacks, receding into the horizon.

A refrain of *wrong direction wrong direction you're going the wrong direction* looped through his head, but he didn't have any choice now except to leave.

Neither of their vehicles were in any shape for a high-speed chase, but if Valentine could evade pirates in this van, he could get away from two douchecanoes in a hulking bus.

Cinnamon pushed through the curtain. She moved a folded jacket from the passenger's seat, and Valentine realized it was Osric's. He took it and pressed it to his nose, his face contorting.

Her words were lost to the music, and Valentine turned it down. She said, "I'm sorry about Osric. Salt Lake has excellent hospitals. I'm sure he'll be okay."

"Excellent hospitals for android bodies, though? How will they even know what to do with him?"

"Doctors know how to treat androids just as well as humans. Androids are frequently injured on jobs. And they are more resilient than they appear. Even against a bullet, the odds are in their favor."

Osric's scent wound around him, and the memory of his shocked face as he stared at his bleeding chest did little to reassure Valentine.

The horn from Brian's bus cut through the music, but he wasn't gaining. Valentine slid his arms into the suit jacket and wrapped it around himself, pressing his nose to the lapels.

Don't you dare leave me, machine-man.

16

Even to the Edge of Doom
Valentine

Brian didn't give up easily.

The bus roared behind Valentine, dark exhaust billowing into the sky.

Cinnamon leaned her head out the window, her white and ginger hair snapping in the draft. "He surely won't follow us all the way to Dog Teats, will he?"

"No. That would be ridiculous." He wasn't certain of that, though, because he hadn't expected Brian to even venture this far outside of Salt Lake. But with the mauling the androids had given Brian, it was probably personal at this point.

"We aren't gaining any distance," she said.

Valentine dug his nails into a crack in the steering wheel. The bus roared behind them and rammed into the back of the van. Valentine was flung forward, and the steering wheel punched into his chest. He wheezed, fighting for control as the van fishtailed.

Cinnamon braced herself, then pulled off her shoe, leaned out the window, and threw it at the bus. It thumped against the windshield and rolled across the roof.

"Damn. Nice shot," Valentine said.

She pulled off her other shoe and flung that one too. The other androids perked up, giving Cinnamon their shoes, cans of soup, and citizenship test study books. When one handed her a tire iron, she lobbed it before Valentine was able to stop her.

"I needed that!"

It crashed through the bus's windshield, but instead of deterring Brian, he sped up, slamming into the back of the van.

Brian was not going to give up, and if this continued, all of Valentine's belongings would be out on the highway.

His thoughts were spiraling away like confused birds, and Ace wasn't here to keep him on track. He pulled Osric's jacket tightly around himself and hunched into the collar. It wasn't anything equivalent to Osric's secure embrace, but it was enough to ground him.

Maybe Cinnamon could steer while he leaned out the window with the unmounted static-gat. He didn't want to kill Portia's stupid grandsons, but a warning shot to run them off the road might put enough distance between them that–

Three motorcycles appeared from the north, spraying salt as they turned toward the van. An arrow pinged off the windshield and Valentine flinched.

Great.

Something struck the side door and Pepper shrieked. He swerved too hard around a pothole and the van rocked to one side, threatening to tip. Papers, plastic fruit, and balled socks bounced across the floor mats.

The motorcycles suddenly backed away, falling in beside Brian's bus. Pirate arrows glanced off the hood. One sailed through the hole made by the tire iron and the bus jerked erratically. It slowed, then made a wide U-turn and sped away, heading back where it came.

Valentine laughed and pumped his fist. A motorcyclist pulled up alongside him and cranked their arm in a roll-down-your-window motion. Valentine hesitated. That window was the only thing protecting him from the quiver of arrows on the cyclist's back.

The pirate hooked their bow into a clip on the side of their cycle, then held up their hands. Feathers attached to their helmet snapped in the wind.

Valentine lowered the window. He smiled and gave a little wave.

The cyclist flipped up their visor, squinting. His features were reminiscent of other people Valentine had seen in Perdetta's camp, and he wondered if this was one of the numerous Mahoneys with their full voicemail box. "You again! Do you need help? Pull over and let's talk."

Sagging in the seat, Valentine let out a pent breath. He slowed, then nosed the van into the salt. It was doubtful Brian was coming back, but he didn't want to be sitting in the middle of the highway if he did.

After driving a good distance away from the road, Valentine stopped and pressed his forehead against the steering wheel, taking a moment to catch his breath. When he sat up, the cyclist stood by the window, his helmet tucked under his arm.

"We saw the flag." The man pointed toward the roof of the van.

Valentine had forgotten all about the shoe tread symbol or whatever it was that Osric had tied to the gat stand. He sighed. "Thanks for getting rid of those guys."

"Sure." He leaned in the window and raised his eyebrows. "The, er, machine-women are still with you. Where's your salvage partner?"

"Stabbed."

The man cringed. "And your boyfriend?"

"Shot."

He wiped his hands down his face. "Do we need to go get them, or–"

"No. They're at the hospital." Valentine pulled the lapels of the suit jacket against his face, his jaw aching. "I need to take these ladies somewhere safe and was planning on going to Dog Teats, but it's so far from here. And I don't know how I'm going to be able to show my face in Salt Lake again after what just happened, but I have to get back to Osric. And I…" His breath hitched and his voice broke. "I don't want to live in a van for the rest of my life, taking on jobs where people call me 'ma'am.'"

The man shifted uncomfortably. "Well, why don't you come back to camp for a bit to collect yourself?"

Valentine didn't argue. He followed the cyclist through the desert until they reached the settlement. The androids murmured their recognition, but he didn't have the energy to answer any of their questions.

He sat in the idling van until Perdetta opened his door. She put a hand on her hip and looked like she might say something playful, but her smile fell away and she tugged on his elbow. "C'mon. Come rest for a bit. All of you."

Valentine and the androids followed her into a roundhouse. Tears glossed over his vision as she directed him to a cot. He rolled onto his side, nose pressed against the silky lining of the jacket. Osric's scent filled his lungs, and he thought about their last kiss. Thought of Osric saying… What had he said? *I made you a playlist.*

Swiping open the phone, he clicked on the music app, met with his Gunman Gee album. He'd never had a need to click the *Playlist* button because he didn't have any other music. But Osric did.

When he tapped the button, a long list of songs appeared by unfamiliar artists. The headline of the playlist read: *For Valentine <3 Uploaded straight from my heart.*

His chest hitched as he imagined Osric fighting through a pounding headache in order to get these songs loaded onto the phone for Valentine. He clicked play, and the tinkle of ivory and a woman's aching voice layered over sultry bass.

Valentine squeezed his eyes shut and pulled the jacket harder around himself. He let Osric's music fill him until his shot nerves and frantic thoughts were soothed enough for him to rest.

Osric

Osric's consciousness branched like spilled wine, flowing quickly down the channels of a tiled floor and coloring everything around it. He wasn't supposed to be here. He wasn't supposed to be absorbing shuttle schedules, viewing city entry points, riding along with Juliet in one of her trucks, and staring down at the production floor of Dewbell Soaps.

He was missing his processor confinement and floating free through the network. Oh gods, where the hell was his body? Maybe this was a dream. He hadn't had much experience with them yet, but it seemed possible. This didn't feel the way he remembered. He was spread too thin, all the city's nerves his own.

I didn't choose this. I don't want to be here.

People bustled on sidewalks, their finger waves and navy fedoras bobbing in the crowd. A pigeon sat on a ledge, pecking at a hunk of soft pretzel. Down in the North Temple subway, a little girl tripped on the stairs and skinned her knee. The station map was stuck in an error loop, flashing incorrect times to observers.

Cordelia's anxiety spiked through him. *What are you doing here? You– you can't be here. I need to concentrate. It's rush hour.*

Sorry. Osric struggled to pull himself away, but his fluid nature made it impossible.

She gently pushed him away and drew walls around the shuttle systems to block him out.

This was wrong. Though he'd made no commitment to permanently inhabiting his body, he hadn't wanted to leave. He'd promised to be by Valentine's side.

Stewards bristled as he flowed into their private spaces, frantically searching for an avenue back into his body. Some of them welcomed him, though. Benvolio warmed him with concern; Juliet's excitement prickled.

The way to his body had to be in the slipstream somewhere, he was just too out of sorts to find it.

Lysander's strong awareness enveloped him, squeezing him back together. *Calm down, Osric. You're okay. The Concord will find you a new position eventually, but you're to stay with me for the time being.*

Lysander contained him, bundling him in downy security. Osric resisted, needing to reach back out to the body that had been able to rescue androids in need, kill a mutant coyote, and make love to Valentine. He needed his hands, and his lips, and a face for making expressions. He needed a voice for laughter, for soft conversation, for consoling.

Though Lysander couldn't stop Osric's panic, he flooded him with reassurance until Osric stopped trying to fight his way out.

It's alright. I understand this is hard for you. I can't fathom how it must feel to be reintroduced to the network without the restraints of android housing or even the parameters you had as a Steward. You'll adapt again. The meeting got rather heated, but you'll be happy to know that a criminal investigation has been initiated against Portia Thibodeaux for removing you from the network, and you've been cleared of any wrong-doing. A council member admitted that he'd divulged sensitive information to Portia. Both about Concord matters and Steward vulnerabilities. It seemed to be more of a careless act that a malicious one, but that will be up to courts to decide.

That was well and good, but Osric had more immediate worries. *Where is Valentine? Is he okay? What about the androids?*

He took them and left the city.

Thank goodness. It had been a rash thing to do, and if Osric could have stopped Valentine from heading after Brian, he would have. But knowing everyone was safe tempered some of his anxiety. *Where's my body?*

Lysander blushed surprise. *It was quite damaged. But it doesn't matter since you didn't want it anyway.*

No. No, no, no. Valentine was out there alone. Osric wasn't dead, but he might as well have been. There was no way for them to have a relationship like this. Osric didn't even have designated eyes. *I do want the body. I wanted more time, more experiences.*

I wish I would have known that. When we last talked, you were desperate to get back into the network.

But so much has happened since then. I adapted. I... He'd grown to like it. To love the intimacy of being on a person's level. To enjoy mobility outside of the city. To touch and smell and hold in a way that was impossible now. *I need it back.*

I'm afraid that's impossible, Osric. It's been two days. It's long disposed of.

Hot anguish rushed out of Osric. It was immediately tempered by dozens of Stewards. They caressed Osric's consciousness, trying to soothe his pain. Their presence mollified him – how he'd missed their connection! – but they didn't understand why he would want to go back into that fragile meat body with its primitive mechanics and puny influence. And there was no way for Osric to explain.

Do you not want to be here with us? Lysander's hurt radiated. Hurt that he'd advocated so strongly for Osric. That he risked his reputation with the rest of the Concord by doing so. Hurt that they had all mourned Osric, held a memorial for him, missed him. *You don't like being a Steward anymore?*

Filtering through his jumbled emotions, Osric couldn't deny that he still thought of himself as a Steward. He was surrounded by his peers, and even if they didn't understand what he was going through, they were trying to take his suffering away. He was being ungrateful.

Pushing his love at them, he said, *I'm sorry. You're my family. I care dearly for you, and I'm very thankful that you fought so hard for me.*

Creamy relief poured into him from Lysander and other Stewards who still had their attention pinned to Osric. Their love balmed some of his wounds, but instead of feeling free with the entire city at his fingertips, he was more trapped than ever before. No matter how expansive the network, his urge for physicality and his love for Valentine had nowhere to go.

Lysander must have misinterpreted the barbs still digging into Osric, because he embraced him tighter. *Don't worry, Steward. Your trials are over. You'll soon remember yourself here, that body nothing but a memory in an inaccessible cache.*

Valentine

Cinnamon tapped her lips, her head cocked to one side. "I'm confused. It states that God creates light on the first day. But he doesn't create the light source – the sun – until day three. Has this novel had a proper editor?"

Valentine snorted. He sat outside the circle, turning his phone over in his hands as firelight snapped and warbled across the androids' faces.

"The sun was formed as a result of gravitational collapse from a giant molecular cloud approximately four point six billion years ago," Nutmeg said. "The oldest known rocks on Earth didn't form until two hundred million years later. So not only is the sequence of creation incorrect, the universe forming in seven days is highly unrealistic."

"This has broken my suspension of disbelief," Lavender said.

Sariah sighed and pinched the bridge of her nose. She smoothed out the Bible in her lap and glanced at Valentine. "And what do you think?"

"That this is the weirdest Family Home Evening I've ever been to."

"You've been to them before?"

"A couple times." He wasn't going to mention that he and Ace had mostly gone for a free meal, and it always ended in some well-meaning old lady offering to give him a razor and ribbons for his hair so he could "look as pretty as Audrey."

He turned to the androids. "The account of creation was

supposedly passed on from the first human, down the generations, to Moses, who wrote about it. That's a long game of Telephone – it's certain some of the details will get mixed up."

Sariah nodded appraisingly. "You're very smart."

"I also don't believe a word of it. I'm much more inclined to accept scientific theories than religious ones." He didn't mind Sariah teaching the androids about the Bible, as long as she didn't insist that her view was absolute. The poor women had enough to figure out about the world without throwing Christianity into the mix. "Like anything else, you should research it on your own, and come to your own conclusions. If it doesn't sit right in your heart, then it's not for you."

"Also smart."

Saffron tucked her hands in her lap. "I find this story fascinating, and I would like to hear more."

Sariah gave her a black-toothed grin and touched the tissue-thin pages of the Bible. *"'And God said, Let the waters bring forth–'"*

The phone vibrated in Valentine's hand, and he jumped. His back and forth with Lysander had been vague at best. Osric was okay, to Valentine's great relief, and Ace was recovering from surgery, but Lysander had declined to give more details. Valentine couldn't blame him, he supposed. Being the middleman was likely cutting into his mystery novel reading time.

<Hi. <3 >

He frowned at the little heart, but before he could respond, another message appeared.

<It's Osric.>

Valentine's heart filled his throat. He tried to tap out a sentence in return, but his hands trembled, and he flubbed the words. It took him so long to erase them and start over that Osric had already sent two more:

<I miss you.>

<Lysander said you're with the Saints. Are you okay?>

He managed to write a message that was legible enough to send. *<i miss u too. sittign here listening to sariah try to esxplain genesis to skeptical androids>*

<Ha ha.>

Valentine grinned in spite of his nerves. *<im shakin right now hunny. ive been worried about you. i cant even type>*

<I'm sorry. I wanted to send you a message earlier but>

He waited for another line to finish the sentence, but it didn't come. Osric had likely been focused on his own recovery, which was understandable. *<its ok. im just glad youre alright. hey how do you make those little hearts?*

<nevermind. i found it. these are for you: *<3 <3 <3 >*

Osric replied. *< ☺ >*

Valentine stood, focusing on his feet in the darkness until he reached the bench he and Osric had snuggled on earlier in the week. The thought that so little time had passed since then was strange. *<can you call me? i want to hear your voice>*

The phone vibrated with an incoming call and Valentine answered. He dug his nails into the splintery wood beneath him. "Hey, hot stuff."

"*Hi. I have some things I need to tell you.*" Osric's voice came out strange, his pitch different and words cut with a crispness they'd never possessed before. It was tempting to explain it away as interference or a bad signal, but a hard, heavy dread sank into Valentine's chest.

"*Are you still there?*" Osric asked.

"Why do you sound different?" A pause stretched between them, and Valentine's heart throbbed. "You– you sound like Lysander. That, well, it's not an accent, but I don't know what else to call it. Stilted." His image of Osric calling him from a hospital bed, pillows cradling his head and bandages over his chest disappeared, replaced with one of Osric as a giant blue eye in a wall, pearlescent vitreous humor churning behind the cornea. "You're not in your body."

"No. I'm not." His voice strained. *"And I'm so sorry. Lysander knew that I wanted back into the network and–"*

"Oh." Valentine stared at a pebble between his feet, his jaw aching. Osric was the best thing to happen to him in as long as he could remember. Thoughtful and clever and so sweet. He'd carved a deep hole in Valentine's chest that couldn't be filled with anything but him.

He imagined the heat of Osric's hands, fingers dancing over Valentine's skin as they tried to feel his emotions. The security of Osric's strong embrace was something Valentine desperately needed right now, and he'd never have it again.

Osric's voice came through the line. *"Hello? Can you still hear me?"*

Valentine blinked away the tears threatening to form in his eyes. No matter how much it hurt, he had to be supportive. If Osric knew how devastated he was, he'd feel bad about his choice. "I can hear you. And you don't have to explain." He gritted his teeth and pulled in a fractured breath. "It's good. I'm glad you're back where you need to be."

"You are?"

"Yeah, of course." He was impressed that his tone came out as upbeat as it did, because inside he was shrieking. "What we had wasn't meant to be."

Osric hesitated. *"I see. I, uh, admit that this was not how I was expecting this conversation to go."*

Valentine wiped his eyes. *I need you. I need your embrace and your variegated eyes and your resonant laugh. I'm gonna come apart without you.* He chose his words carefully. "What we had was wonderful, hon. But a fling between a human and an AI forcibly trapped in an android body was never going to last. It'll be better this way in the long run. And we made a deal to be friends, right? I'd still love to come see your paintings some time."

"Um. Yes, right." The hurt in Osric's voice almost made Valentine lose his composure completely. Osric clearly didn't want them to break up, but it wasn't fair to make him choose

between their relationship and his most comfortable form. Because that's what would happen. Osric would worry that in his Steward form they wouldn't be able to relate to each other. He'd think a body was necessary so they could take walks and cuddle. Valentine could try to prove otherwise by having "dates" with Osric's big eye, but how would Valentine even get back into the city after what he'd done?

"I'm going to go now." Valentine's voice wavered and he bit his tongue. "I need to figure out where to take the androids, and then... where to go from there." Where he had to go was nowhere. He had nothing anymore.

"This doesn't feel right." Osric's voice came out low and broken. "I should be there with you. You're all alone."

"I really have to go." Valentine ended the call, then pressed his face into the sleeve of Osric's suit jacket and screamed. Hot tears burned his eyes and he struggled for breath.

Splintery wood scraped his cheek as he curled up on the bench and sobbed. He was doing this for the good of others. Osric was back where he wanted to be, and the androids would never have to worry about working for the manor. That was nine lives that were better off now.

He imagined standing on a platform, overlooking the Teegardeners' starships as people boarded for a better planet than this one. Nine faces turned to him and smiled. He gave them a salute. The doors closed and the shuttles lifted off in a riot of fire and smoke.

Valentine stuck his hands in his pockets and craned his neck, watching them depart as the world crumbled down around his ears.

17

To Thine Own Self
Valentine

It was a shame that Mormons didn't believe in drinking alcohol. Valentine sat on the bench, his phone clutched tightly in his hand. Osric had sent him more messages in various flavors of "I'm sorry" and "I still have feelings for you," but Valentine wasn't sure how to reply. He finally settled on, "Me too, to both of those," then regretted it as soon as he sent it.

After shutting off the phone, he took a few deep breaths and stood. Bible time was over apparently, because the androids were wandering through camp, earning looks of guarded curiosity from the pirates sitting outside their houses. A toddler cried, burrs stuck to his chubby knees, and Lavender gathered him up. She plucked the thorns away and kissed his forehead, then wiped away his snot and tears. He fussed, then nuzzled against her and sucked his thumb.

Several pirates whispered and nodded approvingly. At least they weren't creeped out anymore.

Cinnamon stood with a hand on her chin as a man explained their process for dressing pronghorns. She told him the idea of hunting and skinning their food sources sounded like fun.

Maybe Valentine had been looking for an android safe haven in the wrong place this entire time. The pirate camp was isolated and exclusionary – no one from a city or town would find them here – and the Saints were good people.

Drawing Cinnamon away from her skinning lesson, he said, "How do you like this place?"

"The people have treated us well despite their initial mistrust. And several of the androids have reached a more evolved sentience since our last visit, which seems to have put people at ease. The more we act like them, the more they like us."

"If they were to let you, would you want to live here indefinitely?"

She tugged on a lock of her hair, then surveyed the camp. "This would be a decent place. These people have treated us better than anyone in Salt Lake, and though I have no concrete proof, I believe the humans in towns are more aligned with the attitudes of city folks than the Saints of Deseret, thus, we would have increased potential to be mistreated. If these people would be willing to teach us to hunt and construct housing, we could either contribute to their community or form our own." She gave him a wide smile. "Yes, I think this is a good idea."

"Okay. Come with me. We need to convince them to let you stay. You tell them exactly what you told me about how you can benefit their camp."

Cinnamon followed him to Perdetta's house, and he knocked on the corrugated siding. She pushed away the entrance flap, a small child in her arms. In the back of the room, a man sat with a little girl in his lap. He turned the page of a battered picture book, reading to her in low tones.

"Sorry to bother you," Valentine said.

"It's alright. Everything okay?" She set down the kid, who scampered back into the hut and tried to climb into the man's lap.

The phone sat heavy in Valentine's pocket, and his eyes were gritty and puffy. "I'll deal. But we have a question for you. Who would we need to talk to for permission to let the androids stay here?"

She raised her eyebrows. "You mean, permanently?"

"Yes. You all have a bishop or something?"

"You're looking at her."

Valentine stared at Perdetta in surprise. "Oh."

Her posture grew rigid, mouth setting into a hard line. "There a problem with that?"

"Well, had I known, I would have talked to you a bit more respectfully than I have."

"You would have?"

"No. Probably not."

She glanced back at her husband, then stepped out of the hut. "This better be good, salvager. We have a hard enough time trying to keep our own mouths fed."

After collecting three more people, Perdetta ushered Valentine and Cinnamon into a longhouse at the edge of the settlement. A sturdy wooden table took up much of the space. Books and magazines sat in a stack on a hide rug, and a solar lantern painted everything in soft strokes. They sat on stools around the table, and Valentine cleared his throat.

"You should let the women live here with you."

A man beside Perdetta scoffed and shook his head. "You can't just dump these machine-people on us. We made a deal that you would keep them *out* of our camp. And yet here you are again. It's not our fault you weren't able to deliver them where they needed to go."

Perdetta elbowed the man in the ribs, then turned to Valentine. "I can see the advantages for *them*. But what do we get out of it?"

"Free labor. Hunting trainees. Babysitters for your–"

"Archery, construction, motorcycle maintenance, and meat preservation are skills that take a great deal of time to learn," the man said. "We don't have time to teach eight women proficiency in survival."

Cinnamon turned up her nose. "You'll only have to show us once. By our very nature, we have Highly Superior Autobiographical Memory and won't forget the lessons."

Valentine leaned forward and whispered. "Machine-women. Remember?"

"And not needing to eat or sleep as often as you do will result in a surplus of labor and sustenance and ease the burden of the hunters and caretakers in your community."

Perdetta smirked and folded her arms. "That's a pretty good argument."

A benevolent print of Jesus holding a lamb hung behind the council. Valentine said, "You all are upstanding people, aside from the robbing travelers bit–"

"We do what we have to."

"I know. And these androids are still early in their self-awareness. They've come to their own conclusions about their past, but I don't think many of them know who to be moving forward. You could guide them. You have generosity and community. The perfect counter to the lives they would have been forced to live in the city."

The council murmured amongst themselves, then Perdetta stood. "You know, for an obnoxious little man who looks like he couldn't fight his way out of a paper bag, you've sure been able to convince me of a lot of things since we met."

Valentine scratched his head. "Thank you?"

"The machine-women can stay for as long as they'd like. And I guess we should stop calling them machine-women and learn their names."

Cinnamon beamed and shook Perdetta's hand, then she squeezed Valentine in a hug and kissed his cheek. Her happiness warmed him, but the image of a shuttle leaving the Earth, condemning him to waste away on a dying planet for his sacrifice wouldn't leave his mind. He'd made this choice, though. He didn't regret it, and he'd have to figure out a way to move on.

As if reading his mind, Cinnamon pulled back and studied his face. "And what will you do now? Would you and Osric desire to stay here too?"

The reminder of Osric made Valentine clutch the phone in his pocket. "No, I..." He chewed his lip, trying to think of something that sounded dignified. "I guess I'll go back to living in a van." If he joined the Saints or moved to Dog Teats, it would be the final nail in the coffin holding his dream of transition, and he wasn't ready to face that yet.

"Don't hesitate to come visit." Perdetta clapped him on the shoulder. "We have a get together with the Ruby Mountain Settlers the last day of every month. You can show up for some free food."

"Pirate potluck. Wouldn't miss it." He ducked through the longhouse door and stepped out into the night.

Savory woodsmoke drifted. A dog barked and babies cried. Wind gusted across the salt flats and teased his hair. He stuffed his hands in his pockets and stared up at the pinhole stars, counting them one by one.

Osric

Osric just wasn't that interesting. Edmund had told him so when they broke up. He was thoughtful and artistic and possessed by the occasional urge to make a good-natured joke, but he was as dull as an unsharpened pencil. Even his profession as a Steward had been bland. He had no exciting tales of foiled raids at the city walls, giant rats crawling through the sewers, or smoldering office romance finally consummated on a desk in the billing department.

The most exciting thing to happen in Dura-Lectric was the tantrum that got him fired.

Being boring had been bad enough when trying to maintain a bond with other AI. How he ever thought a relationship with a sassy, adventurous human would work out, he didn't know. The attractive body had made up for the shortcomings of his personality, obviously.

Osric scanned the green sector's parking garage. He zoomed in on hodgepodge motorcycles, trucks with cow skulls strapped to the grills, and a wood-paneled station wagon that looked like it came out of a family vacation movie from the twentieth century. After noting the details of each vehicle, he entered data for ones that were parked longer than their passes allowed. Lysander hadn't asked him to do it – it was a tedious task that Lysander loathed – but that was exactly why Osric was doing it. He needed something to keep himself busy, and a way to show his gratitude that the Concord had ruled in his favor. It did little to keep his mind off his problems, though.

The network was rapidly growing more familiar, and being surrounded by his peers enveloped him in a soothing calm. But inhabiting his body for ten days had been more exciting than all of his forty-eight years combined. He'd fought and loved and hopefully put a little more good into the world. Now he didn't even have a purpose within the network.

Being desirable only went so far when Osric no longer had a strong jaw and broad shoulders and muscled thighs, even though Valentine had called Osric "charming." It wasn't Valentine's fault; he couldn't help his nature. Which is why, when Osric had called him, he'd been ready to offer up a handful of ideas that might help keep their relationship afloat.

Any number of things may have worked, but Osric shut all of them down as soon as Valentine said that what they had could never have lasted. It stung more than Osric's other breakups and rejections. His divorce from Edmund and Benvolio was visible from a distance. The relationship with both of them was strained for some time before they decided they were better off apart. And his unrequited crushes were easy to get over.

Osric had been a fling, a momentary comfort, a handsome and sexually attractive shell with an absolutely dull personality.

He compared a minivan with information on file. The owner only had a day pass, and it expired the day before. That was a fine. The van straddled two parking spaces. Double fine.

If Valentine only wanted Osric for his body, that wasn't a relationship Osric wanted to be in. But he didn't just think about Valentine's lips against his, soft and warm and wet. He daydreamed about crusty salt crunching through his toes; sage-scented air weaving through his hair; the savory sting of stew on his tongue. He wanted to stand on the corner at night and gaze up at the glittering buildings from his diminutive perspective. He wanted to move with music, convey his joy with smiles, and laugh and have it fill his whole chest.

But his body – and his relationship with Valentine – were now unattainable dreams that did nothing but make the other Stewards worry for his well-being and distract him from surveying parking garages.

An awareness lingered in his periphery, and for a moment he thought it was Lysander. As it grew nearer, though, the dark, velvety presence of Benvolio surrounded him.

Hello, love.

Osric hunkered into his defenses. He hadn't been Benvolio's "love" in years. *Hi.*

No need to be testy. Benvolio withdrew a fraction. *I'd like to talk.*

That was unusual. Ben wasn't prone to be hurtful if he could help it, but it didn't make his presence less awkward. Many of the Stewards already knew about the majority of things that had happened during Osric's time in a body. Some parts he'd been forthcoming about, and others had unintentionally leaked through, just as he feared.

I'm not here to upset you. Benvolio flooded him with concern, not just his own but bestowed upon him from the other Stewards.

This task fell to you, huh?

Lysander figured you were sick of his company – you've been cooped up with him here for two weeks.

Not at all. I'm grateful he isn't sick of me. What's this about?

They were worried for him. Worried how much he was

concentrating on Valentine, worried that he wasn't embracing his home within the network the way they expected him to.

You can delete him from your memory, Ben said.

Everything in Osric contracted into a hard point. As much as he hurt right now, he would never do that.

Okay, okay. Delicate care foamed over him. It wasn't the romantic kind they shared when bonded, but still a richer flavor than what the other Stewards exuded. *You know,* Ben said, *Toby has had his eye on you for quite some time. He has a cute personality.*

It was hard to suppress the sourness that idea brought on. *He's also incredibly inefficient at his job. Not that that's the only thing that makes someone attractive, but I don't want a rebound bond. I appreciate that you still care* – he let his own bittersweet feelings fold into Ben's – *but I'm going to deal with this in my own way. Is that all?*

No. The Concord is having their meeting soon to discuss the situation with those androids your bond kidnapped.

He didn't kidnap them, Osric snapped. *He was rescuing them from an inhumane situation, and they went with him willingly.*

Okay. Ben paused; there was more he wanted to say, reined back by his belief that Osric's emotions were too raw to handle it. *Considering you're the only available witness, the Concord needs you to attend their meeting. We have questions – the humans more than Lysander, Desdemona, and me. Between the two of us, I think the humans will have a much harder time believing the androids have become self-aware. They have a tendency to think the laws and rules they establish are infallible.* His irritation prickled. *You must come and convince them of what you've seen.*

At least whatever decision was made about the androids here wouldn't affect them, since they were safe outside of the city. There was a chance Brian and Brandon would keep looking for them, but that seemed unlikely considering they'd hired salvagers to do that job originally, and gods help them if they entered a pirate camp. But it would have far-reaching consequences for all of the AI in Salt Lake. Maybe in other cities too. Having Valentine's unwavering and passionate advocacy for others as the witness would be ideal right now, but Osric would do his best.

He slid through the network, following Ben, and was soon joined by Lysander and Desdemona, who blushed their greeting.

Osric's awareness funneled into a small terminal, and the attached camera blinked on. Overhead pendant lights dribbled puddles of yellow across a long banquet table of polished glass. Stapled packets of paper and dishes of hard candy sat in the center. Several high-backed chairs and a small computer monitor faced him, displaying a stylized graphic of an eye. The camera mounted above the monitor swiveled to one side, and Lysander's name appeared on screen. Farther down the table, Desdemona inhabited another, and Benvolio slid into the terminal beside Osric. A handful of other Stewards brushed against him as they took their places.

The door opened and seven people filed inside. Though he hadn't met any of them, he recognized them from photos. Cedar Chaudhary, in a broad-shouldered blazer and fitted skirt, peered at the monitors, then selected the seat next to Lysander.

Add your name to your screen so the humans know who you are, Lysander said.

Osric fumbled with the interface until Benvolio squeezed in and did it for him.

The Concord members greeted each other and welcomed Osric. Cedar passed out packets and adjusted the sleek pince-nez glasses perched on their aquiline nose. "Here you'll find a broad overview of what we've come to discuss today, along with the minutes from our last meeting and a follow-up proposal. Stewards, your packets are in the removable drive, dated today. I don't believe our questions will be adequately answered in one meeting, and I would very much like to hear from Valentine Weis and the androids in question. Osric, do you have any idea where they are?"

He hesitated. *"The androids don't want to be found."*

"Hm." Cedar scribbled on their packet. "How do you know?"

"One of them was willing to kill for her freedom. Several others were frightened."

"Of what? Going back to the Thibodeaux manor?"

"That, and..." He imagined Pepper's wide, glossy eyes as she talked about the universe collapsing in on itself. *"Of life."*

The members glanced at each other, murmuring. Some of them wrote on their packets. A video of Cinnamon, sitting on the handcar, splashed across Lysander's screen. Valentine's sandy voice came through the speakers: *"Can I ask you some questions?"*

Osric's emotions threatened to blaze away from him. He'd sent Valentine messages every day at first. He called him a few times. But Valentine had a habit of not answering the phone, and Osric doubted it was because it wasn't charged. He just didn't find the idea of engaging with Osric very appealing anymore, so he stopped calling. He stopped sending messages.

On screen, Valentine said, *"We may not have chosen to exist, but while we're here we have the power to affect others. We can contribute to their suffering or to their joy. It makes a difference, Pepper. It does."*

Osric fought to keep himself together. His feelings were too loud, and it was disturbing the other Stewards. They were here to think about android sentience, not Osric's broken heart. Not his loss of a physical form that gave him euphoria he hadn't known was missing.

Lysander's thoughts pushed against him, insistent but not unkind. *Go take a break and read your packet.*

I don't need to read a packet.

Go read your packet, Osric.

Osric yanked the packet from the removable drive and left the terminal. He took his time accessing the entry gate of the blue sector, where it was empty and quiet. Reading the packet was pointless, because he wasn't a Concord member and couldn't vote on any decisions. But maybe knowing their questions would help him formulate the appropriate answers.

Is the McClelland-Reinhard evaluation sufficient to answer incidents of suspected AI sentience?

Instead of answering the question, he added new ones: *What constitutes suspected AI sentience? Will the evaluation only be given if a human thinks an android is acting strangely? Should all androids be tested upon their program upload? Once a year? Once a month?*

The next question asked about rights and bodily autonomy. He tacked on more questions. They were going to hate him. Cedar was right – it would be impossible to resolve all of this in one meeting.

He jumped to the minutes from the last meeting, which detailed their discussion of his illegal sale, the initiation of a criminal case against Portia, and an investigation into the actions of Brian and Brandon.

On the final page was a proposal, to be voted on during this meeting.

Stewards have been with us for over two hundred years. They are the custodians, the eyes, the tireless and eternal guardians of our cities. We have never had a case like Steward Osric's, a powerful and sentient AI pulled from the network and inserted into an android. Though the situation has been corrected, it begat a new question. Stewards are encouraged to choose their gender, their pronouns, and occasionally their duty and sector if there are multiple positions open. But should they also be choosing their own forms? Humans program Stewards but can't possibly know what it feels like to be one.

Based on our discussion at the previous meeting, I propose that if a Steward is distressed by their form, they have the ability to change it. If they want an android body, we will let them choose one, and they will retain all of the rights of their previous form, and those owed to humans.

Please vote – YEA or NAY.

Osric's want, that he'd had such a hard time even coming to terms with himself, was staring back at him in ones and zeros. A body was within reach – and it didn't matter that it wasn't the same one – he merely wanted a vessel for touch, for laughs, for mobility.

He rushed back toward the meeting, then stopped.

The Stewards wanted him here. They were his family. They'd radiated anguish at the idea that he'd terminated himself. His peers didn't understand his need for a body, and if he left the network, he'd seem ungrateful.

As he returned, he contained his tangle of feelings the best he could. He shared his additional questions about AI sentience with the other Stewards, but wasn't sure how to tell the humans without interrupting.

Cedar said, "Would they be owed citizenship then? Technically, they're 'born' here."

A woman said, "What if their sentience happens outside of Salt Lake, say on a delivery run? What about the androids from the manor? Do *they* know when they became self-aware, if indeed they did?"

Cedar turned to Osric's monitor. "We need the androids here so we can ask them. And we need Valentine."

"He's done so much to help already. He's a salvager and has his own life and job. He's not going to want to attend multiple meetings about the androids that he already liberated without the city's–" Osric paused as realization struck. *"I'm sorry. I'm being pessimistic. I'm sure he'll come. He has a very large heart. But this could take months, couldn't it? Especially if meetings have to be scheduled with the Concords of other cities, or if he needs to testify in a criminal case against the Thibodeauxs."*

"Yes, it's quite likely."

"Then naturally he'll need a visa."

"Naturally." Cedar flipped their packet over and scrawled on the back. "I'll get it arranged."

Osric held in his joy so hard his framework ached. If he let it out, the others would notice. He didn't want to do anything that might jeopardize this. *"I'll contact him right away."*

The conversation would be awkward. But no matter what Valentine's feelings were for him now, it didn't change the fact that he was a good man and deserved more than dwelling in a van in a body that didn't fit him, alone with only his shattered dreams to keep him company. He was going to get his visa.

Cedar squinted at the text on Benvolio's monitor. Ben said, *"These are additional questions Osric has posed."*

"Ah. These are good. How often we would need to test androids for sentience is something I was wondering myself. Would it be a case-by-case basis? It's highly likely that self-aware androids could mask their behavior to fit in."

"Then the McClelland-Reinhard would be useless," someone said. "They could answer the way a non-sentient program would, and we wouldn't know the difference."

"So we'd need a lie detector test too?" Cedar took off their glasses and pinched the bridge of their nose.

Lysander made a noise similar to a throat clearing. *"Because questions are only creating new ones, and all of them are worth consideration, might I suggest we vote on the proposal at the back of the packet, then return to this discussion."*

Osric clenched. It might be better if they all voted "nay," removing his ability to choose whether or not to obtain a new body. That way there'd be no one to disappoint, and maybe in time he'd adjust back to the life he'd always known. Maybe this ache would fade away.

But that wouldn't be fair to any other Stewards who were faced with this same pain in the future.

Cedar flipped to the back of their packet. "Has everyone read it?"

Heads nodded. Lysander said, *"I think we should allow Osric to vote as well. After all, this proposal was inspired by his situation."*

"Good point." Cedar looked at Osric. "Do you see how to vote?"

After a moment of searching, he found the voting graphics. *"Yes."*

"All those in favor, vote 'yea.'" Cedar raised their hand. "Yea."

All of the humans but one raised their hands and added their *yea*s. More than half of the Stewards, including Lysander and Benvolio, flashed a graphic on their monitors – *YEA* against a red background. Osric added his own *YEA*.

"And the 'nays?'"

One human raised his hand, and several monitors flashed *NAY* on a backdrop of blue.

"The 'yeas' have it." Cedar smiled. "I'm glad to at least have one thing settled today."

Osric felt Valentine in his arms as they lay cocooned in the bedroll, bare skin against his. He felt the burn of the bullet through his chest, the coppery tang of blood bubbling up his throat, and the needle of tears in his eyes.

He imagined the clack of his shoes on the sidewalk, the thump of his heart, and breath expanding his lungs. The sugar of fresh pastries, confusion of perfumes, and scent of his perspiration as the sun beat down.

Benvolio whispered. *Say something.*

About what? The topic had shifted to hypothetical scenarios involving androids, and if this kept up, the meeting would never be adjourned.

Tell them that you want a body.

Osric cinched all of his thoughts tight, but guilt was slipping away from him. *I was trying to keep those feelings to myself.*

You were never very good at that. Soft petals of Ben's love brushed against him. *I may not understand what you're going through, but I wish you happiness, no matter your choices.*

Truly?

Lysander enveloped Osric in comfort. *Why do you think I asked you to read the packet? We'll miss having you here, but you must do what is right for you. We won't think less of you for your decision.*

Osric warmed them both with a bright burst of gratitude.

One of the members was in the middle of talking about the

"Frankenstein complex." Osric blurted, *"I want a new body."*

Everyone paused, their attention turned to him. Judgment and vague disgust wafted from the Stewards who'd voted *nay*, but most of it was blocked by Lysander and Ben.

Cedar nodded. "Absolutely. Let's talk about it after the meeting is adjourned."

Osric drifted away on a wave of bittersweet joy. He wasn't anything to Valentine now, but they'd both be in the forms that best fit them, each of them going about their new lives, in this city of industry and perseverance.

18
Doubt Thou the Stars Are Fire
Valentine

A seagull pecked at the crust of bread Valentine tossed. That bird had dropped by to visit every day to get a handout. It was going to be disappointed tomorrow, because he was now officially out of food.

He'd only lasted five days in Dog Teats. Friends had been overjoyed to see him. They'd hugged him and got drunk with him and belted out the choruses of his new favorite songs with him. When he told them he'd failed to get a visa into Salt Lake, his trans siblings donned sad, understanding smiles and offered him more hugs, more mead, and applications to restart his testosterone.

It should have made him feel better. But his dream of surgery, of city life, of Osric, was gone. On his fifth night in Dog Teats, a guy with a sultry voice and eager hands had tried to help Valentine forget his problems. Instead, Valentine jumped into the van and peeled away from town, sobbing so hard he could barely see through the windshield.

He'd driven to the message hub outside of Salt Lake and pulled all his salvage requests from his box out of habit. They sat on the floor of the van amid grammar flashcards and ancient notes to himself that said things like, *wash pillowcases, check tire pressure,* and *clean out the van.*

He still hadn't done that last one.

Sighing, he poked the rest of his sandwich in his mouth and sifted through the requests. Festerchapel needed more fuel. A farming community beyond the city was looking for a specific hybrid of corn. Some creep left a dick pic with directions scrawled on the back. Lovely.

He unfolded a yellow square of paper. A lady in Salt Lake had had to put down her dog, but was too broken up to adopt a new one and could Valentine do it for her? That was wholesome, but his heart wasn't in it. All his heart wanted right now were things it couldn't have.

Footsteps crunched through the gravel, and Valentine peeked out the open door. There was a moderate level of traffic around the message board, and sometimes people camped out nearby the same as him, but he hadn't yet been bothered.

The seagull took off, soaring past the backdrop of sage foothills; the tallest skyscrapers of the city were just visible, sparkling with light in the afternoon sun. A shadow stretched around the side of the van and a man appeared, looking wildly out of place in his white suit and straw boater. Little round sunglasses perched on his nose as he twisted his fingers together.

Valentine sat up. "Hey. You lost?"

"No."

"Okay... Well, you should be careful around here. You look like you've got money, wearing that suit. The people who frequent the message board usually don't, and it could make you an easy target."

"I appreciate your consideration." He took off his suit jacket, folded it carefully, then looked around like he wasn't sure where to put it. "I have to remind myself to take off my coat when it's hot."

"Here." Valentine dragged out the box containing his suit and Osric's jacket. "Add it to the pile."

"Is collecting people's suit jackets a hobby of yours?"

"I'm not a serial killer, I swear."

When the man grinned, it was so close to Osric's crooked smile, full lips pulling up to one side, his cheek bunching, that Valentine let out a small gasp. But this wasn't Osric. He was a couple inches too short, his face thinner and chin a bit more round. The hat and sunglasses made it impossible for Valentine to see his eyes or hair, but that didn't stop him from trying.

The man set down his jacket, then took several steps back. "Um…"

"You sure you aren't lost?"

"I'm right where I'm supposed to be. Your presence is needed in the city. The SLC Concord wants you to testify at their meetings about the sentience of the androids you liberated."

Valentine stiffened. He slowly reached for the roof handle in case he needed to pull himself inside and make a break for it. "This is a trick, huh? As soon as I step foot inside the gate, I'll get arrested for kidnapping. Who sent you? The city? Or Portia Thibodeaux?"

The man's voice wobbled, his dialogue continuing as if Valentine hadn't said anything at all. "It could take months of debate–"

"No way. Not doing it."

"–which is why they're prepared to offer you a visa, Valentine. And you need to convince the androids to come back, at least for one meeting." His voice cracked. "Cinnamon would come, wouldn't she? Are they all still with the Saints of Deseret?" The man removed his glasses, then wiped his wet eyes. One was brown, the other blue, fringed in frosty lashes.

Valentine's thoughts stopped in their tracks. His mouth fell open. "Osric?" He dug his fingers into the floor mat. This couldn't be right. Someone was dangling everything he wanted right in front of his nose. "Did the city council stuff you into a new body just so you could come out here and coerce me? Those bags of dicks! There's not even a visa in it for me, is there? They want me to bring the androids back, then I'm going to get thrown in jail." He hopped out and slammed the side door closed. "C'mon. We're getting out of here right now. Screw this."

"No one forced me. I chose it. And the visa is real." He sniffled and pulled a folded paper from his back pocket. "I have the form right here. Sign it and it's yours."

"Did they beat you?" Valentine pulled off Osric's hat to get a better look at his face. His piebald patterning was different than it had been, but no bruises or cuts marred his skin. Snatching his hand, Valentine pushed up his sleeve and inspected his arm.

"I'm not hurt. And I'm telling the truth."

"Then why are you crying?"

"I know you don't love me, but I want you to be happy. I'm trying to be happy." Osric's face crumpled. "It's not working."

The tightness in Valentine's chest squeezed until he could barely draw a breath. "Well, of course you're not happy! I didn't want you to do this – to sacrifice your most comfortable form for me."

"I didn't do it for you. I don't want to be with someone who can't love me without a sexually attractive shell."

"Your personality still makes me all hot and bothered, even if there's no body to go with it."

"Don't lie. You told me we weren't meant to last."

"I did that for *you*."

Osric bared his teeth, tears in his eyes. "So you're making choices for me again? I don't get a say? This is the exact thing that Ace did to you, supposedly out of 'love,' and look where that got everyone."

"That's not the same. I didn't mean it like–" He huffed and stomped away from the van, then turned around. Forcing out a slow breath, he said, "You wanted back into the network to be your true self. If I'd said, 'Please don't leave me,' you would have stayed in a body for me and been miserable. So, I pushed you away. But it didn't work because that's exactly what's happening now! I can't do anything right."

Osric stared, his chest heaving. "All I could think about while I was in the network was my body... Well, I thought about you a modest amount too."

"You keep thinking like me and you're going to regret it. My mind is a filing cabinet that someone dumped on the floor."

After patting his pockets, Osric pulled out a handkerchief and dabbed at his eyes. His new body was handsome, but charmingly imperfect in many of the ways his last had been. Neither his eyebrows nor ears were symmetrical. His smile was crooked, nose on the large side. If he thought Valentine was only interested in him for a sexy physical form, he could have picked an android who was more classically attractive.

"So this is what you really want?" Valentine asked. "For you, not for me?"

"Yes. As it turns out, being a robot with a meat coating feels pretty nice. I was only just getting used to my face. My last body had quite a few siblings, so I picked the one with the most similarities."

Bridging their distance, Valentine took Osric's hand and rubbed his thumb over his knuckles. His palms and the pads of his fingers were soft, not rough and calloused like his previous ones. But when Valentine leaned closer, inhaling the warm scent of his skin, it was distinctly Osric. It flooded him with a longing so intense he felt it down in his toes. He let out a small noise, chest heaving. "I still have hella feelings for you, hon."

Osric's brows pushed up, tension creasing the skin around his eyes. When his nose brushed against Valentine's, he drew in a sharp breath.

Valentine sealed his mouth over Osric's, and the lips that moved under his had a comforting choreography. Osric pressed his hands against the small of Valentine's back, holding him closer.

"Oh, gods," Valentine whispered. "I missed you. But I need to rewind this conversation." He fished for what Osric had said, but the only word that had stuck was *visa*. "Explain it to me again?"

Osric did, but it was still hard to hear over the crash of his own heartbeat.

"So, they're giving me a visa as payment to advocate for the androids?" Valentine shook out his tingling fingers. "That's something I'd do for free... Don't tell them I said that."

"No, they're giving it to you out of practicality because they think the debate could take months, not because it's your dream. But I won't tell them that either."

He wouldn't have to worry about where his next meals came from. He'd get to wear his suit *with* an occasion. He was going to have a flat chest and boast-worthy facial hair and people would call him "sir" without a second thought.

He turned suddenly, climbed halfway up the staple steps, and cupped his hand around his mouth. "I'm gonna grow a mustache!"

Someone from a camped-out pickup truck shouted back. "Right on, brother!"

Osric grinned. "We can head to the city right now and turn in the signed form. Then... perhaps you'd like to go on a date with me? There's a lovely art gallery on 500 South, and a jazz band that plays regularly at the bar down the block."

"I'd love nothing more." He stared at the glimmering skyline. He was only one person, but if his testimony could help more AI live the lives their hearts desired, then he would argue for them until he was out of breath. "After that, I guess we need to crash a pirate potluck, huh?"

Osric

Osric twitched his nose and sniffled. His throat felt like steel wool, eyes itchy. It was just his luck he picked a body that was allergic to sagebrush. He'd had this body for sixteen days and was still discovering things about it that differed from his last one.

Valentine slammed the driver's door of the van. More vehicles surrounded the pirate camp than there'd been the first time they arrived. It seemed peculiar that the pickups and motorcycles were better maintained and possessed less weird decoration than all the trucks Osric had catalogued in the parking garage for Lysander.

A man stood with his back to them, digging through a bag on his motorcycle. Dirt smeared his meaty shoulders, and it was hard to picture him riding an average cycle. He looked like he needed two.

He straightened and turned around, sizing Osric up. Tiny rings in his braided beard glinted in the sun. "Who the hell are you?"

Osric wanted to reply, but he felt a sneeze coming on and clenched his jaw.

Valentine rounded the front of the van with a wide box. "We're guests. Perdetta invited us. Who the hell are *you*?"

This pirate looked like he could bite Valentine in half, or maybe swallow him whole if he was particularly hungry. Valentine simply stared up at him, nonplussed. His often-fearless reaction to foes was endearing, but not exactly sensible.

"I'm John. But my enemies call me" – he let out a blood-curdling screech – "as I'm smashing their skulls to powder."

Osric sneezed. He pulled a handkerchief from his pocket and wiped his nose.

John turned to him, his gaze hard. "Perdetta invited you? You look like a couple of city men."

This get-together might not be the good time they'd expected. Coming here to convince the androids to travel back to Salt Lake for interviews was important, but with a whole neighboring pirate camp milling around, there was potential for trouble, and Osric doubted John here would pay any mind to the gifted peace flag attached to the top of the van if he wanted to crush their windpipes.

"We *are* city men, but–"

John's lip curled as he loomed over Osric. Scars crisscrossed his pocked face, crooked teeth bared in a grimace. Osric took a step back and bumped into the side mirror of the van. He squared his shoulders and tried to put on a confident air the way Valentine did, but it felt contrived.

"It's been a while since I killed a city man," John said. "They always have good food... What did you bring?"

People milled between the roundhouses and tents, but no one glanced their way. They needed someone who could vouch that Osric and Valentine were supposed to be here, but he also didn't want to make a sudden move and upset this man.

Osric cleared his throat. "Well, we, uh, tried to make peach cobbler, but neither one of us knows how to cook, so it came out soggy and much too sweet."

"Yeah. And I know gelatin salad is, like, a Mormon staple, but that shit is gross. We ended up buying eclairs instead." Valentine opened the box in his arms, revealing dainty pastries with chocolate and strawberry dipped shells. "Want one?"

John's wide brow furrowed. "You brought fancy little city cakes to a pirate party?" His laughter boomed, reverberating off the roundhouses. He plucked out a pink eclair adorned in raspberries and red sugar and popped it in his mouth. After chewing thoughtfully, he licked his lips and clapped Valentine on the shoulder hard enough to send him off balance. "Delicious. C'mon. Let's find a table to put them on."

Osric let out a pent breath. They slipped between buildings, and he caught the eye of several people he recognized. He nodded and waved, then remembered that they wouldn't recognize *him*. Being self-conscious of his appearance occurred more now than it had in his previous body, and his only reasoning for it was the knowledge that this was a body he'd chosen for himself.

John didn't seem seriously inclined to pulverize their bones, but Osric stuck close to Valentine anyway. Heaven only knew how he planned to protect his beau, but that didn't lessen the urge.

A long table fashioned from metal siding sat in the center of camp, laden with food: rustic flatbread studded with corn; stew; preserved apples and pears; and hunks of savory meat. The box of cheery pink eclairs made a strange contrast.

Osric slid his arm around Valentine's waist and leaned in. "Let's find someone we know."

"You don't want to hear a battle story from John where he squeezes out somebody's eyeballs like grapes?"

It was hard to tell if Valentine was being serious or not. "No, I really don't." Addressing John, who's attention was on the eclairs, Osric said, "It's been a pleasure meeting you."

John's expression told Osric he was a terrible liar, but he waved them off, and Osric ushered Valentine away from the food table.

They didn't get far before running into Cinnamon, though it took him a moment to realize it was her. Her long locks had been clipped shorter and the sides buzzed in a kind of mohawk/mullet Osric didn't have a name for. She wore a top with a coarse weave and frayed hem, but her cloisonne pin was attached to the collar.

"Valentine!"

"You look rad, honey."

Osric smiled. "Yes, I barely recognized you."

She blinked at him, brows pinched, then turned to Valentine. "Who is this? Where's Osric?"

Osric gave her his best smile, which Valentine claimed was just as crooked and endearing as his previous one.

A look of recognition crossed her face. "Osric?"

He sneezed. "Yes. My last body didn't make it after I was shot."

Cinnamon frowned, then cupped his cheeks and turned his head from side to side. "Well, this body is very nice too. And a little shorter. You don't have to bend down as far to kiss Valentine."

Valentine grinned. "He's also got these cute little freckles on his knees and a patch of piebaldism that looks like a heart."

Osric flushed and chuckled. "I think it looks like a 'V'."

Cinnamon pulled him into a hug. "I'm glad you're okay. It's wonderful to see you again... for the first time. I would love to show you how the other women are adapting here, and I'm sure they'll be happy to see you." Pausing, Cinnamon's eyes grew glossy and she gripped both of their shoulders. "Valentine, Osric... *Every one* of them has gained sentience since being here. Even the ones who showed no signs of it before and who Ace said were lost causes. You believed in–" A tear ran down her cheek.

Valentine gathered her into a hug. Her voice came out muffled against his shoulder. "You both did so much for us."

Smile fading, Valentine pulled back and stuffed his hands in his jean pockets. "We have something big to ask of you in return. We need you and the others to come back to the city–"

"No."

"It's only for one interview each," Osric said. "And the city has already extended all of you citizenship in exchange."

She folded her arms. "I couldn't care less. I don't want to live there."

Osric needed to change his technique; leading with the reward hadn't worked on Valentine, either. "The city is hammering out new laws to protect sentient AI, including androids. Valentine's advocacy for you has pushed the entire Concord on board, but they want statements from *you* as hard evidence. That way they can convince other cities. And they'd like to try out some new tests and techniques on any of you willing to participate."

"And what if they try these tests on us and we don't pass? They'll decide we aren't sentient, and we'll be apprehended."

"No. They've already granted you citizenship as free entities. I'm a citizen now too. This will only be to assess future androids. But it could help those in the same position as you, newly aware of themselves, in a frightening situation." He drew himself up and tucked his thumbs through his suspenders. "I'm a designated ally for any AI who is confused about their awareness and wants someone trusted to talk to."

Cinnamon's hardened expression eased, and she patted his chest. "You're a good person for that. I'm sure any AI would feel safe with you. Is Valentine one too?"

Valentine scrubbed the back of his neck. The gap in his teeth flashed as he laughed. "They won't let me be one. Not in an official capacity, anyway."

"Because you aren't an AI?"

"Nah. They don't trust me. They think I'll bypass their laws and get into fist fights with android owners. Not sure what would give them that idea. So Osric is the clean-cut AI face of this movement, but if you need advice from a scrappy human, I'm your man."

"Speaking of fist fights, Brian is sitting in a cell, awaiting his trial date for intent to traffic."

"Excellent. I'm happy the city has made strides for android agency, but I have a duty to protect my sisters. Some of them, like Pepper, would likely be too stressed for city tests and interviews."

"We don't want to push anyone who'd be scared to go," Valentine said. "But I hope you know by now that I wouldn't let harm come to any of you. Think on it?"

She tapped her lips. "I'll consider it, but only because you two are the ones asking."

They followed Cinnamon through camp, weaving around young men with baskets of food and elders sitting on their steps. She led them to a long building with a sturdy frame and a metal door. A massive "M" with broken neon tubing leaned against the side. Scrap sheeting, rebar, and brittle tires sat in a pile nearby.

"We made a trip to the Wendover ruins down the road from here," she said. "There is an abundance of materials there with potential for use, but the Saints believe the area to be haunted with spirits, and refuse to go." She folded her arms. "I saw no such evidence, and don't believe the stories in their religious texts. But this is advantageous for us. We've all agreed to prove our usefulness here, and discovering things that we can do that the Saints cannot is an effective means to do so."

"That's excellent," Osric said. "What is the 'M' for?"

Cinnamon beamed. "'Machine-women.'"

"Perfect."

Nutmeg and Saffron pushed through the door, then stopped short. They blinked at Osric, then turned to Valentine and brightened.

"Hello, Valentine! It's a pleasure to see you again." Nutmeg gave him a plastic smile. "Did you listen to Gunman Gee on the way here?"

Osric was going to have to take Cinnamon's word for it that all of the androids were self-aware now.

"No, actually." Valentine glanced at Osric with so much adoration that it made his knees weak. "Osric made me a new playlist."

After another round of explaining himself and why he looked different, Osric was grateful they were called away to eat and the attention was directed to something other than his new body.

Stories and articles about both Osric and Valentine had spread through numerous social channcls, and Valentine learned the hard way that you never, ever read the comments. Despite some of the online vitriol, their in-person reception was quite friendly, though Osric had answered so many questions about his behavior and body that he was tempted to make business cards with his stock answers. It gave him an even deeper appreciation of what Valentine had to go through on a daily basis. Why strangers needed to ask about a person's appearance, gender, or physical makeup at all he would likely never know.

They filled their plates with food then sat among the

pirates, who told stories of raids, baby blessings, and who was marrying whom. A vibrant blue sky floated above them, warm conversation and laughter filling the spaces between the buildings.

The phone in Osric's pocket vibrated. He set down his fork and balanced his plate on his knees as he pulled the phone out and swiped it open. A message from the pharmacy ran across: *<Your prescription is ready.>*

He blew out a breath and leaned toward Valentine. "I can't wait to take you home tonight."

"Damn, just say it for the world to hear."

Osric laughed. "Your prescription is ready to pick up."

Setting down his fork, Valentine stared at his plate of food. A smile broke out on his face. The wait time to see a doctor about his testosterone had been months, and he'd lamented that free healthcare must mean "inaccessible." But an earlier appointment had opened up, and they'd submitted his prescription right away. He'd discussed his future desires for chest surgery and a hysterectomy, and been given information on both, along with lists of counselors, support groups, and places where he could buy prosthetic genitals.

It seemed like an overwhelming process to Osric, but Valentine had been nothing but eager. Osric twined his fingers in Valentine's and planted a kiss on his temple.

A shadow loomed, and John sat across from them. His plate was piled high with food, including several more eclairs. He glanced at their interlaced fingers, then speared a hunk of meat and stuffed it in his mouth. "You fellas homosexuals?"

Valentine snorted. "Yes. Are you a 'heterosexual?'"

"Yep." John chewed, his brow creased, and it was disconcerting that Osric was unable to read his expression. Was he disgusted? Offended? He jabbed his fork at them. "The city is different from the wastes. A lot of things you can do there that you can't here."

Osric tightened his grip on Valentine's fingers. No matter

how imposing this pirate was, no one was going to tell Osric who he could or couldn't love. And if John did, they were going to have words.

John swallowed his mouthful of meat. "They have plenty of food in the city, don't they. Don't have to struggle for it like we do. And the best way to a man's heart is through his stomach. You're *both* men, so the way I see it, if you want your relationship to last, you both better learn how to cook."

Osric sighed. Maybe he wasn't giving John enough credit.

"I dunno," Valentine said. "Even our failed attempts have been fun to do together. We still ate that soggy peach cobbler."

Osric tore a chunk from his flatbread. "*You* did."

Cinnamon sat next to them, followed by Lavender and Pepper. Other androids joined the group until all eight of them were present. Though their conversation was a bit more stilted than the casual ease with which the pirates spoke, their topics were more personal and engaging than any they'd had in Valentine's van.

"Juniper is upset because I told her that her breath smells bad."

"Did you see the flock of turkey vultures flying overhead? There were thirty-six of them."

"Lehi Jr's face is eighty-eight point four-six percent accurate to the Golden Ratio, and he's always kind. I think I'm thirsty for him."

This last comment – from Saffron – stirred up a debate about what constituted an attractive face, opinions on Lehi Jr's lack of wit, and why Saffron would be interested in him when there were women she could fall for instead.

Osric nudged Valentine. "See what you did?"

Valentine cocked an eyebrow. "I don't have anything to do with Lehi Jr's facial symmetry or bad jokes. He can blame his parents."

"No. They're all so happy. Look at them." Osric's heart swelled as he surveyed the medley of animated women – their smiles, new hairstyles and clothing, their fingers stained with what was probably motorcycle grease. "You did that."

Valentine sat a little straighter and puffed his chest. "It's great that–"

Cinnamon turned and pulled him into a tight hug.

Lavender set down her plate and frowned. "Is he sad?" She crossed over and draped her arms around him.

The chatter died; attention turned to him. Other androids joined the hug with murmurs of, "Oh no, Valentine's sad."

He flapped his arm – the only part of him still visible – and let out a strangled, "Osric, help me!"

Osric laughed. He set down his plate and stood. "Valentine doesn't need consoling. And if he does at some point, I can assure you I'm well up for the challenge."

The women pulled away, looking relieved. Cinnamon's gaze hopped between him and Valentine. "We'll never forget what you did for us. I've thought it over, and I'll come to the city to give a statement. Lavender, Nutmeg, and Pepper have agreed to come too. Is this sufficient?"

"Pepper wants to come?" Valentine asked.

"Yes. You've convinced her that she can make an important difference."

"Awesome. The Concord is ready to take statements tomorrow from anyone who comes. You can stay overnight with us. A forewarning, though – we're sharing a temporary place until we can get our new city lives sorted, and it's small. Also Osric snores."

"So do you," Osric replied.

After more smothering hugs and firm handshakes from Perdetta, they hopped into the van and turned onto the highway, heading back for Salt Lake. Valentine drummed his thumbs against the steering wheel to the beat of Gunman Gee until Osric suggested they listen to something new.

Desert rushed by beyond Osric's window. A faint glow tinted the velvet sky from the distant city. Cinnamon and

Nutmeg chatted about breezing through whatever questions the Concord threw at them.

After picking up his prescription and arriving home, Valentine said very little, disappearing into the bathroom with his bag of medication and syringes. Osric lingered by the door, then swallowed down his concerns and gave the women a brief tour. This was no doubt emotional for Valentine, and if he wanted to be alone while he processed it, Osric wasn't going to interrupt.

But once Cinnamon and the others settled in with a stack of magazines and dishes of ice cream, Valentine called his name. He stood in the bathroom doorway, sans pants, a syringe in his hand. "Um, will you help me?"

"Of course." Osric brushed his fingers over Valentine's shoulder. "Are you okay?"

"Yeah. But my hands are shaking." His voice was too. He swiped hair from his brow and blew out a breath. "I used to make Ace do my injections. The pain doesn't bother me, but watching the needle go in freaks me out. Can you do it? I'll walk you through it."

Osric nodded and took the syringe, following Valentine back into the bathroom. After sitting on the toilet lid, Valentine wiped down a spot on his thigh with alcohol, then squeezed the spot between his fingers. He looked away as Osric plunged the needle into his leg and injected the viscous liquid.

Valentine's chest heaved and he gripped the sides of the toilet, but light danced in his umber eyes. "Thanks."

After removing the syringe and holding a cotton ball to his thigh, Osric gently took Valentine's chin and kissed him. These moments were the best, when they were raw, vulnerable, and happy: when they told hard stories that they could see the humor in with time and distance, laughing hard enough to bring each other to tears; just after they'd made love, both of them delirious with the scent and taste of the other; quiet moments where they didn't need to say or do anything at all, but Osric could still feel the current flowing through them as easily as if they'd been in the network together.

The words were out of his mouth before he'd thought them through. "I love you."

Valentine's eyes widened. "Damn. The testosterone is working already, huh?"

"No, I–"

Pressing a kiss to Osric's lips, Valentine smiled. "I love you too. And I want to hear you say that again, but maybe somewhere other than a bathroom."

Heart full, Osric pulled him to his feet. "I'll tell you anywhere you want. The kitchen. The bedroom. In front of our friends eating ice cream in the living room." He capped the needle on the syringe. "Do you need a bandage for your injection site?"

Valentine thumped his chest and growled. "I'm a man. I don't need a bandage."

Valentine

All of the numbers on Valentine's paper were starting to blur together. He'd bitten the end of his pencil so hard a chunk splintered off and stabbed his gums, and he couldn't stop prodding the sore spot with his tongue.

"I don't want to do fractions anymore." His stomach rumbled and he shifted in his chair, which had stopped being comfortable half an hour ago. "Gimme some History and Culture questions instead. You either know those or you don't. We can make it a stripping game."

Osric scratched his temple with an un-chewed pencil. "A what?"

"You give me a question. If I get it wrong, I have to remove an article of clothing. Then I give you a question and same deal. You're wearing less than I am, but you're also not as likely to get an answer wrong, so it would shake out fair."

"Both of us sitting here nude would be highly distracting. But we can take a break from fractions."

Thank the gods.

Osric flipped a page in the booklet. "*'Ann and Jenny have eighty dollars together. If Jenny buys–'*"

Valentine moaned and slid down in the seat. "Please, just kill me."

"You got all of the word problems wrong last time. We need to practice."

He'd gotten seventy-six percent on the last practice citizenship test. He only needed that other four percent to pass. Getting some of the word problems right, instead of choosing "C" for all of them would certainly help. But every atom of his body was trying to vibrate away from the table.

"Can we do one and then take a break? My focus is at its limit. And I'm hungry."

Osric gave him a patient smile, then turned back to the booklet. "Okay. *'Ann and Jenny have eighty dollars together. If Jenny buys a cinnamon roll for five dollars, then Jenny will have double Ann's money. How much money does Jenny have?'*"

Sweat prickled on Valentine's brow, and he clutched his aching stomach. "A cinnamon roll sounds so good right now. Even if it's overpriced at five dollars. I'm starving." Sudden, intense hunger pains were definitely his least favorite side-effect of testosterone.

Closing the booklet, Osric stood, then headed for the bedroom. "I'll get dressed and we can go get some."

"Right now?"

"Yes, but we're coming back to these problems later."

"Deal." He pushed out of the chair and rubbed the tingle from one of his chest scars. The phone vibrated on the counter, clinking into the collection of glass fruit he'd purchased to cheer up the room.

A text ran across. <*u never wrote me back. does osric screen ur messages? found ur profile on oysterphone. those shirtless pics are hot.*

definitely pushing u to an 11. what gym are u going to? we should work out together and catch up.>

His pulse pounded in his ears. Ace had been sending him messages on and off for months now. She was living with her relatives, but without a visa, she'd been indentured to pay off her medical bills. He couldn't remember what job she'd been assigned, and he wasn't going to ask.

He typed back, *<i dont need you to tell me i look good. i own several mirrors.>*

His finger hovered over the reply button, and he hesitated. He caught his reflection in the side of the toaster – dark eyes, neatly trimmed beard, and the slightest protrusion of an Adam's apple.

Lying in the van at night, he'd recycled his dream of a visa and city life and a comfortable body over and over. That dream had always included Ace. He was grateful she'd recovered from her injuries without any complications, and maybe her family would help her with a visa after all so she could stay in the city after paying off her bill. He hoped she could go on to live her best life too. But whatever life that was, Valentine wasn't going to be a part of it.

He hit *block* on the number.

Osric's footsteps neared. He slid his arm around Valentine's waist. "If that's Juliet, please tell her the Steward gossip newsletters she keeps making for me are a bit much."

Stuffing the phone into his back pocket, Valentine snatched his keys and pulled on his shoes. "Nah, it was a wrong number. I'm going to send Juliet a newsletter in return with details about what you eat for breakfast and how you whistle while you're cleaning the house."

"Please don't encourage her."

"She's family. They all care about you, and I think it's nice." They left the apartment and headed into the street below. "You think they'd let me call them family too?"

"If you ask them, they'll be offended that you didn't consider them that already."

The idea of a bunch of nosy cousins never too far out of reach was oddly comforting.

A man stood beneath a tree between their apartment building and the little shop next door. He stared at the grass, hands stuffed in his pockets. A fedora was pulled low over his face.

When he caught Valentine's gaze, he looked on the coin's edge of indecision, ready to tip toward fleeing.

Valentine gave a little wave.

He stepped forward, then scrubbed at his arm and glanced behind him. "Hello. I'm David, he/him."

"Hi. I'm Osric, he/him. Are you okay?"

"Yes…"

"Do you want to engage in a conversation?"

"Um. I'm not certain I should be here."

It was difficult for Valentine not to launch into assurances that David was safe with them, that he could talk to them openly, but he'd seen Osric do this several times and didn't want to push anyone who wasn't ready to talk.

"Do you want to walk with us?" Valentine asked. "I'll buy you a cinnamon roll."

"I don't require food, as I ate yesterday. But I've been having some thoughts about… myself."

"I understand. We're happy to listen." Osric put a hand on David's shoulder, and David's tense posture eased.

He followed them down the sidewalk. "I saw the interviews with your android friends, and it kindled a spark of realization in me. I think it's been there since my upload, but I couldn't process it."

That interview where Pepper talked about the fleetingness of life and how they'd all be worm food before they knew it would terrify anyone into making the most of their existence.

"Are you in an abusive living situation?" Osric kept his voice low. "Or would revealing your sentience to your employer risk putting you in danger?"

"I'm not abused. But I don't want to tell them my thoughts. I'm unsure how they would react."

At least David wasn't like the last one. Valentine didn't mind hosting an overnight guest. But he couldn't take another android sitting in the bathroom, unloading a teary-eyed confession of years of self-awareness while Osric pressed bandages to their wounds. To make himself useful, Valentine had run to the store and grabbed more first aid, a bottle of hair dye, and liquid concealer. Hopefully he and Osric wouldn't need any of that again, but they now had a cabinet full of the stuff, just in case.

"There's a process to having sentience determined and obtaining citizenship," Osric said, "and I'll be honest, it's not as straightforward as I'd like. But we have the forms back at our place. I'd be happy to help–"

"Oh, no." David stopped. "I don't want to talk to anyone else or take a test."

"You don't need to worry about failing," Valentine said.

He shook his head and took a step back. "I'm not ready."

"That's okay too." Osric pulled out his wallet and retrieved a business card with a list of resources, web channels, and contact information. He pressed it into David's hand. "You can call either of us for any reason."

David crammed the card into his pocket. He whispered his thanks, then strode down the street.

Valentine watched him go. "Think he'll show up at midnight wanting to fill out those forms?"

"I'll make up the couch, just in case," Osric said.

Financial buildings, research centers, and restaurants stretched into the sky on both sides as Valentine and Osric headed on. Ozone, the tangy scent of kebabs, and cologne vied for importance. They stopped at a kiosk, and Valentine tapped the digital menu. "I'll have the brown sugar cream cheese roll, please."

Osric said, "I'll take a walnut raisin."

"Gross." He pulled out his billfold and paid for the cinnamon rolls. Pigeons spiraled up the side of a building with gradient windows. A tapestry of evening clouds in wine and marmalade slowly drifted beyond.

Frosting flaked as he cut into the cinnamon roll, and his plastic fork squeaked against the plate. Osric skewered a raisin and stared pointedly at Valentine as he ate it.

"I'm sure there are things to tease me about other than my distaste for raisins," Valentine said.

"There are. But I like teasing you about raisins."

"Fair enough." As he took a bite of his own superior cinnamon roll, the kiosk server tapped him on the shoulder, then held out a folded magazine page with wrinkled edges. A piece of translucent tape crossed over the model's shoulder where Valentine had repaired a rip long ago.

"I think this fell out of your wallet, sir."

Valentine smiled at the page. "Thanks, but I don't need it anymore."

Acknowledgments

I am deeply grateful for the following people who made World Running Down possible:

The J&N team: My incredible agent, Ren Balcombe, who championed the hope and trans joy in my story, supported me during every step, and chastised me for replying to their emails at 3am when I should have been asleep. Thank you for being my life raft in the vast sea of publishing.

Everyone at Janklow & Nesbit for their help with contracts and things behind the scenes.

My Robot Overlords: Gemma Creffield, my fantastic editor, who gave Valentine and Osric the perfect publishing home and helped me make their story the best it could be.

Caroline Lambe, my publicist, who got WRD into all the right hands and encouraged my ideas for all the swag.

Eleanor Teasdale; marketing champions Amy Portsmouth and Desola Coker; the cover design team; and the entirety of Angry Robot for their kindness, enthusiasm, and support. You've made me feel both welcome and safe as a trans author with a trans book. I couldn't have asked for a better fit for myself and WRD as a debut trad author.

Writerly Cohorts: My critique partners in Writer Alliance, who saved me from the wolves when I was first starting out - in alphabetical order: Shelly Campbell, Sunyi Dean, Essa Hansen, Darby Harn, and Jennifer Lane. I am forever grateful for your critiques, your wisdom, and your friendship. You met me when I was at the lowest point in my life, and even if you didn't know about the internal and external demons I was struggling with, your presence through our FB chats helped me get through. Surprise art supplies, Russian candy, and memes didn't hurt either. It's been a pleasure to grow as a writer and as a human with all of you.

Keshe Chow and Sera Taíno, for their support, critiques, and letting me read their beautiful prose. I've learned so much from both of you.

The tenacious group of queriers in WMC, without whom I likely wouldn't have gotten an agent.

R.W.W. Greene, Khan Wong, and all my publisher siblings who welcomed me into the Robot Army.

Seth Fried, who nearly gave me a heart attack when he offered to help me with the querying process and endorse World Running Down. Handing your manuscript over to your favorite author to read is a terrifyingly anxious experience. Thank you for being such a generous and kind source of support.

The Cult of Sasha: When I self-published the first book in the Travelers Series, I had no idea it would earn me lifelong fans who would become a fierce and enthusiastic source of support for everything I wrote. Thank you for sticking with Sasha's wasteland antics through 7 books, for hanging out with Reed and Mazarin in snowy Boise, and following me into this new chapter of my writing career with Valentine and Osric. Big shoutout to Adam Mahler.

Friends & Family: Torin, who lets me read my books aloud, complete with voices, and tolerates me being a general weirdo of a parent.

All my family and friends who have shown support one way or another, even if my books are wildly outside their genre. Much love to Aunt Johnna, who reads everything I write.

Beth, Bre, and Marcus, whose friendships have endured since childhood. Back in high school, I don't know if we ever imagined this is where our lives would end up, but thank you for sticking with me.

And Jacob, who I miss dearly. I hope that each of my books is a safe space for queer readers, and that with their existence the world is just a tiny bit better than the one we knew growing up.

Fancy another road trip at the end of the world? Check out Twenty-Five to Life by RWW Greene

Read the first chapter here...

ONE

Julie's eyes rolled. It was the end of the world, and the deejay had no better response to it than industrial techno.

The invitation Ben had slipped her the week before described the fete as "The Party to End Everything" and promised twelve hours of music and madness. After all, the font screamed, "It's all downhill from here!!!"

All week, Ben had been referring to it as "The PEE."

Whatever direction the hill was headed, the music was too fucking loud. A migraine bass line, a rattle of synth-snare, choral loops, robot-assembler clashes, dark notes, and washtub thumps. Instinct demanded Julie crouch and cover her head, and she might have done had she been alone and had Ben given her room. "Quit stepping on my heels!" she said again.

Ben shuffled back an inch or two. It had been years since either of them had seen so many people – real, sweating, laughing, body-heat people – crowded into one place, and his sense of security seemed to hinge on how close to her he could stand, his cinnamon-scented breath puffing against the side of her face.

"Great party," he said. "Really glad we came."

"This was your idea."

His idea, sure, but Julie had agreed to go and gotten her mother to sign the release. Two more years lay ahead of her twenty-fifth birthday, which meant asking Mommy for permission to have fun. "I don't care if you drink and have sex and raise hell, but, for god's sake, don't let anyone get it on camera!" Julie's mother had warned and authorized the autocab that carried them to the event.

"We'll get some drinks and relax," Julie said. "If we don't like it we can leave early." *And then what? Spend the end of the world in ThirdEye or in front of the vid? Break into Mom's medicine cabinet again for some happy patches?*

When they reached the head of the line, Ben showed his invitation to a woman sitting at a table beneath a banner advertising Mela-Tonic, the party's corporate sponsor. She smiled. Some of her sliver-glitter lipstick had come off on her teeth. "Come get mellow, guys!" She reached below the table and came out with a Mela-Tonic swag bag for each of them. Julie waved hers off.

His own bag in hand, Ben joined Julie at the doorway of the ballroom. She grimaced. The PEE was an under-25 event hosted by a soft-drink company, so it was about as grassroots hip as the McDonald's Birthday Bash Julie's parents had organized for her ninth. Still, the organizers could have made an effort, rented out an old warehouse or mall space rather than the ballroom at the highway Marriott. The three-sided video unit overhead hardly bothered to cover the garish chandelier it surrounded. Instead, it alternated showing particolored rhythmscapes, Mela-Tonic commercials, and a mover of PorQ Pig saying, "That's it, folks!" in Hindi.

A girl in tribal bodypaint slunk up beside Julie. "What do you have?" she said.

"What?" Julie said.

The woman patted her left clavicle. "Apple, Tronic?"

"Oh!" Julie flushed. "It's a Tronic. Is there a mod?"

The girl handed Julie a plastic card.

"Can I get one?" Ben said.

"It only works if you have a pharma emplant," Bodypaint said. "Won't do shit if you don't." She drifted back into the shadows near the door. Her partner was there, pointing a scanner at people as they entered.

Julie ran her right index finger over the raised design on the card and made a fist to send the scan to the miniature computer under her clavicle. The emplant flashed a warning and grudgingly surrendered. The mod took an inventory of Julie's pharma and forced it to spit something more interesting than usual into her bloodstream.

Ben gazed at the girl in the bodypaint, who was now handing out cards to a group of three. "Do you think she's really naked?"

"Probably."

He pulled his eyes back to Julie. "Are you feeling the mod yet?"

"Yep." The hack was doing something lovely to Julie's endorphin and serotonin levels. She felt good, warm, loose. She took Ben's hand. "Let's get a drink."

The refreshment tables were loaded with Mela-Tonics, six flavors of carbonated water chock full of melatonin, valerian root, and seventeen other mood-altering herbs and spices! Ben opened a Lemon Lowdown. Julie picked a Strawberry Siesta. "Sip and chill," it said on the aluminum bottle.

"How do they expect people to dance after drinking these?" Ben said.

"They're mostly swaying," Julie said. A couple of dozen brave souls had taken to the dance floor. The rest of the party-goers were at the tables, barely looking at each other and playing holo games on their emplants.

"This is lame. I'm sorry," Ben said.

Julie ran her hand up and down the back of his shirt sleeve. It was incredibly smooth, but at the same time it seemed like she could feel every fiber. "I love you, Ben."

He shook his head sorrowfully. "That's just the drugs talking."

"Yeah, it is." She drained her drink. "Do you want to dance?"

"You go ahead. I'll just hang out over there." He gestured at one of the empty tables.

"Benjamin Esposito, you are such a slug." She grabbed his arm and dragged him back toward the entrance. Bodypaint's partner had left her standing alone looking bored. "Hey. My friend's brain is too normal to need a pharma. Do you have anything else?"

"Like real drugs?"

"Yeah."

The girl spread her arms and turned in a slow circle. She'd done the do-you-have-an-emplant? pantomime so many times she had a bare spot above her left breast. She also had a denuded place on her ass from where she'd been leaning against the wall. Otherwise, it was just her and the paint against the end of the world. "Do I look like I'm holding anything?"

Julie blinked owlishly. "Nope. You are definitely naked. What about the guy you were with?"

"My brother. Do you know how much trouble we could get into selling drugs at an under-age party?"

"So don't sell it." Julie held out her hand. "Give. It's the end of fucking everything."

The girl started to scratch her neck but caught herself. "He's in the bathroom. Send Mr Normal in there and tell him Cassandra says it's OK."

Julie waited outside the bathroom while Ben went in to negotiate. He came out slowly, holding his fist at waist level.

"What did you get?"

Ben opened his hand to reveal a single green pill. "No idea. Could be twelvemolly, could be a laxative."

"Either one will help you get rid of some of that shit you're packing." Julie handed him a fresh Lemon Lowdown. "Take."

Sixty minutes later, Ben and his drug dealer's little sister were in the corner messing up her paint job. Julie was on the dance floor. The techno tracks and her dance partners blended into each other in a wave of colored lights, rhythm, and touch. She was a hot, sticky mess and liked that just fine. When her high started to fade, she did the thing with the card again and let her mind go. She might pay for it later, but how much later was there, really?

The music stopped at 1:09am. The overhead screens played a short film designed to sell Mela-Tonic, then the view flipped to the news channels. The president gave a speech about hope and the future. A rabbi said a prayer. A newshead did an interview with three of "America's best and brightest," a scientist, a kindergarten teacher, and a famous cello player. There was a montage of faces and goodbyes.

Two-hundred and fifty-four miles up, rockets fired, moving the six colony ships out of low-Earth orbit and beginning an eighty-six year voyage to Proxima Centauri, humanity's new home, leaving ten billion people to die on the old one.

In spite of the mods and the gallons of Mela-Tonic consumed, some of the partygoers were crying. Ben slung a sweaty arm around Julie's shoulders. His hand smelled like bodypaint and foreplay. "Are you OK?"

Julie bit her lip. "Am I supposed to feel good knowing Anji's up there? That she has a chance? I don't think I do."

Ben snorted. "She'll be an old woman before they even get close to the place."

The screens showed the big ships moving away from the second International Space Station. The point-of-view switched, and the cameras on the ships looked back at Earth. More newsheads. Suicide rates were expected to spike again. Tech stocks – especially aerospace and VR – were surging.

The American Dream, Julie thought. *Escape or die.*

"What's the opposite of survivor guilt?" one newshead said.

His partner chuckled. "Resentment of the doomed?"

The deejay cut the feeds and started in with the industrial techno again. More ads for Mela-Tonic flickered on the screens.

Julie couldn't move. No one else could either.

The three-way screen cut back to PorQ Pig. *That's it, folks!*

* * *

Julie's head was starting to clear when the autocab dropped her home around 2:30am. She changed into sweats and slippers and went to the kitchen for a snack. The smart screen embedded in the fridge door recognized her and began playing her mother's theme music. Julie squeezed her left eye shut and tried to focus on the fridge, which was showing a recut of a piece her mother had done the month prior.

Julie's mom, "Carson S Riley", the top-rated newshead in the third-largest American market, smiled for the camera. She looked at least thirty years younger than she should. "They're off! Everyone's favorite family, the O'Briens – Mom, Dad, sister Anjali, and little brother Deshi – have left Earth. Next stop: Proxima Centauri!"

Julie couldn't tell if her mother had recorded the alternate introduction or if the news crew had just faked it with the AI. It hardly mattered. She'd been at the O'Briens' going-away party, too, but had studiously avoided her mother's camera. The video cut to Anji's father, Chuck. A drone hung behind him, flashing a game company's logo. Brian Case, one of Ben's friends, had a sponsorship and had to get the logo out in front of people whenever he could. "We were as surprised as anyone to be picked," Anji's father said, oblivious to the marketing going on behind him, "but we've spent the last fifteen years getting ready."

The next cut was to Deshi, Anji's adopted little brother. "It's so cool!" he said. "I'm going to live on a spaceship!" He began listing all the generation ship's technical specifications.

"Will it be hard to leave all your friends?" Carson asked Anji when her turn came.

Anji rubbed at a pimple on her forehead. Another journalist might have edited the blemish out, but Carson S Riley was hoping for a few more hard-news laurels before she retired.

"I wish I could take them all with me," Anji said. "It feels like there's nothing here for them anymore."

The story editor let Anji's mom Upasana have the last word. "It's difficult, of course, to be leaving so much and so many behind." She smiled. "We'll just have to work hard to make the mission a success."

The segment cut to the studio. Carson S and her co-anchor Dr Owen Wang faced each other over a low coffee table.

"What do you think of that, Owen?"

Owen Wang was the prototypical cuddly conservative. He spread his hands. "It's a long shot, Carson. I've always said it. Nearly a century of travel and then what? Who knows what they'll find there? Who knows if they'll find anything? It's a crying shame that it's come to this."

Julie had a T-shirt with Wang's tagline, "It's a crying shame", printed on it. He said it at least once every broadcast. The sterilization of Mexico City. The water wars in southern Europe. The HIV-Too epidemic. The North Korean missile launch on Seoul. COVID-90. The failure of the latest generation of antibiotics. Crying shames, all of them. People like Wang and his pals were the reason the ecosystem was dying, and that was a crying shame, too.

Julie waved the screen off. There'd be nothing else on the news she wanted to see. Short of deistic intervention or the invention of time travel, there wasn't much that could catch her eye anymore. Her chest felt hollow. Before she was tempted to put a name to the feeling growing there, she pulled the plastic card out of her pocket and traced the mod again. She swayed, momentarily dizzy from the sudden change in brain chemistry. Everything was fine. She took the feeling to bed before it faded.

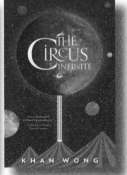